FACTORY FORTNIGHT

William S Allin

JOKApress

Electronic book -
ISBN-13: 9781739171742
ISBN-10:1739171742
Paperback -
ISBN-13: 9781739171759
ISBN-10:1739171759

Cover design by William S Allin using images by AlienArtRevolution via Etsy

FOR:

Odette, the ambulance team, paramedics, nurses, doctors and everyone else at the University Hospital of Wales for keeping me here; and,

Family, friends and everyone else who keeps me going (not forgetting George - woof, woof)

WSA x

CONTENTS

ARRIVALS AND DEPARTURES

Water ran through his hair, down his cheeks, around his neck and reached his back, soaking his shirt. This was not just perspiration; this was a full-on sweat.

"For God's sake!" He resisted the temptation to add 'woman'. It would provoke an adverse reaction, and they were hot and stressed enough as it was. "No matter how much you squeeze the case, we are over our weight limit." He walked away from the suitcases, wiping his fat, sweaty face on his sleeve. Resting one hand on the back of a chair, he grabbed the two-litre plastic bottle of water and took a long, slow drink.

"I just thought that if we pressed all the air out, it might be lighter," his wife said.

"But there is not that much air in the cases!" Pouring more water down his throat, he reflected on his last utterance. "There again, with more air inside, the cases might be lighter…." He realised too late that he had thought aloud.

His wife was already working on the zip of the smaller suitcase. "Right, let's open this and shuffle the clothes. Get more air in."

"It's not going to work." She folded her arms and stared, telling him he needed to provide a more detailed explanation. He tried to recall his chemistry lessons some forty years earlier. "I think we would need a light gas like… er… helium, which is lighter than air… but I'm pretty sure we won't get a canister of that from the shop down the road." He adopted his most sympathetic expression. "Look, love, let's face it. We can either pay for the extra weight or take the bottles out and leave them here."

"This wine is much cheaper than it is at home." She narrowed her eyes as she did mental arithmetic. "I think we had it for about a third of the price we'd pay normally."

"Yes, but the airline charges a fortune for excess baggage. You know how they are. If they had a chance, they would charge us for peeing during the flight. They are hardly going to ignore this amount of excess baggage."

She was not about to concede readily. "Are you sure the weighing scales are accurate?"

They were repeating themselves, but now was not the time to lose patience,

"As I said, they are, as far as I know." He sipped the water, took a deep breath, and sighed. "I don't like it any more than you do, but we have bought too much stuff. If you want to take the wine home, we must leave something else behind, such as gifts for the kids and grandkids...."

She did not let him finish, and her tone told him the issue was non-negotiable. "We are most certainly not doing that."

"Okay...okay, so it has to be the wine."

"We could leave your whisky? You are the only one who drinks whisky; we both drink wine."

He had reached the stage where he no longer cared.

"Let's remove the whisky and a bottle of wine and see how we get on." With the water bottle placed securely on the table, they unzipped the bags, moved items around, extracted them, and refilled them. They then re-zipped the bags and put them on the weighing scales. They repeated the process until they agreed to leave behind whisky, a bottle of Rioja, and several of his older T-shirts and tops. Technically, they were still marginally over their baggage allowance, but they hoped this would go unnoticed by the check-in staff.

He locked the bags and hauled them to the front door.

"I'll nip to the bathroom to wash my face, and then we can wait for the bus." He glanced across the table and saw his wife scribbling on paper. "What are you doing?"

"The lady I booked this place with told me the owners would use the apartment after us. I'm leaving a note to thank them for lending us their place and telling them we had a fabulous time. You never know, they might remember this if we ask to come here again. It's a lovely place. If we must leave the bottles, we might as well get some kudos for it."

He nodded and smiled. "That's a great idea. Good thinking, but what about the clothes?"

"I'll leave another note asking them to donate them to the Spanish people, possibly their cleaner. They don't make very much money, and I'm sure they'll be able to find a use for them."

"That's a lovely idea. Come here and kiss me."

"Bugger off! Not until you've wiped that sweat off your face." She reached into the pile of discarded clothes and picked up an old white cotton T-shirt. "Here, use this. It'll save your shirt and don't forget to have a wee. We have a long bus journey ahead."

"Right, you are love. Cheers," he said, wiping away the sweat. He dropped the T-shirt onto the table and headed for the toilet.

Roughly 40% of the 128 privately owned apartments at the Playa Apartmentos were owned by Germans. The Germans adhered almost religiously to the complex's rules, which dictated that only owners and their families should use the apartments.

A combination of Dutch, French, Russian, Spanish, and British owners owned the remaining properties. These non-German owners did not care about the rules. The Brits, the second-largest community, often advertised their apartments for hire and were more than happy to let the properties to total strangers requiring holiday accommodation.

Lucia García-Ramírez had been cleaning the apartments for over eleven years, and the site rules did not interest her. All she cared about was the money she earned.

July was always busy, and Lucia was exhausted as she arrived at the last of the six apartments earmarked for cleaning that day. She silently cursed the outgoing residents for the lack of care and the mess they left. She was not happy that her employers expected her to clean so many apartments in such a short space of time. The cleaning was relatively quick and easy. The tiled floors and painted walls make them easier to wipe down. The time it took to change bed linen, towels and remove the rubbish always slowed things down.

She unlocked and secured the door to keep it open and heaved her trolley full of cleaning materials and fresh supplies into the two-bedroom apartment's main living area. The influx of fresh air brought instant relief. The wind blew paper across the room, but Lucia did not worry. She was pleased to see that the place was reasonably clean. There was an odd stain on the floor, and a few dishes had been left unwashed, but any resentment evaporated when Lucia spotted the whisky, wine, and clothing on the table. Her mouth opened into a wide grin as she inspected the clothes. The clothes were too large for her family to use, but there were places they could be sold. These were not in bad condition, but she had to wash them well. They stunk of body odour and cheap aftershave.

The clothes were a good consolation prize, but Lucia was most excited by the unopened bottles of Scotch whisky and Rioja. She picked up each bottle in turn, studied it, kissed it, and then carefully placed it on the shelf of her trolley, hiding it under the clean towels.

She instinctively knew the items were her reward for a job well done. Lucia placed the clothes into the dirty linen bag, picked up the paper, and tossed it into the black rubbish bag without reading it. With renewed vigour and a broad smile still on her face, she set about cleaning the apartment in readiness for her employers' arrival from England.

It had been a long and arduous journey, not helped by a delayed departure. The flight itself only provided limited entertainment for two small boys.

Charlie and Harry were hard enough work at home but placing them in a confined space for two and a half hours, with nothing to do, was a recipe for disaster. Sitting on the bus to their resort, Jon Oliver wondered if the holiday was a good idea. He was exhausted already and had another 13 days to survive. Never mind sun, sea, and sangria. All he wanted was sleep, sleep, and more sleep. Not for the first time that day, he wished his boys would behave like reasonable human beings and sit quietly to give their old man a break.

Daisy, his five nearly six-year-old daughter, sat serenely in her summer dress and sandals, chatting to her mother about everything she planned to do during her two-week holiday. Her brothers had no concept of time and could not see further ahead than the here and now. They were more interested in the window levers, the bell button, the space under the seats, other people's possessions and, generally, anything and everything which denied their father a few minutes of peace.

"Charlie, give the gentleman his hat back! Harry, I've told you not to press that button because the driver now thinks we want to get off." He gently but firmly eased the twins into a sitting position, placing his left arm across their legs as he apologised to the man in front and held up his spare arm to the driver, who shook his head before moving the bus again.

"How much further is this place?"

His wife examined the streets outside.

"I'm not sure. It's been a few years since I was here, and it's changed so much."

"Great!"

His wife leaned forward and ruffled his hair.

"Cheer up. It can't be much longer. The driver said it would take about ninety minutes, and it's nearly that now."

The boys stood again and turned to face their mother and sister. Charlie tried to get his leg over the back of the seat, but Jon pulled him back. Harry used a different approach and leaned over as he prepared to fall at his mother. Jon only just caught his legs in time.

"Whoa, sit down here, you two, be good boys. Not much

longer now." He turned to his wife. "I hope you're right about the ninety minutes being nearly up. I can't face extra time with this pair."

At Palma airport, Elizabeth Kingston patiently waited on the plastic bench, holding the handles of two suitcases. She was looking forward to her first holiday in seven years, her first without her husband in twenty-five years, and only her second visit to Majorca.

She desperately wanted the holiday to go well. The previous six years had been a nightmare, the most challenging time of her life. The stroke that struck her husband, Kenneth, was ghastly but was nothing compared to the horrific discoveries she made later. The findings made her realise that her husband was not the man she once thought he was.

After six years of strife, life improved slightly for the Kingstons when Nick, her only son, secured a post with a new enterprise established in the village. The business provided online security software for local businesses. Mr Shanklin, who used to be Nick's IT teacher, developed an innovative software programme that not only defended computers from viruses and hackers but also sought out the source of the virus and identified, then traced, the sender.

His software immediately attracted significant interest. The fledgling company secured a portion of a disused bank building on the edge of Barry docks to develop the programme and other computer security services. Mr Shanklin provided Nick with full training, paid him well, and enrolled him on a part-time course at a local university to study for a degree in forensic IT. Many teachers thought Nick would have had a degree before now had it not been for the unfortunate events.

Nick phoned his father's brother to celebrate the change in fortune and booked one of his apartments in Majorca. The apartment was free, but they paid for their flights.

They booked their holidays for the last week of July and the first week of August. Kenneth Kingston always refused to take a holiday during this period, as he regarded it as "factory fortnight" - when factories closed, allowing the workers to take a well-earned break. Kenneth would never stoop so low as to go on holidays with factory workers or other working-class people.

As Nick returned to his mother with bus tickets in hand, he thought it ironic that not only were they on holiday during factory fortnight, but Kenneth Kingston's son was, to all intents and purposes, a working-class factory worker.

"Right, Mum. It's bay number 27, and the bus goes to Cala Millor. The driver will know where to drop us off."

His mother rose from the seat, smoothed the hem of her best summer dress, and slipped her feet into her orthopaedic clogs. Then she grabbed the handle of the smaller suitcase. "You lead, and I'll follow. Any idea how long it would take?"

"About an hour. The bus is full of people from that side of the island, which means we are heading straight there," said Nick, taking the heavier case. "I picked up a bottle of water to have on the bus."

"I'd rather have a cup of tea, but I can wait until we arrive."

Her son smiled as his mother waved her hat to cool her face.

"I'll text Eddie and tell him to put the kettle on," Nick winked at his mother as they exited the airport and started searching for bay 27.

Gemma Potter sat quietly on the bus, thrilled at the prospect of being on holiday. She had been to Majorca before but not to Sa Coma or as a threesome. There should have been four travellers, but Zoe, Gemma's friend from university, withdrew after a misunderstanding. Gemma's companions sat behind her, busily chatting away while their thumbs worked the buttons on their mobile 'phones.

"Look at this gimp," said Sara, the blonder of Gemma's two companions. "I mean, who goes on holiday with their mother?" She studied the lady's greying hair, formed into a scruffy loose bun, and whispered to her friend. "It might be his gran."

"Total loser," said Kylie Best, the other blonde. "Have you seen what he's wearing? I wouldn't let my granddad go out in a shirt like that."

Sara Grant pulled a face. "And those jeans were so last century. He looks like something out of the ark."

Gemma said nothing but watched the boy ensure his female companion was comfortable before taking his seat. She agreed that his appearance was nothing to write home about, but something about him appealed to her.

The boy glanced up and down the bus, catching Gemma's eye. He smiled at her, and her friends commented immediately.

"You've pulled there, Gem. Two minutes in Majorca, and you've caught one already. Good going, girl! That must be a record even for you."

Sara screeched as she slumped back. "Shit, Kyle, she's got to stage one, and we haven't left the airport."

"Pre-stage one," said Gemma defiantly. She knew other passengers would have heard her friends' comments, so she blushed as she focused her attention on the back of the seat in front.

"Never mind, Gem," said Kylie, ruffling her friend's hair. "Your luck might improve when we get to Sa Coma."

"It can hardly get any worse, can it?" said Sara.

Her two companions laughed loudly. Gemma cringed and smiled weakly at the boy as he turned to face her again.

The taxi driver took the money, thanked the gentleman for the generous tip, and wished them a pleasant stay.

"Grassy arse," said Will Hopkins with a broad smile. "Let's find apartment number 206 and store these cases. Then we can head for the bar." He surveyed the street and spotted a 'Happy Bar' sign close to the apartment block. "That'll do me, and it's within crawling distance. What do you think, Ben?"

His father-in-law, Ben Moran, forced a smile and nodded. "It looks great."

Ben's daughter, Shirley, took his arm.

"It's okay, Dad, there's no rush. We'll stay in the apartment if you don't want to go out. Will can go if he wants."

"No, I'll be fine. I want to see if San Miguel does taste better here. It's pretty shit at home. "

"Nice one, Ben," said Will. "I am ready for something to eat too. The food on the flight wasn't bad, but there hadn't been much of it." He stepped onto a raised kerb by the pub's entrance to get a better view of the bar. "It looks like they do meals. I can see people eating in there. What do you reckon? Steak and chips all around?"

"I'd rather chicken," asked Ben.

"Have what you like, Dad. You can get anything you want around here. They cater for us Brits."

Ben nodded and made his mouth smile once again. His daughter had nagged him to accompany them on this holiday, and he had only relented when he saw an opportunity to do something he had been thinking about doing for a while. Not that Ben would do it just yet. He wanted Shirley to enjoy her break first. There was plenty of time for him to sort himself out. He lifted his bag and walked up the steps to the entrance.

Later that evening, a much-delayed family get-together occurred in one of the larger apartments.

Edward Kingston, known to friends and family as Eddie, loved playing the host at parties and gatherings. He poured himself a glass of cheap champagne and raised a toast to the people sitting on his balcony.

"To the family, especially those no longer with us."

All bar one raised their glasses immediately. The exception was his nephew, Nick, who gritted his teeth and took a deep breath before extending his salute. "To the family," he said quietly.

Eddie ignored his nephew's disrespectful behaviour. The boy was still angry. His father, Kenneth, Eddie's brother, had left them in the mire, but Eddie saw no reason they should dwell in the past. They had survived, prospered even, and their lives were on the up.

"Are you okay, Elizabeth? Have you settled in all right? Let me know if there's anything you need."

His sister-in-law smiled warmly.

"We're fine, thank you, Edward. It's a lovely apartment."

"I hope it's not too small. I am sorry I couldn't give you the three-bedroomed one. My estate agent let it to a prospective buyer."

"It's fine," Elizabeth replied.

"Are you sure you don't mind being on the bed settee, Nick?"

"He'll be fine," said Elizabeth. "It's got everything we need. Hasn't it, Nick?"

"Yes, it's great, thanks. I'm looking forward to getting in there tomorrow." He pointed at the pool. "Mum prefers the beach, but I'm keen to have a good swim."

"That's why I love this place. You have the best of both worlds. The pool is outside your balcony, and the beach is just beyond that gate. You can please yourselves."

Eddie's daughter arrived at his side. "Can you lend me some money, Dad? I forgot to go to the cashpoint."

"How much?"

"Hundred should do it."

He took the cash from his shirt pocket and handed her ten and twenty euro notes.

"Aren't you taking your cousin along?" He glanced at Nick. "I'm sure he'd be much happier with you youngsters rather than stuck here with the oldies."

Louise's face showed her father had said the wrong thing, but she tried to bluff her way through.

"Er… he can come if he likes, but I'm going out with the girls. It'll be a boozy night with Candice and Becky."

"It's okay…I'm a bit knackered anyway," Nick lied.

"Maybe next time?" Louise's smile was as fake as her eyelashes.

"Yeah, maybe," said Nick.

His uncle had not given up.

"Where's Don? Has he gone out yet?"

Louise knew exactly where her brother, Donald, was and where he was going but had no intention of landing him with their sad cousin.

"He's gone to see Christiano. I think they are working, but they might be out later."

"If you see him, remind him that Nick is here. They don't get to meet up very often."

"I will." She fibbed as she smiled and waved goodbye.

Leah Oliver and Daisy climbed wearily up the stairs to their apartment.

"Mum, why couldn't we use the lift?"

"Because it's dark, and the mossies are out."

"Do mossies live in lifts, then?"

"Not always. I think they live in the open air but like damp places."

"So why can't we use the lift?" Daisy's confusion was evident.

Leah continued. "The problem is that people use the lifts when they return from the pool and don't always dry themselves properly. The water drips onto the floor of the lift and stays there. That attracts mossies. They also like it because when people like us get in the lifts at night, we can't see the mossies, so they are free to bite our legs and arms and suck our blood. If we used the lift now, the mossies would have a party on us."

Daisy shook her head. "I'm using the stairs all the time. I don't like mossies, and I don't want them having a party on me."

"Quite right," said her mother, resisting the temptation

to chuckle.

She opened the door. The hall and lounge lights were on, but the apartment was quiet. She put her finger to her lips, telling her daughter to remain silent, and edged toward the open bedroom door on her left. She had thought she would share this room with her husband, Jon.

Her hubby was sprawled out on the bed, fast asleep, with a child at each side. The three wore few clothes. Jon wore the shorts he had changed into earlier, Charlie wore pants, and Harry had on his nighttime disposable nappies. He was getting better in the potty training department, but as they had only borrowed the apartment, his parents thought it safer to revert to him wearing nappies to bed.

The trio looked contented. The boys' heads rested on Jon's shoulders, and their little bodies lay sleeping, curled up in a foetal position, one the mirror image of the other.

"But the boys are supposed to be in my bedroom," Daisy whispered.

"Not to worry, love. I'll sleep in with you tonight. We'll have a girly night in."

"Great," replied an excited Daisy, softly clapping her hands. "What's a girly night in?"

Leah quickly improvised an answer. "Well....we'll have supper..." Daisy started a question, but Leah was ready with the answer, "Yes, I bought tomatoes. Then we'll play a game and perhaps draw some pictures. Afterwards, we'll go to bed and discuss what to do tomorrow. How does that sound?"

"Brilliant," said her daughter, wrapping her arms around her mother's leg. "I love a girly night in."

"Let's leave them here, and we'll unpack this bag." She caught her daughter's hand, and they walked to the lounge/diner. "I'd better plug a mossie killer in their bedroom before we close the door." She placed the carrier bag on the counter and picked up her mobile. "But first, I'll take a quick photograph of the three sleeping beauties. What do you think?"

"Yes," said giggling, dancing Daisy

At the other end of town, Isabella Sanchez sighed into her third glass of wine. It had been an eventful first few hours in Majorca. She would make damned sure things improved.

The so-called boyfriend she had travelled thousands of miles to see had called her a selfish, arrogant bitch, told her he never wanted to see her again and asked her to leave his apartment. He no longer wanted anything to do with her.

She regretted speaking to Carlos in the way she had, but if the stupid prick didn't understand that she would never allow him extended credit, that was his problem. She had warned him of the dangers of mixing personal affairs with business dealings. It was not as if he couldn't afford to pay his bills. He was enjoying an affluent lifestyle; if he could afford that, he could pay her what he owed. She suggested he relax and enjoy her company while she was visiting the island. She would be off to Bilbao in a few days to visit family. She had made a massive effort to come and see him. He should shut up and be grateful.

It was not his response that had upset Isabella; it was the fact that she never thought he would have the nerve to say those things. She felt foolish initially, but that turned to anger. By the time she had left, she had been fuming because he was the first man to finish with her and, to rub salt into her wounds, she had travelled halfway around the world on a journey that never seemed to end, for the privilege. Her only consolation was that travelling business class meant a comfortable flight. Isabella pitied the losers in economy.

Jet lagged, weary, and with nowhere to stay, she wandered about, dragging her case behind her. A friendly, well-dressed German man stepped out of his jeep and asked if she was okay. Isabella had encountered enough Germans for one day and told him to mind his business. When he suggested that he was only trying to help, she said he could help by fucking off. She was no stranger to tough-talking. It had been part of the reason why she was so successful. People knew she was nobody's fool.

Isabella spotted a sign in the window of a rundown bar advertising internet services. She found a clean seat, ordered a bottle of white Rioja, and paid in cash. First, she asked to see and taste the options. Isabella ignored the change but obtained a wireless access code. Then, she took out her laptop to search for nearby hotels.

The Hotel Mediterraneo in Sa Coma looked like the best hotel on this side of the island. It had great reviews and all the facilities she needed. Isabella made a reservation for a prestige double room for two nights via the online booking service, which she charged to her business credit card.

Isabella asked the barman to arrange a taxi to take her to the hotel, but his boss interrupted their conversation. He said he would be happy to give her a lift. He was heading to Sa Coma anyway, and it would be his pleasure to take her. The journey would take no longer than 5 minutes. He insisted she was not inconveniencing him. The hotel was en route. Spotting her unfinished wine, he said there was no rush; he could leave when she was ready.

Isabella thanked him. She guessed the man was in his early twenties. He looked very young, tanned, and confident, considering he was English and seemed genuine enough.

Isabella finished her bottle of wine and asked for his name, the vehicle's make, and the registration number. With this information, she phoned the hotel to tell them she was on her way. Isabella said if she hadn't arrived in ten minutes, the hotel would call the police and instruct them to question Donny Kingston, who was driving a Porsche. She checked, and they took down the correct vehicle details.

Louise, Becky and Candice spotted and latched onto Gemma, Kylie and Sara as soon as they arrived at the club. Introductions were made, and the gang's attention turned to the serious business of enjoyment.

The six downed a second round of shots and threw back their heads, laughing.

"Another," shouted Kylie.

"Same again," said Sara.

Candice and Becky exchanged knowing glances.

"This is going to be quite a night," said Candice.

Louise focused on two men who left the VIP area to survey the crowd. She smiled at them as she nodded. She gently placed a hand on Kylie's shoulder, looked back at the shorter, olive-skinned man and nodded again. The man held up a thumb.

When the new round of drinks arrived, Louise squeezed between Kylie and Sara to grab a glass. Emptying the contents into her mouth, she turned to face the two men and subtly pointed at Sara's back. She nodded toward the taller man. He smiled before he became distracted by something in his pocket.

The taller man held out his mobile for his friend to see. The men shared a joke, laughed and slapped hands in a high-five. Neither man ordered a drink as they leaned against the stage bar, studying the six girls. They knew three of them and guessed the others had just arrived on the island. There was no rush to get acquainted. They would get to know them soon enough. The taller man had to return to his lady companion and introduce her to his friends.

Tracey Stone's boyfriend, Jordan Stevens, was waiting to meet her when she arrived back at Stansted Airport after two weeks in the sun of Majorca.

A broad smile spread across his face as he saw Tracey walk through the door marked 'Arrivals.'

"Hi babe, welcome back. I have missed you so much."

Tracey kissed him and wrapped her arms around him.

"I've missed you too, hun." She started to cry. "I've missed you so much. I never want us to be apart again."

"What's the matter, babe? Didn't you have a good time?

She pulled him closer and whispered, “It was okay, but I wish I had stayed with you.”

“Were your friends no fun?”

“They were okay, but we wanted to do different things.” Tracey could not tell him she had not gone with work colleagues, as he believed. Jordan had no idea that Tracey had travelled to Majorca alone to see someone she had met online.

“Where are they anyway,” Jordan said as he looked around. “I was hoping to meet them.”

“They err must have passed you. My luggage arrived after theirs, so I told them to go on. I’ll see them next week.”

“Never mind.” He kissed her again. “I’m glad you’re home.”

“Me too,” said Tracey, speaking the truth for once.

Twenty minutes earlier, Tracey contemplated catching the first flight back to the sun. Life in Majorca was so much better than at home. The people were more adventurous, and she could be whomever she wanted and do as she pleased.

Everything changed as she waited for her luggage on the carousel. With nothing else to see or do, she switched on her mobile and looked at her messages. Her heart skipped as she noticed that her lovely new man had sent her a text with a photograph. She opened his message, and her heart sank. Her beautiful new man was nothing but a dishonest lowlife shit. Her dream of a new life disappeared.

The picture was hardly flattering, and the text beneath was disturbing. Tracey knew a return to the island was out of the question. Chastising herself for being so stupid, mentally thumping herself for her gullibility, Tracey fretted about what Jordan would do if he found out what she had done. Her guilt and shame overwhelmed her when she realised how pleased he was to see her again.

Her island lover had no idea she was an auxiliary nurse. He believed she was a successful landlord with several properties. What was she thinking? How on earth would she have maintained the pretence? She could not afford the lifestyle. She had splashed the cash, wiped out her savings, and was close to her credit card limit.

She should have realised that her false claims would have repercussions. What was her father's adage? If something seems too good to be true, then it probably is. She should also have known the gorgeous Portuguese man who contacted her out of the blue was only chasing the money she claimed to have. All his fawning over her at the resort, making her feel special, was just a ruse to access her cash.

Why had she registered with that dating site? Jordan was a decent, hard-working bloke who treated her well. He was a bit boring, a typical lad's lad, but he would never hurt her. Jordan could never find out what she had done.

Tracey would close the account and get a new mobile number. If the lover boy tried to contact her again, he would be disappointed, she would forget about him, and he would give up soon enough.

Climbing into Jordan's van as he placed her bag in the back, she realised things were not simple. Although she had not used her real name, her photos appeared on several of her friends' social media pages. The guy was good with IT, so tracing her would not take much effort.

There was no alternative but to do as the message instructed. She would pay him monthly. Tracey would need to create a fictional crisis in her pretend business. It would have to be severe enough to convince him that Tracey couldn't pay the whole amount. The guy would have to accept that something is better than nothing. She would pay what she could. There was no way those images would appear on the internet.

Ben Moran stood back to admire the complex.

It consisted of three accommodation blocks arranged around the pools and gardens in a horseshoe shape. The rear block housed the one-bedroom apartments, and the two on either side contained two or three bedrooms. The apartments increased in size the closer you were to the beach.

Underwater lights illuminated the two pools in the centre of the horseshoe. The smaller pool was circular, with steps on one side and a small ladder on the other. The larger rectangular swimming pool was attached to it. Several tiled pillars blocked the path between the two pools. The larger pool had a diving board at the far end and ladders around the perimeter.

The surrounding grounds looked immaculate. The area around the pools was concreted and had sun loungers scattered around. Beyond the concrete were large grassed areas littered with colossal palm trees lit by spotlights at the base. All the balconies of the ground-floor apartments had ladders that allowed easy access to the grass and pools.

Ben was very impressed with the accommodation and had mentioned the fact to his daughter and son-in-law over dinner. They stayed in a three-bedroom apartment with views overlooking the beach and the pool. The balcony would be in the shade in the morning, and Ben thought he might enjoy breakfast outside. He wondered who Will would know who would have a place like this but would not ask too many questions. He rarely got answers.

His son-in-law had many contacts and could always be relied on to get to the front of the queue if someone offered a bargain, no matter how dodgy the transaction. The mysterious benefactor must trust Will. The apartment was on the market for over a million euros. His daughter had joked that Ben should make an offer, but it was too late.

Ben admired the view one last time before returning to the bar. Will and Shirley had undoubtedly done him proud. Their first day had been delightful, and he felt everything had gone smoothly. The food and drink had been as good as Ben could have wanted. The resort had everything he needed. The apartment was plush and roomy, with intense water pressure in the shower, and was ideally situated. The flight from Manchester had been on time, and he had not felt any nerves during the trip.

He usually became nervous during a flight but quickly settled into this one. He enjoyed the view from his little window and relaxed. He guessed that his state of mind was because he intended to die on this holiday and did not care how or when it happened. In some ways, it might be easier if the 'plane crashed as it would save him from looking for a way to make his suicide look like an accident.

Less than a mile away, behind the hypermarket, Isabella Sanchez roused from a stupor, pulled her body upwards and blinked hard as she checked her surroundings. She was on a wooden bench under a large tree.

Isabella was relieved to see she was dressed and pleased to find her bag and shoes beside her. Her head was swimming. Her bottom, tops of her legs and private parts felt a little tender. Fear began to grip her as she checked her underwear.

How the hell did I get here? What happened to me? Where is Donny? Where am I? She thought, comforted that her clothing appeared intact.

The last thing she remembered was kissing Donny at the Cavern Club. The next thing she woke up here. Had she been drugged? Had Donny laced her drink? Why would he do that? Why was she here? Whatever the reason, she didn't want to remain there longer than necessary.

She grabbed her shoes and bag, stood up and looked around. She saw a hypermarket but had no idea where she was or how far away the hotel might be.

The ground between the bench and the hypermarket car park was uneven, with many deep holes, so she took her time and worked hard to maintain her balance.

Eventually, she reached a solid concrete path and put on her shoes, ready to walk to the hotel, wherever that might be.

A voice called her name.

"Isabella, Isabella, wait. Where the fuck have you been? I've been looking all over for you."

She turned and saw Donny running at her. His shouting made her wince.

"I...I'm not sure. One minute I'm with you in the club, the next I wake up there...on that bench. What did you do to me? How did I wake up in there?"

"What do you mean? What have I done? Where have you been?"

"Shh! Can you stop shouting? My head is banging."

Donny did as she asked, talking in more muted tones.

"But where have you been? I've been worried sick about you?"

"Wasn't I with you?"

"Yeah, but then I grabbed your arse, and you were outraged..."

She touched her backside, wondering if that was why it hurt. She felt groggy. Her mind was foggy, making it difficult to think clearly.

"...and then you stormed off. By the time I told the others I was going with you, you were gone."

Isabella folded her left arm across her ribcage and rested her right elbow on it as she pulled at her face. "I remember kissing you at the bar...."

"Yeah, you came to give me a hand to carry the drinks."

"...and what happened after that?"

"You tried to climb on the wooden partition but came down heavily. I almost cried for you." He put his hand to his groin. "It looked excruciating. You seemed to find it funny and carried on as if nothing had happened. I ordered the drinks, and then I kissed you."

"I remember that, but not climbing on anything."

"You can ask the barman. He thought it was hilarious."

"Okay...so what happened after that?"

"We had a bit of a snog, and I got carried away. I grabbed your arse in both hands and squeezed it. You went apeshit. You pushed me away, saying I should not grope you in public and that you deserved more respect. Then you stormed off."

The bit about her not liking being fumbled in public struck a chord; she had always been the same. “Why can’t I remember? I feel dopey. Could someone have spiked my drink?”

“Not that I know. You drank a lot of Sangria at the club, and they make it strong.”

“Maybe that’s it then. I’m just drunk.” She rubbed her temples, not convinced by the explanation. Overindulgence in alcohol had never previously left her feeling this way.

“I’d say so. You had already downed a bottle of wine at my bar, and then we had a couple more glasses at your hotel.”

She remembered both these things but could not recall leaving the club. “I can’t believe you let me go off alone,” she said.

“You didn’t give me a chance. I had just ordered the drinks and couldn’t run off without paying for them. I returned them to the gang and told them I was going after you. I thought you would be outside waiting for me. I had the shock of my life when there was no sign of you. I’ve been looking everywhere. How did you end up here?”

“As I say, I don’t know....” She yawned into her hand. “I think I must have been confused. I might be jet-lagged. What time is it?”

“Just after four.”

It had been a long day. “What time did I leave the club?”

“Around midnight.”

“I’ve been missing four hours...Fuck! I have no idea how I got here.”

“Well, at least you’re safe now. Come on, let’s get you to the hotel.”

“Is it far from here?”

“Not at all.” He pointed to a junction beyond a bar. “If we nip down that road, it’ll be right before us.”

She looked around the deserted car park and the neighbouring area.

“But why here? I would have no idea where I was going.

Why did I end up here?"

"Don't know. You might have caught the free train to the holiday village."

"Train?"

"It's a tractor that looks like a train engine, pulling carriages behind it."

"But I wouldn't have known where I was going. I would have taken a taxi, surely."

Donny shrugged. "I have no idea what you did. Perhaps you couldn't find a taxi and spoke to the train driver who let you off there, but you took a wrong turn."

That seemed plausible. "Does the train run at that time of night?"

"There is one at midnight. It brings the party animals down from the holiday village into town. The train drivers are helpful and often pick up stragglers going this way. They'll drop you off on the way. If I've been fed up and wanted to go home, I've caught it myself."

This seemed a credible explanation. "But why can't I remember getting the train."

"You did have a lot to drink. The air might have hit you for six when you stepped outside."

"Maybe…but it's strange how I cannot remember storming off. That would have happened indoors. I can remember you kissing me, but then nothing until now."

"Let's not worry about it tonight; I'm just really pleased…and relieved that you are safe. Come on, let's get you to your hotel."

She let him put his arm around her waist and lead her. Her head was thumping, and her throat was dry.

"You know you're not coming to my room?"

Donny stopped dead. "I never expected to. I want to get you to the hotel safely. I'll leave you at reception and call you later."

"Okay." Isabella thrived on certainty and found that she could not remember the last four hours intensely unnerving.

At the hotel, she kissed Donny's cheek, thanked him and said goodnight.

Entering the lift, Isabella hoped to summon more memories by the morning. She despised not being in control.

The man stretched and then scratched his bare belly. The workouts had produced positive results, but he could lose a few more pounds. He listened for noise. The room was as silent as the world outside. He had expected the surroundings to be more raucous, but he wasn't complaining. He liked quiet. It helped him focus on the tasks at hand. This job required his undivided attention. This one promised to be his most significant challenge for many years, possibly his most dangerous assignment ever.

He looked again at the list of tasks he had prepared and couldn't think of anything he wanted to add. Work would start the following morning. It was time for sleep.

SEIZURE

(6 YEARS AND 6 MONTHS BEFORE THE HOLIDAY)

The day began like any other at St David's Private School. Fourteen-year-old Nicholas Montgomery Kingston registered his attendance and shuffled along the corridor to start his first lesson.

He enjoyed history and was confident he would meet his teacher's expectations by achieving a high grade in the GCSE examination the following year. His father would be disappointed with anything other than top grades. Nick had no intention of letting anyone down.

As usual, he sat next to Simon Mayhew, a full-time boarder Nick had befriended the previous term. He opened his book and put his pen and notepad beside it on the desk. Electronic devices, such as laptops and tablets, were strictly forbidden at St David's.

Mr Meadows had just commenced his opening remarks, which usually involved a gentle joke about something that had happened to him in the previous days when the door opened. Mrs Judges, the Headmaster's secretary, stepped in.

"Sorry for interrupting you, Mr Meadows, but the Headmaster wants to see Nicholas Kingston."

Mr Meadows was immediately curious. He struggled to think of why the Head would want to see Kingston. Nicholas never put a foot wrong. He was always a quiet, punctual, polite, well-presented boy who submitted his homework promptly. As far as Meadows and his colleagues were concerned, Nicholas was a model pupil. This intervention could only mean that something had happened at home or to a member of Kingston's family. He turned to see the boy waiting for permission to stand and leave. He nodded.

"Right off you go then, Kingston, but make sure you take

your book and bags with you just in case you have to leave in a hurry. Don't forget to catch up. Mayhew will let you have a few notes, won't you, Mayhew?"

The pupil mumbled an agreement as Nicholas said, "Yes, sir. Thank you, sir."

Kingston followed the lady down the long, empty, silent corridor and through a door marked "No Students beyond this point – unless by prior arrangement". They stopped at the Head's office, and he waited as Mrs Judges tapped her knuckles on the door before opening it.

"Nicholas Kingston for you, Headmaster."

"Thank you." He waved for the boy to enter. "Come on in, Nicholas. I imagine you are wondering why I wanted to see you."

"Yes, sir." Nicholas' nerves were evident and difficult to control. He had never had to visit the Head's office before, and he racked his brain for any trace of what he might have done to justify the summons.

"Your mother has telephoned to say that your father has been taken ill. They have taken him to the hospital in Cardiff. There is probably nothing to worry about, but I have arranged for Mr Shepherd to take you to the hospital in the school minibus. He has to collect some provisions in the City so he can drop you off at the same time. Run along to the car park, and he'll be waiting for you there."

"Yes, sir, thank you, sir." Nicholas turned to leave the room.

"We all hope that your father will get well again soon. Please pass on our best wishes."

"Yes, sir, of course, sir."

Elizabeth Kingston rose to greet the school caretaker and her son.

"Thank you for bringing him. I hope you haven't been put out."

"Not at all, Mrs Kingston. I was due to come into town

anyway. I hope your husband gets better soon." He looked at Nick. "I'll see you then, Nicholas. Look after your mother."

Nicholas nodded and said, "I'll try."

Mother and son sat in the waiting area until a doctor appeared and invited them into a consulting room. He explained that Mr Kingston had suffered a stroke that left him unable to speak or move his limbs. He was currently unconscious. The medical staff would do all they could for him and, as soon as possible, take him for a scan to establish the damage caused.

Mrs Kingston had many questions for the doctor, but Nicholas said nothing. He had no idea what a stroke was, let alone the impact it could have, but his mother's reaction made him realise that this was serious. This news sounded like it could be significant, but at that moment, he had no idea how life-changing.

He awoke with a start. He was fully clothed and had spent the night outside the duvet. For someone who spent months each year sleeping in hotels, he never learned his lessons. He should have brought a firmer pillow. His neck ached, and he massaged his shoulder muscles as he entered the toilet.

"What time are they arriving?" His companion was slipping on her trousers.

"One-ish." He stretched again as he plugged in the kettle. "We'll have time for breakfast before the fun begins."

Ben Moran said nothing as his wife adjusted his tie.

"There, that's better; you look every inch the entrepreneur."

The French word sounded funny, pronounced by a lady with a strong Brummie accent.

"Entrepreneur, eh? I never thought I would be an entrepreneur when I made car parts in the factory."

"And now you are. Isn't it strange how things turn out?

When we met, you were a lowly assembly line worker with ambitions of becoming a supervisor. Here we are today, still together thirty-three years later, and you've got a chain of shops, three petrol stations and a couple of kiosks."

"We've got, you mean. You own half of everything. I wouldn't have had any of it if it wasn't for you."

"Don't be daft. You've done all the hard work. To think we started it all from a dingy corner shop in Dudley selling sweets, fags and booze."

"Great oaks and all that," said Ben. "They were hard days, though, weren't they? I got worried when the bloody supermarkets started opening massive stores everywhere."

"Yes, but I am so proud that you stuck with it. You have done very well, Benjamin. You've done very well indeed." She kissed his cheek. "Are you ready to face the press? Moran's Mini Marts are about to open their newest store, so let's generate publicity."

They left the car and walked a few yards to their new premises, where a crowd, including journalists, awaited their arrival. This new store would be their most prominent and the first outside their native West Midlands.

A footballer from a nearby team cut the ribbon and gave autographs while Ben joined the press representatives.

"This is a lovely area," he said to the reporter from the Cheshire Times. "It is far too nice an area to be ruined by the development of a sprawling supermarket with acres of parking spaces filled with 4x4s. We need to cut pollution and save the planet, so I firmly believe that shopping in the local community is the answer. I am delighted we acquired the old village school and converted it into the latest addition to the Moran's Mini Marts chain." He pointed at the shop sign with the three overlapping Ms. "We provide a wide range of fresh, locally sourced produce at competitive prices. We also strive to protect and maintain the character of a town or village. That's why we convert rather than build. We renovate rather than demolish. Our philosophy is to preserve, not destroy. We don't use articulated lorries to transport our goods. Most of our fleet have electric or hybrid engines, so Moran's Mini Marts not only restore old buildings that would otherwise fall into ruin, but we also help the environment."

"What do you say about the rumours that you gazumped a local social enterprise group who wanted to acquire the site to use it as a craft centre?"

He had expected the question.

"Of course, we feel sorry for anyone who missed out, but we did nothing wrong. We completed the purchase while the other parties were dithering. Let's not forget that the local education authority needed the money from selling this site to complete work on the new school. So, if you think about it, we are helping the wider community. Plus..." He swallowed. He was about to make his big announcement. "I am delighted to be able to announce today that Moran's Mini Marts have purchased the old railway buildings on the edge of the village and plan to convert them into units for use as a craft centre. Not only that, but our stores will, in future, carry a range of locally sourced craft products to help widen the market and strengthen local enterprise." He did not mention that the railway company from whom they had purchased a disused station six miles away had made the acquisition of the other buildings a condition of sale or that the craft centre users would pay rent.

"Do you intend to open more stores in this area?"

"We do, and we are already negotiating on several sites."

"So we'll see a lot more of you in Cheshire in the future."

He looked at his wife and smiled. "Yes, we are so impressed with what we have seen that we are considering buying a house up here."

Jon Oliver loathed working in the cold. His hands ached, his muscles groaned, and his saw seemed to have difficulty going through the wood. Summertime was different. This was a lovely site. The views of the Malvern Hills were breathtaking when the sun was shining. The location was a pain in the arse on bleak, short winter days. The winds took your breath away in the wrong sense. Add a dusting of snow, and the conditions were impossible. It was okay for the bricklayers and the plasterers; they got time off for bad weather, but carpenters could continue working.

Still, it should not be for much longer. One of the contractors working on the site had asked him if he would be interested in changing jobs. He wanted someone to act as project manager for his new developments, and Jon's experience and qualifications made him the ideal candidate. Jon had attended an informal interview and heard the job was his. His starting salary was the only outstanding issue; they had already moved much closer to what he wanted.

Jon had no qualms about leaving the company that had employed him since he left education. He knew they would let him go in a heartbeat if push came to shove. His mother thought it was better the devil you know, but Jon was relaxed about the move. If it didn't work out with the new firm, he was confident someone else would need a good carpenter.

The project management experience offered by his prospective employer would bring him closer to his ultimate goal of running his own business. He hoped it would become a reality in less than six years. He had been saving hard, assembled many connections and ensured he kept his financial and other commitments to an absolute minimum. It was evident that his girlfriend Leah was not overjoyed at the prospect of a long engagement but said she understood the reality of the situation. There was no way that Jon could settle down until he was his own boss.

He would take advantage of Rob Cromwell's offer and gain the necessary experience, and then the world would be his oyster. He and Leah would get married and have a baby one day, but not yet.

Ben Moran was used to getting his way, and he was

infuriated to hear that he would not get planning permission to convert a disused cottage hospital in Cheltenham into retail units.

"You told me that it would be a fucking formality."

"I said no such thing. I told you from the outset that the council would never allow it. If you remember, I said three of the big five inquired about clearing the site and building a new supermarket but got kicked back. The council wants shops closer to the town centre, preferably smack bang in the middle."

"I'm sure that you suggested their objections related to the demolition of the buildings..." Ben was not allowed to finish his sentence.

"No, you assumed that. I said I don't think anyone cares about the old hospital buildings. They would never be listed. The council's refusal to allow retail development in the suburbs has always been an issue. They'd probably be delighted if you used the hospital site for a warehouse or distribution centre, but you have no chance of a shop."

"We don't need another warehouse. We need to convert that building into shops. It's my fucking building. I should be able to do what I like with it." Ben took a deep breath and shifted the mobile to his other ear. "Seeing as though you are no fucking use, who do I need to speak to?"

"No point. There is no one. The full council has committed to the town centre regeneration strategy regardless of party politics."

"There must be someone. I'll ask my lodge contacts for names. One or two of the councillors must be persuadable. Perhaps we should consider enhancing their areas. They may need a new playground or something."

"Good luck with that. The council leader is female and doesn't belong to a lodge. She rules her members with an iron fist, so God help them if they cross her."

"So what do you suggest? Should we sell it?"

"Who to? You were the only one daft enough to buy it. It

had been on the market for years."

Ben did not like to be reminded of his mistakes. "Any decent fucking building surveyor would have warned me about potential problems beforehand."

"And any sensible fucking businessman would have read the report I prepared, not slung it in a drawer without even reading it and then plough on in the expectation that he would automatically get his way."

Ben's eyes widened at the usually mild-mannered building surveyor's outburst. "Enough negativity. What are my options?"

"Hmm, you could try to sell it, use it for another purpose, or let it decay, hoping the council changes its policy."

This last option gave Ben hope. "Is that likely?"

"You never know in local government, but they have a strong majority, and the next elections are not due for a while."

"Is the site likely to get vandalised? Will I get bounced into forking out more money to keep it safe?"

"I think you should be okay. It's out of town and not close to any residential areas. The windows are covered, and the gates are secure."

"That's the first bit of good news you've given me. I'll be in touch."

There was no doubt the woman was deranged. She was crazy. On-lookers must have wondered why she kicked off like that in a public place. How could she react so angrily and loudly to a question about whether she wanted a Chinese or an Indian meal that evening? It was a simple question, and not one that anyone could have anticipated would generate such an adverse reaction.

She clarified that she didn't want either meal, at least not with him. She stood and hit her companion about the head before sweeping her hands across the table. The teacup's contents adorned his shirt, and the remains of his beans rested on his lap. He was relieved that her breakfast plate missed him when she threw it. She had tossed it like a frisbee and screamed when he ducked. The salt, pepper and vinegar caught him on the chest. She shouted at him again, calling him names, and then stormed off.

The other customers learned she intended to return home, leaving him alone, which was all he deserved. She never wanted to see him again. They probably thought he would do well to stay away from her. She needed professional help.

The café owner waved away his apology and refused his offer to pay for any damages. He sensed everyone was keen to see him depart the premises without delay.

He entered the clothing store *'The biggest and best choice in Weymouth'* via the rear entrance. Collecting the first polo shirt, jeans and baseball cap he came across, he paid in cash before nipping to the changing room.

He double-checked that his purchases did not have security tags. The last thing he needed was the store detectives' attention. He placed his stained clothes into the carrier bag and left the store, wearing a new outfit, via its High Street exit. He pushed his sunglasses onto the bridge of his nose and pulled the cap down on his head.

A newspaper was acquired en route to the pub, where he planned to have a pint and relax. She would return to the B&B and pack her belongings. He would have to wait a while before collecting his things.

It would be just the one pint as he needed to drive later. The B&B booking had a night to go, but he thought getting out as soon as possible was safer. It would take about two hours to return to Plymouth, where his visit would also be short. It was time to move on. He rarely remained in one place long; he seldom got the chance. The job took him nationwide, often with a minimum amount of notice.

The Anchor bar stood on a corner, three streets from the seafront. He had seen it as they passed by on arrival.

The signs proclaiming "Regional Pub of the Year" were hard to miss but did little to attract business. He was a little taken aback but delighted to find the place empty. The only other person in the bar was a man sitting on a stool, sipping a soft drink while studying a newspaper. His entry prompted the man to get up and walk behind the counter.

"Hello. What can I get you?"

He surveyed the taps. "A pint of the IPA, please. Is it always this quiet on a Saturday, or did word get out that I was coming?"

"Haha. It'll get busier later. I'm glad for some peace." He checked his watch. "It's nearly one, and some of my regulars will start arriving shortly. Then the holidaymakers will come in later to watch the racing. We have a cocktail promotion between 4 and 6, followed by live music. It'll be banging here this evening."

The barman placed his pint on the counter, accepted the note, and thanked the visitor for the offer to keep the change.

The visitor took his pint to the table beside the door to the toilet and spread his paper to examine the horse racing pages.

The beer tasted slightly off, but he did not want to make a fuss. He would sip it slowly.

After making his selections and entering them on the mobile app, he took out a pen and found the page with the crossword.

He had filled in three answers when two men entered the bar. The larger one barked instructions at the other and then walked towards the toilets. He stopped directly in front of the man with the newspaper.

"What are you doing there?"

The visitor looked up. "Who? Me? I'm just having a pint and doing my crossword." He was calmness personified. His voice was even and soft, his mannerisms passive. He gently stroked his bushy beard. "Significant, five letters."

"Never mind that shit. You are in my seat."

"Am I? I do apologise; I didn't see anyone's name on it."

"I always sit there."

"How was I to know that? I've never been in here before."

"Move."

"Why can't you sit somewhere else until I've gone." He pointed at empty seats. "Look, there is stacks of room, and I won't be staying long."

"But I want that seat."

He could not remember the stock response, but he thought it was something like, "Just because you want does not mean you'll get."

"Do you have any idea who I am?"

"Nope, I haven't got a Scooby, sorry."

The newcomer leaned on the table, making it wobble. Beer spilt onto the newspaper.

The visitor grabbed his pint. "Woah. You almost spilt my pint then".

"If you don't move, Taffy, I'll empty that pint over your fucking head."

Taffy had already assessed the man, estimating him to be about six feet tall, thirteen stone and very beefy. To emphasise his physique, the man had worn a sleeveless vest, and his thighs looked too big for the shorts. A dog tag hung from a gold chain around his neck.

The man was not happy. Taffy thought the man sounded more than a bit pissed off.

Taffy remained calm. "As I said, I'll leave when I finish this pint. You can have your seat back then."

"I want my seat now." The man lunged forward.

The move was easy to telegraph. Taffy stood, pint in his left hand, grabbed the man's hair with his right, and dragged the head down so that his knee collided with the attacker's chin. There was a faint grunt before the unconscious man slowly sprawled across the floor. Taffy took the dog tag and another sip from his pint. The beer somehow tasted worse.

"Meaty," said Taffy, returning his mind to his crossword. The paper was wet. "Shit."

The man's companion stopped chatting with the

barman and moved quickly across the room toward him.

"What have you done to him?"

"Knocked him out, I think."

The second man looked nervous and anxious. Glancing at the bar, he saw that the barman had mysteriously disappeared. He focused his attention on the Welshman.

"Do you know who he is?"

Taffy thought the men could have been brothers. Their facial features were very similar. "I have no idea. He asked me the same question. Does anybody know him?"

The man looked at the bar again. There was still no sign of the barman. It was too late to back out now.

"You cheeky bastard." He swung a fist at the stranger but missed. Taffy stepped aside, still holding his pint. He rammed his foot into the back of his opponent's knee and wrapped his free arm around his neck as the man fell forward. He squeezed until he was lifeless.

Taffy dropped the second newcomer onto his motionless friend, keeping the dog tag that came away from the second man's neck. He looked at it briefly and put it in the same pocket as the first one.

The barman returned to see the outcome and found it difficult to close his mouth.

Taffy put his glass on the counter and said, "Sorry about that. For some reason, they took exception to me. By the way, the IPA tastes off. I think the pipes need cleaning."

"Do you know who they are?"

"Don't you start. Does everyone around here have amnesia today?"

"That's Frankie Nuggets' son, Graham, and nephew, Gus." The barman rubbed his fingers across his mouth, wondering what to do next. "He won't be happy."

"Who? Frankie Nuggets?" He looked at the ceiling and then around the walls. "Why do they call him that?"

"Because he owns a chain of chicken nuggets shops along the coast."

"Ah, right, I imagine he doesn't only sell nuggets, but Frankie Chickenburger doesn't sound as threatening."

"I wouldn't laugh about it. Frankie will go apeshit when he finds out what you've done. He'll probably want to kill you."

"I'd better get going then, but before I do." He reached over the bar, poured the remaining beer into the sink, and smashed the glass on the counter, retaining the base with sharp vertical strands.

The barman raised his hands. "I don't want any trouble...I won't tell him anything."

"I believe you, but there's one more thing I need to do."

"What?"

Taffy pointed at the camera behind the bar. "I have to see your CCTV."

"It's through the back."

Taffy followed the barman to the backroom, still holding the broken glass. He was pleased that the CCTV recorded events on a standalone computer with a plugged-in video screen. He moved the mouse, tapped a few instructions on the keyboard and then hit the enter button. The images disappeared.

"The brewery has only just installed that."

"All I've done is erase today's footage. You can reboot it when I've gone." Taffy put the glass to the barman's neck.

"No need for that. I won't say anything."

"I know, but this is for your own good. If Frankie pizza...."

"Nuggets."

"...aye him. If he sees you are unharmed, he'll think you didn't try to help his boys. You can tell him I threatened you with the broken glass. I'll give you a cut on the neck to make it more convincing. It'll look like I forced you to show me the CCTV."

"But I'm on Warfarin...it makes me bleed a lot."

He grabbed a nearby tea towel and threw it at the barman. "Keep the pressure on the cut using this. I won't hit anything dangerous. You'll probably feel little more than a scratch." He grabbed the man's ear, gently lifted his head, and stabbed his neck with the glass. "Did you feel a little prick? Ha ha, the old ones are the best."

"Ouch." The barman put the tea towel on his neck

"Now, after I've gone, you should call Frankie Fish Fingers and tell him what's happened. Does he live nearby?"

"If he isn't in the area, he'll send his boys around."

"Noted. I need to get a move on." Taffy picked up his bag and left the pub.

He took a taxi back to his B&B and trotted into reception.

"Your girlfriend has already checked out. Will you be staying tonight?"

"Unlikely..." He accepted the key the man held out to him. "...but is it okay to let you know later?"

He did not wait for a response. Taffy jogged up the stairs to the room, changed his clothes, put his most recent purchases and soiled clothes into his leather case, and exited via the fire escape.

Taffy left the B&B's grounds through a gate at the back, which took him to a lane. He walked to the main street and strolled along the pavement until he reached his car. As he started the engine, he saw a Range Rover and a Jaguar speeding toward him. They passed by and turned right.

She was waiting at the rendezvous point and smiled as he stepped out, leaving her to drive.

"Any trouble?" She asked.

"Not unexpected." He sat in the passenger seat and lifted a small laptop from behind the driver.

"Jesus, Snowy, I know you like your theatrics, but that performance was well over the top."

"You could have held back a little. Throwing the plates and condiments was unnecessary. I am not sure those stains will come out."

"I'm after the Oscar for best actress." She put on her seatbelt. "It makes life more interesting, but you get me to do some weird shit."

"As I always say, having a valid back story is essential in this job."

"I know so that if things go wrong...

"That's right." Snowy's focus was elsewhere. The laptop powered up quickly, and he tapped the screen. A password box appeared. He took out the dog tags and copied the details on it into the computer.

"That worked. Let's get these details to the Prof before anyone notices what's happened."

Frankie Laing was fuming. Someone had ambushed his son and nephew at their local, which was unheard of. Who would be stupid enough to do such a thing? He doubted it would be anyone he knew. Was someone stepping in on his territory? Was he being sent a message? If so, by whom?

Frankie would have to react, but how could he when he had no idea who was responsible?

Philmepint, the barman at the Anchor, had done well. He had given them a detailed description of the man. Phil had surprised Frankie with his bravery. The stranger had threatened him with a broken pint glass and forced him to access the CCTV system, but Phil had remained composed enough to ring Frankie immediately afterwards. Frankie would never have put Phil down as someone to stay calm in adversity, but he had. The stranger could have returned to slit Phil's throat, but the barman hadn't considered the danger; his priority was to call Frankie. Phil was very modest about his role. Frankie would ensure he got his reward.

Thanks to Phil's quick reactions, Frankie's men were quickly on the Welshman's trail. The loss of the CCTV inside the pub didn't matter; he owned the taxi company, and tracing the Welsh guy in a baseball cap was easy.

The trail led to a B&B. His men arrived just too late. The idiot in reception had handed the room key to the man moments before and had not seen him leave. He thought the tourist was still upstairs. Frankie did not understand how the receptionist did not notice the made-up address in the register or why they had not invested in a more modern IT system. How many people pay in cash these days? Why hadn't they checked the guests' addresses like normal people? The visitors made the booking over a week before. He had a name. Mr Bound, first initial 'E', but he guessed that was probably fake too.

Smashing up the hotel room had not appeased him, and Frankie was still livid when he arrived home.

His boys returned with copies of the CCTV from shops in the High Street and updated him on witness statements. Locals spoke of an incident involving a Welshman and a girl at a local café. The girl launched a tirade of abuse at the man, threw a plate of food, and stormed off. Frankie watched the CCTV footage of someone fitting the Welsh man's description leaving the clothing store and carrying a bag that probably contained his soiled clothes. From there, the man made his way to the pub. Cameras picked up his departure from the Anchor. He saw the man jump in a taxi, but the footage told Frankie little that he did not already know.

Putting the pieces together, Frankie calmed down. He had no idea why the Welshman was in town, how he got out, where he went or what had happened to his girlfriend, but Frankie surmised that his son and nephew had picked on the wrong man at the wrong time. Frankie would have been annoyed had a girl embarrassed him like that and would have taken it out on the first person to irritate him.

He wished he could learn more about the man. Not many men could floor Gus, let alone Graham. Frankie could use someone like that.

Now, where had he put his mobile?

Matilda Laing almost leapt from her seat when she saw the money had arrived in her account. That would teach the old bastard. She wished she could have been there when he discovered what had occurred.

Elizabeth and Nicholas Kingston ate silently in the vast dining room at their property just outside Cowbridge. Elizabeth had trouble comprehending what had happened. Nicholas was unusually quiet, even for him.

"Would you like a dessert? There is ice cream, or I think we have the remains of that strawberry cheesecake from yesterday?" The words of the Beatles song came to her mind.

"No, thank you, Mum. I'd better see what homework we have. I'll be in my room."

"Okay, love. I'll be in the lounge if you want to chat."

Frankie Laing's view of the Welsh bloke who attacked his son and nephew had gone from loathing to admiration to hatred. He had just learned that the boys had lost the dog tags, which had the account information for two of Frankie's hidden overseas accounts. He thought he had been so clever by hiding the cash to stop Matilda's lawyers from including it in the divorce settlement.

He had split the money equally between four banks and had given each of his children the details for one of the accounts. The boys got dog tags, and his daughter had a bracelet. The account numbers and passwords had been engraved on the back. Now two were missing, which meant somebody, whoever had employed that fucking Welshman, had access to half his money.

Determined this incident would not be repeated. He destroyed the remaining dog tag and bracelet and put the account details into a notebook. Frankie added the list of numbers necessary to access the accounts to a DVD of a family holiday. The DVD would never be required. Frankie had an excellent memory and was confident he would easily recall the information when needed. Nobody was going to get their hands on that money.

He had a strong feeling that Matilda had set up this attack. The more troubling question was whether one of his three children and nephew had informed her. Frankie spent all evening racking his brain and could not believe any of the four would have betrayed him. He thought it more likely that one of them had mentioned the existence of the accounts to someone close. That person must have gone running to Matilda.

Frankie pledged not to rest until he had identified the informant and caught the Welsh man. He would enjoy inflicting punishment.

DAY 2 - SUNDAY 25 JULY

Gemma Potter was the first of the three to rise. She stumbled out of the bedroom, grateful for the cool tiles under her bare feet, and plodded to the kitchen area, where she opened the fridge. The metal block shuddered as she pulled the door handle. She grabbed the bottle of water and emptied some into a glass. Gemma sipped the liquid and placed the bottle against her forehead.

It had been a spectacular evening, a fabulous start to the holiday. The boys had been great company and, for once, had not tried anything. Louise laughed off Gemma's questions about the boys being gay. She said her brother, Donny, was a little shy. His best mate, Christiano, was the son of a Portuguese diplomat and was always on his best behaviour for fear of doing anything that might embarrass his mother.

Candice had backed up Louise's tale by telling her that while Donny and Christiano enjoyed a good laugh, they rarely tried anything on with girls they had just met. Candice suggested the pair were perhaps too well-mannered and had no idea what they might be missing.

Gemma wasn't sure she believed what they told her, but she was surprised when both men left early. Donny went first, chasing the loud South African woman who appeared annoyed at something, and Christiano was not far behind.

Whatever the reason, Gemma was not disappointed that the boys did not try it on with her. Neither was to her liking. They were too smooth and full of themselves, readily splashing the cash. She preferred the look of Barty, Donny's friend, who turned up as they left the club. She wondered if he would be around the next time they visited.

The hot Majorcan sun broke through a gap in the curtains. Gemma saw that the weather was nothing like at home in Cheltenham. She would need strong sun protection, and her fair skin would burn to a crisp if she were not careful.

She peeked through the curtains and looked at the crowds of tourists gathered around the complex's pool. There was not much chance of three beds together. The beach might be quieter. Beyond the well-manicured lawns lay the promenade and the beach and sea. Many more people covered the golden sands, but there was no shortage of space.

The sight of someone jogging by took her by surprise. She could not believe that anyone would run in this heat. Narrowing her eyes to get a better look, she recognised the runner as the lad they had joked about on the bus the previous day. This time, he was without his mother, and his outfit looked more modern. He wore knee-length shorts and trainers. His upper body was bare with minimal movement as he ran steadily, oblivious to the heat. In a moment, he had gone, disappearing around the bend.

Mummy's boy or not, he's fit. She wondered where he was staying as a smirk spread across her face.

Jon Oliver knew his peace had ended when he felt movement on his left arm. Harry was awake; it would not be long before the world knew it.

"Dad, Dad, I need a drink." The toddler pressed his hands into Jon's chest. "Dad, Dad, I need a drink." Harry beat Jon's torso as if it were a drum. "Dad, Dad, I need a drink."

There was no alternative. Jon opened his eyes and forced a smile. "Okay." He blinked several times. "Just give me a minute, and we'll get you sorted." He eased onto his right side and gently removed his arm from under Charlie's head, replacing it with a pillow. His elder son rolled away from him, stretched out his left arm, and slept on.

Jon sat up, yawned widely and rubbed his eyes. He had no idea what time it was but guessed it was early. His body craved sleep, but that was a forlorn hope with a wide-awake Harry on the case.

"Right, let's go and look at what Mum and Daisy bought last night." He put his index finger over his lips. "Let's see how quiet we can be. I wonder if we can get to the kitchen, get a drink and not wake anyone up. Shall we give it a try?"

Harry nodded enthusiastically, his tiny index finger covering his lips.

Isabella Sanchez stumbled out of bed. She was pissed off. Her backside and private areas did not hurt as much, but Isabella's pride had taken a beating. She found that very painful and difficult to handle.

She felt a little nauseous as she pondered various options about why she had no memory of events. She wondered if someone had drugged her before attacking or sexually assaulting her. She surely would have remembered if somebody had raped her. There would be evidence. She had checked herself in the bedroom mirror. There was minor bruising, but that might have occurred when she showed off in the bar, as Donny suggested. The marks appeared consistent with a tumble onto a wood block, but she was no expert. Isabella hated not being able to remember. She needed to know.

She again retraced the events of the previous day. Having arrived at the airport to find Carlos and his brother waiting to meet her, the three had gone to Carlos' apartment, where he had ended their two-year relationship. His brother clapped as Carlos slammed the door in her face.

She roamed until she found the bar. Donny took her to the hotel, and she bought him drinks in the hotel bar to thank him. They discussed her day, and he listened as she cursed her ex-boyfriend for being a bastard.

Donny took her mobile number and called an hour later, inviting her to a club. A car came to collect her. She was ushered into the VIP area and given more to drink. Donny and his friend Christiano were great company but were very young. Some other men in their group were closer to her age, but she found them boring and stupid and had no qualms about telling them how she felt.

Donny and Christiano seemed more interested in the younger girls with Donny's sister, but, in fairness to them, they paid Isabella lots of attention.

She recalled trying to hit on Donny, as she thought a night with a toy boy might help improve her mood. She followed him to the bar, where she kissed him. She had recollections of him groping her. After that, her memory was non-existent. The next thing she recalled was regaining consciousness on the bench.

She studied her backside in the mirror. Bruises had appeared on her cheeks, which were sensitive to touch. Thinking a bath might help, Isabella ran the water, adding every vial of the complimentary bath salts.

Ben Moran had woken to the dulcet tones of his son-in-law singing in the bathroom. Will had a good voice that befitted someone who had once performed in clubs, but Ben was unsure of the appropriateness of '*Love to love you baby*' at 7:30 am. He did not raise the issue when he joined his daughter at the balcony table and poured himself a cup of tea.

"Did you manage to sleep, Dad?"

"Yes. I slept well, thanks. What about you?"

"Not bad. I managed to get a few hours before Will started snoring. I knew letting him have that brandy was a mistake."

Ben smiled.

"I thought it was you."

"Cheeky bugger," said his daughter, laughing. "I do not snore!"

"Well, your mother did," replied Ben without thinking.

The silence was awkward but over quickly as Will stood in the doorway. "Morning Ben. Did you sleep okay?"

"Fine, thanks."

"Good." Will had turned his attention to his wife. "Is

there any tea left, love? I'm gasping."

Sunday was a day of rest for Rebecca 'Becky' Saunders.

On the other six days, she worked with her father in the family shop in Cala Millor. Her mother substituted for her on Sundays, as she had weekends free from her main job.

Hearing that her parents were moving to Spain, Becky imagined a life of sun and sand. She had certainly not expected to have to work for a living. When the move became a reality, three weeks after her sixteenth birthday, just over a year before, Becky's father suggested his youngest daughter should continue her education at a Spanish college. Becky had other ideas. As far as she was concerned, her schooling was over.

She enrolled on a business course but played truant until the college wrote to her parents, informing them they had dropped their daughter from their register. Nigel Saunders had been horrified and stopped her allowance or, as he called it, 'pocket money' and gave her an ultimatum. She could either enrol in another course or find a job. While she was making her mind up, she would work with him in the convenience store. Her father reminded her that he thought she was a bright, intelligent young lady who spoke Spanish well and should take her opportunities while she was young enough to enjoy them. Becky smiled, nodded, apologised, and assured him she would knuckle down.

Then, three months ago, Christiano Gomez entered her life. He called into the shop asking if she had a plaster. He had fallen and grazed his knee. Becky helped him clean the wound, applied a sticking plaster and gave him a bottle of water. She did not think the injury was severe, but she sensed the fall had shaken Christiano.

He told her he was twenty-four, the son of Portuguese diplomats, and obsessed with photography. Christiano said he and his friend Donny ran a successful business from a nearby internet café and invited her to see it.

Over the following weeks and months, Becky learned

that Christiano, who hated to be called Chris, and Donny picked up unsuspecting tourists, whom they then secretly filmed in compromising situations. These videos went on their website, and subscribers paid to see them. Christiano explained that he would continue until he had enough money for a photography course. His parents would not help him as they expected their son to follow them into public service.

Despite initial reluctance, Becky agreed to help the pair get introduced to visitors. Louise and Candice quickly became her friends, and Becky found it all rather exciting. She was thrilled when the boys handed her a share of the money they made from their website. Becky was even more delighted when Christiano kissed her as they walked from the club where the five had celebrated a successful week.

He called the next day to apologise, but Becky assured him there was no need. She had liked it, admitted she fancied him and would be happy for it to happen again.

On their next date, Becky asked how Christiano could go with other women while saying how much he wanted to be with her. She accepted his explanation that picking up tourists was merely a job and meant nothing. He did not put his heart and soul into it. He felt differently about Becky and cared for her but would not rush her into anything. Christiano was concerned that he was older and people might get the wrong impression. He suggested they take their time. Becky was adamant she did not care what other people thought. Thus began their relationship.

Two months, two weeks and three days after their chance meeting, she and Christiano had sex for the first time. Her parents had gone to Alcudia, where Becky's older brother lived, to stay for the weekend. She wasted no time in inviting Christiano to sleep over. Becky felt terrific when Christiano lay back on the bed, repeating that it was the best sex he had ever had.

Becky had been appalled to hear that Donny's girlfriend, Candice, had agreed to have sex with another man to help the boys and their good friend, Grigor. She sought reassurance from Christiano that she would never be expected to do that. The look on his face told her she was safe. That would never happen.

Becky stretched and considered what she should wear that evening when she and her friends took the three tourists to Grigor's club. She was looking forward to it, but not everyone in her little gang was so enthused.

Louise suggested these three could be trouble. She thought Gemma might prove difficult.

Becky knew that Louise could be a drama queen, and her predictions did not always come to fruition. Lou had dismissed Becky's plans for her and Christiano to be together forever and laughed that the relationship would never last. Becky smirked as she thought about how wrong Louise was. She and Christiano were tighter than ever, and Becky would ensure they stayed that way.

Jon's 'phone rang just as his wife and daughter entered the kitchen.

His wife shook her head, "Already?"

Jon shrugged. "I have to take it. Only be a sec." He retreated to the balcony to speak to his boss.

"Good morning Rob." He checked his watch and calculated the time back home. "It's only eight am, and it's a Sunday. You're up early."

Rob Cromwell, the owner of Cromwell Construction, was not one for pleasantries. "I'm teeing off at nine-thirty and wanted to sort this out before I go," he said.

"What's the problem?"

"Where are we with the Kelly job? I can't find any record of you placing the concrete order."

Jon had delegated the task to Rob's son. Richard was learning the ropes, ready to take over the business. "Rich was looking after the Kelly contract. Have you spoken to him?"

"He's away with his girlfriend and won't return until

this afternoon, so I'm ringing you. Can you check that the concrete will arrive tomorrow and get back to me?"

"But I'm in Majorca..."

"Don't I know it? God knows how much this call costs me. I told you this was not a good time to take a holiday. It won't take you long. Get back to me before nine." Cromwell rang off.

Son or no son, there was no way he was getting away with it that easily. Jon accessed his address book on the phone and pressed Richard's number. The call went straight to messages, so he left a short, terse message but knew it would do no good. Richard rarely returned his calls. Jon's next call was to the personal number of his contact at the concrete supplier.

"Ian, Jon here. I'm very sorry to call you so early. Yes, I know what day it is, but I must check something."

Ten minutes and much grovelling later, Jon placed an order to be delivered the following morning. He texted his boss to confirm everything was under control. His boss responded that he knew his son would not have let him down.

The sign advertising free Wi-Fi was a deal clincher.

"This one looks okay, Mum. Shall we try it?" Nick was already on his way into the café.

"Why not?"

Elizabeth Kingston placed her bags on a chair. "If they make coffee, then it'll do me." Her eyes scanned the bi-lingual menu. "I might have a cake too. What about you?"

Nick had also decided. "I'm having two bacon rolls, orange juice and a coffee."

His mother smiled. "Are you going to have a cake for dessert?"

"You never know. I'll see what yours is like."

The waiter arrived, took their order, and left them with a jug of water and two glasses. Nick filled one and emptied it again very quickly.

"That's better," he said, refilling his glass.

"How far did you go this morning?" Elizabeth casually checked out the other three customers. One couple was devouring a full English breakfast, while a lady who appeared local sipped coffee as she examined a till receipt.

"Not too far. I went out the front of the apartment block, around the bend, past the cafes onto the promenade and then ran down to the next town. There is a lovely little bridge down the end, just before you enter the next place."

"Any idea what it's called?"

"No, not yet, but we can walk there later if you fancy it."

His mother nodded and sipped her water.

The lady with the receipt spoke to them. Her accent was Spanish.

"That is Sillot. It is old, not as modern as Sa Coma."

"Gracias," said Elizabeth. "Is there much to see in Sillot?"

The lady shrugged. "It depends. There is now a nice walk along the…how you say…promenade?" She saw Elizabeth nod. "There are also a few good restaurants and bars there. It is also on the way to Porto Cristo, so there are plenty of buses, but it is quiet in Sillot. If you want nightlife and entertainment, then this end and…" She moved her hand in a circular motion and then pointed beyond the hypermarket, "…down there towards Cala Millor, are better places, I think."

Elizabeth smiled.

"Sillot sounds ideal to me, but Nick might prefer a bit more life. Thank you for that. My name is Elizabeth, and this is my son, Nicholas."

"Call me Nick."

"Hello, Elizabeth, Neek. I am Lucia."

"Your English is excellent," said Elizabeth.

Lucia smiled as she shrugged. "I learn a lot as I clean apartments. If I don't speak English, I won't get the job. They know no Spanish."

"Yes, I know what you mean. We do tend to expect everyone to learn our language." Elizabeth eased back in her seat as the waiter delivered her cake. "Gracias, "

"Da nada," said the waiter. "Your coffee and sandwich are coming in a moment."

The cake looked delicious, but Elizabeth did not eat it until the waiter returned with Nick's food. She turned to Lucia again, this time speaking Spanish.

"That looks good. Do you know if it is homemade?"

Lucia was surprised to be speaking to a Brit in her native language. "*Yes, it is my brother's place. He trained in Barcelona and opened here two years ago. He makes all the cakes himself.*"

"*Was it your brother who served us?*"

Lucia shook her head. "*No, that was his brother-in-law, Alfonso. My brother Raphael also has a shop in Cala Millor and spends much time there. My son Javier works there too. This one is more convenient for me, and I stop on my way home from work after I go to the supermarket.*"

"*We also went to the shop,*" said Elizabeth, pointing to her shopping bags and beach equipment. "*It is very reasonable.*"

Lucia shrugged. "*Maybe.*"

Nick had a decent knowledge of Spanish, which his mother had tutored him, but he lacked the confidence to use it. He listened to the exchange without contributing. On the other hand, his mother relished the opportunity to speak a language she had learned many years before but seldom got to practice these days. She was in her element.

Leaving the ladies to their conversation, Nick picked up an English newspaper and only looked up when he heard them chuckling.

Ben, Will, and Shirley walked to Sillot and back, planning to spend the afternoon by the pool. Will selected three empty beds close to the complex's back wall and removed his bright yellow shirt, exposing his beer belly and recently acquired tattoos.

"I'll have a minute to let lunch settle down and then take a dip in the pool."

Shirley tossed him a plastic container. "Make sure you

put some cream on. You'll burn in no time in this heat."

Will smiled in Ben's direction. "She's a fuss, isn't she?"

Ben nodded. "Someone has to look after you." He chose the end bed and settled down for a read. He wasn't interested in the book but thought it best to go through the motions.

The beach was heaving as Elizabeth and Nick stepped over the small wall, looking for a suitable spot to plant their umbrella. They guessed that hiring a sun lounger and shades would be expensive, so they bought a chair and umbrella to use as needed. Elizabeth much preferred being on the beach to sitting around the pool, so she selected the one free spot close to the few trees scattered across the beach.

Nick quickly erected the umbrella, placing rocks around the base to help keep it in place. Once camp was established, he went swimming, leaving his mother to read. She kicked off her shoes and buried her feet in the warm sand. Later, she would stroll in the water, hoping the salt would help her cracked heels.

It had been years since she had done so. She liked the feeling and was determined to make the most of it.

Christiano and Donny hunched closer to the monitor, snickering at the images on the screen.

"Here's a good bit," said Donny. "Grigor goes for it. The poor cow knows nothing about it."

"How much did you put in her drink?"

"A little more than usual, but she was such a bossy bitch. I thought she needed bringing down a peg or two."

Christiano smiled as another man joined Grigor with the unconscious South African lady. The two took full advantage, one at the back, the other at the front.

"Jesus, look at Raul. I had no idea he was so big. He is angry at her for calling him stupid." Don shook his head. "They are giving her a right roasting."

Christiano cackled as a third man, a mutual friend,

pushed his penis into the lady's mouth, playing to the camera as he did so. "Barty's an idiot."

"Those two aren't letting up, are they?"

"It's a good thing she didn't bleed."

"That was more luck than judgment, by the looks of it. I should have told them to go a bit easier. She might have got hurt."

"Tough shit," said Christiano. "Those men paid for a good time, and she deserves nothing less after what she called them. Did you clean her up afterwards?"

"Of course.."

"Where did you leave her?"

"I was going to leave her outside her hotel, but she started to come around. I'd only managed to get her onto the bench behind the hypermarket when she came to."

"Did she remember anything?"

"Don't think so. She was very sore." He grinned. "I told her she had tried to walk the wooden beam at the bar and slipped."

"Good thinking."

"I thought so. I've promised to check later to see how she is feeling."

Christiano's eyes returned to the video. "This is great footage. I'll start to work on pixelating the faces."

"While you're doing that, I'll get us a coffee."

"And Danish."

They slapped their palms together.

"Good call."

Jon had joined his children at the water line and was busy digging holes and building castles in the fine sand. It was proving to be a thankless task. No sooner had he dug a hole than one of the boys filled it in again. They demolished the castles equally as quickly. Daisy sat quietly, nearer the sea, building a walled fortress. Jon smiled as she carefully dug a road from the wall to the castle.

His daughter had inherited her artistic skills from her mother. He watched her as she walked up the beach to the trees, collected a few pebbles and brought them back for decoration. The twins lost interest in their father's activities and wandered to observe their sister. They readily agreed to help when she asked them to get more stones. They were safe enough, so Jon stayed where he was, letting the water lap over him.

Ben put down his book and, instead, read the leaflet he had taken from the stand on the wall outside the estate agents. It provided details of trips from Sa Coma.

A couple looked like they could help him in his mission. One tour visited the Cape of Formentor, which offered breathtaking views. Another involved a tour of various attractions, including Santanyi, which also involved cliffs. He would consult his guidebook before choosing.

"It's hot in that sun," said Jon returning. He moved his sun lounger closer to his wife.

Leah looked up with a worried look on her face. "Where are the kids?"

"Relax, they are just over there. All three are fine. They have plenty of factor 50 on." He nodded toward the children. "It looks like Dais has made friends with a young German boy, although I am not sure he is too happy she is telling him what to do."

Leah smiled. "I think her brothers often feel the same way," she said, returning her attention to her magazine.

Jon rubbed his shoulders as he watched the children playing.

Charlie and Harry happily ran back and forth, collecting stones in their little plastic buckets. They dropped them in a pile just outside Daisy's expanding kingdom. The German lad was laying roads to the walled fortress from other castles he had erected nearby. Daisy told him off for building too close to hers, and the boy crawled away.

Jon began to think that the holiday might work out fine. It would be perfect if the kids entertained themselves. That would be an unexpected bonus. A scream from Daisy shattered his peace. Jon saw his daughter holding her hand, which appeared to have been hit by a rock dropped by the German boy. The lad stood still, blankly staring as the little girl ran to her parents. Jon rose and met Daisy halfway.

"He dropped the stone on my hand! He dropped the stone on my hand!"

Leah sat up and accepted Daisy as Jon placed their daughter into her arms. She checked the damage. The back of her daughter's hand was red, but the stone had not broken the skin, and there was no blood.

Jon looked for the boys. They stood in silence, eyes peeled on their sister. The German boy had dropped to his knees and started digging again, oblivious to what he had done.

The brothers looked at each other and then at the German as they returned to the building site. The German boy pointed at something and then shouted at the twins. Without any warning, the boys slapped the German with their plastic spades. One caught him in the face, the other on his back. There was not a lot of power in the slaps, but the boy screamed, jumped up and ran away sobbing.

Jon collected his sons, told them what they had done was naughty, and placed them on a lounger as Leah cradled a crying Daisy. Their daughter had a towel around her. The brothers looked at Daisy and burst into tears themselves.

The promise of ice cream eventually calmed matters, and Jon slipped on his shirt, ready to walk to the shop. The arrival of a furious German man shouting at him delayed his progress. Jon looked at Leah, who shrugged. He saw his children staring nervously at the angry stranger.

"I am sorry, I don't understand," Jon said.

His comments turned off the man's volume control, and

Jon saw others on the beach staring at them.

"I am sorry, but I cannot understand what you are saying."

A Welsh lady wearing a sarong over her swimsuit appeared out of nowhere. "Can I help? I speak a little German."

"Yes, please," said Jon without thinking.

The woman spoke to the man in measured tones. She pointed to the water's edge, at the sand fortresses, then at Daisy, at the stones, and finally at the boys. The man uttered a response, and the lady shook her head. The German took in what the lady had said before speaking again. When he did so, the lady asked Leah if she could show him the little girl's hand. Leah showed her daughter's arm; the mark was evident, and the man nodded. He leaned toward Daisy and said, "I am sorry." Daisy cuddled up closer to her mother. The German spoke to the lady who translated.

"He asked me to tell you he is very sorry about his son's actions. He will go back and admonish him not just for dropping the stone on your daughter's hand but also for lying about it." She looked at Jon. "He told his father that you slapped him."

Jon's jaw dropped. "I would never do that." He looked at the man and shook his head. "I would never do that."

The man nodded and held out his hand. "Sorry," he said again as they shook hands. "I hope your little girl is okay."

"What did you say to him?" Jon asked the lady as the German shuffled back down the beach.

"I told him what happened. I saw it all from over there."

"I am so pleased you did. Your German is excellent."

The woman smiled. "How would you know?"

Jon laughed. "I suppose I wouldn't, but you got the message across."

"He seemed to understand me, so I must have made some sense." She looked at Leah. "Is your daughter okay?"

"Yes, thank you, she'll be fine. She's more shaken than hurt."

The lady spoke to Daisy. "And what is your name?"

"Daisy," she said in barely more than a whisper.

"That's a lovely name. Do you feel better now?"

Daisy nodded.

"Good, and how old are you, Daisy?"

"She's five," said Leah.

"Nearly six," said Daisy.

The lady smiled as she saw two other faces staring at her. "I am pleased that her brothers stepped in to protect their sister," she said.

The boys looked at her and then at their parents.

"Yes," said Jon. "But we don't condone that sort of behaviour."

"Sometimes, you need to show bullies that they won't beat you," said the lady. "I think that little German boy has learned a valuable lesson."

A young man arrived at her side. "Everything okay, Mum?"

"Yes, everything's fine."

"Your mother just helped us avoid an international incident," said Jon.

"It was just a misunderstanding." Elizabeth turned, ready to go back to her seat.

"I don't know how to thank you," said Jon, scratching his arm. "Can I get you both an ice cream?"

Three hours in the sun was enough for Ben, who announced his return to the apartment. He declined Shirley's offer to accompany him. He had his key and suggested he might have a nap. Shirley watched him enter the building and did not relax until she saw him opening the patio door.

"He seems to be enjoying himself," said Will, arching his neck to look at her.

"Hmm, I must admit that he seems much better than I thought."

"That's a good thing, isn't it?"

"I'm not sure. I get the feeling that there's something on his mind, something he's not telling us."

"Maybe you are just worrying too much." He flexed his arms and legs, extending them out from the recliner. "Relax. It's your holiday, too, remember."

Shirley sat back and swung her feet onto the chair. "You're right. I'll try."

"But before you do, can you put some cream on my back? I want to lie on my belly?"

"Mummy, mummy, Harry's feet are too hot in his trainers, and the sand gets in them."

Leah feared this might be the case. "Shall we get you a pair of sandals, Harry?"

Her son nodded.

"Are you sure?"

"Yes."

"Will you wear them?"

"Yes."

"Okay, then we'll get some the next time we go to the shop. What about you, Charlie? Do you want a pair?"

"No. Sandals are for girls."

"They are for boys and girls."

"Daisy wears them, so they are for girls."

"Daddy wears them, too."

"Daddy is a girl."

"I'd leave it at that if I were you," said Jon, whispering. "I think we'd better watch our little sexist thug."

"Good night last night." Louise took a beer bottle from the fridge and joined the two men ogling the monitor. She twisted off the cap and discarded it into a bin.

"It was." Donny pointed at the screen. "It was very productive."

Louise rested her head on Christiano's shoulder as he leaned in to watch the screen. "Is that the South African?"

"It is," said Christiano. "That bloke with the huge penis is Raul. He is a business acquaintance of Graham's."

"I know. I met him at the club just before the four of you left."

"Graham told us to set him up with someone and to make sure we filmed it," said Donny."Isabella fell into our laps."

"How did you get her back here?"

Donny spoke again. "Grigor had his car. Getting her in and out of the car was hard work. Once we had gotten her into the pleasure palace, she was no trouble."

All three laughed.

"What business does Graham do with Raul?" Louise asked.

"No idea," said Donny. "He said the video would be an insurance policy, so I am guessing he either sees Raul as a threat or wants something from him."

Christiano nodded. "Sounds plausible, but I think their relationship might change once Graham has this footage."

Louise took a drink. "Graham said Raul was married with a few children, so he would probably prefer the film to stay private."

Christiano caressed Louise's left buttock as he stood. "It is up to Graham what he plans to do with this just so long as he pays us."

"Talking of plans," said Louise. "How long must we wait for Becky to work for us? I had hoped we would have used her and dumped her before she turned seventeen. She is a pain in the arse."

"She refuses to come with me to the Palace, so I have not yet been able to put her on camera. My parents are going out for a meal later this week. I will invite her over then."

"I'm going to Christiano's place this afternoon to make sure the equipment is fully charged and ready to go," said Donny.

"I thought you might," said Louise, patting Christiano's bottom.

Elizabeth paddled in the sea, leaving Nick under the giant palm trees. It felt good doing nothing. He stretched out on the oversized beach towel provided by his uncle. It was old with frayed edges and faded colours, but Nick did not care. He was used to having other people's cast-offs. It would not be for much longer. His time was coming. He and his mother would soon be enjoying the good life again. Nick could hardly wait. In the meantime, he would do nothing besides relaxing in the sun. It made a pleasant change.

Nick's peace was broken by a large Senegalian man wearing several pairs of sunglasses hanging from a long gold chain around his neck. The man also carried two doctor's cases and wore an outrageously bright orange shirt.

"Looky looky, many bargains."

"No, thank you," Nick said. "I have everything I need."

"I recognise that accent. Are you Welsh? Like Gareth Bale?"

"Yes, although I'm not as good at football."

"Not many people are. He had a gift."

"I'm impressed you recognised I was Welsh."

"Your countrymen and women are everywhere."

"Are there many here now?"

"Plenty, my friend. Would you like to come and meet them?

"Not really. You have a good ear. I only said a few words."

"Should I have waited until you started to sing?"

"Not unless you wanted to clear the beach." Nick took a drink from one of the two bottles of water he had placed against the tree. He saw his visitor looking at the other and reached for the spare. "Would you like a drink?"

"I would. Thank you." The man poured half the bottle down his throat. "I usually carry one, but I dropped it in on the headland, and there are no shops between there and here." The visitor wiped the top of the bottle and held it for Nick to take.

"You keep it. I can get another if I need to. We are staying close by."

"Thank you. That is very kind." He opened one of his cases. "Can I interest you in something? I have special rates for friends to repay your kindness."

Nick smiled. "No thanks. I'm fine. I don't want payment. It is only a bottle of water." The man nodded as he closed the case. "You can tell me something, though."

"What would you like to know?" The man had picked up his other case and was readying to depart.

"Your English is excellent."

"Thank you."

"So why do you need to say things like looky, looky and many bargains?"

The visitor laughed. "It is part of the game, my friend. When tourists see me, they think I am stupid and not as bright as them. They believe they can get a better bargain." He tapped the side of his nose. "But Banda knows his market." He winked at Nick as he walked away. "Looky looky," he shouted, leaving his deep, hearty laugh ringing in Nick's ears.

The boys were irritable, and Leah knew why.

"They need a siesta," she said. "Shall we head back to the apartment? We could have a drink while these three get their heads down?"

Jon yawned, "I might need a kip myself. All this relaxing is exhausting."

The boys played in their bedroom before Charlie crashed on the sheet he had dragged to the floor. Harry followed shortly afterwards.

Daisy did not want to play with her brothers. She read in her parents' bedroom. She was fast asleep when Jon nipped in to change his shorts. He placed Daisy's book on the bedside table and then went next door to lift Charlie onto the mattress and remove a toy lying under Harry's cheek.

Confident that the children were comfortable, Jon

ensured the bedroom doors would not shut, checked the apartment's front door to ensure it was locked securely, and joined Leah on the balcony. She had poured the wine.

"This is the life," said Jon, taking a full glass. "Cheers!"

They tapped glasses.

"Cheers," said his wife, sipping her wine. "Hmmm. This was only cheap, but it's very nice. I might get more bottles and put them in the fridge."

"Great, it would be lovely if we get a bit of time like this every day," he said before apologising. His phone rattled in his pocket, and he said he had to take it.

"Hello,"

"Where are we with the quotation for the old church hall?"

"I left it with you last week."

"Where is it then?"

"No idea. I put it on your desk. It's in a quotation folder. You know, the yellow ones."

"I know it's a yellow folder. I'm not stupid."

Jon said nothing. He listened as papers shuffled and Richard uttered expletives.

"It's not here. My old man told me to ensure the quotation gets submitted tomorrow. He'll go mental when I tell him you haven't done it."

"You'd better not tell him that. It's not my fault. That was supposed to be your job. I was only helping you out."

Richard continued to shuffle papers. "The bad news for you is that I'm here, and you're not. Do you realise how much you've pissed him off?"

Jon could guess. He had also anticipated that the quote would get lost and had stored a copy. "Go into my office." He knew Richard would use a cordless phone and could hear him marching over the stone floors.

"Right."

"Top drawer, first cabinet."

"Yeah."

"Look under "c for the church hall."

"Got it." The call ended without a goodbye or a thank you.

Sara and Kylie returned from their shopping expedition to find Gemma talking to Candice and Becky.

The four exchanged greetings.

"Great night last night," said Candice.

"It was fab," said Sara. "I was a bit hung over this morning, though."

"A bit," said Gemma, laughing. "You looked like Frankenstein's sister when you got out of bed." They all laughed. "I am happy to see that you've recovered now."

"Yes, we had a burger and chocolate milkshake in the café in the hypermarket. I feel a lot better."

Becky patted Sara's arm. "I knew you'd be a party animal. Where do you fancy going tonight?"

"No idea," said Sara. "You're the locals. Where do you recommend?"

"Christiano and Donny have tickets to a party in the bar at the old bull ring. It's called Grigor's and is about five miles out of town. Would you like to come along?"

"How do we get there?" Gemma asked.

"Taxi, I suppose," said Sara.

"How much does that cost?" Kylie reflected on the previous evening. She could not afford to keep spending at the same rate.

"I can probably get a friend of my father's, Jakey, to take and collect us," said Becky. "He has a minibus that he uses for airport runs. I'm sure he'd do it for a few euros each, no more than 20 euros each way, and there'll be a load of us."

Kylie liked that price. "How much are the tickets?"

"They are free," said Candice. "Christiano and Donny know the owner. They do work for him. Donny said it would be free entry and drinks, but he told me to warn you that sometimes these parties turn into orgies. People are at it all over the place."

"I'll get my camera ready," said Sara.

Jon and Leah sat on the sofa of their apartment and kicked off their shoes. They had taken the children to an English bar nearby, where Daisy and Leah had danced while Jon entertained the boys in the outdoor play area. They swapped periodically, but Daisy did not think her father was as good a dancing partner.

The menu was limited, but it was food the kids liked. The chef also provided extra tomatoes to keep Daisy happy. Afterwards, they let the children look in the gift shops. Daisy bought a hairband, and the boys got soldiers. Jon guessed that most of the plastic army would get buried and lost the following day.

"I'll get us a drink," said Jon, leaving his mobile on the table to go to the fridge.

Leah turned off the ceiling light, turned on the air conditioning, and closed the curtains. She was tempted to sit on the balcony but feared the mossies.

The room was lit only by the light from the cooker hood, and she thought it created a lovely ambience.

Jon's 'phone rattled and then buzzed, and he returned to answer it. Leah took it before he had a chance. It was his boss. Leah pressed the decline button and switched off the phone.

"That might have been important."

"It can wait."

"But there might have been a problem with the quote."

"I said it could wait. Rob doesn't pay you enough to take calls when you're on your first proper holiday in years. Whatever it is can wait until the morning." She put the mobile in the pocket of her trousers. "I thought you were getting us a drink."

Ben, Shirley, and Will had strayed into nearby Cala Millor, where they found an Italian restaurant. After enjoying a three-course meal, they visited a karaoke café, so Will could show off before taking a taxi back to the Happy Bar for a nightcap.

Will ordered three brandies and three beers and would not take no for an answer. Ben joined the toast, downed his brandy and ordered another round. It had been a long time since he had a hangover, and if he didn't have one on this holiday, he would never have one again.

Elizabeth and Nick meandered leisurely back from the old town of Sillot. They had enjoyed their meals at a quiet Spanish restaurant off the beaten track, a haven of peace compared to the rowdy English pubs they passed on the seafront.

Nick leaned on the railings at the side of a bridge, watching the ducks go about their business. His mother stood by his side.

"It took us a long time to get here, but here we are."

Nick smiled. "Indeed. We should make this a holiday we won't forget quickly."

His mother put her hand on his shoulder. "I do hope so."

Wherever Gemma looked in the bustling club, she saw older men chasing much younger women. She was uncomfortable and wasted no time communicating her feelings to Kylie.

"Never mind a bull ring. This place is more like a cattle market. These girls don't seem to have any taste."

"Or many choices," said Kylie pulling a face as a younger girl nearby kissed a much older man. "It's not my kind of place."

"Shall we go?"

"I'd say yes, but where can we go? We are in the middle of nowhere. The taxi isn't due for hours, and we can't run off and leave Sara."

A large man with a face dripping with sweat approached

them and asked, in broken English, if they wanted to dance. Both smiled but declined politely. The man shrugged, turned his attention to a young lady on another table and grabbed her backside as they entered the dance floor.

"Classy," said Gemma.

Christiano and Louise returned from dancing.

"Are you having a good time, ladies?" The Portuguese asked.

Kylie looked at Gemma, who spoke for both of them.

"It's not our cup of tea, to be honest. We prefer places where the men are our age and not older than our fathers."

Christiano looked shocked. "I am so sorry." He glanced around. I did not realise that." He called Donny, who was chatting with Sara by the bar. She followed him as they joined the others.

"Donny, the girls are not comfortable. We must go somewhere else."

"What? why?"

"Look around you, Donny. Grigor must be catering for the older customers tonight."

Donny nodded. "Yes, I see what you mean. I hadn't noticed." He looked at Sara. "We were too busy chatting."

Christiano spoke again. "I am so sorry, girls."

Louise stood and said. "If you give us five minutes to say goodbye, we can all return to town. There is a club in Cala Millor called the Cavern. Let's go there."

"How do we get there?" Gemma asked.

"I'll get Becky to sort that. I can see her over there," said Louise. "I'm sure Jakey will be happy to have an earlier collection time. She can give him a call."

"Shall we wait here, Donny?" Sara asked.

"No, I don't like the thought of you girls being around these slimy old geezers. You might be better off waiting outside. I tell you what, hang on a moment." He turned to his sister. "Lou, I'll take the girls outside and look after them while you and Christiano go and thank the main man."

The girls followed Donny to the exit, where he spoke with an enormous man in a suit. The man let them wait in the foyer, and Candice and Becky joined them momentarily before stepping out for a cigarette.

"Fair play to Christiano. He's a real gentleman," said Kylie. "Not many men would leave a place just because we weren't comfortable."

Sara agreed. "Donny is the same, though, isn't he? As soon as he knew that we didn't like it. He wanted us out of here. I must admit that I hadn't noticed so many slime balls."

"You were too busy chatting up Donny, I suppose," said Kylie.

"Well, I wouldn't say no," said Sara.

"You never do," said Kylie, giggling. "And I certainly wouldn't say no to Christiano."

Gemma listened as her companions sang the praises of Donny and Christiano but made no comment. She neither trusted nor liked their male companions. They were pleasant enough, but something about them did not ring true. In her experience, twenty-something-year-old boys never behaved so impeccably.

Louise got kissed twice on each cheek and given a cash bundle before Christiano shook hands with Grigor and Graham.

"That video was excellent. It will prove very useful."

"Glad you liked it," said Louise.

"We have almost finished pixellating the one featuring Raul. You can have that in a few days," said Christiano.

"Good." Grigor eased his hand up the skirt of the teenage girl sitting on his lap. She turned and kissed him, and he turned his face away from her toward Louise.

"Why do you never star in any of the films? You have a great body; my friends would pay good money," said Graham.

"I am merely the organ grinder." Louise giggled smuttily, "I manage the operation and help the boys find suitable girls, but I am totally off the menu. I am very selective about who I go with." She winked at Christiano.

"That is a pity. My friends like girls like you." Grigor handed the teenage girl a glass of champagne and encouraged her to drink.

Graham blew a kiss at Louise. "Might you have more girls available in the next few days? I have another business associate coming in on Friday."

"We'll certainly see what we can do," said Louise.

"He likes them young. Do you have anybody suitable in mind?"

"Possibly," said Christiano. "She may not be keen initially, but I am sure I can persuade her."

"That is what I like to hear. I don't know how you do it, but keep it up."

"Providing the tourists keep coming, we will use them. We selected three new ones yesterday. One of them, Sara, looks promising. She seems keen on Donny," said Louise. "I do not think Gemma is interested. We might have to separate her from the other two."

Christiano agreed. "If we can get her out of the way, getting Kylie to make a movie would be easier."

"You should be so lucky, lucky, lucky, lucky," sang Grigor, squeezing the teenager's breast as he nibbled her neck.

DISCOVERY

(6 YEARS 5 MONTHS BEFORE THE HOLIDAY)

Ben Moran strode around the living room of the large, empty house. It was ideal for their purposes: it had lots of space, a vast garden, a great neighbourhood, and a price he could afford without borrowing money.

"What do you think, love?" His wife folded her arms, trying to keep warm.

"I like it," he said. "I like it a lot."

"Good." Cheryl Moran looked at the estate agent. "You think they might accept our offer?"

The agent took out his mobile. "Well, it is a little lower than they wanted, and there has been quite a bit of interest, but I'll advise them that they are not likely to get another cash offer of this size. Are you looking to complete it as soon as possible?"

"We are," said Cheryl. "We want to get this sorted quickly. We liked it as soon as we saw it."

The agent nodded. "I'll see what I can do for you. Excuse me a minute."

"And if you succeed, we'll give you a quarter of the money we are saving as a bonus," said Ben.

"But that's...." He was going to say it was against the company's rules, not to mention immoral and technically illegal, but he had bills to pay like everyone else. "...very generous of you. In cash?"

"Of course," said Ben.

Cheryl waited by her husband's side as the man left the room to make a call.

"It was a bit of luck finding this," said Cheryl. "After some of the places we have visited, this is a real palace."

The pair gave the downstairs another look.

Cheryl ran a hand over the kitchen worktop. "It's lovely, isn't it?

"It is. Thank God for mobile 'phones. A few years ago, we would have had to find a call box and make an appointment. Now we can ring and say we're here. If you want the sale, come and meet us."

"As you did, and he did. I have a good feeling about this, Benjamin.

"Me too," said Ben, spotting a smiling estate agent re-entering the room.

The lady at the bank was welcoming and friendly.

"Come on in, Mrs Kingston, and you must be Nicholas."

"Yes."

She shook his hand.

"Pleased to meet you."

The lady waited for Elizabeth and Nick to sit at one side of the table before sitting on the other.

"How can I help?"

Elizabeth Kingston took a deep breath.

"My husband has always tended to manage the finances, but, sadly, he suffered a massive stroke last month ..." She breathed deeply again. No matter how often she uttered those words, saying them was not getting any easier. "...so now Nick and I need to take control. I thought a good start would be establishing what accounts we hold in joint names and what I need to do to gain access to the accounts solely in my husband's name."

"I see. First, I'd like to say how sorry I am to hear that news, and I wish your husband a full and speedy recovery. "

The doctor's prognosis was not good, but Elizabeth saw no reason to disclose that now. She smiled weakly and said, "Thank you."

"Secondly, we must run through a few security issues before I can provide any information. These won't take long, but I am sure you can understand why we must verify who you are."

"Of course," said Elizabeth, taking a passport, utility bill and purse from her bag.

"I must also clarify that if your husband has any accounts solely in his name, we need you to obtain a power of attorney over his estate before we can let you have any details. Is that clear?"

Elizabeth had assumed this would be the case. "Yes. I'll speak to our solicitor about that once...." She struggled for the right words. "...once things have become a little clearer."

Shirley Kendall, nee Moran, signed and returned the paper to the suited lady sat opposite. "That's it then. I should be a single woman again very soon."

"Once the decrees come through. I cannot foresee any problems."

Shirley hoped her solicitor was correct. She knew her husband, Cole, could be temperamental and obstinate when he wanted to be, but she hoped his new partner would convince him of the benefits of ending this marriage amicably.

Cole might not listen, but the recent arrival of his third child might also help him see sense. He was not generally a nasty man, at least not to Shirley, but he certainly had a darker side. Stories had reached her about him losing his cool with others. Cole was also manipulative, controlling and forceful.

The pair had lived apart for several years, and Cole now lived with Caitlyn, a younger lady, and their baby daughter, Kim. Somehow, he had managed to maintain a presence in Shirley and her children's lives. Cole turned up uninvited and unexpectedly, demanding attention and often forcing their children to cancel other arrangements to spend time with him.

Her son, Thomas, 11, dreaded his father attending his football matches. Cole frequently threatened other parents, making the sidelines uncomfortable for spectators. The team manager twice banned Cole, but it made no difference. Nobody stood up to him. Thankfully, Thomas was one of the team's better footballers. It would take a brave coach to omit him from the first eleven.

Rosie was a year older than her brother and a strong swimmer. Cole insisted on attending the galas. Shirley dreaded the thought of any lad paying her attention in her father's presence.

Her soon-to-be ex-husband followed their daughter on all her social networking sites, demanding that she give him her passwords. He regularly embarrassed Rosie with his comments and made threats if he found anything her friends said insulting or offensive. He almost always did.

Towards the end of their relationship, Cole spent long periods away from home and embraced his return to single life. When he returned home between jobs, He would disappear without notice and spend many nights away from his family.

Shirley became more and more unhappy. While he had never raised a finger at his family, she worried it was only a matter of time before one of them did something to provoke him. It was a huge relief when he said he was moving out.

Shirley had considered divorce but never took action. They had been together since she was seventeen and Cole was twenty-four. Now, three months short of her thirtieth birthday, she decided to formalise the separation and get as far away from Cole as soon as possible.

She discussed the matter with her father, declining his offer to pay someone to break Cole's legs but accepting the offer to facilitate relocation.

When her parents found a new home, and they had rung earlier to say they had visited one they both loved, Shirley and the two children would take over their old house. She had warned Cole they would be moving, and he was less than enthusiastic. Shirley explained that she had a more prominent role in the family business, requiring her to be closer to the centre of operations. The alternative was for the children to stay with their father full-time. She knew that would be a nonstarter. There was no way his new love would tolerate it.

Shirley was excited at the prospect of moving back to the Midlands. Life in King's Lynn had been great initially, but as Cole's construction business expanded, so did his ego and physique.

Working for unscrupulous business people, Cole had recently gotten involved in several dodgy developments. He grew close to known criminals and began to think he was untouchable.

Cole was also obsessed with fitness, and he trained four or five times a week. The weights and readily available steroids bulked him out, and he considered himself invincible. However, he was becoming unpredictable and erratic.

Returning home would be a fresh start for her and the children, but it would also put many miles between them and him.

Snowy tutted as his latest selection, a sure-fire winner, finished sixth in a seven-horse race. That was the last time he listened to his tipster friend.

His mobile rattled, and he answered it as soon as he read the caller's name.

"Hello, Prof. I didn't expect to hear from you so soon. What's up?"

"I have another job for you. This time, it is a clean one, so there is no need for fisty cuffs."

"Thank gawd for that. What is it?"

"We've undertaken a due diligence exercise on behalf of a company considering securing additional funding for expansion."

"In other words, you've checked that the finance bods won't find anything untoward?"

"Exactly. Overall, everything looks fine, but we've identified an employee who raises a few questions."

"Why? Does his background set the alarm bells ringing?"

"No, nothing like that. He must be earning extra cash,

but I can't figure out how. The accounts balance, no stock has gone missing, and everything seems fine."

"So, what is the problem?"

"This employee earns a little more than minimum wage yet drives an expensive new car, lives in a mortgage-free home, and has a taste for fancy gadgets."

"Male or female, or can't I ask?"

"Male."

"Perhaps he won the lottery or something. He might have received an inheritance."

"No, we checked all that."

"Does this employee have another job?"

"Nope. He works the graveyard shift at a garage, and his only other interest appears to be playing games on a computer."

"Maybe he gambles?" Taffy thought about his latest bets and hoped this employee was doing better than him. By the sounds of it, he was.

"That would be for you to find out. I am sure a man with your skills can discover what's behind this?"

Snowy never enjoyed delving into anyone's personal life, but he wanted a challenge, and the money would be handy. If his initial theory was correct, and this person was winning on the horses, then maybe Snowy could learn something. He saw no reason why he should not share the good fortune.

"Okay, send me the details. When do I start, and where am I going?"

"ASAP and the West Midlands. I'll put everything you need to know in the email."

"Thanks."

"Did I mention there is a bonus for early resolution?"

"How soon is early?"

"We must complete the exercise before they seek the extra cash in the new financial year."

"So I probably have about three months? That should be plenty of time."

"You have to allow time for us to prepare the report, so you probably have a couple of months. And Snowy..."

"What?"

"Don't get too cocky about it. We thought something was amiss with this guy weeks ago but haven't found anything. If he is up to anything, then he hides it well.

"I can start next week." He hung up and glanced around the tiny bedsit. He would not be sorry to leave this dump.

Later that evening, Elizabeth and Nick sat around the dining table at their enormous house in Cowbridge, shuffling papers and asking questions.

"There should be a lot more money. Where has it all gone?" Elizabeth picked up another bank statement. "This shows cash in this account before someone transfers it to another. Where is it now? We have no record of where it went; it just shows it as transferred."

"It must be in one of Dad's accounts," said Nick. "I have added it to the list of questions we should ask Douglas Watson on Friday."

Elizabeth had arranged for them to visit Watson and Carnaby, the family's solicitors. "Good idea." She reached over and placed her arm around his shoulders, saying, "I don't know where I would be without you." She kissed his head. "I am sure Douglas can help us. We'll sort everything out very soon. Just wait and see."

Nick nodded and smiled at his mother. The smile was for her reassurance. Despite his inexperience in such matters, Nick felt that his father's financial situation might be more complex than his mother believed.

Jon Oliver had been stunned to hear Leah's announcement.

"I thought you said the pill's effects would last a while."

"That's what the nurse said, but she also warned us that we should use condoms while I was off the pill as there was a bigger risk."

"But it was only a few days…I thought we were safe, what with you having your period."

She held up her hands. "I have no answer. I am sorry. It's just one of those things."

It was a pretty big thing to him. "But you are sure?"

"Yes, I tried two home kits and then went to the doctor." She had no wish to ask the question but needed to know where she stood. "Do you want to get rid of it?"

He took her hand in his. "God no…unless you want to?" She didn't. "Then we'll manage somehow. It'll be fine. We would get married one day anyway, so why not now."

It was not exactly a romantic proposal but a fair point. "What about your plans? You wanted to set up your own business."

"Yeah, well, I still can. It might take a bit longer. We'll need to get a house and arrange a wedding. If you want to marry me, that is."

"Of course I do."

They kissed.

"Right then, we'd better tell our parents, and then I'll need to hand in my notice after telling Cromwell that I'll take the job."

"Why? What's the rush?"

"I was planning to leave anyway."

"I know that, but why do you have to rush? We have six months before the baby's birth."

"I thought we'd have a honeymoon, and my boss is not likely to be delighted if I ask him for leave and then disappear shortly afterwards."

"Honeymoon?"

"We might not have another holiday soon, so let's make the most of this. It's my treat."

"Fine by me," said Leah, kissing him again. "Can you afford it?"

"Yes. I had to work a month in hand when I started, so I'll

get that back. I can also use some of my savings."

She was less happy with this proposal. "You'll need that to start your own business."

"Cromwell will pay me more than I am on now. I'll soon top up the coffers."

DAY 3 - MONDAY 26 JULY

Jon awoke early. The truth was he had barely slept. Cromwell would not be happy that Jon had not taken his calls. His boss was bound to ring back. The prospect of a bollocking had been playing on his mind all night. Jon had no idea what he would say.

He set up the coffee machine, poured himself a glass of water and sat on the balcony to drink it. The air was warm, the sky clear, and the complex eerily quiet. Two feral cats faced each other on the outer wall but then separated. A maintenance man quietly swept up fallen leaves and litter.

The cleaning got interrupted by the young man whose mother had spoken to the German on Jon's behalf the previous day. The two men exchanged greetings in Spanish, and their words echoed around the empty concourse. Jon watched as the lad walked through the gate, taking care to lock it again, and departed the scene. Jon relaxed in the plastic chair, closed his eyes and drifted off, not in such an energetic way as the boy but equally as rewarding.

Nick had no planned route for his run. He departed the complex, turned to his left, avoiding the staff sorting the outside tables at the burger bar, and trotted up the wide carriageway to the Red Lion English bar. Taking a right at the junction, he stepped onto the raised concrete boardwalk and went to Cala Millor. A sign suggested his destination was 3.5 km away. There and back would be just over 4 miles, and Nick could easily cover that distance. He was pleased that he had set off earlier than the day before when the heat made running challenging and almost exhausted him.

As they discussed the previous evening, Gemma and Kylie sucked their orange juice through straws poking out of the top of the plastic cartons.

"What happened to you then?"

Gemma let the juice wash around her mouth before she swallowed. "I came back here."

"On your own?"

"Yes, on my own. We weren't all as lucky as you and Sara."

Kylie sniggered. "I think Sara was luckier than me. They were going for it in the club. Christiano was initially reluctant to kiss me."

"But you made him."

Kylie chuckled. "Yeah, you know me. I forced myself on him."

"Do you know why he is like that? He seems to be keen on you."

"And he is always telling me that he is. Louise told me that he is quite shy with girls. His mother is a feminist and a staunch supporter of women's rights in Portugal. His parents brought him up to respect women. He gets nervous that he might overstep the mark. He is such a sweet guy."

Gemma had heard this story twice from two sources but doubted it was true. "Really? And you believe that?"

"Of course. Why wouldn't I? It certainly makes a change from the blokes back home. They try to get into my knickers whether I want them to or not. Christiano prefers to take it slowly. I think I can change his mind, though."

"Well, if anyone can, you can," said Gemma, squashing the empty container and tossing it into the bin.

Jon stirred to the noise of someone dragging away a heavy pipe. The maintenance man had opened the metal covers at the side of the pool, which covered underground storage space, and was making slow progress down the steps.

An older man sat on the edge of the diving board, waiting for approval to enter the water. The janitor checked the readings on the monitor and then re-emerged, waving to the man to ensure all was clear. The man dived into the pool and began to swim in lengths. Jon started to count how many the man completed but grew bored after 24 and decided it was time for coffee.

Will's "Bohemian Rhapsody" recital was almost as high-pitched as his "Love to Love You Baby", but Ben did not comment. He had had the best night's sleep for ages and, arriving for his morning coffee, found that Shirley had been out to buy him a newspaper and his favourite cake.

"I made filter coffee this morning, Dad. Will found the machine in the cupboard. We got coffee from the hypermarket."

"Lovely love, thanks very much."

The pain au chocolate melted in his mouth, and, coupled with the rich-tasting coffee, it almost made him glad to be alive.

When his phone rattled at 8.30 am, Jon was reluctant to take the call. He waited until the rattling stopped before studying the screen. He had missed three calls, which his log confirmed were from his boss, and had two recorded messages to review. He accessed his messages and listened as Cromwell ranted about not being happy that he could not speak to him. The first message sought urgent confirmation that Jon had sorted the problem with the housing association. The second was related to payment for scaffolding. Both jobs had been Richard's responsibility. He turned the mobile over his hands, pondering what to do next.

Leah decided for him. She snatched the phone out of his hands. "That's it. I won't have you worrying about work for the whole fortnight. You are supposed to enjoy this break. You know what the doctor told you. You need to relax." She switched off the phone, removed the back, and extracted the SIM card. "I'll keep hold of this," she said, returning the mobile.

"But..."

"No buts. Your children and I demand your undivided attention for the next fortnight. Cromwell Construction can wait. We'll deal with what we have to when we return, but for the remainder of this holiday, you are not taking any work calls."

"What if somebody else tries to contact me? Family or someone?"

"They have my number and can ring me if it is urgent." Leah dropped the SIM card into her shorts pocket. Noise from next door told her the children were awake. "We'd better sort breakfast. Those three will be eager to get out and about."

"Hola Lucia, Buenos días," said Elizabeth Kingston, entering the small café bakery with her son.

"Buenos días Elizabeth, Buenos días Nick." Lucia prepared two chairs for the arrival of her new friends.

Nick waved, then went to the counter while his mother joined Lucia.

"Dos cafés, por favour," said Nick before turning to the ladies. "Lucia, would you like something to drink?"

"No gracias," she held up her cup. "I have one, thank you."

A young man spoke to Elizabeth, and Nick became worried. He relaxed when the visitor kissed Lucia, calling her 'Mama'.

Elizabeth spoke in Spanish. She introduced Nick as her son and pointed at the man, saying, "Nick, this is Lucia's son Javier."

The pair shook hands.

"Your mother tells my mother that you like fighting, yes?"

Nick wondered when Mum had disclosed this detail but did not dwell on it. "I like the Mixed Martial Arts."

"Si, MMA, we have that on the satellite channels. It is very violent, no?"

"It can be, but it helps to keep me active."

"Do you play other sports?"

"I was the pitcher for the school baseball team."

"Baseball? You play baseball? I thought that was only America and Japan."

"For some strange reason, it is popular where I live."

"Are you good as a pitcher?"

"Not bad."

"Do you also play football?"

"Yes, but I'm not very good at that."

Javier waved away the confession. "None of us is very good, but we play on Friday at the cage in town behind the big hotel. We start at nine when it gets cooler. We play the game, then we...er...as you say, have a few beers and food. You are welcome to join us. If you would like to play, then that is good too. Just tell my mother."

"I haven't any kit."

"Da nada, you can play as you are, we have..." he patted his chest "... er...training tops..." he checked he had said the right thing.

Nick nodded. "Bibs."

"Bibs si, we have bibs to tell the teams. We run, we kick, and we sometimes fight." He chuckled. "But we have fun, and then we celebrate. If you would like to play, then let me know. "He kissed his mother again and spoke to her in Spanish before returning his attention to the visitors. "It is nice to meet you, Nick. Good to see you again, Elizabeth. I must go."

Again? Nick thought. When did you meet her before?

Becky twirled her short blond hair while waiting for Christiano to frame the photograph. She had taken the day off, claiming to have period pains, and her father would have to manage alone.

"Okay then, look at me...smile...no, make it a dirty smile, like you are trying to seduce me without saying it. That is better, much better. Open your top a little. Beautiful, beautiful, show me everything you have."

The camera constantly clicked as Christiano gave new instructions, and Becky complied. He eventually put down the camera and removed the last of Becky's clothes, leaving her naked on his bed.

Will had it on good authority that Castell Punta De N' Amer's ancient watchtower on the 200-hectare Punta de N'Amer headland was worth a visit. The point lay mid-way between Sa Coma and Cala Millor. His friend suggested the walk would take about 45 minutes from Sa Coma.

Shirley was unsure whether her father would enjoy looking at a display of weapons and learning more about the tower but was pleased that Ben seemed keen. His interest rose after Will mentioned that the views out to sea were supposed to be spectacular, and a bar at the top sold drinks and snacks.

The walk took them alongside a small riding stable on the resort's edge, opposite a burger restaurant and the beach.

Ponies were left to roam inside fenced areas, and enterprising youngsters offered horse food for sale out of large baskets. Shirley paid for a few carrots and wandered up to the fence. She was not alone for long. A horse strode up to her and let her stroke its head while it munched on a carrot. Her father joined her and patted the horse.

"You used to love horses when you were little."

"I still do, but not as much as Will. He spends a fortune on them every weekend."

Ben placed his arm around her. "You've been a great daughter, Shirley. I love you, and I'm proud of you."

This unexpected display of emotion surprised Shirley, but her response was instant. "I love you too, Dad. I'm pleased to see you smiling again." She nudged his shoulder with her head. "But what's brought this on?"

"Nothing. I just thought that perhaps I haven't told you often enough."

"I think you have. You always have. You've been a great father. I don't know what I would have done without you."

"It's what fathers are there for."

"But you didn't have to give us all that money. Are you sure you can afford it?"

"I have plenty - more than enough. Anyway, I'd like you to use it. I won't need it all."

Shirley wondered what her father meant but didn't get a chance to say anything more.

Will appeared and asked, "Didn't I lose twenty quid on that nag last Saturday? And I'm not talking about you, love!" He ducked away as Shirley tried to thump him.

Christiano had established an improvised studio in his parents' dining room and had taken many photographs of Becky in various skimpy outfits. After he had finished the photography, he took her to his bed.

"What competition is this?" She kissed his hairless chest as she gathered her clothes.

Christiano remembered his lie. "It is for novice art photographers in the magazine I buy."

She put on her bra and knickers. "But it's not sleazy, is it? It is a tasteful competition."

"Of course, it is like I said. The judges only publish the winning photographs and destroy all other entries. Entrants can only submit photographs of dressed models, nothing else. The best ten photographs win prizes. That is why I want you to be my model. I want to have my best chance of winning." He put his arm around her shoulder. "Thank you for doing this, Becky. I know you are not comfortable being my model."

"I don't mind. I am pleased you don't want me to do what Candice does for those men at Grigor's."

"No, I want to keep you all for me."

"Good. You will make sure the shots are tasteful."

"Of course, you don't need to ask. "

"Thanks. My father would kill me if he knew I'd modelled for you."

"Don't worry. Your father won't find out unless we win

the competition and he buys the magazine."

"He doesn't read magazines."

"Then we are safe." Christiano kissed her, and Becky responded eagerly.

"Before we make love again, I have a small favour to ask you."

"What is it?" Becky had her arms around his neck and her mouth by his.

"I would like a few more shots. Is that okay?"

"Why do you need more photos? You've taken loads already."

"I know, but they are soft pictures for the contest. I want something a little more...seductive."

"Why?"

"Because sometimes when I have to go with other women, I cannot get aroused, so I like to...err...fantasise about you."

"Really?"

"Yes. It works every time. I try to visualise your face just before we make love. When I know that you are ready for me."

"Honestly?"

"Yes. You have a special look. Very alluring." Becky said nothing as she took in his words. "You are so special to me, Becky. When you look turned on, it makes me very hard. I would also like to have that image to use when I am alone. "

"So you only want photos of my face?"

"I do." He handed her a pink sex toy. "But if you use this and enjoy it, you will look perfect. Plus, you will be ready for me when I have finished taking pictures."

"I am not sure. These photos wouldn't be artistic. They would be pornographic. How do I know you won't sell them?"

"How can you ask such a question? I would never do that, not to you. These photographs are only for my use, and I only want to capture your expressions. If you like, I will give you the camera immediately so you can delete any you don't like."

Becky knew that Christiano could be devious; that was part of the attraction, but she was wise to him. Initially, he wanted to take these photos in the flat above the shop, but Becky refused. There were hidden cameras dotted around that place. Her little group had helped persuade many girls to pose for Christiano on the pretence that he was harmless.

She felt happier having these photographs taken at his home. His parents would never permit him to install cameras here, so she was not worried that they might be a bit saucier. She trusted him not to show anyone. She and Christiano were an item. He said he loved her. It was customary for a boy to want a photograph of his girlfriend. He would only keep the ones she liked. The others would get deleted.

"So you want me to use this, but you will only take photos of my face."

"And shoulders but no boobs and certainly nothing lower."

"And you promise I can delete what I don't like."

He nodded, she agreed, and Becky's underwear hit the floor again.

Christiano picked up his camera and started snapping, focusing on her face as promised. Subtly pressing his foot onto the button under the bed brought the hidden video cameras to life. He moved carefully, avoiding the cameras' line of sight, as a smirk spread across his face. This little film would show Becky pleasuring herself before Christiano joined her on his bed. Later, he would pixellate his face and any other identifiable features.

It had taken him three months, but Christiano knew that once this session ended and he enjoyed her again, Becky would have little choice but to do what he and his friends demanded. If she refused, her father, family, and friends would quickly learn that young Becky had become an internet sensation.

Jon held on to Charlie as his brother paddled off. Harry

got to grips with the armbands and quickly moved around the bigger pool. Charlie, on the other hand, was not so keen. If Jon had let him go, he would happily have stayed in the same position, going around and around. Charlie tapped his shoulder and whispered in his ear.

"Dad, Dad, I need a wee."

Jon looked around. Apart from him and the kids, the pool was empty. "Just wee in the pool."

Charlie looked as if his father had said the silliest thing ever. "No, I can't. Mum said we have to wee in the toilet or the potty."

"I know that, but it is also okay to wee in the pool if you need to."

"But I want to go to the toilet."

He smiled at his son, hoping he was providing reassurance. "If we get out now, we will have to dry before going to the apartment, which might take a long time. Have a wee in the water. Nobody would notice, and Mum won't mind."

Charlie fidgeted in his armbands. "But I can't reach my willy."

"That's okay. Wee through your bathers, just let it out. Mum can wash them afterwards."

"Mum said I have to take down my pants to wee and give my willy a good shake when I have finished."

The logic was unchallengeable, but Jon didn't fancy the trek to the apartment. A new approach was needed.

"That's right. Normally, when you are in dry clothes, you must do what Mum says, and you've been a very good boy lately. We are very proud of you." He kissed his son's cheek. "When you are in wet clothes or a pool wearing bathers, it is okay to wee through them. Nobody will give you a row, but you mustn't fuss. It would be best if you weed quietly. The water will wash it away, and nobody will know what you did."

Charlie did not look convinced. "Are you sure?"

"Yes." There was only one thing for it. "Daddy just had a wee, and nobody said anything, did they?"

His son was shocked as he looked around the pool. Everything seemed the same. "No." He thought about it again. "Okay, I will wee."

Jon turned him to face in the opposite direction. "Good boy, but it is always better to wee away from Daddy because the water flows to the drain quicker."

Ben, Shirley, and Will sauntered from the riding stable to the Castell Punta de N'Amer. The road was sandy and uneven, running past agricultural fields and wooded areas with infrequent sea views. During the hour-long walk, the only wildlife on view was an abundance of ants.

Reaching the Castell, Will walked up to the top, leaving Ben and an exhausted Shirley to get the drinks at the bar.

"The views are terrific," said Shirley.

"Spectacular," said Ben, pointing. "You can see right round to what is it called, Cala Millor over there."

"I needed this, though." Shirley poured the ice-cold lager down her neck. "That's better. If he's not quick, I'll be drinking his too." She turned to look at her husband in his newly acquired leather cowboy hat. "Look at him. You could swear he was bloody John Wayne."

Ben smiled, watching Will act like the idiot at the top of the Castell. He and Shirley waved as Will stopped performing long enough to take their picture. Ben hoped it would make a lovely memory for them. The views were magnificent, and the bar was worth remembering as an ideal place to enjoy a quiet beer. Sadly, as there were no cliffs, it was not the place to fulfil his mission.

Elizabeth and Lucia met up after Lucia finished work and wandered around the shops like old friends. They ridiculed the latest fashions and laughed as they each modelled unsuitable outfits.

Lucia held up a dress and told Elizabeth she would wear it well. She had the figure for it. Elizabeth thanked her for the compliment but couldn't afford the dress. Lucia suggested she put it in her bag, leave without paying, and move on to the next shop. Elizabeth was shocked.

Lucia picked up a pair of sandals, telling Elizabeth they were the type she liked but were always so expensive. Elizabeth suggested that was because they were Italian. Lucia tried them on even though they were outside her price range and commented that although they would be ideal for work, there was no way she was paying that much for them.

Elizabeth spotted a mother and daughter she recognised. "Hello, how is your hand?"

Daisy cowered into her mother. Leah rubbed her head.

"It's okay, Dais. This is the kind lady who helped us yesterday when you had the stone on your hand."

Daisy held up one hand, and the grown-ups studied the small bruise.

Leah spoke again. "I meant to thank you for helping us out yesterday. Honestly, I'm scared of what those boys might do next."

Elizabeth smiled at Leah. "Are they twins?"

"No, but most people think they are. They were born within ten months of each other."

"Were they born in the same year?" Elizabeth asked.

"Yes. Charlie was born in January and Harry in November, but he's already almost the same size as his brother."

"They used to call that Irish twins." Elizabeth shrugged. "I don't imagine that term is acceptable these days."

Leah shook her head while Lucia looked confused.

"Are they good boys?" Lucia asked.

"Put them together, and they can be a real handful." Leah closed her lips and raised her eyebrows. "They can be a nightmare. It sometimes feels like we are rearing the Kray twins."

Elizabeth laughed, but Lucia did not understand the reference. "Clay twins?"

"I will explain later."

Leah looked at Elizabeth. "We are most grateful for your help."

"It was not a problem. Just so long as Daisy is okay." Elizabeth bent her knees to get nearer the child. "Did it hurt?"

"Just a bit," said Daisy quietly.

"Well, you were very brave." Elizabeth looked at the shelf. "Have you seen any shoes you like?"

Daisy shook her head. "Not yet. Mum said they are over-priced rubbish."

Leah pulled a face and gasped.

Elizabeth chuckled as she stood up. "Out of the mouths of babes...."

"They hang me every time," said Leah.

Lucia stepped forward. "If you would like to buy your daughter good shoes at a fair price, go to my friend's shop in Porto Cristo. You can get there on the bus." She reverted to Spanish and spoke to the shop assistant, who handed her paper and a pen. Lucia wrote out the details. "I used to buy all my children's shoes there. They are on the hill out of town. It is worth the trip because the prices are excellent."

Leah looked surprised at the intervention of the Spaniard. Elizabeth explained that Lucia lived in the area. She spoke to Lucia in Spanish before explaining to Leah that she had told Lucia about the incident with the German boy.

Lucia looked shocked, reached down to take Daisy's hand, and rubbed it. "It looks very sore. He is a nasty boy, but you are brave and do not cry."

"No," said Daisy, stepping away from her mother. "It is not so bad now."

"Good girl," said Lucia.

Leah turned to Elizabeth. "You speak Spanish too. How many languages do you know?"

"Five. Spanish, German, French, Italian and Welsh."

"So that's six, including English."

"Yes, but she struggles with English. That's why she

brings me," said Lucia.

Elizabeth laughed. "That's true enough."

"Have you been friends long?" Leah asked.

"What day is it?" said Lucia.

"Monday 26 July," said Leah.

"About twenty-four hours," said Elizabeth, still chuckling. "We met yesterday."

"Wow! I thought you were old friends."

"I think we are now," said Lucia.

"I'm not that old," said Elizabeth, grinning. "I may look old, but I'm not that old."

"Nor am I," said Lucia. "I am only 26; this sunshine makes me look much older. Wait until you have been here for two weeks. You will look just like me."

All three laughed, leaving a worried Daisy wondering what was so funny about looking old.

Nick returned from his swim and checked his mobile. His boss left a message saying he was ready to proceed with Nick's project. Nick smiled at the prospect, collected a drink, and wandered to the balcony.

His uncle, aunt, and cousins were outside their apartment, to the right of the one Nick was using. Eddie waved as Louise and Donny appeared to smirk. His aunt tapped their arms as if she was telling them off. Nick held up his drink. He could not wait to see Chris' work's results. He had a good feeling about it.

The Cavern was only half full, but it was still early evening. Gemma and Sara wandered over to a booth as Kylie fetched the drinks.

"Who are these people?" Sara asked, pointing at the framed photographs on the wall.

"That's the Beatles."

"The Beatles? Who are they?"

Gemma stopped and stared at her friend. "Are you

telling me you've never heard of the Beatles?"

Sara shrugged. "Never."

"They were the biggest band in the world and are still revered today." She pointed at the image of the band. "That's John, Paul, George and Ringo."

"Were they a boy band then?"

"No...well, they were boys but weren't a boy band as such. They weren't a manufactured group."

"Were they any good?"

"You could say that. They sold millions. My father loves them." She glared at her friend. "And you've seriously never heard of the Beatles?"

"Nope. My dad won't let us play pop music in the house. Before I moved into my flat, I could only watch TV at my grandparents' place. They never watched anything good."

Gemma knew that Sara's family was very religious.

Sara pointed to the wall. "Who is Sargeant Pepper?"

"He was huge back in the day, too," said Gemma, relieved that Kylie had arrived with the drinks. The history lesson could end for now.

Nick studied the information on his mobile again. As his grandfather used to say, his dreams might be fulfilled with a fair wind and a modicum of good fortune. He hoped they would be. They deserved a break.

The music grew louder as the room filled up. The drinks remained cold and massively overpriced.

"I'm not sure how long my money will last at this rate," Kylie said, half-shouting into Gemma's ear.

"I know. Let's get a few bottles in and drink before coming out. These prices are ridiculous."

Kylie turned as Christiano grabbed her waist.

"Would you like to dance, lovely lady?" He took hold of her hand, raised it and kissed her fingers.

Kylie looked at Gemma and pulled a face as she

shrugged. "Why not? Look after the drinks, Gem?"

"Of course."

Gemma rested against the post and watched the dancing. Sara and Donny laughed as they attempted a few intricate steps, while Kylie and Christiano just went for it. She had to admit that Christiano was an excellent mover.

"Can I get you a drink?"

Barty had probably had enough already. His eyes were glassy, and his breath reeked of alcohol.

She raised her half-full glass. "I'm okay, thanks. Have you had a good evening?"

His words came slowly and slurred. "Yeah, we've been to Cody's bar in Cala Bona. It's a happy hour, so you buy one and get one free.

Gemma nodded, thinking of another way her group could save money.

"Are you sure you don't want one?"

"Yeah, go on then. I'll have a gin that I can put in here. The barman put lots of tonic in the last one."

Barty returned and handed her a tall glass almost full to the brim. "Here you are, a large Gin and plenty of tonic water.

"Lovely," said a disappointed Gemma.

Barty was not in the mood for conversation. He seemed likelier to fall asleep and sipped his brandy through half-open eyes. When Christiano and Kylie returned, they laughed and poked fun at Gemma's 'catch'. She smiled politely.

Donny came to join them, waving and blowing kisses at Sara as she went to the loo. Gemma felt a bit nauseous at the insincerity of it all. Donny laughed because Barty had closed one eye. "Come on, Bartholemew, where are your manners? It's rude to fall asleep in a female's company unless they fall asleep first." He punched him in the stomach.

Barty doubled over and vomited. The splash missed his friends' feet by millimetres and caused a commotion amongst the other revellers. Donny grabbed Christiano's shoulders.

"We'd better get over there," he said, pointing to the

seats. "You know how touchy Paco can be about making a mess in his club."

They led the girls to the seating area on the other side of the bar, leaving their friend to be picked up by the security team and dragged off the premises.

The waitress arrived, taking orders for drinks.

Gemma held up her two drinks. I'm okay, thank you."

"Champagne. Five glasses." Donny said.

Gemma and Kylie exchanged glances. Gemma spoke for them. "I can't afford champagne."

"Nobody is asking you to," said Donny. "This is on us. We've had a bonus, and we like to spend it on friends."

"Fair enough," said Kylie. "Count me in."

"Thank you," said Gemma. "That's very generous. Will he be okay?"

"He'll be fine," said Christiano. "He is always the same on a Monday. He has too much at Cody's and then comes down here when he should go home. He is a menace."

"Idiot," said Donny. He put his hand on Gemma's knee, squeezing it tightly before stroking her thigh. She moved his hand. "The problem with Batholemew is that he does not know how to treat a lady. He has no class. He has no respect." He pushed out his lips and blew her a kiss.

Christiano laughed, and Gemma felt uncomfortable and slid away. She did not want to be accused of stealing a friend's man again, and she wished Sara would return quickly to keep her sleazy new boyfriend occupied.

"I still think Rob Cromwell has a nerve. You only work for him; he doesn't own you." Leah was still annoyed by Jon's request that he check his messages.

"But we are swamped at the moment. We've had more work than ever, and Rob only suggested postponing it.

"We booked this holiday months ago. He had a bloody cheek, asking us to rearrange at such a late stage. We'd have lost a fortune, plus it's okay for him and Dickhead to take holidays when they want."

Jon did not mention that Richard had just taken another unexpected short break. "He saw sense in the end, but he does expect me to answer my 'phone."

"And I expect you to give us two weeks' undivided attention. If Rob Cromwell can't manage without you for a fortnight, he needs to buck up his ideas or pay you more, preferably both." She stood ready to go to the kitchen. "Do you want beer or wine?"

"Wine, please...and can I have the sim card."

"No, you can't. Now stop asking. You're worse than the kids."

Jon threw his hands up in the air and groaned in frustration.

Elizabeth thanked Lucia for the splendid meal. They hugged and kissed cheeks before the taxi driver opened the back door and encouraged her to enter.

Her friend gave the man clear instructions and reminded him of the price she had agreed to with his boss, which caused Elizabeth to laugh and the driver to curse.

Elizabeth learned that Lucia and her husband had separated but remained friends. Lucia said he had initially found it hard to cope with the unexpected new addition to her family but now believed her husband adored their young grandson. He was initially outraged that his daughter was expecting a child outside of marriage, and relations between the two remained strained.

Elizabeth smiled when she saw the child giggle when his grandmother, mother, and uncle fussed over him. She had helped feed him, although she sensed a reluctance that Lucia assured would pass when he got to know her better. By the end of the evening, he was much calmer in her company.

Leaving the taxi and walking across the short car park to the entrance door, Elizabeth knew she had much to be thankful for. Although she had her share of worries, her son was doing well. He had become a fine young man, and his confidence had blossomed because of his many new experiences since his father died.

She wondered what Nick would have been like had her husband been alive and the family money still in the bank. In some ways, she was pleased that Kenneth had not been around to see Nick grow up. He would probably have stifled their son's development, bullied him into doing what he wanted, and probably turned Nick into something he was not.

Snowy reflected on a most productive day. He had the address of his target's office and was reasonably confident he also had the man's home address. He would confirm that detail tomorrow. For now, he had to be patient and follow his timetable. There was little point in rushing, as he could not leave the island before his designated departure date. If he finished the assignment too soon, he risked identification and possible retribution.

OPTIONS

(6 YEARS 2 MONTHS BEFORE THE HOLIDAY)

Jon was not sure what to do. His wife was fed up with being pregnant and wanted the baby born. He could offer no sensible suggestions.

Yet another sleepless night had resulted in a miserable start to the day. He needed to get to work but could not leave until his mother-in-law arrived. To make matters worse, Leah had no idea what to do with herself.

Reassurance was his best option. "It won't be much longer now."

"You keep saying that." Her hands rested on the edge of the worktop. "It's okay for you. You can go off to work to see your mates. You haven't got to suffer all this."

Jon was about to suggest he was suffering enough, but this was not the time. "Shall I get you a drink? Do you fancy a glass of orange juice?"

"I am sick to death of orange juice. Get me a large glass of Shiraz."

"You know I would if I could."

"It was a joke." Leah waddled toward the living room. "I think there are some tomatoes in the bottom of the fridge. I'll have them with a splash of mayonnaise."

"Coming right up," said Jon. He still didn't understand why his wife found that combination so appetising.

Elizabeth Kingston rested her elbow on the wooden arm of her chair and ran her fingers over her lips and chin, a reaction she had had to lousy news since she was little.

"To summarise, you're saying that you tracked the transfer of several hundred thousand pounds from our bank accounts to a bank account in Gibraltar. However, we have no idea whose account it is or what happened to the money after that."

The solicitor nodded. "Yes, that's right. We could investigate further, but it might prove costly. To be honest, there is no guarantee that we will ever know whose account it is, let alone recover any missing funds. It might be a case of throwing good money after bad."

"Good money that we simply do not have anyway."

"Exactly." In recent years, he had usually dealt with her husband and had become used to his abrupt, impatient manner. Elizabeth was different. She remained calm and dignified, considering her response before speaking. Douglas had no idea how she had coped with the devasting news that had come her way since her husband fell ill.

"What about life insurance? I know that Kenneth took out several endowment policies when we first married. I helped him pay for some of them."

Douglas Watson shook his head. "Sorry, they got cashed in about 18 months ago. The money went into Kenneth's account. It's all gone."

"All of it?"

"Yes."

"How much?"

"Quarter of a million."

Elizabeth sighed as her hand returned to her mouth. That suggested over half a million pounds were missing. "Does he have a pension?"

"There is one, but we are still checking on that. There appears to be a problem with the beneficiary's nomination. It appears Kenneth failed to name you."

"Typical. Can we contest that?"

"We can try."

"And we are sure Kenneth had no other accounts where he might have hidden money?"

"Not unless he created fake identities or had accounts in other banks. We doubt he had the wherewithal to undertake the former, and if he had accounts elsewhere, he would either have funded them from other money we know nothing about, or they have lain dormant for quite some time."

Watson explained that the UK banks had confirmed ownership of the accounts to which Kenneth had paid money. However, they did not know the owner of the bank in Gibraltar.

Payments to other UK banks covered various finance agreements. Of which there were plenty.

Elizabeth reread the list. "He owed money everywhere."

"Sadly, yes. The debts related to the purchase of the cars, the caravan, the boat plus mortgages on the houses here and in France."

"That we now have to pay for?"

"If that is what you decide to do." Watson nibbled his bottom lip. "There is always an alternative."

Elizabeth knew what he meant. "Thank you, that is not an option."

"You could always file for bankruptcy?"

"That is also something I am not prepared to consider. Nick and I have discussed this, and we will repay everything Kenneth borrowed. We will sell what we can and repay the rest over time."

"I admire your fortitude, Elizabeth, but you must be realistic. The houses should recover what you paid for them, but the market in that part of France is slow. In addition, the car, caravan and boat might only raise half of what you owe to the credit company."

"But the boat is practically brand new."

"It is, but Kenneth paid over the odds for quick delivery. Depreciation erodes 10% per annum, and interest gets added. Kenneth went with a finance company rather than the bank, so the rates are higher. You would still be paying these debts for many years to come. If you filed for bankruptcy, you could start again and rebuild your life, and it would be like nothing had happened in a few years. Your credit rating would be back to normal in about six years."

"But I will know what happened, and I cannot face the prospect of being declared bankrupt. Nick and I are not going down without a fight. That poor boy has already suffered enough and has inherited enough baggage from his dear father without having the further stigma of bankruptcy."

"Lots of people go bankrupt these days. There is no stigma….."

"Maybe, but I want to retain whatever dignity and integrity I have left. Not many teenagers have to deal with what Nick is processing. His father is dead. Everything he has known is falling apart. He knows we must sell the house, furniture, cars, and boat. Even that won't be enough to sort out the mess, and everything else will have to go too. We cannot afford his school fees, so he must join a local comprehensive wherever we live." She stopped to shiver. They had not yet found alternative accommodation. "And all this when he is about to begin his GCSEs. No, bankruptcy is not an option. We will pay everything back within six years."

"I admire your integrity and determination, but if things get too tough, keep the alternative in mind."

Elizabeth was all too aware of how tough things might get. "I will."

"That reminds me. You realise that the company will stop Kenneth's salary payments. There might be some death in service benefit. I can look into it."

"Thank you."

"But it might be better to prepare for the worst-case scenario."

Elizabeth nodded as her index finger circled her lips again. "I have already, don't worry. We'd better get the house on the market and find somewhere else for us to live." She rose from the chair, collecting her handbag as she did so. "You must let me have your bill so I can sort that before the vultures start circling."

"Elizabeth, I wouldn't dream of charging you. Our

families go way back, and if I cannot do a favour for an old friend, then what kind of man am I?"

"Thank you, Douglas. You are very generous. She leaned across the table to shake hands. "It is probably better that Kenneth didn't pull through this."

The solicitor looked intrigued. "Why? Do you think he wouldn't cope with the changes?"

"It's not that. I would have fucking killed him for what he has done."

Snowy initially believed that the Prof and his team were barking in the wrong forest. The account software and CCTV footage painted a picture of a model employee. Paul Telford paid all monies into the till and did everything by the book. If anything, the lad might be too clean.

Research showed that Telford had inherited the house from his uncle, and his brother, Kevin Telford, was the car's original owner. It appeared Kevin sold it to his brother when he hit a lean spell, and things had not improved for the elder Telford sibling. There was nothing suspicious about any of this.

When Snowy broke into Paul's house, his doubts appeared. He found the biggest television he had ever seen. It filled the whole lounge wall, and the plush sofas used to watch the screen had leather seats and recliners on each end. The kitchen was impressive and still looked new, while the garden was immaculate. The hot tub was top-of-the-range. The house contained so many gadgets it resembled a set on a shopping channel.

The guy was either good with money or had other means to finance his lifestyle, one that paid in cash. Snowy thought he might know what it was. He started to watch the filling station.

On his third night of surveillance, Snowy saw a car pull into the garage. He switched on his laptop to view the live feed from the CCTV in the booth. The driver waited for the pump to be activated. Telford pressed the button, allowing fuel to flow, and the man inserted a fiver's worth of fuel. Snowy had spotted the same man doing the same thing two nights earlier but had not tracked the man's movements afterwards.

This was the exciting bit. Here was the moment of truth. Snowy was confident this would provide the evidence needed to solve the puzzle. He started his engine, still watching the screen, as the customer walked to the kiosk and slid the money into the tray.

Snowy's eyes studied his laptop. Telford had a rather unusual way of extracting the money. He placed his hand over the notes and slid them onto the counter. Snowy had spotted this two nights ago.

Please hand him the receipt, Snowy thought.

Telford obliged, placing a receipt in the well. The man returned to his Vauxhall and drove away, unaware anyone was watching him.

Snowy activated the camera he had secured on the passenger side of the dashboard.

The driver only drove a short distance before pulling off the road into a disused factory forecourt. Snowy parked far enough away to be invisible to the people he was observing. The Vauxhall pulled alongside a Polo, and the driver exchanged the receipt for a small bag. Nobody left their cars, and the transaction was over in seconds. The Vauxhall drove away. Snowy smiled.

Cromwell Construction gave Jon the job of supervising the renovation of a community hall, and the project went well. Rob Cromwell visited the site to review the work.

"Nice job, Jon." He ran his hand across the new bar area. "Very nice. You've done well here; we've come in on time and under budget. Great job."

"Thanks, Rob. The team have been brilliant. They really worked their socks off."

"And to think that if you hadn't checked my figures,

bloody Clemence would have won this contract too. I'll make sure you get rewarded. Talking of which…" He looked around to make sure nobody else was in earshot. "I'd like a word with you."

Jon appeared concerned.

"There's Nothing to worry about. I have put a few more irons in the fire. If things work out as I hope, we can take on more work. I want to expand the business."

"Great news. I'll need to earn as much as I can. Leah is due any day now."

"I know. That's why I've been thinking of giving you a promotion. How about you set up a team and lead some new projects?"

Jon liked that idea. "That would be great, Rob. Thank you." He remembered something. "But I must take a fortnight off when the baby arrives. Can this wait until after then?"

"Of course, it can. We haven't had any green lights yet, but I like to prepare things in advance.

"Brilliant." Jon's mobile rattled. "Sorry, Rob, it's my mother-in-law. I'd better take this." Rob motioned for him to carry on. Jon's listened to his excited mother-in-law. "Okay, I'm on my way." He ended the call and turned to Rob. "Got to go, Rob. Leah's gone to the hospital. It might be a false alarm, but her mother's panicking."

"That's why God made mothers. Get out of here, go to Leah and let me know what's happening."

It was time for his big reveal, and the following evening, Snowy sat opposite his client in her favourite curry house in Birmingham's Edgbaston district.

"How did you discover Paul was dealing drugs from our filling station?"

Snowy snapped a poppadom and took a bite, washing it with lager. "Receipts and sleight of hand."

"What? How?"

"If the customer wanted drugs, the money for petrol and

drugs would go into the cash well. Paul would cover the cash with his hand, meaning the camera could not pick up that the customer handed over more than required. Paul would turn in his chair, using his body to hide that he was taking his cut before opening the till. The buyer got a receipt exchanged for drugs in the car park down the road."

"But the receipt could have been legit."

"It could have been, but Paul frequently handed over a receipt without printing one. I initially thought that perhaps he was giving receipts for more than the value of fuel sold, possibly in some VAT scam or something. When I started the stakeout, I saw the kiosk had more visitors than petrol sales. Some people bought chocolate, and who takes a receipt for a Mars bar? All the on-foot customers went in the same direction after leaving the forecourt. After that, it was just a case of following them. When I visited the garage this morning, I found a stack of receipts for various amounts hidden in a bag under the till. The receipts get traded for drugs."

The waiter arrived and placed the food on the table.

"Your curry looks delicious. Do you mind if we share?" She smiled at him.

"Do you mind if we don't? Snowy doesn't share his food."

"But you can have some of my biryani."

"Hmm, tempting, but if I had wanted biryani, I would have ordered it."

His companion shrugged. "That puts me in my place. I admire your honesty." She sipped her wine as the waiter made a space available for the rice and naan. "My ex-husband wouldn't know honesty if it slapped him in the face."

Snowy was not sure it was his place to ask too many questions. "My mam always told me to be myself and say it as I see it. If someone likes or dislikes me, they base their decision on the real me." He held out his arms. "In all my glory!"

She covered her mouth as she chuckled. "Did you just call yourself Snowy?"

"I did." He waited for the question. It was not long

coming.

"Why Snowy?"

"It's because I am whiter than white...." She was not falling for that one. "...my middle name is Ira, I R A, and the Welsh word for snow is Eira, E I R A. When my friends at school found out about my middle name, my nickname became Snowy. It has stuck with me ever since."

"Why Ira?"

"After Ira Gershwin. My father was a jazz nut."

"That is what I call a fan."

"He was bonkers about jazz, particularly free-form. It was the only music we were allowed to play in our house."

"And do you still like jazz?"

"I never did. I loathe it in all its forms. I always have. I think free jazz is for people who can't be bothered to learn or understand a tune."

Ben Moran had no patience with jobsworths. "It is quarter to ten. Nobody will mind if I park here while I pop in there," he pointed at a bar, "to let my wife know I am here."

The security guard held firm. "I am sorry. You are on private land, and I must insist you move on. We've had problems with abandoned cars, and the owners have had to pay for disposal."

Ben pointed at his car. "This is a top-of-the-range Jaguar. Do you think that I intend to abandon it here?"

"That's not the point. You cannot park here. If you do, I will have to contact the police to have them move you."

Ben had heard enough. "The police won't give a shit about me parking here for five minutes. In any case, I'll be gone by the time they arrive. Now get back into your little box before I ring James Cook." The name meant nothing to the security guard. Ben pointed at the for sale sign. "He owns Cook and Jarvis, who are selling this site. He is a personal friend of mine, and we've done several deals together. He won't be best pleased when he hears you have been abusive to me."

"I haven't been abusive."

"But he doesn't know that, so shut up and get back in your cabin before I make you unemployed."

They ended their evening at a pub down the road from the curry house. Snowy fetched the drinks and was about to place them on the table when a man bumped him.

"Watch where you are going, mate," the stranger said, sounding overly aggressive and becoming more threatening by stopping to stare at Snowy.

Snowy placed the drinks on his table and turned to face the intruder, six inches taller and leaner. "I think you need to watch where you are going. Mate. You walked into me, and I very nearly spilt my pint."

"Not my fault if you can't hold your beer."

"Very funny. If I had lost my pint, you would have had to buy me another."

The man smirked and then pressed his face into Snowy's. "Oh yeah, Taffy. You're sure about that, are you?"

Snowy nodded. "Pretty sure."

"Are you trying to make something of this? Do I need to take you outside?"

"You are quite attractive, so I wouldn't mind." He put his palm on the man's chest. "However, before we do, I must advise you that I attended karate training twice weekly for seven years. I also took home many prizes at national and international competitions. I am not saying this to impress or scare you. I need to inform you of these facts for legal and insurance purposes. You know, just in case anything happens outside that you might later regret,"

The stranger took a step back as he eyed Snowy up and down. Snowy did not move. The man's expression softened. "Sorry mate, I've had a bad day but shouldn't have taken it out on you. Can I buy you and your good lady a drink?"

"No need, mate, just be more careful in future."

"I will."

Snowy held out a hand. The man shook it and then went on his way.

"I'm impressed," said his good lady as he sat down. "You defused that well. Did you really attend karate training twice weekly for seven years?"

"Why do you need to ask? Doesn't my physical condition tell you?"

She chuckled again. "It tells me that you've probably won a few pie-eating competitions in the last few years."

"That hurts." He rubbed his belly and pushed out his bottom lip, feigning upset.

She kissed his cheek. "I'm only joking. I like a man with a bit of meat on him."

"You are not a cannibal, are you?"

She had to cover her mouth as she snorted. "You are a boy you are. So is it true?"

"Is what true?"

"About the karate training?"

"Remember what I said in the curry house. My mam raised me always to tell the truth. I can be economical with it, though. I took my nephews to classes because their parents worked afternoons. They won many titles."

He smiled as his companion giggled again.

DAY 4 - TUESDAY 27 JULY

Donny Kingston yawned, shook his head, got out of bed and joined Candice by her dressing table. She handed him the rolled-up note. He sniffed the white powder through the improvised straw, changed nostrils and sniffed again. Shaking his head, Donny blinked repeatedly, stretched his eyes, gasped and groaned. "Shit, that's good."

"Hey Nick, come over here a second."

Nick crossed the grass to join his uncle. "What's up?"

"Nothing. I just wanted to check that you are both having a good time."

"Yes, we are, thanks. Mum loves it."

"What about you?"

"Yeah, it's good."

His uncle had expected a more gushing response. "I'm glad, but I thought you would have come over to see Donny and Louise. They haven't seen a hide nor hair of you."

"They don't want me hanging around with them, and anyway, I probably couldn't afford to go to the places they do."

Edward reached into his back pocket and took out a wallet. "I can let you have money."

Nick thought it was a bit late for that. "No, you're okay. We're doing fine." Nick was going to add the words without charity but thought better of it. He sensed his antipathy towards all things related to his father was showing. "I've never been one to splash the cash, so I wouldn't know what to do with it now."

"I want you to know I am not doing this out of charity...."

You could not sound more condescending if you tried, thought Nick.

"...think of it as a delayed birthday present I never sent you." He held out several notes and was disappointed as Nick stepped back. "Look, just take it. Go and have a good time."

Nick resisted the temptation to say what he wanted; this was not the time. "Thank you, but as I said, I don't need money to have a good time. I've learned lots of ways to enjoy myself. In any case, Donny and Louise have their friends and interests and won't want a cousin they haven't seen for ten years butting in and cramping their style. I'll be fine unc. Don't worry about me."

"Graham and Grigor have another job for you."

"I thought I was done with that. You told me I wouldn't have to do it anymore."

"I said you would not have to do so many. We still need you to help with the special ones."

"Do I have to?"

"Yes. It's not my fault you look younger than you are. Anyway, this job pays well."

Her left hand was starting to ache, so she used her right.

"Who is it, and what do I have to do?"

"It's an acquaintance who is on holiday with his family. You have to seduce him. He will be at the Bull Ring while his family enjoys a pirate show elsewhere. Catch his eye in the VIP room, show him you are interested, and take it from there."

"How much?"

Donny thought he deserved a reward for his efforts and told Candice lower amounts than he had agreed with Graham. "They'll pay you 200 for turning up. Another 300 if you get him to touch you in public, get him to the room, and you get another 500. You'll have an extra 1000 if you do the deed."

"Bloody hell, he must be important."

"He is. He has some property that they want."

"2000 would come in useful."

"Minus our cut, of course."

That would wipe out half of the money. The response

was less enthusiastic. "I would do it if you took a smaller cut."

"You know the arrangement. You wouldn't have the work if it weren't for us."

She wouldn't be doing this work in the first place if it weren't for them. "Couldn't we split this 50-50?"

"We could, but only if you get him into bed and keep the sheets off."

Candice did not like the camera capturing her naked. "Is that necessary?"

"It is if you want 50%."

Money beats modesty. "Okay then. When is it?"

"Friday night."

"I can't make it Friday. I have to work. There is a large birthday party coming in."

"I'll get someone to cover for you at the restaurant. Graham said this has to be you. Our guest has a taste for younger girls and likes redheads."

"Where would I take him? The usual room?"

"Yes, Christiano and I are going over there to set up on Thursday. We'll be at the club with you. Christiano can make the introductions and then disappear, and I'll direct the cameras from next door. We'll both be on hand should you need us."

That was not much reassurance. Candice would take her knife. A previous punter had been rougher than she liked, and she doubted her guards would be much of a deterrent if things turned nasty. They were not fighting material. In his current flaccid state, Donny wasn't sex material either. She withdrew her hand. "You ought to go a bit easier on the coke. It's getting more and more difficult to get you going."

It isn't coke. It's the company, thought Donny, who said, "Never mind, let's leave it for now; I've got to be somewhere."

Leah looked after the children, leaving Jon to swim in the sea. She was seriously concerned about him. He had been having dizzy spells and feeling light-headed. The doctor told him that his blood pressure was far too high, and if that carried on, he was at risk of a stroke, amongst other things.

She hoped she had not made matters worse for him by removing the SIM card and refusing to let him have it back. At least by only worrying about what Cromwells might have said to him, he wasn't rushing around trying to sort out problems from a long way away. What he didn't know couldn't hurt him, especially when he was too far away to influence matters.

She longed for the day Jon could tell the Cromwells where to go, but she knew such a move would not come anytime soon without intervention. There was no way he would leave until he had secured something else. The Cromwells kept him so busy that he had no time to find anything else. It was one long, vicious circle.

There was always her grandfather's house. The probate would be approved soon, and she would be allowed to take possession. They had discussed whether to do the place up and sell it or move in. She liked the idea of them starting their own business. The stables would be an ideal workshop and play area for the kids, and she might squeeze in a design studio. They could finance the works by selling their house, it would take a while, but there was no rush. In the meantime, Jon could make a living doing odd jobs; people would always need a good carpenter.

Charlie's laughter made her think about her children and their future. Jon was determined to ensure they were provided for and would not risk that by acting recklessly. In her view, his main priority should be to ensure he was around to see them grow up. The best way of doing that was to get him away from Cromwell. The schools around her grandfather's house were much better than where they lived, which would help the children, too. She waved at Jon as he paddled in the water. Leah needed to persuade him to change his lifestyle but would have to tread softly. Jon never reacted well if he felt she was forcing an issue.

Gemma wasn't particularly pleased to learn she would spend the day alone. That had never been part of the plan. She wasn't stupid or naïve and fully expected the holiday would involve the odd romance or two but hadn't anticipated her two friends going off together for a whole day.

"Have a nice day," she said through gritted teeth as Christiano, Kylie, Donny, and Sara climbed into Christiano's jeep. They tooted as they drove away.

The prospect of an extended period at the hotel did not fill her with relish. The other residents were okay, but there were far too many unruly children for her liking. The beach was an even less attractive proposition. She could not go for a swim without worrying about her possessions, and it would be hot for her to lie on the recliner all day. She had little option but to take the opportunity to explore. She would wear her new shorts and the colourful flip-flops that she had rescued from the charity shop back home.

Elizabeth and Lucia crossed the road to escape the men, encouraging them into their restaurants.

"*The prices they charge are ridiculous*," said Lucia. "*If you want to eat in this town, stay away from the seafront*."

Elizabeth knew these restaurants would be just the places her husband would choose. He enjoyed flaunting his wealth and letting everyone know he could afford the most expensive eateries. Not that he would have ever let them visit Majorca. That would be what ordinary people did. He would have insisted they go to Italy again.

She loved the places they visited during their time together but had grown tired of her husband's attempts to ingratiate himself with the locals, especially when his knowledge of Italian culture and application of the language was so much worse than he liked to believe.

Kenneth would never have agreed to go on a coach trip like Lucia and her planned to do the next day. That would have been out of the question. He would have booked a taxi if he hadn't wanted to drive a hire car, even though the lighthouse at Formento was many miles away.

Lucia announced their arrival at the beachfront coffee shop and placed their order.

The coffee was tasty and Italian, but Lucia refused to accept that the cake was as good as that in her brother's place.

"No es posible," she insisted as Elizabeth teased her.

Crossing the road by the hypermarket, Gemma spotted the boy from the bus sitting alone in a café. He was paying close attention to something on his phone and did not notice her enter. She thought she would see if she could remedy that situation.

She ordered a latte and stood by his table.

"Is anyone sitting here?"

Nick glanced at her and said, "Doesn't look like it. Help yourself."

That was hardly a rapturous welcome, but Gemma sat anyway.

"Was that a Welsh accent?"

Nick looked up again. "Yes. Is that a problem?"

"No, not at all. It's just that I thought I recognised it."

"Ah, right."

"What are you doing? Texting? Surfing the net?"

"No, I'm working."

His tone had not softened. "I didn't mean to disturb you. I'll sit somewhere else."

"That's up to you." He held up his hands. "Sorry, I am just a bit preoccupied with this message. You're not bothering me in the least. I'll stop once I have sent the reply. How does that sound?"

"Great." She thought of a suitable topic for conversation.

Nick put down his mobile and smiled. "Right, all done."

"Thanks," she said. "Didn't I see you on the bus from the airport?"

"You did. I was the sad gimp who goes on holiday with his mother and wears shit clothes."

Gemma's eyes widened, and she swallowed hard. "How did you hear all that?"

Nick shrugged.

"I never said any of those things."

"Didn't you? I bet you thought them."

"Shit! Yeah, I guess I did...sorry. Look, can we start again? I'm Gemma." She held out a hand.

He caught her fingers, shook them and said, "Nick."

"It's nice to meet you, Nick."

Nick nodded, his lips closed tightly.

Engaging him in conversation was going to be more challenging than she imagined. The waiter arriving with her coffee gave her an idea. "Can I get you a drink or something...to apologise for being rude on the bus?"

Nick eyed her suspiciously. He was still wondering what was behind this intervention. "Yes, go on then." He ordered in Spanish. *"I'll have a filter coffee, thank you."* He laughed at the waiter's response.

"What's so funny?" Gemma asked.

"He said you're much younger than my usual female company."

"What? Do you meet many girls in here?"

"He was talking about my mother."

"Oh, right." Gemma nodded. "Where is she today?"

"She's gone to Porto Cristo."

"On her own?"

"Well, I think she is old enough, and I gave her clear instructions not to talk to strangers".

Gemma poked out her tongue. "Ha ha."

"She's gone with a friend."

"A friend? I thought there were just the two of you."

"There is."

"So, have you been here before?"

"Where? The coffee shop?"

"No, Sa Coma."

"This is the first time."

"Are you here with other people?

"No, it's just Mum and me. My uncle and his family live here during the summer, but we haven't seen much of them."

His coffee arrived. "Cheers."

Gemma raised her cup and nodded. "So, who has your mother gone to Porto Cristo with?"

"Bloody hell, they say the Welsh are nosey." He chuckled, letting her know he wasn't being serious. "I will explain to save you from asking so many questions. She's gone with a Spanish lady, Lucia, whom she met the other day. She and Mum get on like a house on fire. Lucia has two days off and mentioned yesterday that she was catching a bus to Porto Cristo. Mum asked if she could join her, so they went together. Lucia is going to take her to the caves. They are thinking about booking a coach trip tomorrow. Is that enough?"

"I wish I'd known I'd have gone with them."

"Why? Where are your friends then?"

"They've copped off with a couple of local lads. They are taking them to some lighthouse on the north of the island."

"Didn't you want to go?"

"I wasn't invited. I wouldn't have gone anyway. It's not my thing, and I'm not into playing gooseberry."

"Didn't they have a friend for you?"

She thought of Barty and his unfortunate incident the night before. "No. A girl we met, Candice, has promised to fix me up with someone, but I am not sure my tastes are quite the same as hers."

Nick recalled the chat with his uncle and cousin on the night they arrived. He was sure that she had mentioned Candice. "Is this the same Candice that is friendly with Louise?"

Gemma looked surprised. "It is. They're mates. Candice likes Louise's brother."

"Donny. Short for Donald."

"How do you know them?"

"They are my cousins."

"Shut up."

"I'm serious."

"Really?"

"No, I just made it up…yes, really."

"But they are minted…." She knew she had said the wrong thing before Nick had said a word. "I'm sorry. I didn't mean to say it like that."

"Why not? It's the truth. My uncle does have a lot of money, but you wanted to ask how I dress so shit when I have rich relatives."

"Yes, sorry, I was thinking along those lines."

Nick was not offended. "It's a story of contrasting fortunes. We were the wealthy ones until my father died six years ago. We never found out what he did with our money, and we've struggled ever since. My uncle, my father's only brother, on the other hand, has seen his business boom in the last three or four years, so he's gone up in the world while we've bounced along the bottom."

"Didn't he help you out?"

"We didn't want his help. Mum and I managed just fine, and now I've got a new job. Plus, this man I know has traced a large chunk of the missing cash and thinks we can get the money back soon."

"Good for you." She pointed at the phone. "What job do you do?"

"I work for my old schoolteacher. He developed computer security programmes that have proved popular. We are working on other ideas, but most of my work currently involves updating and improving older programmes. I get to test them and learn about online forensics."

"What's that?"

"We help trace things. Viruses, hackers, money transfers, trolls, that sort of thing."

"Does it pay well?"

"It will eventually, but I'm only learning the ropes."

"I hope having money won't turn you into a spoilt brat like your cousins."

It was Nick's turn to look surprised. "Don't you like them?"

Gemma put her hand to her mouth. "Sorry, me and my big mouth. I have no right to slag off your family."

"It's okay. I don't like my cousins much either. We are only staying at my uncle's apartment because he let us have it for nothing. What's wrong with them?"

"Louise is such a fake, but it's not just her, to be honest. Her brother thinks he is uber-cool. He's like, everybody loves me, everyone must look at me, I can have anything I want. He gets on my tits. He's such a wanker." She put on a posh accent. "More champagne, everyone? Let me buy that. I'm loaded. Have you tasted my shit? It's 18-carat gold, you know!."

Nick chuckled. "You really don't like him then?"

"No...he seemed good fun at first, but having spent the last couple of nights with him and his greasy mate Christiano...."

"That's a bit racist."

"I didn't mean it like that; he also thinks he is smooth and slick, but I think he is a slimeball. I can't believe they are as squeaky clean as everyone thinks. It must all be a pretence."

"I wouldn't know." Nick placed his elbows on the table and his hand around the coffee cup.

She wasn't sure whether he was bored or irritated. "Sorry, I don't know what came over me. I've just met you, and I'm bombarding you with vitriol. I have no right to offload my prejudice on you."

"They are long words for a swede basher."

"You cheeky swine!" Gemma looked hurt. "What makes you think I'm a swede basher?"

"Now let me think...your accent is West Country through and through. You'll be telling me next that...." Nick adopted his best Somerset accent, which he developed listening to recordings of The Wurzels, "...you can't read, and you can't write, but you can drive a tractor."

Gemma screeched with laughter. "That's so not funny. Why do you think we speak like that?"

"The Wurzels."

"Wurzels? How did you hear the Wurzels? They were popular when my father was young."

"My mate's dad loves them. He plays them while we use his garage," said Nick.

"Weird, man, but we do not sound like that."

"Yup, you do." He put his cup to his mouth. The coffee was strong and hot. "Donny isn't the flavour of the month then, is he?"

"No, not really. As I said, something about him doesn't ring true. Take this morning. He and Christiano came to collect my friends Sara and Kylie, and he was gushing about how wonderful Sara looked and how lucky he was."

"You sound a bit jealous to me."

"I'm not. Really. I just hate insincerity. He was banging on about how Sara would catch the eye of all the men in the restaurant. She is pretty, but his comments were way over the top. Those two blokes are so full of bullshit. I cannot believe my friends fall for that crap."

"Restaurant? I thought you said they were going to a lighthouse."

"They are, come on, keep up. The four are stopping at Candice's parents' restaurant on the way back."

"Oh, I wondered what Candice's parents were doing these days." He cackled, "So Donny, Christiano and your friends are likely to be gone all day?"

Gemma thought Nick might have had an idea. "Yes. I am all alone with nothing to do."

Before she could ask if he had anything in mind, Nick's mobile pinged, and he picked it up long enough to read a message. He checked his watch. "Well, it's been lovely meeting you, Gemma, and I hate to be rude after you bought me coffee and slated my family." His smile gave him away. "But I have to be going; I have work to do."

"Aren't you on holiday?"

"Yes, but it was a last-minute thing, and I agreed to help my boss with a new project. He has installed a software package for a client and needs me to test it remotely."

"How do you do that? Laptop?"

Nick held up his mobile. "No, it is all on this, but I can't do it from here because it is secretive stuff, and I need to go somewhere more secure." He shook her hand. "I might see you again, but in the meantime, enjoy the rest of your holiday, and if I were you, I'd find some new friends."

I had found one already for a moment there, thought Gemma as Nick left the café.

Jon handed Charlie a fresh spoon. "Try to keep hold of this one a little bit longer." He groaned as Harry dropped his onto the floor. "Not you as well."

The boys ate their sandwiches and earned a treat, but Jon could not fathom why they always made such a mess of dessert.

"I'll get another, Dad," said Daisy, trotting to the basket holding the cutlery.

Leah got out the camera and took a picture of her sons with faces covered in chocolate ice cream. The boys beamed on cue, Harry had his spoon on his lips, and Charlie held his spoon by his nose.

"Are you sure you don't fancy a walk, love?" asked Will.

"No, I'll be fine. I've got a baguette and a bag of crisps, so I've sorted my lunch. You go and enjoy yourselves."

Ben wasn't sure whether he wanted to go, but it would allow him to book his first coach trip. He decided to start with the visit to the Cape of Formentor and had hoped that Shirley would change her mind, allowing him to stay put.

"Come on Ben. That bar we visited last night had a pool

table and satellite telly. We can catch up on the news while playing a few games of pool and enjoying some real chips."

"Sounds great," said an unenthusiastic Ben.

Nick grabbed his keys and towel and entered the pool area for an afternoon in the sunshine.

He stretched the towel across a plastic lounger, hid his belongings under it, kicked off his shoes and dived in. He had just completed his fifth length when his uncle's shadow appeared on the water.

"Hi Nick, are you on your own?"

"Mum has gone to Porto Cristo to see some caves."

"Didn't you fancy it?"

"Nah, not my cup of tea. I thought I'd get some exercise."

"Ah, right, good. I'm glad you are here, and I am sorry to interrupt, but I need some help. I seem to have a bit of trouble with the laptop. I think it's attracted a bug of some sort."

Nick put his elbows on the poolside and rested his head on his arms.

"What sort of bug?"

"I don't know. I was checking my emails and opened one that I thought was from...an old business contact, and the next thing I knew, the damned machine was not responding as it should. I appear to be losing messages and files without deleting them."

"Don't you have a security system?"

"I do, but you know how quickly these hackers learn. I fear I might not have kept the virus protector as up-to-date as I should have. I know you're on holiday, but would you mind having a look? I would ring Donny, but he's gone for the day."

Nick climbed out of the pool. "Yes, of course, not a problem. I expect it is some form of a virus. It's probably nothing too serious. I'll dry myself and be right with you."

His aunt was in the kitchen and offered him a drink.

"No thanks, I'm fine at the moment."

Eddie led him into his den at the back of the apartment.

It was a small area, separated from the main bedroom by two elaborately decorated wooden screens. He pointed at a laptop on the small desk.

“There it is. I'll just log you in.” Eddie grabbed his desk diary and opened the back cover. “I can never remember which password opens what.” Nick smiled politely. Eddie typed in the details and then replaced the book. “You wait until you get to my age.” He stood aside to let Nick access the machine. “Will it take long?"

"No idea, sorry. It depends on how far it has spread and how quickly I can download the recovery software from our website."

"But you think you can sort it?"

"Yes, I think so, but I can ring my boss and get advice if I can't.”

“Mr Shanklin, you mentioned him. Is he good?”

“Red hot. He’s worked for Microsoft, Google and IBM, so he’s dealt in software and hardware. There’s not much about computers that he doesn’t know.”

“I thought he was your teacher?”

“He was. He had enough of travelling the world and returned to Wales to retire but somehow became a teacher. It was lucky for me that he did.”

“Lucky for me, too, if you can sort this out. I’ll stay to watch and learn if you don’t mind.”

“No problem. Is there a network, or is this a stand-alone?”

“Mine is stand-alone. I don’t let the kids use it. Donny uses his office laptop, but Louise isn’t savvy regarding IT, so her laptop rarely gets switched on. I should sell it, but she only complains when I suggest it.” Eddie shrugged. “We all share the router, and I know that Donny sends videos and stuff to his mates, but they can’t access my machine.”

“Right, so the virus should be limited to this.” He patted the laptop. The software will sort it.”

“Great...where do you get the software from?”

"I have it here." He held up his keys with a memory stick attached. "I tend to take this with me wherever I go, just in case of an emergency. It is available via our website, at a cost, of course."

"How much do I owe you?"

"Sorry, I didn't mean it like that." Nick waved his hand. "Don't worry about it. You're family, so no charge."

He plugged the stick into the laptop, pressed a few buttons and pointed at the screen. "It's identified something and is isolating it. It looks like there are quite a few on here. It could take some time."

His uncle looked impressed as the screen lit up with messages updating them on its progress.

"Okay, we need to install the removal software now that it's identified what we are dealing with. This takes a few minutes. Can I be cheeky and have that drink after all? I didn't realise how thirsty I was."

"Yes, of course," said his uncle. "Do you want a hot drink or something cooler?" He looked at his watch. "It is afternoon now. Do you fancy a beer? "

"That would be great."

"I'll join you."

His uncle returned with two beers and stood to watch images of viruses disappearing into a bin.

Ben and Will returned from their lunch rather the worst for wear. Shirley shook her head as the pair staggered through the door.

"Sorry, love, we got talking to a man from Sussex…" said her husband.

"Who wanted to talk about Ethics," said her father. He looked at Will and burst out laughing. "Get it? Ethics, Essex, classic. That was an old Two Ronnies joke. I used to love the Two Ronnies." He fell onto the sofa. "Comedy is not as funny these days."

"Must be the way they tell 'em," Shirley said.

Her father pointed at her. “Frank wotsit, he was good. I liked him,” Ben repeated Shirley’s words, trying his best to use an Irish accent.

Shirley loved seeing her father resembling the man she used to know. “Can I get you two a drink?”

“Not for me, thanks. I need a siesta,” said Ben, unsteadily shuffling to his bedroom. “It’s the way I tell them. Ha ha ha.”

“I’ll have a beer, love, if there’s one there,” said her husband.

“I get you a cup of tea,” said Shirley. “I think you’ve had enough beer for one afternoon.”

Will took her father’s place on the sofa. “Okay, love, whatever you say, anything for an easy life.”

“I wish,” said Shirley. By the time she had filled the kettle, her husband was asleep, and her father was snoring loudly.

“So, what do you do back home?”

“That’s lovely.” Gemma sipped her cocktail through her straw, smacked her lips and responded to his question. “I’m a student.”

“What are you studying?”

“Brewing and distilling.”

“Seriously?”

She nodded.

“That is so cool. What do you intend to do with your degree?”

“I want to help my father. He makes craft beers, only on a small scale at the moment, but I’d like to help him expand the business and branch out into ciders.”

Barty was very interested. “That sounds like my ideal job! Do you need a product sampler?”

It was a typical response, but Gemma giggled as if she hadn’t heard it before. “Probably, one day.”

Barty seemed nice and was sober for a change. Gemma was warming to him. She had always liked his appearance, but his behaviour left much to be desired. Tonight, at least, he was making an effort. "Would you like to dance?"

"Yeah, great," she said as Barty took her hand, and they joined Christiano, Donny, Kylie, and Sara on the dance floor.

A couple of songs later, Gemma leaned toward Barty and asked if he would like a drink.

"Yes," he said, retaking her hand.

"What would you like?" Gemma had her purse at the ready.

"I'll have vodka and coke, please."

Gemma had expected him to ask for beer like before, but she did not make an issue of it. "Okay."

"Put your money away. These are on me. Vodka?"

"Yes, please," said Gemma. "With a coke and no ice."

"Right," he pointed at the seats beside the bar. "Grab a seat, and I'll bring them over."

The drinks were accompanied by more chat until Barty made a move. He held her tightly and kissed her.

Okay, Gemma thought, easing away. That was a strange move; the tongue could have stayed in his mouth. She smiled at him, adjusted her position and kissed him. Gemma said nothing as he touched her breast through her dress.

The kissing continued until Barty broke away. "It is boiling in here. Do you fancy a breath of fresh air?"

Gemma nodded and walked with him to the door.

"Shall we take a walk on the sand?" he said as they waited for the bouncers to stamp the back of their hands.

That sounds romantic, thought Gemma. "Yeah, great," she said.

They walked down the beach to the water's edge, where Gemma took off her shoes to paddle. Barty grabbed her from behind, putting his arms around her waist and held her tight. "I think you are really hot." He moved his lips from her ear to her shoulder.

Does that constitute foreplay in Majorca? Gemma thought as his teeth nibbled her flesh.

Barty moved the strap of her dress and kissed her bare shoulder. "Shall we have a sit-down?"

"Yeah, fine." Gemma slid the strap back into position. She wished she had covered her shoulders; the nibbling had not been a pleasant experience. She retook his hand and was confused when he led her to the middle of four towers of sunbeds stacked on the beach. "What?"

"Wait a second." He shifted the towers until they formed the outer perimeter of a square, took two beds from the top and dropped them into the middle. "Gives us a little more privacy."

"You've done this before," said Gemma, putting her shoes and bag onto a bed. She put her arms around his neck.

Barty kissed her again, pulling her with him until they sat on a bed.

The necking continued. He eased her backwards until Gemma was horizontal. His mouth moved from her lips to her neck and back as his hands pulled down her shoulder strap. Gemma wasted no time in putting it back.

Their lips locked. Barty tried a different approach and grabbed her right breast. His grip was awkward and tight, and Gemma gently moved his hand away. She resented the mauling. If this was going to happen, and there was no guarantee that it would, then it would be on her terms.

"Let's just kiss for a bit and see where we go," she whispered. Barty seemed to comply.

Mouth on mouth, tongue touching tongue, his body close to hers started to do the trick for him. Gemma became aware of his erection pressing into her leg. She tried to ignore it, hoping he might explode prematurely.

Barty shifted slightly, and Gemma thought her wishes had come true but realised he had only moved to secure a better position for his next trick. His hand moved up the front of Gemma's dress as their mouths locked. She immediately pushed it away.

"Not yet. I'm not ready,"

"I am." Barty used his weight to stop her from breaking away. His hand was on her knickers, and his fingers pressed through the cotton.

"I don't want to do this, not here, not now."

"I do."

"Get off," she said.

Barty's hand ventured further. "Come on, Gem, stop teasing. You know why we're here and want it as much as I do."

"Get off," she repeated as she clenched her fingers around his groin, squeezing him tightly. Her legs were ready to attack.

"That hurts."

"Sorry, let me get some cream. I told you to be careful."

Jon thought he had completely covered his shoulders with sunblock but must have missed bits. "It's only a small patch."

"I know, but it only takes a small patch." She gently applied Aloe Vera cream. "You need to take better care of yourself."

He knew what was coming. "I'm feeling much better."

"Good, but what happens when we get back? Within a week, you'll be worse than ever." She kissed the back of his head. "I think you need to seriously consider working for yourself."

He reached back and patted her leg. "I know, but it's not the right time. The kids are too little, and it's a big risk going out on your own at any time. At the moment, it would be impossible."

"Money isn't everything. I keep telling you that. Working for the Cromwells is not doing you any good. I have never seen you as stressed as you have been in the last few months."

"That's because Richard is new. He'll soon settle in."

"Will he?" She stopped smoothing his shoulder. "He's been there six months, and you still have to run around after him. He was supposed to ease the burden on you. He's giving you twice the grief."

"He'll get better."

"You keep saying that, but when? I don't think he'll ever improve, not while he has you around to do all the work."

Leah had made the same comment several times, and he knew she was right. Richard was supposed to learn the ropes to allow the business to expand. He was expected to assume control when his father eventually retired. Richard did not meet the expected standards despite Jon's patience and support. He was lazy, disinterested and unreliable. Jon knew it, Rich's father knew it, and the customers knew it. However, knowing a problem is one thing; doing something about it is another. Rob's answer to his son's shortcomings was to expect Jon to do the work. New contracts were delegated to Richard, but Jon took the flak when issues arose.

"I'll have a word with Rob when I get back. I'll tell him that I expect things to change and give him a deadline for improvements. If things don't change by the date I set, I'm out of there, and we'll go for Plan B."

"Nothing is going to change, Jon. He might give you a pay rise and promise you the earth, but it'll all be lip service. Within a week, everything will be back to normal. Nothing would have changed. The kids and I want you to stick around. We don't want you to have a heart attack or a stroke. Where would we be then?"

The same thought had crossed his mind and was one reason sleep had become difficult. "I'll be fine. It's just a temporary blip."

"I am sure that's what your father said."

That cut to the quick. "My father's situation was different. He didn't look after himself. He smoked, drank too much and ate the wrong food."

"But he had a weakness there." She touched his chest. "You already know that your blood pressure and cholesterol levels are too high, and you are only half the age your father was when he had his first heart attack. You have far more stress in your life than he ever did." She hadn't intended to sound so sharp. "Look, love," she kissed his ear. "All I'm saying is that we need to find a way of giving you an easier time." She nibbled his ear lobe. "We should seriously consider selling our house and moving into my grandfather's place." Her lips moved across his shoulder while her arms explored his upper body. Her left hand caressed his chest. Her right entered his shorts. "We can do the renovations at our own pace, convert the stables into workshops, and then you can be a self-employed carpenter, and I can open a design studio. We can use the rest of the land to grow vegetables and provide plenty of open space for the kids."

"Sounds great," said Jon, tilting back his head until their lips met.

Neither Ben nor Will was in the mood for drinking. Shirley, on the other hand, was ready to party.

"Come on, you boring old farts. We're on holiday. Let's have a cocktail."

"I'm not sure," said Will. "My stomach is a bit off."

"Go on then," said Ben. I'll have a Majorcan sunrise."

"What's that when it's at home?" asked Will.

"Not sure," said Ben. It says here it has local liqueurs and wine in it. It's worth a go."

"I'm having a Sa Coma sling," said Shirley.

"Are you sure?" Will looked concerned. "You had a Margarita last time. Should you mix your drinks?"

"I'll be fine. I want to see if I can get through the list."

Will held up the card. Cocktail descriptions filled both sides. "There are a lot of them. This could be quite a night."

"I'm not going to drink them all tonight, you soft bugger. I aim to complete the set by the time we go home."

"In that case, I'll have a long slow screw against the wall."

Ben and Shirley looked at each other and said in

harmony. "Not in here, you won't!"

They giggled as Will groaned.

With his mother safely delivered to the apartment after dinner and engrossed in her book, Nick felt fidgety and in need of a walk. He assured her he would be fine and set off on the route he had taken for his run that morning.

Only parts of the road were well-lit, and Nick had to watch for potholes in the pavements. He was amazed at how the drunken revellers he encountered avoided injury. They paid no attention to him.

On the outskirts of the town, he saw a cheaply erected sign advertising the "Cavern Disco Bar". The sign pointed toward the seafront. Nick recalled the name from the conversation with his uncle. His cousins were said to be regulars there. Nick wondered if they might be inside now but did not intend to find out.

He was hoping that the night air would make him sleepy. It hadn't helped so far, and Nick wondered if a dip in the sea would do him good. The night was warm, and the sky was clear. It was ideal weather for a late-night swim. He set off down the long, empty road to the beach.

The Cavern Disco Bar was no more than the basement of an old hotel. It was certainly popular. Cars, motorbikes and scooters filled the car park. Waifs and strays sat on and leaned against surrounding walls, trees and cars as they chatted, smoked or kissed. Some looked like they required a moment of recovery. Hefty security men stood on each side of the entrance, and a third wandered around the perimeter, checking for signs of trouble. He gave Nick an uncertain look as he passed by. Nick had no intention of stopping. He was keen to find the beach and the sea.

He found the playa two hundred metres from the club and spotted directions to the Castell among the array of signposts. Lucia had mentioned the watchtower and the magnificent scenery. He thought he might run there the following day.

The beach was empty apart from the thatched sun shades on top of wooden poles and piles of sun beds standing irregularly across the golden sands. The moonlight cast shadows across the sands as the gentle waves of the Mediterranean lapped up on the shoreline. Nick heard voices, and his eyes scoured the beach again. He saw nobody and decided that whoever it was probably didn't want to be disturbed.

He slipped off his t-shirt and trainers and walked onto the beach. The sand was cool underfoot. As he passed a pile of sun beds, Nick heard a girl's voice which appeared muffled and anxious. He could not determine what she was saying but listened to a male voice telling her to stop moaning. She knew why they were there.

Nick moved closer to the beds, which had been positioned to provide privacy for whoever was at the centre. He looked and saw two more beds, one occupied by the couple. The girl punched out at her companion as he wrestled with her clothes, his hands trying to keep her in position. It appeared to Nick that the girl was winning. The boy screamed as the girl brought her knees up to her belly and pushed them into the boy's chest, sending him backwards into the stack of beds.

Nick was about to leave them to it when he heard the boy threaten the girl about her choices and raise his hand. Nick stepped into the barricade. The boy tried to lie on the girl, who held something in her hand, but her legs fended him off again. He hit the sand but quickly got back up.

"Bitch."

Nick stepped forward. "Excuse me. I think she's trying to tell you that she wants to go. Leave her alone."

The boy faced him. "Fuck off, mate. Keep your nose out." He turned back to the girl.

"Get off her." Nick dropped his trainers and shirt and grabbed the boy, pulling him back and smashing his fist into his face. The boy crashed into the tower of plastic beds, which wobbled as the boy slid onto the sand.

The girl climbed off the sunbed and pushed down her dress, mumbling thanks in Nick's direction. He was amazed that he knew her.

"Gemma? Are you okay?"

The girl looked embarrassed. "Yes. Thank you."

Barty shouted, "I fucking warned you, twat."

Unfortunately for Batholemew Smith, he was slow across the sand and did not pose any real threat. Nick had ample time to assume his fighting stance. He caught the boy with a punch under the chin. Barty's feet left the ground, and he landed on the sand again, uttering a forlorn "Shit."

Nick stood, ready to strike, but Barty was on all fours and moving away. A foot hitting his backside spurred him on, and he crawled toward the club.

The girl took a deep breath as her attacker shuffled away.

"Are you sure you're okay? Did he hurt you?" Nick asked.

"He didn't get the chance, but I would have used this if you hadn't turned up." She showed him a canister of pepper spray.

"Where did you get that?"

"They gave them out in Uni." The girl smoothed her face and hair and then looked at Nick. "You must think me stupid, but he seemed so nice."

Nick offered no comment. He picked up his shirt and put it on.

"Don't feel you have to dress on my account." She pulled a face. "Sorry, I really shouldn't have said that. Sometimes, I have trouble keeping my mouth shut. You probably think I'm a right tart."

He smiled. "Nah, not really. You swede bashers are all the same."

She slapped his arm. "Cheeky." She looked for Barty, who was now on his feet and walking to the road. "Do you think he'll come back?"

"Don't know." Nick saw the boy had almost made it to

the road. “I’d better not hang around. He might return with reinforcements.”

The girl collected her bag and shoes. “Are you going to Sa Coma?” Nick nodded. “Can I walk with you? I don’t fancy going back in there.”

“What about your friends? Won’t they worry?”

“Unlikely, but I’ll text them to say I’ve moved on.”

“Shall we walk, or should I get you a taxi?”

“Why would I need a taxi? Do you think I won’t make it if we walk?”

“No, I am not saying that. I was thinking about your shoes. You’ve had a drink, and I don’t want to have to carry you.”

“You sarky swine.” Gemma chuckled. “I’ll be fine if we stay on the beach for a while. I can carry my shoes.”

“Okay then, let’s move before your boyfriend returns.”

“He’s not my boyfriend. His name is Barty. I met him in the club.” She worried that she was making a terrible impression. “I didn’t meet him tonight. I’ve seen him here a few times, but tonight was the first night that….”

“It’s okay; you don’t need to explain yourself to me. Ready?”

“I am. Are we going around the headland? I hear the path is good, but it will be dark.”

He held up his ‘phone. “It’s up to you. I have a torch on here, but we can return to the road if you’d rather?”

“You’re a right little boy scout. Lead on.” They had only gone a few steps when she spoke again. “So, do you often do this?”

“Do what?”

“Rescue damsels in distress. Put yourself at risk for strangers.”

Nick grinned. “You’re not a stranger, though, are you? Anyway, I was hardly at risk. He didn’t seem to be much of a fighter. If I'd given you time, you would have finished him without my help.”

Gemma admired the modesty but shook her head. "I don't think so somehow. I am not sure what would have happened if you hadn't turned up. I hope my pepper spray would have worked."

"Well, I did turn up, and nothing happened, so you and your pepper spray live to fight another day. " Nick glanced at her, smiled, and added, "In any case, you bought me a coffee, and I am obliged to protect you."

"My hero."

He laughed as they walked on. "I never expected to see you there."

It was her turn to look at him.

"What? Why do you say that?"

"Well, you must have agreed to go off with him, so you must have expected something to happen."

"Jesus, are you always so direct? You do think I'm a tart."

"I didn't say that. I was just wondering why you changed your mind."

"What? Now, you think I'm a prick teaser, too? Thanks very much."

Nick stretched his arms as he apologised.

"I'm sorry, I didn't mean it like that...I was just wondering how a pretty, bright girl like you could end up in that situation with...a dickhead like that?"

Gemma liked his words and how he said them but was unwilling to let him off gently. "Well, I must attract them because now I'm walking home with a dickhead like you."

"Touché." He saw her smile and shrugged. "Yes, I suppose it's out of the frying pan and all that."

Gemma smiled again. "As I said, I've seen him in the club, and he is usually nice. He tends to arrive pissed, but I always thought he was harmless. He was sober this evening and seemed interested in me. He asked me to go for a walk. I had no idea that they set the beds up like that. I realised what he wanted, and when I told him I wasn't ready, he suddenly became aggressive. I should have known that he was only interested in one thing. Then you turned up. I can assure you that I had no intention of shagging him."

Her frankness surprised him, but he tried not to show it. "Glad to hear it, not that it is any of my business."

"He's a friend of your cousins. They were there, by the way. Louise seemed a bit off. It was as if she didn't like Sara being with her brother." From Nick's shrug, she guessed he wasn't interested in his cousins' antics. "I still can't believe you are related to them."

"Why not?"

"For one thing, they are always so smartly dressed and, well...you're not."

Nick stifled a chuckle. "Are you always so rude? I'll have you know this is top-quality gear." He quickly dropped the pretence. "To be honest, this is the best I can afford at the moment."

"Well, it looks good on you."

"Yeah, sure, that's why you and your mates were laughing at me on the bus,"

"I wasn't laughing at you. I told you that earlier."

"Only because I think you were embarrassed for me."

"I might have been embarrassed, but it wasn't for you. My friends made the comments. I quite liked the look of you. When you smiled at me, they said I might have a chance, so I blushed."

"Thanks for that."

"What? Blushing?"

"No, thank you for telling me the truth and for saying that you liked how I looked. I don't think anyone has ever said that to me before."

"Come off it. You can't expect me to believe you've never had a girl tell you that she thinks you're nice. I may be a swede basher, a tart, and a prick teaser, but I'm not that stupid."

"No, I'm serious. I've never really bothered with girls, not in that way."

"Are you gay?"

"No, at least, I don't think I am. I fancy girls and have female friends from school and stuff, but I've never had a girlfriend."

"Really?" She stopped walking and stared at him. "You've never had a girlfriend?"

Nick shook his head. "No. I've never had time; honestly, I haven't thought about it...until now. I've always been too busy working."

"I would never have thought that. I imagined you having loads of girls chasing you. What with you being so hunky, well-dressed, and extremely offensive!" She waited for a reaction.

Nick hooted. "No need to be sarcastic."

"Seriously though, I think the girls in Wales don't know a good thing when they see one."

Nick did not usually get lost for words. He was unsure what to say. "Come on, let's get moving. At this rate, it'll take us all night to get back." He put his hands in his pockets

"Suits me," she said. "I'm in no rush. I'm enjoying myself." She put her arm through his. "I can't believe I am sharing a romantic, moonlight walk across this gorgeous beach after being rescued by a fit Welsh virgin."

They shuffled on, unaware that someone loitered in the shadows of the shops opposite.

Snowy waited for the young couple to continue their moonlit stroll before stepping out of the doorway and walking up the road.

The sign showed that M&G Import and Export Limited occupied part of the property, but the evidence suggested nobody had been inside for some time. Rubbish littered the parking area, and various posters, advertising circuses, and festivals slowly fell away from the windows. The paintwork needed refreshing, and a window upstairs had a hole.

A door opened, and Snowy instinctively sought a hiding place. The large waste bins provided cover and let him see what was happening. He hoped whoever was there did not plan to dump rubbish. The only excuse he could think of involved pretending to be drunk and acting pissed was never his strong point.

The adjoining property housed an internet café and bar. It looked like the café was closing for the day. A long-haired man double-checked all doors before getting on his moped. Snowy sighed as the bike farted its way up the road.

He took another look around before calling it a day. He would return in the daylight. Snowy had to collect his order of fish and chips before the takeaway closed.

"So, have you had a boyfriend?"

Gemma withdrew her arm, stopped and pulled a face. "Yeah, of course I have. I'm not…" she was going to say 'weird' but thought better of it. "I'm not with anyone at the moment, though."

"Why is that? I'd have thought all the farming boys would be after you."

"I know. Prize breeding stock like me." She shook her head again and giggled. "You are a cheeky bastard. I had a boyfriend…of sorts… until a few weeks back, and then I dropped him."

"Why? Did you argue or something?"

"Not really. I just got fed up, and it wasn't as if the relationship was going anywhere." She stopped and watched another couple walking hand in hand on the promenade. "It was time to move on."

Nick had walked ahead. He waited for her to catch up. "I take it he wasn't marriage material?"

Gemma found the comment hilarious. "Christ, no. He wasn't great stage two material." She laughed loudly. "Marriage to Mac? Shit no. That was never going to happen."

"Stage two?"

Gemma's head bowed. She knew as soon as she had spoken, the phrase would take the conversation in a different direction. Gemma licked her lips, preparing to speak. "My friends teased me a lot when I was younger because I lived my life in stages." His expression changed. "I know it sounds weird, but if I went to the shops, I would verbally run through the steps in my mind. Stage one is making sure I am suitably attired. Stage two, I know what I need to get. Stage three, gather a bag, my keys and money. Stage four is how to get to the shop. Would I walk, take a bus, or can I drive there? Stage five...you get the picture. I used to run through all the steps in my brain. I always had a step-by-step plan."

"So your last boyfriend didn't know what you wanted?"

Her turn to look confused. "What?" She thought about what she had said. "No, I developed stages for different situations. The girls used to take the piss out of me. I don't vocalise it so much anymore except if I need to plan coursework or something."

"So you and...this bloke were at Stage two? What does that mean?"

"Okay." Deep breath. "I once wrote an essay about how every successful relationship goes through stages."

"What class was that? Marriage Counselling?"

"No English Lit. We were studying 'The Taming of the Shrew' by..."

"Shakespeare. We studied it, too."

"Right. The teacher gave me top marks but made me read my essay in class. After that, the girls started to use my stages to describe how serious or not they were."

"Isn't it a natural thing? You either like someone and want to be with them, or you don't."

"There is more to it than that. Knowing where you stand is important to decide what happens next."

"I see," said Nick, not understanding. "What are these stages."

Gemma continued. "The first is Connection. You know when you first meet someone and decide that you like them and want to take things further? Many of the blokes I've met never got through that stage."

"Your friend back there, for instance."

"Exactly," said Gemma. "Stage two, which I call the Coupling stage, is where you'd get to know each other better."

"That just sounds like a continuation of step one."

"It is to an extent, but I think of it as when you begin to build a relationship and commit to it, perhaps by not seeing other people, etcetera."

"So if that bloke, Barty?" She nodded. "If he had played it cooler, would he have been in with a chance of stage two?"

Gemma forced a shiver. "We'll never know. If he always behaves like that, he wouldn't get beyond stage one."

Nick resisted the temptation to smile. "What happens at stage 3?"

"I call this the Critical stage where you start making decisions as a couple, possibly by living together."

"Why is that critical?"

"It's a risky stage. Family and friends might now see you as one unit." Nick looked lost. "It's hard to explain, but if one of you gets invited to something, it gets taken for granted that the other will be there too. One of you might resent the loss of individuality and inability to make decisions without consultation."

"Jesus, that's a mouthful. You've clearly explained this before." Gemma nodded. Nick spoke. "So are you saying that once you reach stage three, you must discuss everything before making decisions?"

"Not always, but if it affects the partnership, then certainly. You might live together, but you should never assume you can decide for someone else."

Nick thought about his parents and how his father made decisions without consulting anyone. "I see," he said. "You must have thought a lot about this."

"I did. Stage 4 is Consolidation, where things like children, cars, and the like come into the equation. Stage 5 is Companionship when you grow old together."

"Sounds ideal." Nick scratched the back of his neck. "The

five Cs to contentment. Perhaps you should write them down? You'd make a fortune."

"Now who is being sarcastic?"

"Sorry, I meant it as a joke. I like your theory but can't comment on it. I've never reached stage one."

"What is this then?" said Gemma. "We've connected."

Nick pursed his lips and nodded. "I suppose we have."

Gemma thought she saw something shiny and swept her foot over the sand. It turned out to be a chocolate bar wrapper, so she covered it again. "Anyway, there are a lot more stages. Those five are the good stages, but many couples fail because they try to rush things or their relationship is not strong enough to survive."

"What do you call the bad stages?"

"Well, in no particular order, the Cancellation stage, where one of you gets dumped; the Cheating stage, which I think is self-explanatory. In the Crisis stage, problems appear, and arguments might occur regularly. The Catastrophe stage is when something happens from which the couple never recover, losing a child, for instance, and then the Carer stage, where maybe one of you gets seriously ill, and you stop being equals. There are more, but you've got five dark and five light stages to go on with."

Nick considered where his parents stood in Gemma's stages. It was a dark one.

"Stunned you to silence, have I, Taffy?"

"Not at all," Nick said as he thought of something to say. "So Mac, is that his name?" He saw a nod. "He wasn't long-term material?"

"No chance. He was too needy. We met in Edinburgh, where I go to university. We'd only known each other a few weeks, and he wanted me to move in with him. We had fun, but it was never anything serious, at least not to me."

"Was he a student too?"

"No, he worked for my friend...ex-friend's father." She was relieved that Nick had not pressed the issue.

"Have you ever got to stage four?"

"I haven't gotten past stage two yet. I have plenty of time to do that. I want to finish my Master's degree first."

They walked on slowly, discussing her studies, and Gemma was relieved that Nick asked many questions but did not resort to cliches or jokes about the potential benefits of knowing a brewer.

The pair reached a point where the beach briefly ran out, and they had to rejoin the promenade. Nick held out a hand to help her with the step.

"You are a gentleman, but I could have done that alone."

"Sorry. A force of habit, I suppose." He stuffed his hands into his pockets.

"Don't take offence. I liked it. It's a nice thing to do." She put her arm back through his.

They walked in silence for a moment or two. Gemma sensed Nick had something on his mind. "Come on, out with it."

Nick glanced sideways, wondering how she knew. "Oh, err, I was just thinking…as we've sort of cleared the introductory stage, whether I would have a chance of moving on to stage two?"

Gemma pulled his arm with both hands as she stopped walking. "Are you asking me out, Taffy?"

"Yes. I…am…if that is okay."

"Really? You're not being sarcastic?"

"Yes and No. Yes, really and no, I am not being sarky."

"In that case, I accept. Thank you. What are you doing tomorrow?"

Nick outlined his plans and asked if Gemma would care to join him. She agreed, much to Nick's delight.

"Thank you. Can I buy you a drink to celebrate?"

Gemma looked around. There was not a bar in sight. "Where?"

Nick took her hand and led her across the tarmac to a vending machine outside a tobacco shop. "You can have a beer or a soft drink. What do you fancy?"

"What are you having?"

"I think I'll have a beer," said Nick, removing coins from his pocket and counting them.

"Then I'll have the same. Thank you."

Nick held out a collection of coins. "Have you got a euro for this? It doesn't take shrapnel."

Gemma giggled as she opened her bag to check her purse.

Ben could never sleep on a full stomach, so he stood on the balcony listening to the sea while watching the late-night walkers on the promenade. Most seemed to be revellers, some of whom enjoyed themselves too much.

The gate opened, and Nick, the lad from the one-bedroom apartment in the top block, stepped into the grounds and waited for the automatic gate to close behind him.

Even though Ben was two flights up, Nick still spotted him and waved as he passed by the pool. Ben waved back, trying to remember what it was like to be young, without a care in the world, with years to go before life began grinding you down.

Nick reread the email and, with a broad smile spread across his face, said. "Chris said he's in, Mum."

"What happens next?" Elizabeth sipped her wine.

"He's following the money trail to see how much he can trace. He only found a small portion of our cash in the first account but said there are extensive links to other offshore accounts."

"Is he confident we'll get some of it back?"

"He is but is not yet sure how much. He'll have a better idea in the next few days when he sees where the trail leads and how much we are talking about."

Elizabeth raised her glass. "Anything would be a big help."

DAY 5 - WEDNESDAY 28 JULY

The stress levels were slowly beginning to recede. There was nothing like a bit of passion for improving the mood and aiding relaxation. Leah's taking the sim card has been beneficial. He could guess where it would be but had not attempted to retrieve it. He was not going to worry about his bosses. They could like it or lump it. Leah had identified a plan, and they would find a way to make it work. They were only five days into their holiday, and it seemed like an age since he had seen home.

This trip reminded him of the holidays before Jon had accepted the devil's coin and joined Cromwell Construction. These thoughts had run through Jon Oliver's head after sex the previous evening before he fell fast asleep.

His eyes opened slowly, and he reached for his watch. It was just after seven. He had no idea when he had last slept so well, and his first conscious thought of the day was non-work related for the first time in ages. He was thinking about sex. Much to his delight, his long-lost friend, the wake-up erection, had returned. He moved closer to Leah, who came to with a start.

From her reaction, he thought she was pleasantly surprised. They snuggled up, caressing, touching and nibbling before she moved on top. It had been a while since they had been intimate in the morning, but they knew each other so well there was no awkwardness. Leah was about to progress matters when a sleepy Daisy pushed open the door and plodded into their room.

"Mum, Charlie keeps taking the sheet off my bed."

She kissed Jon's cheek as she rolled off and pushed down her nightie.

"Okay, love," Leah said, getting out of bed. "Let's go and

sort him out. Then we can make breakfast."

Gemma stretched as she sat upright, the cotton sheet falling away. One of the other two beds was empty and appeared unused.

Kylie stirred. "What time is it?"

"Eight."

"Shall we go out for breakfast?"

"If you want."

Kylie looked at the empty bed. "Looks like Sara struck it lucky last night."

"If you call that lucky."

"Me-oww. What happened to you anyway? You seemed very pally with Barty, but he returned from the beach alone. He reckoned that some bloke pulled him off you and hit him. He was worried about you and tried to get Donny and Christiano to go after this mysterious assailant. They weren't interested. Barty couldn't have been that bothered. He had a beer before hitting on a girl dancing with Kirsty."

"Am I that forgettable?" Perhaps he had better luck with her, thought Gemma. "Barty started okay but became pushy. A bit too pushy. I was about to kick him in the balls and hit him with pepper spray, but a lad called Nick stepped in to help me."

"What happened next?"

"Nick knocked Barty into the sand and told him to beat it."

"This guy saved you?" Kylie sat up, anxious to learn more. "Sounds exciting. Who is this, Nick, apart from being your knight in shining armour?"

"He's the guy from the bus. You know, the one with his mother."

Kylie's eyes widened as her jaw dropped. "The gimpy one? The gimp saved you?"

"He did."

"Shut up. You are joking?"

"No, I'm being serious. Nick sent Barty packing and then

walked me home. He's a sweet guy. I like him."

"Are we talking about the same bloke? The one wearing shit jeans and had a haircut from the last century.

"That's him."

"Shut up. You never went with him?"

"I never said I went with him. He walked me home, that's all. We chatted non-stop as we strolled across the beach and stopped for a drink, talking and listening to the sea. The beach, the moonlight, him, it was all very romantic. He is lovely and quite funny. He made me laugh."

"But you didn't do anything?"

"No."

"Did he try it on?"

"No."

"Is he gay?"

"No, at least I don't think so. I met him at the café yesterday, and we chatted, and then he showed up last night."

"Perhaps he's a stalker."

Gemma roared as she threw her pillow at Kylie. "He's not a stalker. It was just a coincidence that he was out for a walk while I was fighting off Barty."

Kylie tossed the pillow back. "Is this the same Nick that is Donny's cousin?"

"It is."

"But Donny reckons he is a total loser. He never went to university and has bummed from job to job."

"So have you. Does that make you a loser?"

Kylie thought about the comment. "I don't think so...."

"No, it doesn't," said Gemma firmly. "You found your niche, and I think you're a great person, and Nick might be too. Anyway, he's not had it easy." She stopped there for fear of giving away something that Nick might have said in confidence. She doubted he had. Having just met her, would Nick tell her anything others would not already know? "I am just pleased he was there."

"Are you seeing him again?"

Gemma smiled as she nodded. “He’s collecting me at 10; we’re going to some beach up the road.”

“Does he have a car, then?”

“Yeah, he put it in the hold.”

“You know what I meant. Has he hired a car?”

“We’re hiring bikes.”

“You are going on a bike? In this heat?”

“Yup, but we’ll take it easy and stop when necessary.”

I haven’t seen you on a bike since junior school.”

“Well, today is the day.” Gemma got out of bed. “And do you know what? I’m looking forward to it.”

“This I must see, Gem and the gimp on bikes. I’ll be posting loads of photos.”

“Are you sure you don’t want me to accompany you?”

“No love, you go and enjoy your horse ride. Is Will joining you?”

Not a chance,” said his son-in-law, entering the room. “Last time I rode a horse, I could hardly walk for a week.”

Ben winked at his daughter. “I thought somebody with your natural ability would take it to it like a duck to water?”

“Ever seen a duck on a horse?”

Ben and Shirley had no idea where this conversation was heading and shook their heads, awaiting the punchline.

“There you are then. Anyone fancy a cuppa?”

Nick devoured his breakfast cereal while reviewing the information sent through by his boss. The trail looked complicated, but if anyone could crack it, Chris Shanklin could.

Elizabeth and Lucia sat at the back of the bus and watched the other tourists board. Elizabeth recognised one man who sat at the front of the bus. She mentioned it to Lucia.

“That man with the hat on stays at our apartment block.”

Lucia squinted. “Si, Signor Moran. He stays with his daughter and son-in-law.”

Elizabeth was surprised. "Have you met?"

"Yes, I see him the day he arrived, but he is a quiet man. His face always looks sad."

"How did you meet him?"

"I clean the apartment, and the agent tells me that Signor Moran's son-in-law is a valuable client, and I should make sure the apartment is spotless and visit to ensure everything is fine."

"And did you make sure it was spotless?"

Lucia pulled a face and pretended to spit. "I do not need to because all my apartments are spotless once I have finished with them. He was, as you say, teaching a grandmother to fry eggs."

"Something like that," said Elizabeth, offering her friend a mint.

Ben Moran sat by the window, removed his hat and dropped it beside him. Shirley and Will had been brilliant and fabulous company, but he needed this break. He had become so used to spending time alone that being in company stressed him out.

Besides, they had been on the island for five days, and Ben was nowhere near to finding a suitable spot to ensure he didn't have to return home.

The sight of Graham Laing standing not 300 metres from him shocked Snowy. He recognised the man immediately and darted into the nearest bar, sitting in the shade.

Graham had barely changed since the last time Snowy had seen him. He was dressed better, his attire looked expensive, and Snowy thought he would see his reflection in Graham's shoes, but the facial features were identical.

Graham and a younger lad entered a run-down hotel in one of the town's backstreets. Snowy waited in a café opposite and, when questioned, ordered a latte. He fancied a beer, but it was not yet 11 am.

A large white van emblazoned with "Kingston Exhibition Specialists" pulled into the hotel's forecourt, and the driver opened the rear roller door. Five black men clambered out of the back as three more exited the hotel. One took the five inside, and the other two collected large boxes, bringing them into the building. The driver closed the rear door and turned the vehicle around but did not leave the premises.

Forty-five minutes later, Graham and his companion emerged and jumped into the passenger seats. Graham handed cash to the two men, and the driver counted his share before the truck drove away.

There was no way that Snowy could keep up with the van on foot. He ordered a large beer while maintaining his surveillance of the premises.

Nick shuffled his bottom and lay back on his towel. The sun beat down on his chest, and he wondered whether he should have brought the beach umbrella. He dismissed the idea, remembering that transporting it on a bike would have been difficult.

Gemma caught his hand and squeezed his fingers. "It's lovely here and so quiet."

"Hmm," Nick replied.

"Did you say your uncle told you about this place?"

"Yes. I helped fix his laptop yesterday, and we got talking. He mentioned it then."

Gemma and Nick hired the bikes from a shop near his apartment block, and the pair cycled to Costa Del Los Pinos, a hidden oasis beyond Cala Bona, consisting of a sheltered bay, a bar and golden sands. A large yacht lay anchored in the bay, the crew had already arrived ashore, and their landing craft rested on the beach beside two cycles.

Gemma's hand tapped his elbow. "Talking about your family, your cousin and his mate can be a bit kinky, can't they?"

Nick had no clue. "What do you mean?" He saw Gemma

resting on her elbow, waiting to tell a story. He rolled onto his side.

"Well, Kylie told me Christiano takes pictures of topless girls and puts them online."

"What? Are you serious?"

"I am."

"But that is hardly kinky."

"He's asked her to go with him today to pose."

"Why does he need her to pose? There are loads of topless women around."

"He wants Kylie to stand in front of the topless women for him to catch them unaware, and he also wants her to engage them in conversation to make them stand up. He has even suggested she offer to rub cream into some of them."

Nick raised his body and also rested on his elbow. "Is that normal?"

"I don't think so. As I said, it sounds a bit pervy to me."

"And will she do it?"

"Yeah, she can be a dirty cow when she wants to be, plus she fancies him. The only thing is that Christiano is playing hard to get. That won't last. Kylie loves a challenge."

"Good for her." Nick smiled and prepared to resume sunbathing, but Gemma hadn't finished.

She tapped him again. "And your Donny is a bit of a weird one too."

"He's not my Donny." Nick regained his listening position. "But why is he weird?"

"Well…he took Sara to his flat last night."

"Flat? What flat?"

"The one above his bar."

"What bar?"

"Do you know your cousin at all? He runs an internet bar at the top of town with a flat above it."

"I thought it was a café."

"Café, bar, what's the difference? The room has a bed, but Sara says they didn't use it. He collected some things, and they went to a club. Afterwards, he took her back to your uncle's place, and she slept on the sofa bed, but they didn't have full sex.

Nick tried to recall if the girls in school had shared such details but did not have long to dwell on it as Gemma spoke again.

"He was happy to pleasure her but would not have sex."

"Pleasure her?"

Gemma held up her spare hand and extended her index and second fingers, poking them through the air. "You know, he was pleasuring her."

Nick's expression suggested that he had not known until then. "Ah, right."

"Come off it! I know you are a virgin, but you must have seen online stuff?"

Nick shrugged. "A bit…probably not that much, to be honest."

"Really?" Gemma shrieked with laughter. "Do you expect me to believe that? You are verging on the ridiculous!." She found her joke hilarious.

Nick groaned as he shook his head. "But what is weird about that?"

"Well, he said he can get off just knowing he is getting her off. He doesn't need to have sex. I think that sounds strange."

Having limited knowledge of such things, Nick was unsure how common this was, but from Gemma's tone, he doubted it was typical behaviour. "Perhaps he doesn't fancy her?"

"Maybe, but Sara says he let her suck his dick. She couldn't do that if he didn't get aroused."

Once again, her straight-talking came as a surprise. "I suppose so." Nick did not wish to discuss the sex lives of others, especially those he did not much care for and started to recline. Gemma brought his movement to an abrupt halt.

"Anyway, you can't say much. You haven't even kissed

me yet. Not many men get to stage two without a snog. Don't you fancy me?"

"Yes...of course I do."

"Then why haven't you kissed me?"

"I haven't had the chance. You never shut up long enough. You are always too busy talking."

She slapped his arm. "I am not. You are a cheeky bastard." She giggled again before her tone became serious. "Are you a bit nervous about it?"

It was strange how she seemed to know what he was thinking. Nick nodded. "I am a bit, to be honest. I wanted to kiss you last night and this morning...but, I think, the more I thought about doing it, the more nervous I became."

"Are you nervous now?"

"I wasn't."

"It's perfectly natural, you know, not being nervous. I mean kissing."

"I know that but...."

"No buts, try it."

He leaned over, and their lips met. Gemma's mouth led the way.

As they separated, she said, "That wasn't so bad, was it?"

Nick smirked. "No, that was very nice. Can I do it again?"

"You can, but you don't need to ask. If it feels right, then do it. I'll soon tell you if I'm not in the mood."

Nick looked her up and down. Her painted toenails, bikini, skin slowly gaining a tan, and hair tied behind her head. It felt right. He kissed her again, touching her side and pulling her to him. Gemma put her arms around his neck, easing him onto her towel. Nick's hand made its way up her back, enjoying the feel of her skin.

Gemma brought him back to reality when she grabbed his penis through his shorts.

"Oww, what are you doing?"

"Just checking."

"Checking what?"

"That you aren't gay. You didn't seem too sure last night."

"Oh, right, and you can tell that easily, can you?"

"I can."

"And what's the verdict?"

"Promising signs, but you require probably need further examination...and I need to run some tests."

"What sort of tests?"

"Some internal, others possibly oral." She shrieked aloud.

"When?" He reached for her shoulder and eased her forward until their lips met again.

"Well, not here," she said. "What do you think your name is? Bartholomew?"

He laughed. "God no, Nicholas is bad enough."

"Yes, I hadn't realised what an awful name that is, but I suppose you are a saint."

"I was until you arrived."

"Cheesy." She sighed, cackled and then kissed him. "I prefer Nick. "

"Me too. Nicholas reminds me of my father." He lay back, determined to talk about something else. "So when do I get these tests?"

She smirked, "Patience Taffy, let's just say you're on the waiting list." She snuggled into his shoulder and put her arm across his chest.

Snowy followed the man in the brightly coloured shirt down a lane to the beach. The man wore several gold necklaces with sunglasses hanging from them. He also carried two outsize cases, the type that doctors used. He stopped at the beach's edge, partially opened one of the cases, and then walked across the sand, inviting sunbathers to look at his many bargains.

As the road to the Cap de Formentor lighthouse is very

twisty with tight bends and, at some points, steep, the travel company gave travellers an option. They could spend time at the beach or transfer to smaller buses for what the driver called *a roller coaster on a coach* to reach the lighthouse. Lucia insisted that Elizabeth would regret not getting to see the outstanding views.

Ben nodded and smiled at the two ladies who sat opposite him on the shuttle bus.

Jon Oliver felt calmer, and when his wife said they needed to visit the local hypermarket to get provisions, he suggested she should go on her own. He would look after the kids. It would do her good to look around the shops. It would also allow her time to think about his great idea that they should ask the Cromwells to invest in their new venture.

Leah hadn't taken the proposal seriously, but Jon thought she might warm to it. In the meantime, he would benefit from quality time with his children. They would not go far, probably staying close to the pool. Leah accepted his offer, and they parted at the entrance to the complex with a quick kiss.

The pool area was empty apart from one towel belonging to the German swimming in the main pool. Jon knew the guy completed multiple lengths of breaststroke every morning.

He moved the designated sun beds into the shade of the enormous palm trees and covered them with beach towels. The twins were anxious to get into the water but, for once, obeyed their father's instructions to stand on the grass while he set up camp. Daisy suggested it was not a proper camp as they had no tent.

"That's right, love. I suppose it is more of a base than a camp," he said. He removed the twins' t-shirts and squeezed their thin arms through the inflated armbands. "Listen to me, you pair. Make sure you stay in the little pool where I can watch you." He gently held a chin in each hand. "What did I just say?"

"We must stay in the little pool," said Charlie.

"Baby pool," added Harry.

"It's not a baby pool. It is a paddling pool. It is for big boys as well as babies. But you don't go in the big pool unless with your mother or me."

"We know," said Harry.

"Know," added his brother.

"But that pool is mostly for babies, isn't it, Dad?" Daisy asked. She was removing the cotton dress that covered her swimsuit.

"It's not only for babies, Dais. I've seen lots of adults in there this week."

"But adults only go in there to look after their babies."

The twins silently observed this exchange, and Jon knew he had to persuade them that the little pool was for everyone. They were no longer prepared to be called babies; if they thought the smaller pool was beneath them, they would use the larger one. That had all the hallmarks of being a complete nightmare for him.

"Not always, Dais. I've seen several adults in the little pool without a child." It was time to change the subject. "You pair play nicely, and I'll be in to join you shortly. I want to have a minute to start this book. Okay?" He emptied the bag containing the selection of toys onto the concrete floor.

"Yes, Dad," said Charlie, picking up the ball

"Dad," added Harry, collecting the plastic bucket.

"I'll look after them, Dad," said Daisy.

"Perhaps the three of you can play together?"

"Oh, Dad," said Daisy. "You know I can't play with babies."

Fortunately, the twins missed this last exchange. They had already departed the scene. Charlie was walking down the steps, and Harry had launched the bucket into the little pool.

Ben was undoubtedly impressed by the highest lighthouse in the Balearic islands. He was even more interested to learn it had a focal height of 210 meters above sea level and cliffs that fell directly into the sea. He stared at the water below, believing he could perform a realistic slip over the wall and generate enough momentum to roll off the edge.

"Why is that man so interested in the sea?"

Lucia pointed at Ben when Elizabeth's expression told her she had no idea who Lucia was talking about.

"He is probably just taken with the view and surprised that someone built a lighthouse up here. It is impressive."

"There is something about that man. He looks so sad all the time. I don't like that he looks down when he should look up and out. He is not right."

Elizabeth shook her head. *"Just because someone looks down doesn't mean anything is wrong with them."*

"He looks down too much. Why study the earth when there is so much to enjoy up there." She held a finger up into the air. *"Look around you. Nobody else studies the rocks as much as him. I haven't looked down once, and neither have you."*

"Only because it would remind me that I must travel back down that dreadful road."

"But we will not be so close to the edge on the way back."

"So, do you have any brothers or sisters?" Gemma opened the baguette and added a squeeze of mayo.

"No, not really."

The response delayed the approach of food into her mouth. "Not really? What does that mean? You either do or you don't?"

"I think I have a half-brother. I've never met him, but we found out recently that my father was having an affair before he became ill, and his...er...other woman had his baby."

"Seriously?"

"Yes, seriously, his mother wants him to meet me."

"Shit," she said between chews. "How old is the kid?"

"About seven, I think. My Dad died six years ago, and

Mum thinks the baby was about eight months old when Dad died."

"That must have come as a shock."

"A bit, but nothing surprises us anymore after everything we learned about my father. My mother was distraught to learn he was a father again. She always wanted me to have a little brother or sister, but Dad was adamant that he only wanted one child. Then the selfish twat goes off and has one with some woman he's just met who worked behind the bar at the yacht club."

"There's nothing wrong with working behind a bar."

"Sorry, I didn't mean it like that. I still find it hard to believe my father did the dirty on us. "

"That must have been difficult for your mum."

"It was typical of him. He always had to have his own way, the arrogant prick."

The anger in his voice was palpable.

"He was still your father."

"Yes, I know, but that doesn't mean I must like him. The more I think back, the more I realise I never really got on with him."

"Why not?"

"He was not an easy man to like. Kenneth never let his guard down; he had an inflated image of himself and always acted like he was superior. He was such a snob and never did the fatherly things like taking me to the park. That was for common people. He thought he was better than that. He was always too busy if I asked to go anywhere and would stop my mother from taking me. Dad was very controlling and manipulative. He never hit us, my mother or me, but he had this way, you know, he was sort of mentally abusive. My father could say terrible things, but if you reacted, he would turn it around to make it sound like he was the one who'd been hurt. He was clever like that. If you met him today, I'm sure you would think he was charming, but I knew him as a selfish, snobby, overbearing, lying bastard."

Gemma's eyes opened wide, but she said nothing immediately, taking her time to swallow the food. "You really didn't like him then."

"No." Nick smiled, pleased at the chance to break the tension.

"Are you going to meet your half-brother?"

He toyed with his chips. "I'm not sure yet. Mum thinks I ought to for the little boy's sake, but I think that if I do, then they've won. It tells them we don't care what happened or my mother's grief, but I do mind. It hurt my mum, and I care about that a lot."

"He's only a little boy, though. It wasn't his fault."

"I accept that, but he and his mother have been living in luxury for six years, using my father's money while we've been on the bones of our arses."

"Perhaps they didn't know how badly off he had left you?"

His mother had suggested the same thing. "Yeah, maybe, but I still can't believe nobody would have told her. She must have made friends at the yacht club, and I'm sure that word would have gotten back to her at some point." He bit into the bread, washed it down with water, and dabbed his mouth with the napkin. "Anyway, enough about me. Do you have any siblings?"

"Siblings. That's a good word for a Welshie. Yes, I have siblings. I am the middle of three girls."

"If the other two are like you, I feel sorry for your father."

"Oi, cheeky." She playfully slapped his hand. "My father is spoilt rotten by his four lovely angels. We love him to bits. We love our Mum too."

Nick smiled. "What are your sisters' names?"

"The younger one is Kate. She's a gem and is just studying for her A-levels. She wants to be a vet."

"Do you think she'll make it?"

"Probably, she's very bright and determined…yes, before you say it, I know she sounds nothing like me." She pulled a face and stuck out her tongue.

"I never said a word."

"You didn't need to."

"What's the other one called?"

"Carrie..."

"Carrie? Your older sister is called Carrie Potter?" He could not believe this. "Your sister's name is Carrie Potter?" Nick started to laugh loudly.

"It's not her fault; she was around before that bloody wizard became so popular, but she's got terrible stick for it."

"Carrrieeeee Potterrrrrr," hissed Nick before chuckling again.

"Yes, hilarious," said Gemma, keeping a straight face. "She's married now, so she is no longer a Potter."

"Oh right," said Nick, lamenting at the lost opportunity to continue the gag.

"Yes, her new surname is Waits." Gemma took a drink as she waited.

"Her new name is Carrie Waits?" Nick roared again. "She is now Carrie Waits? What is she? A bodybuilder? Couldn't she have married Mr Airbag? She could have become Carrie Airbag."

"Nobody of that name in our village," said a deadpan Gemma before she giggled.

Nick composed himself. "It would have been funny, though, Carrie Airbag.."

"You wait. I'll be telling her what you said."

Nick wasn't sure if that was just a turn of phrase or a genuine possibility.

Jon thought it might be time to let Harry have another go at paddling without the armbands. He put them at the side of the pool, placed his hand under his son's belly and told him to swim. Harry did his best, and Jon followed him across the pool, congratulating his son on his progress. They went back and forth, with Jon keeping a sneaky eye on Daisy and

Charlie, as Harry paddled further unaided on each pass.

"Well done," said a proud Jon. "You'll soon be swimming as well as Daisy."

His daughter's intervention could not have been less subtle.

"Dad, Charlie's weeing in the babies' pool."

"Shhh, it's okay, Dais. I said it was okay for him to do it if he was in the pool."

"But he's not in the pool, Dad...look."

Charlie was on the pillars between the pools, bathers around his knees, urinating into the water.

"Oh sh...sugar!" Jon gathered Harry and waded across the pool to get his brother off the pillars.

Snowy checked his watch. It would soon be time for him to go, but he needed to speak with the salesman. He hoped the man would have reached him by now, but people kept talking to him. Snowy undid his strap, put the watch into his pocket, slipped off his shirt, secured it in the waistband of his shorts, and casually walked up the beach.

"Lookie lookie, many bargains," said the man.

Snowy sat on the edge of an empty sunbed. "Over here, I'll take a look."

A wide smile appeared on the man's face as he got nearer. "Hello, boss. What are you looking for today? Anything special?" I have many good things at low prices."

"I need a new watch."

"What make?"

"How much choice do you have?"

The man sat on the bed with his cases between him and Snowy. He selected three gold watches and invited Snowy to choose.

Snowy studied the offerings and eventually selected one. "How much?"

"That is a lovely watch, my friend. You have good taste, that one is two hundred euros.

"How much? I only want a watch. I don't want your whole case."

"That is a good price. A watch like that would cost many thousands in a shop. How much do you want to pay?"

"Fifty euros."

The man let out a deep heart laugh. "Very funny but no way. I cannot accept anything less than one hundred and seventy-five. This is a top brand."

"And I can only pay seventy-five." Snowy estimated the watch to be worth far less. It was clearly a fake.

The haggling continued until Snowy secured the watch for a hundred and ten euros. It was more than he wanted to pay, but he was sure his boss would see the purchase as a reasonable business expense. He handed over the cash. "Where would I find you if I have trouble with it?"

"You won't have any trouble. This is a fine watch." Snowy did not look reassured. "I am always on the beach, my friend."

"But what if you are not?"

"Ask another seller to contact Banda. I will find you."

Ben looked around for a final time before rejoining the shuttle. He had decided this might be the ideal spot. He would consider the other choices but book another trip here if they were less good.

The area around the lighthouse heaved with tourists, and the cliffside path had signs advising it was unsuitable for children and infirm pedestrians. He would only have to walk a few yards, appear to trip and then pretend that his momentum was carrying him over the fence. That would be that. The inquest would determine "Accidental Death", and the insurance company would pay out.

He studied the landscape, trying to appear nonchalant. Ben could not see any surveillance cameras, but he would have to make his fall convincing. It was likely that any spectators would be too shocked to recall too much detail. He felt sorry for them, but they would get over it. The insurance company would look for signs of any unusual behaviour before the accident. Would a second visit to the same site constitute unusual behaviour? He would need a valid reason, and one came to him immediately. Ben would say that he had to return to capture the magnificent views. He would tell his family he was annoyed that he had left his camera behind on this visit.

He liked his thinking. Ben would subject Shirley and Will to his moaning about the camera for the next few days. He would be careful not to overegg it. Shirley and Will might want to accompany him if he appeared too enthusiastic.

What if they did? That would be a relatively minor problem. Ben was confident he could put enough distance between himself and them in this terrain with a similar number of visitors. They might see him but not be able to stop him.

He hoped he would be alone. Ben felt guilty thinking about Shirley coping with visions of her father's death. He would try to dissuade them.

Ben felt better having devised a plan. He stepped aboard the bus, eager to enjoy his remaining time on the island before returning to spend his last moments at the lighthouse.

Will collected Shirley from the ranch, and they strolled into a nearby bar.

"What are you having?"

"I'll have a large white wine, please. Can you get me a glass of cider, too? That was thirsty work."

"Shall we have lunch here, or do you want to go somewhere else?"

"It's not very salubrious, is it?"

"Neither is the Gulshan in Edgbaston, but I can never get you out of there."

"Good point. Grab a menu then, and we'll take a look."

"Afternoon, gents," Will said to the four men sitting around a table with empty coffee cups and tapas dishes. They did not respond, as they were too busy exchanging cash for each other's goods.

Nick jogged across the hot sand on his toes. He wanted to get to the sanctuary of his towel. The shower had cooled him down, but the feeling would not last.

"That's better."

"Don't forget to cream up again. We don't want you burning to a crisp."

"As soon as I've dried off." Nick lay back on the towel, letting the hot sun work.

Gemma lay close to him, lying on her side. She stretched her free arm and brushed water off his neck. "I'll be happy to rub the cream in if you want?"

"Can I dry off a bit first?"

"Of course." Her fingers crossed his chest. "This is firm; do you work out a lot?"

"I suppose I do. We have classes twice weekly, and I work out with my mates on other days. What about you? You look to be in good shape, so you must be getting plenty of exercise."

"Thank you for noticing. When I was in uni, I went to the gym every other day, but I haven't been for a few weeks. I get enough exercise these days, fending off unwanted attention."

"I can imagine." He stretched.

Gemma moved her hand to his stomach. "You don't mind me doing this, do you?"

"No, not at all. If your hand is up here, you're not trying to pinch my dick."

"What? Like this." Her hand moved quickly to his groin, and instinctively, Nick rolled over, off the towel and into the sand.

"Great," he said, standing up. Sand covered one side. "Thanks for that." He spat sand from his mouth. "I'd better nip in the sea and wash this off."

"The shower is nearer."

"Yes, but the sign at the shower tells you to remove sand before using it."

"I don't think many people worry about that," Gemma said, sitting up. "Hang on. I'll join you."

No sooner had Nick emerged from his underwater swim in the clear blue sea than Gemma wrapped her legs around his waist and her arms around his neck. Nick entwined his fingers and rested his palms against her backside. They kissed.

"You know that you must be careful having sex in the sea as the suction could result in you getting stuck together."

"I wouldn't know," said Nick. "But I wouldn't mind giving it a try."

"Bloody hell, Taffy. I thought being in the water would cool you down."

"Well, you started it, you smutty swede basher."

The refreshment break on the return journey came at the Hotel Formentor, where drinks and food were available. Alighting from the bus, Elizabeth ignored Lucia's comments about the exorbitant prices. She insisted that having endured the steep, narrow bends and fast-moving onward coming cars on the mountain roads, a gin was in order. Lucia could join her, but the matter was not for discussion. Her friend shrugged and appeared reluctant to follow. Lucia smiled and nodded when she saw Elizabeth had her back to her. Elizabeth was a great companion, but it was apparent that she hated getting told what to do.

They took their drinks into the hotel gardens, where they joined Ben Moran, enjoying a cold pint of Guinness.

"Hello," said Elizabeth. "May we join you?"

Ben could think of nothing he would like less but stood and signalled for them to sit. "Yes, of course, please do."

"I'm Elizabeth, and this is Lucia. You must watch her as she is Spanish and can be rude and fiery."

Lucia cursed at her in Spanish before smiling at Elizabeth's response.

The ladies took turns shaking Ben's hand.

"I've seen you at the apartments in Sa Coma," said Elizabeth.

"Yes, I've seen you too; you are with your son."

"It is her toy boy," said Lucia, cackling.

"I wish," said Elizabeth. "And you are with your daughter and son-in-law, I understand?"

Ben did not know how she knew this but nodded. "Yes, Shirley and Will."

"I knew that because Lucia is very nosy and keeps detailed records on everyone staying in the apartments. She knows everything that happens."

Lucia cursed in Spanish again and then said. "Do not believe her. She has a problem that means she cannot tell the truth. It gets her into a lot of trouble. That's why I am here. I am her nurse."

"Oh. I see," said a bemused Ben.

Gemma and Nick returned their bikes and walked to Gemma's hotel, stopping to kiss several times.

"Would you like a drink?" he asked as they passed the bar. He was desperate to spend more time with her.

"We've got some in the room," said Gemma.

"Okay," said Nick, unsure what to say or do.

They walked up the stairs, holding hands and kissing frequently but speaking very little.

"Are your friends in?" Nick asked as they reached her door.

"I don't know. We'll find out soon enough." Gemma opened the door, shouted hello, and was pleased when no reply came. "We're alone. Come on in. You'll have to excuse the mess. We aren't the tidiest."

She walked to the fridge, took out two beers, and handed one to Nick.

"Thanks, I need this." Nick stood next to her.

"Why? I hope it's not to give you courage," said Gemma.

"Nothing has to happen if you don't want it to; I won't think any the worse of you."

"That's very kind of you."

Gemma smiled.

"I really want something to happen," said Nick, playing with the ring pull on his can.

"Me too. Give that here." She put the cans on the table and wrapped her arms around him. Their mouths met again. Neither broke away, and things became more heated. "Come on. You've been fast-tracked." She grabbed his hand and took him to her bed.

Something tells me Nick is not gay, thought Gemma as she held him. "I'll be gentle, I promise," she said.

Lucia, Ben and Elizabeth visited Lucia's local bar and consumed jugs of Sangria. The three chatted, laughed and ate tapas, enjoying new friendships and exploring new cultures.

At the end of the evening, Ben tried to pay, but the ladies told him to put away his money. This would be their treat. He could pay next time. Lucia teased she would find somewhere very expensive.

Ben and Elizabeth left Lucia at her doorstep, with much hugging and cheek-kissing, and then walked back to Sa Coma arm in arm.

Will and Shirley raised a glass and toasted happy days. Shirley complimented Will on his choice of wines and did not object when he ordered a second bottle. He eventually admitted that the waiter had helped him with the selection.

"It's a lovely spot." Her eyes scanned the horizon with the sea on one side of them and enormous clifftop houses on the other. "However, did you hear about it?"

"I looked online, and the reviews are excellent. I might leave them a five-star rating myself. That fish was stunning, and the service has been brilliant." He pointed at the building directly opposite; the gates were opening, and a green Ferrari emerged onto the road. "Now that's what I call wealth. I walked by there earlier this week. The drive is longer than the street I grew up on. Imagine having a house like that, in a place like this, with a Ferrari to drive about it in."

"I wouldn't like it," said Shirley, making a face.

"What's not to like?"

"I never look nice in green for a start."

Other customers had no idea what the man found so hilarious.

"For a swede basher, you're not too bad."

"That's rich coming from you, Taffy."

He placed his palms on her bed, pushed his body above hers, and smiled. "I think it's official that I quite like you."

"I quite like you too, but don't get fanny-struck on me."

Nick laughed. "What do you mean, fanny struck?"

"My father told me about it years ago. It's when a guy thinks he is in love with the first girl he has sex with."

"Ah, right. No, I don't think I am in love with you. You're quite safe."

"I feel safe," said Gemma. "That is the strange thing. It's weird."

"Perhaps you are knob struck?"

She laughed. "There is no such thing and, as much as you may think of this," she stroked him, "They are all the same."

"How many have you seen?"

"As they say in the movies, enough to know what to do but nowhere near enough to write a book. I certainly haven't broken any records." She placed her hands on his face. "This feels strange, y'know. I have only just met you, and here we are."

He lowered his face again, kissed her nose, and then held his head a couple of inches away from hers. "It is weird. The first time I saw you on the bus when your friends were taking the piss out of me, I somehow knew I would like you. When we spoke at the café, I was confident we would see each other again."

"Hmm." Her arms tightened around him. "I think you are ready for the second part of the examination."

Christiano's parents enjoyed eating at their favourite restaurant in Cala Bona, a few miles up the coast from their home on the outskirts of Sa Coma. The fresh fish was always delicious, and twice weekly, they served the house special, swordfish steaks cooked in garlic.

While they waited for their meal, their youngest son served his version of the house special. He had plied Kylie with more than enough Sangria to lower her resistance and was about to perform his masterstroke.

"Kylie, I have never met anyone like you before. You are so beautiful."

"Do you think so?"

"Yes, I do. I am so happy to be with you tonight.

"I am happy to be with you too."

Christiano kissed her again and let her tongue glide over his. He eased her backwards on the sofa. She complied without fuss and did not resist as Christiano's hands explored her.

"Shall we go to my room? It is more comfortable there."

"Okay." Kylie followed him across the wooden floor.

"I hope my room is not too small. I do not get to bring many girls here, certainly not many nice girls. I hope I don't let you down."

"I am sure you won't."

He undressed her, and they lay on his bed. Christiano's mouth started at her chin and worked downwards.

"Kylie, you are so special. I want you to wish that this moment would never end. I want to satisfy you and will do whatever you want." He quietly pressed the hidden button.

Kylie groaned and uttered a breathless, "I'd like that."

Snowy enjoyed a last drink before returning to the apartment. It had been a day of mixed emotions. He had found

Graham Laing's home, but there had been no further sign of him. The man leaving the house in the flashy sportscar was known locally as Grigor, but Snowy knew him by another name. He needed to understand why the man had assumed a new identity and what had happened to Matilda.

In room 317, Jon and Leah were enjoying a bottle of Rioja on their balcony, watching the trees on the promenade blow in the light breeze and the ripples crossing the pool.

The kids were exhausted from their activities and slept soundly in their rooms. Leah had been to check on them and returned wearing only a nightshirt. She clanked her glass against his. "Cheers"

Jon faced her. "Cheers."

They kissed.

Her eyes looked down at her nightshirt, and Jon followed her gaze. She hitched up one side, and he smiled as he saw her bare behind. "I'm just going to the bedroom. Would you care to join me?"

Kylie flopped on him, smiling.

"That was amazing," said Christiano as he eased her onto her back, ensuring her body was visible to the hidden cameras.

"Thank you," she whispered, sucking his neck.

"No, thank you," he said, holding back a sneer.

Jon clenched his teeth and let out a deep, quiet breath, desperate not to make too much noise. Leah kissed and nibbled his neck as he lay down on the bed.

"That was lovely," he said, cuddling her. "What brought that on?"

"Not sure," she said. "I think it's been on my mind all day."

DEVELOPMENTS
(5 YEARS BEFORE THE HOLIDAY)

Cole's arrival at her gates startled Shirley. She watched him via the video camera as he told her he was in the area to look at a job. An old friend wanted him to convert an empty office block into living accommodation. The job would take around six months, and he proposed to move in with his family for the duration of his stay. He was excited about spending Christmas with Shirley and the kids.

Shirley said nothing, but her mind raced through a multitude of excuses. The first thing she had to do was get him away from the house. There was no way he was going to step over the threshold.

"Wait there, and I'll be out in a minute. You only just caught me. I was on my way to the office."

Shirley strolled down the drive, mentally debating what to say.

"Are you on your own?"

"Yes. I've left Prior in charge. Tommy D and Big Norm are with him."

"Are you all staying in the same place?"

"Nah. Me and Prior are in the Grantchester..."

"Nice."

"It's okay. The other two are in a pub down the road."

"The Swan?"

"Yes, that's the one." He looked her up and down. "You look well. You've lost weight. Your hair looks great."

"Thank you, but why are you here?"

"Can't a man visit his wife without a multitude of questions?"

"I am not your wife. Your wife is in King's Lynn with your baby girl."

"Don't remind me. The worst thing I ever did. She never notices if I am there or not. She is so wrapped up with the sprog. I am looking forward to moving in with you for a while. It'll be great to have good company. It'll be just like old times."

"That's not happening, Cole. You've made your bed..."

"I know this comes as a surprise, but think about it. I can spend time with the kids. I can help out around the house, take you out. You must be lonely in there all on your own."

Now was not the time to mention Snowy. "I am used to it."

"Only because you had to be. I'm back now."

"It'll never work."

"As I said, think about it. You probably wouldn't even know I was there. I'll be out early and home late." He shook the gate. "Are you going to let me in then?"

"No, I haven't got time. I've got to go to a meeting. She pressed the remote button, which caused the garage door to open.

"Never mind. I'll call around tomorrow at about ten... make it eleven. Me and the boys are going out tonight."

"Anywhere nice?"

"We are meeting at the Swan at half seven and take it from there."

"Enjoy. Why are you calling around tomorrow?"

"I'm taking the kids out for the day."

"They never said."

"Didn't they." Cole shrugged.

"You have asked them? They do know?"

"Not yet, but they'll be fine with it. I thought you could cook us a nice meal in the evening. I haven't had your lasagne for ages."

He was going to have to wait a lot longer. "It's not convenient. We have other plans."

Cole ignored her concerns. "Change them. You are my family, and I don't see you often enough. It's the least you can do." He put a hotel brochure into the space between the bars.

"I've written my room number here in case you need to get hold of me."

"I've got your mobile number."

"I accidentally, on purpose, left my mobile at home so she can't get hold of me. I don't want her ringing every five minutes. I'll pick up another phone on the way back to the site. I'll give you the number tomorrow."

He walked to his van after repeating how much he looked forward to spending time with Shirley. He suggested she *must be gagging for it*.

Shirley sighed, pressed the button to close the garage door and returned indoors. She needed to think and think fast. She wondered if her father's offer of sending people to hurt Cole was still an option but dismissed the thought as her ex would probably kill them.

Nick Kingston soothed his eye, rubbed his leg and stood. The pain in his right side was immense and debilitating, but he was determined not to cry. Nick grimaced as he straightened, blinking quickly and repeatedly as he reached for his bag. A trainer-covered foot kicked it further away.

"Posh boy thinks he is going somewhere."

The crowd laughed.

Stewart "Wilco" Wilcox looked at the faces of the crowd, smiled, and then punched Nick in the head, knocking him to the ground again.

Wilcox leaned over and grabbed the lapels on Nick's blazer.

"Listen you posh twat. You stay here until I have finished with you. Have you got that?"

Nick said nothing as Wilcox punched him again.

"I said, have you got that?" He grabbed the breast pocket of the blazer and ripped it off. "Oh, dear. It looks like I have damaged his blazer. Who wears a blazer these days anyway?" He held the cloth up as if it were a trophy and threw it away.

Nick watched it land on the grass.

Wilcox searched Nick's other pockets but found nothing. One of the things Nick had learned since joining the comprehensive school the previous Easter was to hide any valuables. He had stuffed the little money in a plastic bag and pushed it down the front of his pants. He had nothing else of any value.

Wilcox searched until he realised there was nothing to find but was not prepared for his moment of triumph to fizzle out like a damp firecracker. He had to leave his audience satisfied and knew how to provide a gusto finish to the proceedings. He unzipped his trousers, took out his penis and urinated over his victim. The crowd cheered and laughed as Wilco raised his hands and wiggled his hips. Piss splashed all over Nick, who curled into a tighter ball but said nothing.

"You think you're so much better than us, but in reality, you're nothing. You are just something that we take the piss out of and then piss on. That's all you are to us, posh boy." He shook the last drops of urine and watched them fall on Nick. "You make sure you remember that next term when you and I meet again."

Nick slowly hauled himself from the floor as the crowd dispersed, brushing the dust and dirt off his trousers. He collected the pocket from his blazer, unsure if even his mother could salvage anything from the wreckage. He thought it was worth a try.

Julian Dawes and Simon Bleasdale, two of Nick's three best and only friends at the school, appeared by his side. Bleasdale had collected Nick's school bag and handed it to him.

"Thanks," Nick mumbled.

Julian stood in front of him.

"We told you to go home at lunchtime. Everyone knew Wilco planned to get you after school today, and you played right into his hands. He lives way over the other side of town. After today, you wouldn't have had to face him until next term."

"But I couldn't just go home without good reason. It

reflects badly on the school." Nick touched the inside of his mouth. The cheek was sore, and he had traces of blood on his fingers.

"Nick, when will you learn that this school isn't like your last place? Nobody gives a shit about attendance records. You are no longer dealing with normal people; the kids here are not nice. If Wilco warns that he is after you, do what you must to avoid him. Wilco is a fucking idiot, a moron, a total waste of space," said Bleasdale. "You should stay out of his way."

"And now nobody will forget that he's pissed on you. That'll stay with you forever," said Julian. "That will be the first thing people say next term."

"But what am I supposed to do?" Nick sniffed his jacket's sleeve. "Phew, that stinks."

A fourth voice entered the conversation.

"We could fight back." Zac Donald, Nick's other friend, joined the trio. "I've told you I've been watching mixed martial arts. Last night, the local rag said a new club is opening in the community centre on Tuesday. The instructor was mentioned in the article and said he'd be teaching different fighting styles. Training involves karate, judo, aikido, jujitsu boxing, and some kendo."

"Kendo. What's Kendo?" Nick asked and added, "Don't say as little as possible."

Nobody else got his joke, and silence fell until Zac said, "I am seriously considering joining. It might help me to defend myself. You three should come with me. The first lesson is free."

Nick shook his head. "I can't do Tuesdays; I work at the garage."

"Change your shifts then. Look, Nick, you need to do something. You've had your arse kicked at least once a week since you arrived. You can't keep on getting beaten up. You have to help yourself. You need to start fighting back." He studied his friend's dishevelled appearance. "You could start by dumping that bloody blazer. That makes you a target. Nobody around here owns a blazer, let alone wears one to school. By wearing that every day, you are just singling yourself out. You are asking for trouble."

Bleasdale put his hand on Nick's shoulder, then quickly pulled it away, remembering what had just happened. "Yuck... Zac may have a point, Nick. It's easier for us at the moment. Wilco and his morons haven't picked on us so much since you've arrived, but what happens when he's had enough of taunting you? He'll be back on to us. We would be better prepared next term if we did some training. My mum reckons that if you stand up to bullies, they back down and leave you alone. I would love to see his face when we stand up to him."

Zac and Dawes nodded.

"Yeah, could you imagine it?" said Zac.

"It would be so cool," Dawes added.

"But are we likely to learn that much in six weeks? It takes years to become a martial arts expert."

Zac was not having any of Nick's negativity. "But it would be a start. We could join the club and train regularly, and, in between, I can get hold of DVDs of fighting styles, etc. We can use my old man's garage to practice and teach ourselves. Anything is better than the nothing we have now."

Nick had grown tired of getting beaten up. He hoped Wilco and his crew would have lost interest in him by now, but the last few weeks had been worse than ever. The repetition was becoming boring, not to mention extremely painful. He could only turn to his mother for advice but knew she would contact the school. That was unlikely to improve matters. The self-help option sounded like it was worth a try.

He considered his circumstances. The garage owner paid him to help for four hours on a Tuesday evening. The pay was terrible, the conditions awful, and his job primarily involved fetching, carrying and cleaning. The man was always rude to Nick and was slow to hand over payment. Nick felt confident he could find a better job, especially now he was on holiday and could work during the day. His search would begin the following morning. He turned to Bleasdale and Julian.

"And you two are up for this?"

"I am," said Julian.

"Too right," said Bleasdale.

Nick looked at Zac.

"What time on Tuesday?"

"Seven."

"Then let's do it." Nick surveyed the smiling faces. "We can be like the Musketeers. Standing firm in the face of adversity. All for one and one for all!" He raised his arm in the air, but nobody else joined in.

"What?" Bleasdale stared at Nick. "The film is called The Three Musketeers, but there are four of us."

Nick started to explain but then thought better of it. "Okay then, we can be the seven samurai, but three of us are on holiday."

Julian and Zac laughed.

Bleasdale looked even more confused. "So we are the four samurai?"

"Yes," said Nick, grinning.

"Then why the fuck didn't you say so? I was hoping we could be the hero turtles! I'd be Raphael."

Geoff Potter signed on the dotted line. This was it. He was finally doing it. After years of being a servant of the big boys, he was embarking on a new venture, working for himself. His wife countersigned and looked at him.

"That's it then, Geoffrey. There's no turning back now."

"No, I suppose not. We have to make it work."

The bank official took the signed forms promising to return with copies.

His wife grabbed his hand. "We'll be fine. We'll still have my wage coming in, and we've put away some of your redundancy money, so we have something to fall back on."

"That is supposed to help with Gemma and Kate's education."

"We have plenty of time to worry about that yet. Besides, I am confident you will be such a success that we won't need to touch it."

"I hope you are right."

Carol Potter pulled a face as she looked into her husband's eyes. "Am I ever wrong?"

Snowy arrived just after four and was alarmed to find Shirley and her two children sitting silently in the lounge. This was not normal.

Shirley explained about the visit from her ex-husband and his plans. It was evident that a day out with their father did not appeal to the children, who said they wished he would leave them alone. They cheered up a little when Snowy promised to accompany them but then feared that their father would not take kindly to a stranger butting in.

Snowy told them not to worry. He would not let anybody force them to do anything they didn't want. If their father did not like it, then he could lump it.

Shirley insisted this was her problem and that she would sort it out. It was not fair for her to put Snowy at risk. She would not let Cole through the gates; if he played up, she would call the police. Shirley accepted that as the children's father, her ex-husband had the right to see them, but arrangements needed to be made. He could not simply turn up when the mood took him. Both children wished their father would go away. They were sick of him interfering in their lives, especially after he chose to leave them.

The atmosphere improved a little when Snowy volunteered to get a takeaway. They could have anything they wanted, and he did not mind visiting more than one shop.

Shirley suggested he could order online and get it delivered, but Snowy said he was unsure what he wanted and, in any case, had to collect his winnings from the bookies to pay for it.

Geoff and Carol showed their three daughters around the premises that would soon become the home of "Potter's Fine Ales". Carrie, the eldest, made the right noises but, in truth, wasn't that interested in what equipment would go where. She wanted her father to succeed, but if that could happen without her involvement, so much the better.

The youngest daughter, Kate, would soon celebrate her tenth birthday and wondered if she could hold her party in the factory unit. She danced around the open space, suggesting where the disco and dance floor might go. She also spotted a great position to place the food table.

Middle daughter Gemma hung on her father's every word. She had always been Daddy's girl and took great interest in her father's interests. Gemma had already decided to spend evenings and weekends helping her father. She would be pursuing a career in brewing.

Jon and Leah Oliver sat watching television while the nearly one-year-old Daisy slept on the sofa between them.

Their baby had become a toddler, and both parents were thrilled when Daisy completed the walk from chair to couch without falling over the week before. The hard part now was keeping her still, and the doting parents appreciated the time Daisy spent sleeping.

A strange buzzing noise disturned Leah's relaxation. "Is that your mobile?"

Jon reached for the table and lifted his phone. "No."

"Well, something is buzzing."

Jon stood and entered the hall to retrieve his jacket. "It's my work mobile. I bet I've missed a call from Rob."

"Work mobile? Since when have you had a work mobile?"

"Since this morning. Rob gave it to me as he was having trouble reaching me on-site."

"Where's your mobile? Why can't he ring you on that?"

"He did, but I never ring him back if I miss a call."

"Why not?"

"It's pay-as-you-go, and I don't see why I should pay for work-related calls."

"And you told him that, did you?"

"I did, so he brought this in this morning. I wish he hadn't bothered. We must have spoken about a dozen times today."

"It's good to talk."

"Very funny. Rob called me from the golf course this morning to remind me to make a courtesy visit to the doctor's surgery we finished refurbishing last week to check that everything is okay."

"What's wrong with that?"

"He reminded me three times yesterday, and I had already been there when he rang."

"It's not a bad thing that he supports you like that. Many bosses would leave you to fail. He's just making sure you're coping okay."

"Hmmm, when he offered me the promotion, I thought I would work alongside Rob, but he's happy to leave everything to me. He occasionally pops in but spends most of his time playing golf."

"He must trust you."

"Then why does he need to ring every five minutes to remind me to do things I have already done?"

"It's a new arrangement for both of you. It'll settle down."

"I hope so. I'd better give him a bell. Won't be a minute."

Two men departed the hotel, deep in discussion followed by raucous laughter. Snowy waited until they had left the grounds before approaching. He checked again. There were no cameras or spectators anywhere near.

"Cole? Can I have a word?"

"Who are you?"

"I'm a friend of your ex-wife's."

"What sort of friend?" Cole did not see the man as a threat and walked until they were very close. "What do you want?"

Cole's companion stood a few paces behind.

Snowy shrugged. "There is no easy way to say this, but I am a close friend of Shirley's."

"What? Are you telling me you are shagging my missus?"

Snowy's voice was calm, and his manner relaxed. "Ex-missus, but, with respect, the nature of our friendship is none of your business."

"Oi, Prior, hark at Lord Fancipants." He stared into Snowy's eyes. "It is my business if you are shagging my Shirley. Not that you will be on the scene much longer. I bet she hasn't told you I am moving back in."

"She did tell me, but I am not sure that is a good idea."

Cole pressed his fingers into Snowy's chest. "And why is that? Not that it is any of your business."

"Because I don't think Shirley wants it, and I am not sure your children do either."

"They'll come round to it. They just need time."

Snowy saw Cole's companion sit on a low wall and puff on a vape. "Hmm, I doubt that. I think they are a bit frightened of you, to be honest."

"They are not frightened. They respect me. Kids should respect their father, and my kids know they must respect me."

"You earn respect. You can't demand it."

Cole turned to his mate. "Do you believe this? This chubby twat is giving me lessons in parenting." He laughed aloud before he faced Snowy again, saying, "Who the fuck do you think you are?"

Snowy shrugged. "I'm nobody, really. I am just trying to help you avoid making a big mistake. You can't force your way into people's lives. It would help if you started by talking things through. Give Shirley and the children a chance to say what they are thinking; then, if they decide they don't want you back, you should return to your new family gracefully, maintaining a modicum of respect."

Cole's humour had quickly turned to anger. "Who are you to tell me what to do? What business is it of yours?" He blew air from his mouth before lurching forward to headbutt the stranger. Cole opened his eyes when he failed to connect. He did not understand how he missed but recovered quickly to swing a punch at the man. Cole felt his knuckles collide heavily with the guy's chin, and his hand vibrated. To his amazement, the man did not fall and quickly hit Cole with two short jabs, catching him below his rib cage. As Cole fell forward, his neck met the man's extended arm and his legs swept from under him. His collision with the tarmac pavement came quickly and painfully. Cole had no time to think about what had happened before the man placed a foot on his throat.

Prior stepped forward to help his friend.

"Please stay where you are," said Snowy. "I might need you to take your friend to the hospital. You can't do that if I break your arms."

"You'll be the one with the broken arm," said Prior, stepping nearer.

Snowy shook his head, disappointed at the response. "Please don't try anything. If you come at me, I will have to take my foot off his neck to get into position to defend myself. You know how it is. If I have to move suddenly, I may inadvertently press down on his throat and could end up crushing his windpipe. He would need a tracheostomy, or whatever they call it, to stop him from choking." He scratched his chin. "Or something like that. He'll probably die anyway."

Prior looked at Cole, who was struggling for breath and finding it difficult to remove the man's foot. "Do you know who he is?"

"Of course. I am not in the habit of standing on just anyone's throat."

"He's got loads of friends."

“That's good to know. I’m happy for him. Now, please sit down while I speak with Cole. I won't hurt him further, and I’ll only keep you a minute.”

Cole nodded as best he could, telling his friend to obey and Prior returned his backside to the wall.

Snowy took out his mobile and pressed the buttons as he spoke to Cole.

“Here is the thing. I also have friends. I got close to some hard men while serving in the forces. We watched each other’s backs and trusted one another. We were a tight bunch. We had to be. It was us against the world. You probably know the stories, but we really did become a band of brothers. You hurt one of us. You hurt all of us. I am happy to say I am still in touch with all of them, and we regularly meet up.“ He was quiet long enough to photograph Cole’s face and study the image. “Not great, but it’ll do. Since I left the forces, I have worked with some seriously dangerous people. They are proper criminals, not plastic hard boys like you. And they all need to keep me sweet. I know where they buried the bodies see, and if anything suspicious happens to me, I have made arrangements for their secrets to come out. They will all be in the proverbial.” He tapped the buttons on the mobile before holding it for Cole to see. “You see what’s on the screen.?”

Cole croaked. “A mountain.”

“Wha?” Snowy turned his mobile. “Sorry, I am always doing that.” He flicked the screen. “What do you see now?”

“My name and photograph.”

Snowy pressed another button. “Can you see who I plan to send this to?”

“Yes, Squadies and..” Cole’s eyes narrowed. “...Clients.”

“Good.” Snowy brought the mobile closer to him. “I am sending your and your mate’s pictures to my friends and customers so they can find you and yours if anything suddenly happens to me or the people I care about. Do you understand?”

“Yes.”

“Good. I am not sure I could say that again.” Snowy

motioned for Prior to move nearer. "That's close enough." He tapped the screen, smiled, let his fingers work on the screen keyboard and sent a second message on its way."

He raised his index finger to Prior. "They'll be looking for you too, but please be reassured they won't leave it there. Nobody you know or care about will be safe. Got it?"

Prior nodded.

Snowy lifted his foot, reached down to help Cole stand, and said to Prior. "Take him."

The man did as he was told and stood behind Cole, holding his friend upright while he struggled to catch his breath.

"You keep an eye on him," Snowy said to Prior before pointing at Cole. "Make sure you call Shirley and apologise for turning up unannounced. Tell her you won't be around tomorrow. You might also like to say that you will see the kids when they are happy to see you. Understand?"

"Yes." Cole rubbed his throat and put his other hand in his pocket for his new mobile. "I'll do that right away."

"Good man."

"But what if anything happens to you by accident?" Prior asked.

"You'd better hope it doesn't," said Snowy. "Now, if you will excuse me, I have to get two Chinese takeaways, one Indian, and I fancy some cod and chips. I might even sneak in a pint while I'm waiting. Enjoy your evening."

Nick showered and placed his school clothes in the washing machine. They were halfway through the cycle when his mother arrived home. She told him she had enjoyed a good day on the market and updated him on her takings. Nick congratulated her on a job well done and dismissed her concerns about the marks and bruises on his face, which he said resulted from an aggressive football match. He had already peeled the potatoes and put them in a saucepan of water.

Ben was not surprised when his wife announced that she had joined the gym. She was always in the market for a new hobby, and he agreed it would be a good way for her to meet people in their new area.

He assured her he would be fine and settled down to a glass of Shiraz, a bowl of crisps, a radio comedy show and his evening paper.

A perfect way to end his working week.

Shirley slipped her arm under the duvet and stroked Will's belly.

"Wha?" he said, stirring from his attempt to sleep and turning to face her.

"Nothing. Can't I rub your belly if I want to?"

"Of course, but I thought you were tired."

"I was, but I've been thinking about what you said to Cole."

Will pulled a surprised face and blinked twice before realising Shirley could not see his expressions in the dark. "Me? Why do you think I said anything? When could I have seen him?"

"When you went to the bookies to collect winnings even though you always place your bets on the app and never win anything."

Schoolboy error. "But why would he listen to what I said? He has no idea who I am. He is twice my size."

"Hmm, but you never seem frightened of anyone, and I think it is strange that you leave to visit an imaginary bookie and collect a takeaway you could have had delivered then, by the time you return, Cole has rung to say he changed his mind about everything the kids and I were unhappy about."

"Coincidence."

"Coincidence, my arse. What did you say?" She kissed his shoulder. "Tell me."

"Well...I did bump into him and suggested he should

change his plans."

"And?"

"And nothing. We had a few words, then I left him to think about what I said and got the food."

She guessed he was not telling the whole truth but played along. "Why didn't you say anything earlier?"

Will sighed as his brain formulated a reply. "Because you told me not to get involved in your personal issues."

"I also told you I wasn't looking for a serious relationship, but here you are."

"I can't help it if you find me irresistible."

Shirley bit his shoulder before she turned his face so her lips could meet his. Will winced. "What's wrong?" Shirley put the bedside light on and examined his chin. "That's bruising. Did Cole hit you?"

"Nah, that's where my jaw hit the counter. Do you know how much fish and chips cost these days?"

Shirley knew she would not get any sense out of Will, so she turned off the light. "I'll make it better in a minute." She kissed him again. "Thank you." She whispered, climbing onto him.

"I'm not sure what I've done to deserve this, but I won't argue."

"Best you don't."

DAY 6 - THURSDAY 29 JULY

Nick saw his uncle drinking coffee on his balcony and walked to join him. “Another lovely day, Unc? Are you doing anything nice?”

“Not really. Your aunt wants to go to Palma, so I guess she’ll expect me to go with her. What about you?”

“Oh, you know, a bit of this and that.” He saw his uncle smile. “I think I’ll do some sunbathing. I better make the most of this weather while I’ve got the chance. It’s never this hot in Barry.”

“Don’t remind me. I’m sure it was snowing the last time I was there, and that was in June.”

Nick laughed. “I meant to ask you if your computer is working okay again.”

“Yes, thanks. All good.”

“Donny and Louise haven’t had any problems, have they?”

“Not as far as I know. Louise hardly uses hers, and Donny is pretty good. He has to be. There are always problems at the café.”

“Is it far to this café? I wouldn’t mind checking it out.”

“At the other end of town. I’ll mention it to him. He can give you a guided tour.”

That would be great,” said Nick, looking at his watch. “I’ve got to be somewhere, so I’d better go. Enjoy Palma.”

“I won’t,” said his uncle, emptying the dregs of his coffee mug onto the flower bed below.

“What time did you get in last night?” Shirley asked as her father handed her a coffee.

“Not sure. It was about one-ish, I think.”

“Well, Will and I were worried sick. We didn’t know

what had happened to you."

Ben did not say they could not have been that worried as they were both fast asleep when he returned. "Sorry, love, I didn't think. We had a few glasses of sangria in a bar in Sillott and then walked back."

"We? Who is this we?"

"Me, Lucia and Elizabeth. I met them on the coach trip yesterday. Lucia lives up the road. Elizabeth is staying in this complex."

Shirley sipped her coffee, thinking about what Ben had told her. "Is Elizabeth the lady with the son? Is she Welsh?"

"That's the one. She lives just outside Barry."

Shirley was about to comment when Will wandered through, scratching his bits through his boxer shorts.

"Well, you dirty dog, we let you out for the day, and you hook up with not one but two hot chicks. You lucky old bugger."

Ben smirked, "They are ladies, not chicks."

"I never knew ladies were into threesomes," said Will. "I've been chasing the wrong ones all these years. Ouch!" He flinched as Shirley tapped his sunburnt back.

She spotted Nick at two hundred yards and walked to meet him.

"Good morning," he said.

"Morning. "She put her arms around him as their lips met. "How are you?"

"Fine, thanks. What do you want to do today?" His hands met behind her back and held her tightly.

There was no awkwardness or hint of shyness, which reassured her that he did not regret the previous evening. "Do you fancy the beach?"

"I do, but shall we go nearer my place? There's more space, and the sand is better."

"Whatever," she said and took his hand.

Holding hands with a girl was strange, but Nick liked the

feeling and would soon get used to it.

Sara and Kylie had the morning to themselves as Donny and Christiano had business to do. They would meet them for lunch at the burger bar.

"She seems keen," said Kylie. She stood by the window watching Gemma and Nick stroll away from the hotel.

"Yeah, she does, which is unusual for her." Sara spread marmalade on her bread. "She normally takes things slowly and avoids commitment. Remember her with Gary Cobbley? She kept him dangling and then dumped him when he suggested they were an item."

"He would never get to stage 2. Bless him. He kept on trying."

"Putting those two together would have been a mistake. They were incompatible."

Kylie's eyes followed the pair as they joined the promenade. "She is quite astute; fair play to her."

"Does it worry you that she doesn't like Donny or Christiano?"

"Not really. Gemma's not always right. Anyway, her taste in men differs from ours; would you go out with Nick?"

"I doubt it, would you?"

"Probably, but then I went out with Gary."

"Shit, so you did. I'd forgotten about that. What was he like?"

"Big cock, small brain. Our Gary was tough to have a conversation with."

"You spoke to him, did you?"

Kylie giggled, "Of course."

"I thought it was all about the sex with you."

"It is mostly, but you must fill the recovery time somehow." Kylie sipped her juice. "Have you and Donny done the deed yet?"

Sara swallowed a corner of toast as she shook her head. "No. I thought we would last night. We went to the flat again, but he repeated that he doesn't need penetration for satisfaction."

"What a strange mantra."

"I get the feeling he's used it before."

"Unlike his dick?"

"Hmm, not with me anyway."

Carrying even more toys and beach equipment, Jon, Leah, Daisy, Charlie, and Harry took the last remaining pair of sunbeds on the edge of the middle row of five.

"It's busier than ever this morning," said Jon, taking Harry's hat off.

"Charlie, stand still while I take your shirt off," said Leah. "It's too hot to be fussing about."

"I want to leave this one on."

"Well, you can't. This shirt is your best one. You know the rules. We take the good one off and put an older one on for you to play."

"But I like the Lego one."

"I know you do. That's why I want to keep it looking smart."

Daisy had removed her dress and looked for her sun hat in her mother's bag. "Mum, where's my hat?"

"Hang on a second, Dais. I only have one pair of hands."

Jon took the hat from his backpack. "Here is it, Dais," he spun it through the air, and it landed on the sand by Daisy's feet.

"That wasn't very clever, Daddy. Now I have sand all over it."

"Sorry," said Jon, returning his attention to changing Harry's shirt.

Gemma and Nick laid out their towels, dropped their stuff and ran straight to the sea. They returned after a brisk swim.

"That's better," said Nick, letting the sun dry him off.

"The water is clear; I could see the fish at my feet."

"Bit cleaner than it is at home," said Nick. "I wouldn't swim in the sea where I live."

"Do you live close to the sea, then? I thought you lived in the valleys."

"We are miles away from the valleys. Our house is about two miles from the sea."

"Is there a beach?"

"Yeah, quite a nice one. Not that I get there very often."

"I'll have to visit you. You can take me to see it."

"Fair enough, we can go on the Gavin and Stacey tour."

"Of course, I knew Barry was good for something."

"It's good for many things."

"I doubt that somehow, present company excepted, of course."

"I am not sure what Cheltenham is good for, though, apart from horse racing."

"Oi Taffy! Less of your cheek. Anyway, I'm not really from Cheltenham. I grew up on the outskirts of Hereford."

"That explains a lot."

"What do you mean?"

"The swede basher accent. Cheltenham people are much posher."

"They are not. "

"Why did you move?"

"My father. He started at a brewery in Birmingham until that closed. Then he went to work for a cider maker in Hereford, and they got taken over. He and his mate found jobs in a small brewery in Cheltenham and worked there until Dad started his own business. Carrie was born in Birmingham, Kate and me in Hereford, but we all live in Cheltenham now."

"And your dad works for himself."

"Yeah. Dad always wanted to run his own brewery, so he bought bits of equipment over several years. Then, when he was made redundant, he started working for himself. He makes craft beers, which he sells to free houses."

"How are things going?"

"It's pretty good so far. Dad is keen to expand production, and I'll help him part-time while I do my Master's."

"He must be doing well if he can afford to employ you."

"The business is building, but Dad needs investment. I've told him he has a year to secure it before I start pushing in full-time."

"I bet he got that message." He turned his head to see her tongue poking at him. "How much would he need?"

"No idea, but it's probably more than you can afford, Taffy."

"At the moment... but in the future... you never know."

"So if you won a million quid, you'd help my Dad."

"I would."

"Even though you've only known me a few days."

"Yes, but only because it sounds like a good investment, not because I'm fanny-struck or anything."

"Obviously. " Gemma reached over the short space of sand and joined him on his towel to kiss him.

"What's that for?"

"Do I need a reason?" The one that followed lasted much longer.

Louise studied the spreadsheet figures. "We have had another good month, but we could do better if we cut back on expenses," she said.

This was not the news that her brother wanted to hear. "You have to speculate to accumulate."

"You sound like Dad, and look how he turned out. Dependent on shipping illegal immigrants across to the mainland to make money. I don't want to be fleecing tourists for the rest of my life." She read her brother's face. "I am not saying we must become misers, but we could save a few euros here and there."

"How do you suggest we do that?" Christiano asked.

"You could ease off on the bubbly, for one thing."

"But the ladies like champagne..."

Louise spoke over him.

"Only because you put it on the table. Kylie and her friends are from Cheltenham. They would be happy with a pint of cider."

"I think we make enough money, " said Christiano.

"I know that, " said Louise. "But I would prefer to keep it to ourselves than spend it on a bunch of slappers."

Nick observed the little boy gathering stones in his little bucket and tossed a few more in his direction.

The boy smiled, scooped them up and trotted back to join his sister, struggling to stay in his sandals.

His brother took over.

"Ah, they are twins," said Gemma. "So cute."

"They are brothers born in the same year but not twins."

"You know a lot about them?"

"They are staying in one of the apartments at our place," said Nick. "They have a sister too. Mum started talking to their mother."

"And before you know it, the Taffia has more members."

Charlie tried to put a large stone in his bucket, but it was too large and made the plastic bucket unstable. As he started the return journey, the bucket wobbled, and the stone fell onto his toe. The boy screamed as he fell back.

Nick winced; Gemma jumped up, picked up the crying boy and carried him back to his mother. "There, there, don't cry. Look, here's mummy."

She handed him over.

"Thank you," said Leah, rushing toward Gemma. "I knew something would happen as soon as my husband went for a swim. Honestly, there's never a moment's peace."

"They are lovely children," said Gemma as Harry and Daisy wandered over, wondering why their brother had screamed.

"Thank you. This one is Charlie," The boy had stopped

crying and was staring at the stranger, his head resting on his mother's shoulder.

"Hello, Charlie," Gemma touched his cheek. "Are you okay now?"

Charlie nodded.

"And this is Daisy."

"Hello, Daisy. Are you having a nice time?"

"Yes, thank you."

Harry stepped forward and held up his hand.

"Harry wants you to high-five him," said Daisy. "He does it all the time."

Gemma gently put her palm on Harry's. "Hello, Harry. Pleased to meet you."

Harry chuckled and ran off.

"I'm Gemma,"

"And I'm Leah. Pleased to meet you."

"And you know Nick," said Gemma as he joined her.

"Yes, his mother saved us from a diplomatic incident." Leah sensed Gemma's confusion.

"Really?"

"Yes, we had a communication problem with a German that she sorted out." Charlie wanted to continue playing, and Leah placed him on the sand. "Be careful."

Gemma turned to Nick. "What are you? A Welsh peacekeeping force?"

"Yeah, something like that." Nick followed Charlie, lay on damp sand and started digging a hole.

"So you're his girlfriend?" Leah asked.

"Not really. We only met the day before yesterday. Nick stepped in when a boy got too keen."

"He looks like he can look after himself," said Leah. "He's very..." she waved her hand before her, trying to think of the right word. "...athletic but not in a muscle-bound way."

Gemma laughed. "I'd call him buff."

"Me too..." said Leah, "...but it would sound a bit creepy if I said it. I'm almost old enough to be his mother."

Snowy stood in front of the beach seller and blocked his way. “Excuse me.”

“No problem. What are you looking for?”

“It’s not what. It’s who. I need to speak to Banda.”

“Why? What do you need him for?”

“I bought a watch from him yesterday, and I need another.”

The man opened his case. “I have plenty of watches. Pick one. I can do you a good price.”

“Sorry, no. I promised Banda.”

“Well, he is working at Cala Bona today. He should be selling in the bars around here tonight.”

“You know the Sunshine Bar?”

“I do. We use it often.”

“Tell him I’ll be there at seven. You do that, and I’ll buy something from you the next time we meet.

“Sure thing, man. Banda will be there.”

Christiano had been expecting a call from Graham, so the request was no surprise. He dropped his mobile onto the desk and swivelled around in his chair to face Donny and Louise.

“He wants Becky to be available next week. Uncle Fester from Alicante is visiting again.”

“What is with these bald old farts and young girls?” Louise exhaled. “I suppose it is none of my business.”

“It is our business, and as you said earlier, it is profitable.” Donny looked at Christiano. “Are you sure Becky will agree?”

“I’ll tell her tomorrow.” He fiddled with the mouse. “I have almost finished this video. Once she sees it, Becky has little choice.”

“Should we arrange a substitute, just in case she refuses?” Louise asked.

Christiano reached out, grabbed her hand and kissed her

fingers. "How can she refuse me?"

"You are a smooth bastard, but we had better have somebody on standby."

"Candice?" Donny suggested.

"No. Uncle has had her. I'll tell Alice to make herself available. We haven't used her for a while."

"You never mentioned that you were good with children."

"Am I? I never thought about it. It's not the sort of thing you say in the current climate. People accuse you of being a pervert."

"That's true. Have you spent much time with kids then?"

"A bit...but in a normal way. My mate has kids."

"Really?"

"Yeah, Zac has a little boy, Jake, and a girl, Angelina. They are about the same age as Daisy. I am their Godfather."

"Bloody hell, so you actually are the head of the Taffia?"

"I am, and you'd better watch your step, or you'll end up with a headless leek in your bed."

"Your mate has twins."

"No, not really. He had them with two different girls."

"What? At the same time?"

"Yeah, pretty much. Jake is the elder by a few weeks. Zach went out with Heather, attended a training camp, and then got off with Cally, a girl in our club."

"Haven't you lot ever heard of contraception?"

"Never had much use for it personally, but I think Heather wanted a baby. She's a few years older than us, and I don't think Cally and Zach expected anything to happen."

"Until it was too late...How many girls are there in your club?"

"Five or six. It's not a massive group."

"And why didn't you get off with them at this camp?"

"I didn't go. I worked most weekends."

"What about weekdays?"

"Always too busy."

"Is Zach with either of the girls now?

"Yeah, he and Cally live together. They rent a house at the moment. He also has custody of Jake because Heather decided she wasn't ready to be a mother. She went a bit...er... odd, really."

"How could you tell? You all seem bloody weird to me." She kissed him. "Here they come."

Daisy, Harry and Charlie, accompanied by their father, brought their buckets to Gemma, who praised their efforts. "Well done, there's a lot of water in there. Let's see if this works."

Gemma and the three kids built several sand castles with channels running down to other castles. The intention was to let the water run down the canal to demolish the castle below. Nick got tasked with ensuring the channels were deep enough.

Gemma invited Daisy to empty the bucket, but they were all disappointed when the water drained into the sand. The twins tried another bucketful, and although the water travelled further, it dried away before reaching the target. Nick dug out some more sand.

Gemma picked up the remaining bucket. "Now, children, you should never do this to anyone unless they say it is okay. Do you understand?" She saw three little faces nod and threw the last bucket of water over Nick's head. The kids screeched, their parents shrieked, and Gemma ran into the sea, hotly pursued by a wet-headed Nick.

Sara, Kylie, Christiano and Donny observed proceedings from the promenade, and the girls giggled as Nick chased Gemma to the sea.

"Typical Gemma," said Kylie. "She's mad as a box of frogs."

"He's going to catch her," said Sara. They guffawed again as Nick rugby tackled Gemma around the waist, and they both disappeared under the water.

"I think it is a bit sad," said Christiano. "It is very immature."

Donny said nothing. He was amazed at how much his cousin had changed. He had always considered Nick to be a sad little mummy's boy. It shocked him to learn that little Nick was no longer little, was undoubtedly not sad and had become attached to an intelligent, pretty girl. Sara's comments about Nick flattening Barty also disturbed Donny. If it was true, then his cousin could look after himself. Barty was no slouch in the fighting stakes. On the plus side, his friend reckoned he had been pissed and caught off guard.

Things would be different next time.

Nick and Gemma had sunbathed enough for one morning and went for lunch in Sillott. They laughed, strolled, kissed and teased along the promenade, eventually reaching the last bar before the small harbour area. They placed their orders and held hands across the table, waiting for service.

"Do you ever touch alcohol?" Gemma asked as their drinks, a cola for her and water for him, arrived.

"Yeah, I would have had a beer the other night if you hadn't pounced on me."

"You made it so difficult for me."

"I could have tried harder to refuse you, I suppose. As far as alcohol is concerned, I've never really had the money, so I've not indulged that much."

"Perhaps we should have a bit of a session one day and see who lasts the longest."

"That would be very one-sided. You swede bashers drink cider for breakfast, lunch and dinner. Alcohol is part of your five a day."

"It is not." She held the glass to her lips, sipping through a straw. "Honestly, you are so cheeky. I'd be out of here like a shot if I didn't like your scintillating conversation."

Nick retook her hand. "I'm glad you want me for something anyway,"

"Hello Neek, how are you? Are you all set for tomorrow?"

Gemma's eyes went from stranger to Nick and back again.

"Oh...er... hola Javier. How are you?"

"I am very well, thank you, and you."

"Great, thanks." Gemma raised her eyebrows, inviting him to make the introduction. "Gemma, this is Javier. He's the son of Lucia. My mother's...sorry, our friend who lives in Sillott.

"It is lovely to meet you, Gemma. Are you here on holiday too?"

"Yes, I arrived the same day as Nick."

"And now you are together. It is funny how many holidaymakers come to this island to meet people from where they live."

She was about to tell him that it was unlikely that she and Nick would ever have met back home, but Javier spoke again.

"So Neek, are you available to play tomorrow? The English boys have challenged us, and we are a player short. We need you to play. I was going to ask Mama to ask your mother, but then I saw you here. It is meant to be, no?"

"Kismet," said Nick, but neither Javier nor Gemma appeared to know what he meant. "Yes, okay, count me in. Always happy to beat the English." He felt Gemma's foot kick into his shin. "Providing I can avoid an injury."

"Go carefully. We need you to stay fit. See you at the cage on Friday. It is that way." He pointed in the direction away from the sea.

"That narrows it down a bit," said Nick. "See you at nine on Friday."

Javier bade his farewells and was gone as quickly as he appeared. Gemma wasted no time in making a point.

"So that's your way of telling me you have other plans for tomorrow?"

"It only lasts an hour."

"And what am I supposed to do while you play football?"

The question and her tone caught him off guard. "I don't know. You could come with me? Javier said there would be food and drink afterwards."

That was not a deal clincher. "That's exciting, but I am not sure I want to sit on the side while you and your new friends run around after a small ball."

"Well, perhaps we could meet afterwards?"

"So now you expect me to sit at the hotel waiting for you."

"Not really. If you don't want to see me tomorrow evening, that's up to you. I just thought that you might."

"But do you want to see me?"

"Of course."

"And yet you still agreed to play football without asking me."

"Yeah, I suppose I did, but I hadn't met you when I agreed to play. I didn't think it would be an issue. It's only an hour, so you can either wait for me, or if you'd rather, we can see each other during the day, and you can do something else tomorrow evening. We could give it a miss altogether."

Nick was unapologetic, which, perversely, came as a great relief to Gemma. She was happy he was not subservient, hanging on her every word. "Okay, then. I'll come along."

Nick looked bewildered, but as the smile widened on her lips, he guessed it had been a wind-up. "Great."

"But you valleys boys are so racist."

"I am not a valleys boy, and I am no racist. Baiting the English is our national pastime. It has nothing to do with racism."

Gemma pulled a face as the waiter brought their food.

"Whose place is this?" Kylie asked, glancing around the sparsely furnished room. There was no carpet, a large bed, a coat hanger, three chairs, a table and a locked cabinet hanging on one wall. Ill-matched paintings hung around the room, all reflected in a mirrored ceiling. A solitary bookcase bearing several well-used books and two speakers stood by the door.

"It is what we call our pleasure room," Christiano fiddled with the padlock on the cabinet. "Here, we can live out our greatest fantasies." He threw back the wooden doors to reveal a multitude of sex aids and toys. "We can try anything you like."

"Shit! I may be adventurous, but this is something else."

He walked to her, dangling handcuffs. "Shall we try a few things anyway?" As they kissed, he slipped the handcuffs onto her wrists. "I will make it very special," he whispered, easing her onto the bed. He secured her left arm.

"Okay, but don't hurt me. I am not into pain."

"I have no wish to hurt you. I wish to enjoy you and give you pleasure." He secured her right hand using a second set of handcuffs. Kylie saw she was bound to the bars of the metal headboard. She tittered as Christiano unbuttoned her shorts.

Will, Ben and Shirley returned from a boozy lunch. Father and daughter dozed on the furniture, leaving Will to sit on the balcony, watching very little happen. The pool had few swimmers. There were several sunbathers, but they were either sleeping or reading. The only noise came from the apartment occupied by Eddie Kingston, who Will thought was having a gathering. There was chatter and clinking of glass.

Shirley was awake and shouted to ask where Will had put the bag containing her reading glasses. Will told her where he had left them, but she appeared none the wiser. He said he would get her the bag and entered the apartment.

Edward Kingston handed Grigor the third bottle of beer and made a toast. "Here's to our continued success."

Grigor winked as they clinked bottles. "It's onwards and upwards, my friend. This latest shipment will be the biggest yet. Three dozen, all are requiring safe passage to the mainland."

"No problem. Usual delivery address?"

"Yes, we'll sort out the paperwork when I return from Ibiza next week."

"We are not handling the other stuff this time?"

"No. I will look after that, but I may need to put the money through your accounts."

"Not a problem, providing my commission stays the same."

"It works for us."

"I'll drink to that."

"What are we celebrating?" Evelyn Kingston asked, joining them.

"A lucrative business model," her husband replied. "White wine?"

"Yes, please."

He went to get the drinks. His wife walked to a small stack of plastic seats in the corner of the balcony.

"Let me get that," said Grigor. "You have my seat. It's got a cushion to protect that pert little bottom."

"Thank you, but I'm afraid it's not so pert these days."

"It looks good from where I'm standing."

He winked. She smiled awkwardly.

Grigor lifted a chair from the pile and then stopped dead, his attention caught by noise from a neighbouring apartment. He stood motionless for a moment.

Eddie returned and gave the wine to his wife. "You okay, Grigor? You look like you've seen a ghost."

"Just remembered something but then forgot why it was important."

"Happens to me all the time," said Evelyn.

"Ah, but nobody would ever forget you," said Grigor, placing the chair beside hers.

Not all apartments changed hands on a Saturday, and some bookings were very last minute. Occasionally, Lucia had a telephone call from an owner asking to prepare the accommodation for arrival the following day.

Fortunately, she had deep cleaned this property the week before. It only required a quick once-over with a cloth and brush, and Elizabeth offered to help.

"*Wow, this is impressive*," said Elizabeth, looking around the three-bedroom apartment. "*It's twice the size of ours.*" She opened the patio doors. "*Look at this view. You can see out into the ocean.*"

Lucia switched to English."This is a lovely apartment. Very modern. The owners live here for months at a time and spend a lot to keep it modern." Lucia gathered the brush and handed it to Elizabeth. "While you are out there, you can sweep the floor."

"No problem." Elizabeth obeyed her instructions. "Do all the owners keep their apartments so current?"

"Current?"

"Up to date, modern."

"No. The English like to rent out their places and don't care how old-fashioned it looks. Your brother-in-law owns three apartments but has only improved the one he stays in. The others have not changed in years."

"He told me he was about to modernise the other two but would delay it until we went home."

"He said that?"

"Yes. That was how we got the apartment at the last moment because he was not letting it again until it was refurbished."

"I think your brother-in-law is…." She struggled to recall her son's words. "…full of shit."

Elizabeth was surprised to hear Lucia say that, but that did not stop her from laughing aloud. "I beg your pardon."

"People around here say that Edward cannot afford to do any work on his properties."

Elizabeth stopped sweeping and encouraged her friend to tell her more.

"He has tried to sell the apartments but has had no buyers. He is asking a lot of money for such old-fashioned apartments."

"I thought his businesses were doing well."

I am only telling you what people are saying. He has other businesses, like the internet café and a share in some clubs, but his main business...the exhibition company...is that right?"

"Yes."

"That one is not doing so good. He has lost contracts and has let his workers go. He rents out his vans to take things around the islands and the mainland. "

"I see," said Elizabeth, sweeping the floor with renewed vigour.

Will stood ready to leave. "So I'll meet you at nine at the Red Lion. Are you sure you don't want to go anywhere else first?"

"I don't," said Shirley. I had more than enough to eat this afternoon. I'll be happy with a quiet drink or two."

"Wimp," said Will, kissing her cheek. "What about you Ben?"

"I'm okay, thanks. I'll read my book for a bit. Perhaps Shirley and I could have a walk before we join you."

Shirley nodded.

"Right, I will see you lovely people at nine on the dot. Please don't keep me waiting. I might get a better offer."

"We'll keep our fingers crossed," his wife replied.

Banda was uncomfortable. The man had lured him here to buy a watch but was now offering money for information about Grigor and Graham Laing. Banda did not like the men but worked for them and knew they were dangerous. He wondered whether this was a test.

"Why do you want to know? Has he done something to you?"

"Not to me, no. The man I work for sent me to find out what I can about Grigor and Graham."

"Why don't you ask them yourself? They live up that road."

"It's not as simple as that." Snowy sipped his water. "Grigor and his girlfriend..."

"He has no girlfriend. He picks up girls when he needs them."

"So Matilda isn't here with him?"

"Matilda is in Palma."

"She is?"

"Matilda is not a woman. It is a boat. Grigor keeps it in Palma marina."

This was news. "The boat must be named after Grigor's ex-girlfriend Matilda. I need to find her too."

"Why are you so interested in them?"

"If I tell you something, can you keep it to yourself?"

Banda nodded.

"Grigor, Graham and Matilda stole something from Graham's father, and his father wants it back."

"What did he steal?"

"I can't tell you that, but his father is ill. He is also furious that they stole his things. He will probably send someone over here unless I can retrieve his belongings, and the pair might get badly hurt."

"They probably deserve it. You should not steal from your father."

"And fathers should not hurt their children."

Banda shrugged. "That is usually true, but Grigor is not a nice man. He keeps bad company. Graham Laing is also nasty. They get what they deserve."

"Then why are you working for him?"

"I have no choice."

Banda explained that he used to run a shop in Senegal, where he lived with his wife and daughter. When his mother passed away, his father came to live with him. The shop did not make enough money to sustain four people, so Banda came to Europe hoping to make money to send home. He paid a trafficker to bring him to Spain, and he arrived in Palma via Malaga and Barcelona. His escort introduced him to Graham and his partner, Grigor.

The original arrangement would have seen Banda get a Spanish passport to allow him to work legitimately. However, Graham told him he would need to pay for that passport, and Banda could earn money by selling goods.

Grigor found Banda a room at the hotel and set him up with a suitcase full of things to sell. All the money from sales had to go to Grigor and Graham, who gave Banda a share. At first, Banda made good money, but the local police started to clamp down on sellers and regularly confiscated goods.

Graham soon changed the rules and expected Banda and his workmates to pay for the accommodation and to buy the goods they wanted to sell. When Banda complained that his income had fallen so low he was struggling to send money home, Grigor offered him the chance to sell drugs. Banda would never do that. He did, however, supplement his earnings by doing menial jobs for the pair. He was not proud of all the jobs he completed and was no closer to getting a passport.

He was desperate to return home, having not seen his daughter in three years. She was nearly eight.

"Why don't you just leave?" Snowy asked.

"Where would I go?"

"You could get a boat to the mainland?"

"That takes money, my friend."

"Couldn't you just hand yourself into the authorities? They would ship you back."

"Graham and Grigor have spies everywhere. They would find out, and Banda would disappear like the others before him."

Snowy needed no further explanation. He slipped Banda five twenty euro notes and said there would be more to come in exchange for information about Grigor and Graham's whereabouts.

"The travel agent next to the bar advertises trips to Soller." Leah placed her shopping on the kitchen table. "I wouldn't mind going there."

Jon looked up from his book and peered into the living room. He had sat on the balcony reading while the children enjoyed a siesta. "Soller? Where's that, and what's there?"

"It's that quaint little place on the other side of the island. The trip takes you to the market in the morning, and after lunch, there is a train ride to Palma, which takes you through lemon groves with great views. The bus meets you there and brings you back."

Jon was sceptical. "A train? Really? Is that a good idea with those two?"

"They will love it."

"I am not sure."

"Bit late now. I've booked it, and we are going on Saturday." She looked around the living area. "Where did you put that tourist guide? I can show you photos of Soller."

"It's next to the television," Jon replied, wishing that photographs of the place would have been enough.

Graham enjoyed standing in his office looking out over the dance floor via the colossal window, mirrored on one side to stop people from looking in.

"You are sure it was him?"

"I wasn't at first when I saw him in town. He moved the same way as I remember but looked different. He's gotten rid of the beard and shed a few pounds. Then I heard his voice. He is staying in one of Eddie's apartments."

"I didn't think Eddie was letting them. I'm sure he said he was trying to sell them."

"He is, but Hermann, the German estate agent, asked him to let our friend stay there for a fortnight."

"How does Hermann know him?"

"Eddie didn't know. He said they were old friends."

"We'd better tread carefully."

"What do you think he'll do?"

Graham turned away from the window, emptied his glass and sat on the sofa. "He's going to try and get the stuff back for our darling dad, I guess."

"Where is it?"

"At the house, by the entertainment system where we left it."

"We'd better move it."

"No need. It's safe enough where it is. Speak to Eddie and ask him how long his guests are staying." He picked up the decanter from the table next to him to refill his glass. "Get Barty to trail our Welsh friend. See where he goes, who he meets, etcetera."

"He will want paying."

"That's fine. He'll spend it in our bars anyway, so we'll get it all back."

"What's your plan?"

"The first thing we need to do is find out whether he is acting alone, and then we can decide what trap we need to lay for the Welsh bastard."

PRIZES
(4 YEARS AND 6 MONTHS BEFORE THE HOLIDAY)

"Please put your hands together for our Student of the Year, Nicholas Kingston."

The assembly hall resonated with applause and cheers as Nick climbed the stairs to join the Headmaster and staff on the main stage. Someone told him to smile, and a camera flash went off as he collected the trophy and vouchers. The Head stepped back, allowing Nick to access the microphone, but he was not the speech-making type. Nick said a quick "Thank you" and then raised the award before pointing it at Bleasdale, Donald and Dawes, pushing his clenched spare fist through the air in a victory salute.

It had been a better year. Nick was the first-choice pitcher for the school's baseball team, and the mixed martial arts training Donald had suggested twelve months previously had paid huge dividends. Nick's upper body had expanded and tightened, his strength and stamina had improved, and his self-confidence soared.

He had no trouble keeping up with the twice-weekly training regime and supplemented this with extra sessions with his fellow samurai. They arranged the additional training periods around Nick's busy work regime, which already involved much lifting and carrying.

Nick had gained much respect from his fellow pupils and lost the "posh boy" tag immediately after he put Wilco onto his back during rugby training. Wilcox initially thought it had been a fluke, brushed it off, and continued to taunt his opponent, but then Nick repeated the performance, making the second tackle much harsher than the first. Nick hit Wilcox with a real boneshaker, leaving the boy spread-eagled on the grass. Wilco's back ached from the collision with the ground.

Kingston then acted out an elaborate mime simulating him urinating on Wilcox, which was even more embarrassing for the bully. The other players howled, Wilco's so-called friends and teammates cheered, and even the usually sour-faced teacher clapped.

Wilco knew then that his days of bossing Kingston had gone. He would need to find a new victim, which would be easier said than done. There were no easy targets. The three he picked on before Kingston were no longer fearful of Wilco. He tried to ignore the sarcastic remarks they made to him. He thought about beating them up but was unsure he could. They looked more muscular than he, much different from the pathetic wimps he used to bully. To make matters worse, if he threatened any of the younger pupils, they would rush to Kingston, who left Wilcox without doubt about what would happen if he tried anything.

Nick studied the shopping vouchers and thought about what he might buy. He was inclined to pick up a few bargains that he might be able to resell for a profit on the auction site. He would put the cash proceeds towards reducing the indebtedness.

The Kingstons had reduced debt levels by over 80%. They had sold everything they could. The houses, the yacht, the cars, Kenneth's suits, shoes, cufflinks, and all gadgets that once occupied the home office, together with Elizabeth's jewellery and expensive knick-knacks, were sold via auctions or private sales. His mother had developed new skills involving baking, sowing and painting, which she put to good use by developing cheaply prepared products to sell at car boot sales and local markets.

Nick himself did three jobs. The first involved weeknight working at a local hypermarket. The second meant working Saturdays at a shop in town, while the third role was at a pizzeria on Saturday and Sunday evenings. The tips were very lucrative. Around all this, he managed to keep his schoolwork on track; teachers expected Nick to leave with nine GCSEs. In addition, his mother taught him Spanish, French, and Welsh, and he maintained a rigorous training regime.

The teachers encouraged Nick to stay on for his "A" levels and to apply to university. Nick had different priorities. He wanted full-time employment so that they could wipe out the remaining debt. It had become a mission, a challenge he was determined to complete.

Nick and his mum still hoped to find the missing money, but the lack of leads made that task very difficult. For now, he concentrated on securing the best-paid jobs to pay their bills. Everything else could wait.

As he stood on the stage absorbing the atmosphere, he was pleased to get attention for something other than being the only pupil in school to wear a blazer.

Ben Moran toasted his daughter and new son-in-law.

"Congratulations on your wedding, ladies and gentlemen. I give you Shirley and Will, the happy couple."

The friends and family gathered in the family home responded by raising their glasses and cheering.

Shirley leaned into her fiancee and whispered in his ear. "I feel like a teenager again."

"I'm not sure I can get you one at this time of night."

She playfully dug her elbow into his ribs.

"Oww." He turned to the small crowd. "You saw that, didn't you? She's beating me up already. I want a divorce."

"Too late, sunshine. You're stuck with me now." She moved from his side to stand in front of him. "Well, and truly stuck." Shirley gave him a huge smacker on the lips.

"And there's nobody I would rather be stuck with." He kissed her as the audience clapped again.

The Potter family gathered around their kitchen table. Gemma sluggishly pulled back a chair, sat, and looked at the floor.

"Look, Gem. Nobody will stop you from working in the

brewery. It's just that Dad needs an extra pair of hands now."

No response. Geoff Potter's middle daughter had not welcomed the news that her father had recruited a new employee. A friend from his previous job was looking for employment, and Geoff offered him a position immediately.

Carol Potter tried a different approach. "Stop sulking, Gemma. Your father needs full-time assistance. You have to go to school."

"I could leave school."

"You'll do no such thing." Carol was close to snapping. "For God's sake, grow up, will you? You need to complete your education. It is important."

Her husband saw merit in calming matters. "You complete your exams, do your 'A levels' and attend university. Once you get a degree, you can return and work in the brewery. By then, I should know if I can make a go of things. If I fail, you'll still have other options, and I can find another job."

The fact that Gemma now looked at them offered Carol some hope. "If you did a degree in marketing, you could help your father promote the business."

"They do a course on brewing and distilling at Edinburgh University. I will go for that."

Geoff nodded, trying to appear encouraging. Carol shrugged in despair.

DAY 7 - FRIDAY 30 JULY

It had seemed like a good idea at the time. A quick jog, as Nick called it, followed by a dip in the sea and a few hours on the beach. It sounded ideal, but the reality was slightly less fantastic.

Gemma had never classed herself as a runner. She used the treadmill at uni and walked everywhere she could, but road running was not her forte. The heat wasn't helping either. She was conscious that she was slowing Nick down and, after three miles, told him to go on. She would meet him later.

Leah and Daisy entered the café with waves and greetings from Elizabeth and Lucia.

"Hola, Buenos dias," said Daisy with a wide smile.

"Ah, you clever girl," said Lucia, helping Daisy onto the seat between her and Elizabeth. "Buenos dias. Como estas."

"Estoy...bien...gracias." Daisy was delighted to get the words in the correct order and gave herself a little clap. She hugged Lucia and Elizabeth, removed her sun hat and dropped it onto the table.

"All we have heard from her are the Spanish words you've been teaching her," said Leah, sitting next to Elizabeth.

"She is never too young to start and has a good teacher to show her how it should be spoken."

"I want to speak five languages just like you," said Daisy.

"Well, I wouldn't bother with Welsh unless you want to come and live with me in Wales. There's not much use for it elsewhere."

The waiter took Leah's order and placed a fresh jug of water and two glasses, promising to return soon.

Leah sipped the water. "It's so hot today."

"It is," said Elizabeth. "A day in the shade for me."

"I've had hot flushes. Jon teases me that I'm on the change."

"Oh Lord, don't remind me. We still have that to come."

Leah's smile disappeared, and her face adopted a ponderous look. She caught Elizabeth looking at her and uttered the first thing that came into her mind. "....er...I hope I have an easier time than my mother. She went through hell."

Elizabeth rested her hand on Leah's arm. "It's okay. I know that I look older than my years. Lucia said the same thing."

Hearing her name, Lucia stopped talking to Daisy and asked, "Que fue eso?"

"I was just saying you thought I was older than I am."

Lucia laughed. "I am sorry, but you..." she touched Elizabeth's head. "...need a new haircut, a touch of make-up and nicer clothes."

"See what I have to put up with," said Elizabeth. "Nick and I have had a tough few years, but hopefully, things will start improving now." She drank the rest of her coffee.

"What happened?" asked Leah. "If it's not too personal a question."

"No, not all. My husband died suddenly, and, well, not to bore you with the details, we thought we would be better off than we were."

"Why? Did the insurance not pay out?"

"Nothing like that, although he had cashed in the insurance I paid for without telling us. We had other money put aside, but when we looked, it had disappeared. We had no idea where and what it went on, but nothing was left. Nick and I had to sell everything and take any job on offer to pay our debts."

"Oh my God, that's terrible. Couldn't you have declared yourselves bankrupt?"

"Funnily enough, that is what my ex-solicitor suggested, but no. Nick and I agreed to pay people back, and we are 99% of the way there. Our friend thinks he has traced the money and can get some of it back. Hopefully, things are going to improve from now on."

"Good for you," said Leah, raising her glass.

The waiter brought her tea and Daisy's milkshake. Leah poured tea into the cup and stirred the teapot before topping up her cup. Lucia asked if she could take Daisy to the counter to teach her some new words.

"Of course," said Leah, reminding her daughter to be a good girl. She looked at Elizabeth again. "Do you mind me asking how your husband died?"

"A stroke, a big one. He fought it and survived for a few months, but.... "

"That's tragic. Did he have high blood pressure?"

"Not that I know of?"

"Had he been under stress?"

"Yes, but we didn't know it at the time. We think it was the stress that brought it on."

Leah fell silent while stirring in the milk.

"What's wrong?"

"Nothing," she said, forcing a smile.

"Come on, you can tell me. It won't go any further."

She glanced at Daisy and then spoke again. "I am a bit worried about Jon. He joined Cromwell Construction because it paid better, but he works too many hours, gets loads of grief from his boss, and always takes calls, even when he's supposed to be off work. Then, when he comes home, he helps with the kids, shopping, cooking and the housework. He needs to slow down a bit."

"Some people thrive on pressure."

"Not Jon. He's already got high blood pressure, and the doctor wants him to take tablets." Leah shook her head. "He can be quite stubborn."

"He doesn't want to take them?"

"No, he keeps saying he'll get more exercise and cut back on work, but it's easier said than done," Elizabeth said nothing, anticipating Leah would continue. "I want him to start his own business...."

"That can be stressful, from what I hear?"

"Yes, but I could help him. My father died..."

"I am sorry to hear that."

"Thank you, but he had been ill for some time, so it was a blessing by the end. He left me his old family home. It's a lovely big house with a huge garden. It also has stables."

"Has your mother passed too?"

"Sorry?"

"If he left you the home?"

"Oh no, sorry, it's not my family home. My parents downsized when my father became ill and bought a flat in town. They loved it there. My grandfather's house and the surrounding land were sold to a supermarket chain for one of their megastores. When they looked closer, they found a stream running near the house. It had become overgrown. The locals objected to the stream getting covered, and the council imposed conditions on the planning permission. The supermarket fenced off the house and a parcel of land. They built on the rest. Just before he became ill, Dad approached them and repurchased the house and buildings for a bargain price. The supermarket sold it on the condition that it became a family home and would not be demolished to build new houses. Sadly, he never got around to doing anything about it. When he died, Dad left the flat and the bulk of the estate to my mother, money to my brother and his father's house to me, plus some money for the children."

"Didn't your brother want the house?"

"I don't know. My father was insistent that it should stay in the family. My brother is unlikely to have kids, plus Dad knew that Jon was good with the tools."

"Sorry, I shouldn't be so nosey."

"You're fine. It's not a problem. I thought we could sell our house and use the equity to renovate the old house. I want to convert the stables into a workshop for Jon, a play area for the kids and a design studio for me. My idea is that Jon could run a carpentry business, possibly taking on an apprentice or two, and I'd do design work. We could sort out the garden together and perhaps grow vegetables and things."

"Sounds ideal. What's the problem?"

"Money. What we make on the sale of our house should cover the cost of doing up the new one, but we'd have little left for living. If Jon took on work to help pay for the renovations, it would take him much longer to finish our house, and he doesn't want the kids living in a building site."

"Could you borrow money?"

"Not from a bank. There would be no income, so we'd struggle for a mortgage until we finish doing up the old house. My mother said she would lend us the money, but I won't accept it. She had a tough time when Dad was ill, and I want her to live a little." Elizabeth nodded knowingly. "My brother is too busy enjoying himself, and his money will probably disappear quickly!"

"Sounds like you need an investor?"

"That's exactly what Jon said, but his answer is to see if his boss wants to invest. That's the last thing I want."

"I can understand that," said Elizabeth as Daisy returned with a novelty ice cream.

"Look, Mummy, Lucia bought me helado."

Nick did not mind when Gemma suggested they go to the beach via the local shops, but he was concerned when she pushed him into a hairdresser's salon.

"Come on, my treat."

"But I haven't booked..."

"I called in earlier, and they said they have space this morning." She patted the seat, telling Nick to sit down.

"What do I ask for?

She reached into her bag and removed pages ripped from magazines. She opened them and showed Nick. "The girls and I think these styles would suit you."

"You do, do you?"

"Yes, we do."

"But what if I don't want a haircut?"

"You need one."

"I can have one when I get home."

"Who does your hair?"

"I always go to Tosca's on the High Street."

"I assume Tosca's other clients are men of a certain age."

Nick was looking at the pages, wondering which style the girls recommended. Gemma pointed at a couple. Nick's eyebrows rose and fell. They were not as radical as he worried they might be. He could not imagine his usual hairdresser being able to replicate the cut. "Now you mention it, Tosca tends to cater to an older clientele."

"Welcome to the 21st Century," she said, agreeing with Nick's choice.

Becky was horrified at the news. "But you said..."

Christiano held out a hand. "I know what I said, but things change. Graham has a friend coming over who expects to meet a young lady. I said you'd do it."

"By meet, you mean have sex."

Christiano nodded.

She stood and walked away from her desk seat beside him. Burying her face in her hands, she thought about what to say and do next. "You promised me I wouldn't have to get involved. You told me you wanted me for yourself. You promised..."

"As I said, things change. Graham is a powerful man with powerful friends. What they want, they get."

Becky folded her arms as she turned to face him. "Well, he's not having me. I won't do it. I am not that type of girl."

"Grow up, Becky. You are that type of girl, and you will do it." Christiano turned the laptop screen so she could see it and pressed play. "Or your family, friends, and anyone interested gets to see this."

Becky's eyes opened wide as she watched her face and

naked breasts appear on the screen. Her eyes narrowed again as she saw herself with the sex toys, and tears formed on her eyelids.

"Bore da, Nick."

The tall, well-built man wore a shirt so colourful it would not have been out of place in a Rio carnival. He dropped his cases onto the sand and put his coat hangers, bearing clothes, over the top.

"Hola, Banda." The pair slapped fingers and then pressed their hands together. "It is afternoon now, so we say Prynhawn da."

"Prenhound dar?"

"Close enough."

"Your hair looks good, man. Very sexy."

"Told you," said Gemma.

Banda looked from Nick to Gemma. "Is this your girlfriend?"

"Well, she is a girl and a friend, so yes."

Gemma studied them both, peering over the top of her sunglasses. Banda stepped nearer, and she took his hand. "I'm Gemma."

Banda shook her fingers. "Banda. Are you from Wales too?"

"England," said Gemma.

"Shame," said Banda, smirking.

"Don't you start with all that racist stuff." I have enough to put up with from Taffy here." Her thumb pointed at Nick.

"Feisty. I like that and good breeding stock, Nick. I will give you 30 camels."

Gemma looked stunned. Nick shook his head.

"No chance I am looking for fifty."

"Sorry, my friend, that is too much for me. She is out of my league."

"Mine too, I think," said Nick.

"Hello! She is listening," said Gemma.

Banda ceased tittering and wiped his mouth.

"Here." Nick handed him a bottle of water.

"Thank you." Banda took a long, deep drink. "It is too hot today. People think I am used to this heat, but they forget I come from Glasgow."

"I can tell from your accent," said Gemma.

"Ha ha ha. Now, who is being racist?" Banda took another drink and returned the bottle.

Nick became aware of three small faces staring at the interloper. "It's okay, don't be shy. Come on over."

Charlie and Harry walked to Nick, and Daisy went to Gemma.

"Are these yours?"

"No, they belong to that couple over there." Gemma pointed at the Olivers, who looked strangely bemused.

Banda turned and shouted. "Hello beautiful lady, hello man."

The Olivers waved.

"This is Daisy," said Nick. Banda shook her hand. Nick added, "Banda has a daughter back home in Senegal."

"How old are you, young lady?" Banda asked, crouching down.

"Nearly six."

"My daughter will be eight in..." He counted out the months. "November."

"And these two monsters are Charlie and Harry." Nick placed a hand on each head as he announced their names, and the boys quickly corrected him.

"I'm Harry,"

"Charlie."

"Sorry, I got you the wrong way around again. "High five, Banda."

Two little hands shot up in the air, and Banda gently tapped each in turn.

"Right then," said Nick. "Shall we see if Banda will let us look at his box of tricks? One thing, though: we can look, but we can't touch. Banda has to sell these items, and people don't like it if too many people touch them. Okay?"

Three heads nodded.

"Right then, Banda, what can you do for..." He checked his wallet. "...a few euros each."

"Plenty, my friend," He put the hangers onto a tree branch and opened both cases. "Lookee, lookee many bargains," he said in his premier salesman's voice.

Christiano told Donny and Lousie the content of his conversation with Becky: "She was not happy, but, in the end, she knows she has no choice. She stormed off calling me names, but she'll calm down."

"She has a few days to get used to the idea," Donny said. "Becky must have known what we had planned for her. She knows what Candice does."

"I never actually mentioned it," said Christiano, sipping water. "I think some things are better left unsaid until it is too late for arguments."

Daisy ran over to show her mother her new fan. Charlie and Harry followed, displaying their yo-yos. Banda slapped Nick's hand, thanked him again and strolled off, searching for his next customer. Nick and Gemma returned to sunbathing.

"When did you meet him?"

"The first morning I was here. I've bumped into him several times since."

"That stuff he sells is fake, isn't it?"

"Possibly, but he has to make a living somehow. He sends most of his money back home."

"He probably makes a bomb."

"I doubt it. Have you seen how many sellers tour the beach? They all offer the same stuff. They must buy everything they sell, live and pay their rent. I bet it's not easy for them."

Ben Moran looked at the list of trips in the window and was just about to enter the shop when a familiar voice called his name. "Hello, Elizabeth, how are you? Where's your partner in crime today?"

"We met for a coffee earlier, but now she has to work, so I'm heading back to the complex for a read. You going anywhere nice?"

"A...er...friend of mine recommended I see Santanyi. He said the views are spectacular."

Elizabeth stepped nearer and peered through the window. "Sounds lovely." She looked at the photographs on the board. Ben, "You'll have a great time."

It dawned on Ben that there might be benefits to Elizabeth accompanying him. For one thing, Shirley wouldn't worry. For another, if he made friends, nobody would think it suspicious if he ended his life on this tour. It was evident that he was enjoying his holiday. Who would suspect anything? "I'm thinking of going tomorrow. Why don't you come with me? My treat"

Elizabeth knew she would be at a loose end as Lucia had to work, and Nick would probably be out with Gemma. There was only so much sunbathing she could stomach. "That would be lovely, but I can pay my way, thank you."

On their way back from a late lunch, Donny Kingston stood in the car park with his two partners in crime. He was not sure about his sister's proposal. "Can we afford it? It sounds like it might be expensive."

"I have spoken to Graham and Grigo. They'll pay for most of it. They have plans for the place next door. It would be cheaper to do the whole building in one go. They want a contribution to the materials."

Christiano joined the discussion, "This place is not very inviting. The building looks old-fashioned and dirty. Look at the old posters peeling off the wall. That sort of thing puts people off." He raised his hands and framed the scene as a film director might. "Imagine the building painted white with the car park cleaned and all the rubbish removed. If we improve the inside, we will attract more customers."

"But the café was only meant to be a front. It is not our main business."

Louise spoke. "I know, but we must find ways to attract new stars. The girls have done well, but we cannot rely on them forever. Candice and Becky are becoming too well-known and won't be useful to us for much longer. I won't be sorry to see them go. The girls they bring are pretty similar. We don't make much from them."

Donny knew that she had a point. The victims were rarely cash rich. "How do you know that painting this place will attract anyone better?"

"It is worth a try. That bossy bitch you found last week walked in. Graham believes she is ripe for the picking because she owns a business in South Africa. She could be worth a fortune. She just turned up here. Imagine if we could attract more like that."

Christiano had another reason for making improvements. "If the tax authorities turned up, they would not believe a place like this takes as much money as we claim. How would your father launder his money then?"

It was a valid comment. "Okay, so when do we start?"

"I am not very good with a paintbrush."

Louise put her arm around the Portuguese. "You fool. Nobody is suggesting we do the work. Graham is owed a favour and intends to get his boys to persuade Manuel to do it. He wants work to start next week. If Manuel refuses, his wife will learn about the girls he sees at the Bull Ring."

"Happy days." Donny put his arm around his sister's shoulder. "But Graham and Grigor have never used that half of the building."

"Not yet. That part of their operation moved to Palma. Grigor and Graham want to open a discount liquor store. I think our darling Daddy might have to carry more than people in his vans in future."

"So long as it keeps him off our backs." Donny kissed

Louise's head before the three returned to their office.

The cage was a synthetic football surface surrounded by a large mesh fence. There was not much space on the sidelines. The fence was only three feet from the edge of the pitch, making corners and throws-in challenging.

Nick knew his limitations as a footballer but was confident he was not letting the side down. He played for the Majorca XI against the Mini Englanders XI or, as Javier's friend Sergio called them, the Infidels.

The Mini Englanders included Donny, Barty, and two other boys Nick had seen hanging around with Donny and Christiano. Barty was quite a skilful player and always appeared to have the ball. Nick took great delight in getting it off him, sometimes legally. In truth, Nick hadn't done much other than tackle hard. It helped that he was much fitter than most other players.

Shouts of 'Ole' filled the air when players hit the mesh, and Nick enjoyed barging Barty into the fence, causing much laughter and shouting from the Majorcan teammates and complaints and groaning from the opposition.

The Majorca XI won 3-1, and the players shook hands at the end of the match.

"Well played, cus," said Donny through gritted teeth. "Nice haircut, by the way."

Nick nodded.

"You did well," said Christiano. "You should have played for England and me for Majorca."

"I was happy where I was," said Nick.

Javier pushed him into the fence shouting "Ole", and Nick took it in good spirits. Sergio shook Nick's hand before he also threw him against the mesh. Again Nick laughed. Barty came to shake hands and, holding his one hand, tried to shove Nick into the metal, but Nick caught him and spun him around, causing Barty to hit the fence before tumbling onto the floor.

"Fucking hell, it was only a joke," said Barty, pulling himself up. "They did it to you, and you laughed, but I try it, and you knock me over. What's your problem?"

"I just don't like people who throw their weight about."

"Is that because I tried it on with your tart the other night?" Barty was standing again.

Nick grabbed his chin and pushed him against the fence. "Watch your mouth."

Barty did not retaliate. "Okay, I didn't mean it. How was I to know you felt like that."

Nick let go, prodded him in the chest and said, "Just be more careful what you say."

The look on Nick's face left Barty in no doubt that the threat was real, and while his gut reaction was to lash out, he thought better of it. This lad had put him down twice, and Barty was not confident about taking him alone. He wanted revenge but might need help to get it. Barty looked at Donny and Christiano, who had been observing developments, and realised they would not support him. He would leave it for now, but this was far from over.

Donny had been more shocked at his cousin's reaction than any of them. He thought he would try to stay on his good side.

"Er Nick, Dad said you'd like to look at our computer system?"

"Yes, I would."

"Why?"

"I'm just being nosey. Since I got the job, I've become obsessed with computers and like to see what's out there."

"Are you free tomorrow morning?"

"I am."

"Call around about tenish." Donny looked at Christiano. "I'll show him around. You've got to go to Manacor."

Christiano nodded. He was also suddenly respectful of his mate's cousin. "Of course, give him the full tour. Perhaps Nick can show us a thing or two."

Hearing his friends fawn over the Welsh kid made Barty more determined to show the cocky twat a thing or two of his own. His chance would come.

Shirley sat back in her seat, sated after a fine meal. "That dessert was to die for. You should have a go at making that when we get home."

Will almost coughed his wine into his glass. "Me? I wouldn't have a clue where to begin. I'd probably end up poisoning you." He gulped it down.

"You are an excellent cook, Will. Now that we have more time, you can practice more. Make a note of the name. There'll be a recipe on the internet somewhere."

Will took a photo of the menu with his mobile.

Showered and wearing fresh clothes, his damp kit stuffed into a plastic bag, Nick joined Gemma by the others chatting by the gate.

"I can't say whether you played well because I know nothing about football, but you looked the part." She ruffled his hair.

"Thank you." Nick watched as the majority of the opposition players prepared to leave.

"What happened between you and Barty at the end? You threw him into the fence."

"Nothing. It was just a wind-up."

"Really? It looked from here as though you were about to hit him?"

"Who me? Never." He smirked. Nick scanned the horizon. "I thought Sara and Kylie might have been here."

"No, they've been stood up…or is it stood down? They have to entertain themselves tonight. The English boys are going to the Bull Ring for a party for some business people, Grigor's friends. We went down there last week. It was awful."

"So, what are your friends doing tonight? They could have come along."

"I suggested that. I knew you wouldn't mind. They've gone for paella in Cala Millor."

"Talking of being stood up, I won't be around tomorrow morning. If you wanted to see me, that is."

"Why?"

"Donny has invited me to see his equipment."

"Oh aye, is that what cousins do in the valleys then? Show each other their equipment."

He tutted, "His computer equipment at the shop. I don't live in the valleys."

"So you say. It's fine, no problem. It's not as if we are joined at the hip. Anyway, I need to do some shopping. I haven't got anything for my sisters yet. Will I see you afterwards?"

"I hope so, but I may not be around tomorrow evening either. I may have to work on a project for my boss, but I won't know until lunchtime tomorrow."

"First, it was the football, then your cousin's equipment, and now it's working on a Saturday night? Are you trying to tell me something? I mean, who works on a Saturday night?"

"I do, sorry, but I might not be. It all depends on how things go tomorrow. If my boss uploads the software, I must test it tomorrow evening."

"Can I test it with you?"

"You could, but you'd be a distraction, and I can't afford to make any mistakes. This might be a valuable customer."

"Can't it wait until Sunday?"

"Not really. I need to test it when their office closes. I can let Chris know what I find, and he can sort problems out on Sunday before they reopen on Monday."

"How long will that take?"

"Depends. It could be an hour, maybe longer. I won't know until I get the testing protocol."

"But you'll be available tomorrow afternoon?"

"Definitely. I'll be finished at Donny's by twelve, so I could meet you at half past."

"Okay," she grabbed his hand, and they followed behind the others walking to the beach. "We can go on the bus to Porto Cristo. I hear it's lovely."

Snowy joined Banda at the bar. He placed his order and added a glass of iced water for his companion. "What's up?"

"Grigor and Graham are going to Ibiza next week. They are looking for a new nightclub, and the two boys from the internet café are going with them."

"Why?"

"I have no idea, but the café will be closed for decoration. Perhaps it is a reward. They work closely with Grigor and Graham."

"How long will they be away?"

"They go to Magaluf on Thursday, then sail out on Friday. They return on Monday."

"Thanks." He took a bundle of notes and surreptitiously handed some to Banda. "Thank you very much."

The Majorcan boys set up the sizeable wood-fired grill on the promenade and took turns cooking. Late arrivals brought more food and drink. They included many females, much to Gemma's relief.

Large cool boxes filled with beer stood at the water's edge, and opened bottles of wine stood on a picnic table. Several unopened bottles of vino remained in shopping bags close to the beer. Plastic beakers were the drinking vessels of choice.

Nick apologised for not contributing to the feast and offered to run to the shop to buy provisions. Javier would not hear of it.

"You are our guest. You are welcome to eat and drink as much as you like."

Ben Moran had left his companions at the Happy Bar enjoying sangria and walked along the promenade. He smiled as he observed the youngsters enjoying a barbecue on the beach. He wondered what his youth would have been like had he lived in a sunnier climate. He had a happy childhood in the Midlands and did most of what he imagined others his age did at the time, including drinking, watching football, chasing girls, and working to pay for it all. He could not recall many sunny days.

He rarely visited the beach, and when he did, it was usually a long trip across Wales to Aberystwyth. He and his mates never lit a barbecue on the beach, and the only beach food they consumed was stale sandwiches and lukewarm tea.

Cheryl had never visited Aberystwyth until she met him. About three months into their relationship, they went for a sneaky, dirty weekend. Their parents believed they had gone with friends to a holiday park, where the girls would stay in one caravan and the boys in another. It had proved to be quite an experience. It was the first time they slept together. The only downside was that, even then, Cheryl tended to snore.

It dawned on Ben that, for the first time in months, thinking about Cheryl had not made him miserable.

With the barbecue cooling, Javier played his guitar as people danced, drank and had a good time.

Gemma pulled Nick up to dance. They could not compete with their hosts. Undeterred, they tried again but found moving quickly on the sand problematic. Gemma gave up. She put her arms around Nick and kissed him as they slowly danced.

"I prefer it like this," she said.

"Me too. More my pace."

"I fancy going for a swim."

"Now? We don't have any kit."

"Who needs a costume?" The glint in her eye was evident even in the moonlight.

"How much have you had to drink?"

"Enough to know I won't be able to do anything if we don't leave soon. That wine is powerful."

"It's nice, though."

"And very strong. How I like it and my men."

"Are you sure you are not drunk already?"

"I might be." They kissed again. "So, are you up for a swim?"

"I am."

They waved farewell to Javier and the others and left the party to walk across the empty beach.

Nick stripped naked, putting his top and shoes on a sun bed, before swapping his shorts for the pair he had worn to play football.

Gemma wore only her knickers.

"Ready?" Nick asked.

She nodded, and they ran into the sea. Shivers disappeared as they immersed their bodies in the water.

"I don't want to swim," said Gemma, her arms wrapped around Nick's neck and her legs dangled by his sides. Nick held a buttock in each palm.

They necked passionately as Gemma removed her underwear and held them in her hand. Things became more intense as the water splashed around them.

The glow from the promenade streetlights lit up the beach down to the water's edge. Shirley pointed at the young couple on the sand.

"They seem to be enjoying themselves?"

Will squinted to get a better look. "The naughty buggers. You know she's got her top off."

Shirley patted his back. "Now, now, don't get jealous. I am sure you were like that when you were young."

"Like what? Cavorting in the sea? I don't think so. I'll have you know that I am from strong Welsh Methodist stock. We didn't believe in such things."

"Are you trying to tell me you never cavorted when you were young?"

"Never. The closest we came to excitement in my village

was pushing over cows when they had fallen asleep standing up."

Shirley howled. "Is that what counted as promiscuity down your way?"

"How very dare you! It took a lot of skill. I was the village cow-tipping champion for three years running. I only stopped because a cow fell the wrong way."

"Is that when you ate all that bullshit you spout out now?"

Will stopped and looked pensive. "Now you mention it. There might be a connection."

Shirley was still chuckling as she spotted her father walking toward them. She waved, turned around and hugged Will's arm tightly for the walk home.

"We managed to avoid the suction problem," said Nick as Gemma's feet dangled again.

"The night is still young," Gemma said, taking her knickers off his head.

DEVASTATION
(TWO YEARS BEFORE THE HOLIDAY)

His wife organised and paid for the short holiday when Ben's father died. She hoped it would take his mind off the news that his mother was seriously ill.

The sudden passing of his dad hit Ben Moran hard. For the first time in his life, Ben felt helpless. He became anxious, waking in the early hours, sweating and struggling for breath. The symptoms started to ease when he took the medication prescribed by his doctor, but then further tragedy struck within a month.

Ben's mother developed breast cancer, and the diagnosis knocked him flat. His sleeping patterns became even more erratic, his attention span shortened, and his mood swings more apparent. The doctor suggested Ben had depression, brought on by heightened stress and anxiety, and recommended a holiday. Cheryl visited the local travel agents and booked the trip as a surprise.

The closer the trip got, the more reluctant Ben became to go. His life had changed so much in such a short space that he craved security, and the place he felt most secure was at home. He argued that he could not go away because he needed to complete the sale of several of their larger stores to a national, cooperative supermarket chain. Cheryl insisted that the legal team could handle that. He had nothing to do but sign the final contract, which would not happen over the weekend.

Cheryl tried to cheer up her husband by discussing how they might enjoy the sale proceeds, but Ben wasn't interested. His outlook had always been upbeat; people commented about how optimism filled the air around Ben Moran, but he knew that was no longer the case. Now Ben felt as if death and gloom had absorbed him. He was in no mood to go anywhere or do anything.

His wife maintained a happy disposition. She made only positive statements and worked hard to sell the trip. They would enjoy three days in Bruges to savour the Christmas markets, the scenery and the food. All travelling would be by rail. Ben disliked flying unless he had no choice.

Ben tried postponing the trip, but Cheryl would have none of it. She reminded her husband he was not the only one grieving; they both deserved the break. They had earned one. His sister, Rosie, and brother, Brian, assured them their mother would be safe. While her prognosis was not good, the doctors did not expect immediate deterioration. They fully expected her to survive beyond Christmas, still two weeks away, and they believed it would help Ben if he got away from family issues, if only for a few days. The family at home would keep them informed of developments.

The trip started well. The pair travelled to London via the hospital in Birmingham to see his mother. She looked frail but was delighted to see them. She told them to bring her back a large box of Belgian chocolates. His brother said not to make it too big as she could not open it. His mother chastised Brian for that comment, and they all laughed about how Mum still ruled the roost. Even the nurses joined in.

Their onward journey to the capital was in a first-class carriage, and they enjoyed the wine and nibbles. Cheryl booked a nice hotel and arranged for them to see an outstanding West End show. They followed this with a classy meal at a Michelin-star restaurant nearby, which Ben said had cost more than he used to earn. He was amazed that he had slept well in the hotel.

The next day, they took a cab to St Pancras, ready for the early morning Eurostar departure. They then joined their holiday party and met their rep.

Everything went like clockwork. All the connections were on time, the weather was dry but cold, and the train was comfortable. Ben enjoyed every moment of the journey from London to Brussels and looked forward to spending a few days with Cheryl in the Venice of the North.

They had an hour to spare before the connecting train to Bruges, so after securing their luggage, he went to get refreshments while his wife shopped for chocolates. He had just ordered two coffees when his phone rang. Rosie was in tears when she told him their mother had suffered a heart attack, and the medical staff feared the worst. He knew then that they would not see Bruges, and, with the help of their holiday rep, they quickly assembled a timetable for their return journey.

Several hours later, they arrived at the train station nearest to the hospital. Regular contact with Rosie informed him that Mum was still alive but only just. Taxis were few and far between on a busy, pre-Christmas, late-night shopping Friday evening, so they waited patiently. The queue continued to lengthen, but eventually, they were next in line. A black cab appeared, and Ben gathered up their bags. At that moment, a man raced across the concourse, stopped the taxi and got in.

Ben ran to talk to the man and held open the door. "Excuse me, but this is our taxi. We're next in line."

"Tough shit, loser, I'm in here now, and I'm in a hurry. Take me to Harwood Golf Club," said the man to the driver.

"But this is our taxi. We've waited, and now it is our turn. We need to get to the hospital to see my mother. She's dying."

"Save me the sob story and fuck off away from the car. I'm late for dinner. Driver, take me to Harwood Golf Club." The man pushed Ben away from the door and then slammed it shut.

Ben looked from the passenger, who said nothing, to the driver, who shrugged and back again. He heard the car getting put into gear and watched as it moved away. The passenger sneered at him, flashed a v sign and then held his hand to his head, his index finger and thumb extended in an "L" for loser shape.

A sad, embarrassed, exasperated Ben looked forlornly after the cab before slowly walking back to join Cheryl. Others in the queue sympathised with him and chastised the man for his impatience and rudeness, but it did not make Ben feel any better. He felt terrible. He wanted to scream, cry, run after the cab, and explain to the man that it was vitally important that he be allowed to take the taxi, but he did nothing.

The taxi took four minutes to arrive. When they eventually got to the hospital, the medical staff informed them that Ben's mother had passed away moments before they arrived.

DEPRESSION
(TWENTY-THREE MONTHS BEFORE THE HOLIDAY)

Most of the week following his mother's death was a blur for Ben. He knew he had participated in the discussions about the funeral arrangements but had trouble remembering what was agreed. He would say a few words on behalf of the family but still had no idea what to cover in his speech. If truth be known, he just wanted the day to end.

His wife had confirmed arrangements to accommodate family members arriving for the sad occasion. He was unsure whether he felt relieved or disappointed that he had played no role.

"It would have been nice to do something useful. I feel so helpless."

She hugged him tightly.

"I know how you feel, but you've had much to contend with in recent months. What with your father's death, the sale, and now your mother dying. It's going to take a while to get back to normal."

"I suppose," he said, patting her back as they parted. "I just wish I didn't feel so shitty."

"It'll get better. Let's get today out of the way, and maybe you can try to enjoy Christmas. I've spoken to Brian and Rosie; they'll come here for Christmas Day. There's plenty of room, so they might also stay the night. Shirley and Will are coming too. The kids are looking forward to it."

He smiled at the mention of his grandchildren.

"They won't want to be stuck here with us old farts."

She playfully slapped his arm.

"You speak for yourself."

They giggled, relieved at the chance to lift the atmosphere.

Jon stopped tying his laces and rested his elbows on his knees before putting his head in his hands. The fingers of one hand ruffled his hair. He was exhausted before he started work.

Daisy had been a dream, but the boys proved more troublesome. They never stopped. Charlie was into everything. Harry had only just started crawling and barely gave their parents a moment's peace. He dreaded what they might be like when they could both walk.

Leah handed him a coffee.

"Cheers, love, thanks."

"Try not to be too late tonight."

"I will, but I can't make any promises. Rob wants that dormer job finished by the weekend."

"I thought that was Peter's job?"

"It is, but he's new and is finding his feet. It doesn't help that the boys won't listen to him."

"He has to show them who is the boss."

"I know and tell him that, but they regard him as a joke. Rob is thinking about letting him go. Richard has another eighteen months in Uni, and then he's joining us. I might have to do extra work in the meantime, but it will only be until Richard comes on board. Rob said he would help me."

"You make sure he does. You can't do it all."

"I will." He took a deep breath. His wife spotted it immediately.

"Are you okay?"

"Yes, I'm fine. I think I've pulled a muscle or something." He rubbed his chest, realising he had said and done the wrong things. Leah looked concerned. He needed a better excuse. "Or it might be indigestion. I probably ate my cereal too quickly."

Gus joined Graham on the deck of his boat. "And this is all mine?"

"Yeah, if you want it."

"What do you mean if? Of course, I want it."

Graham dangled a set of keys. "Then it's yours."

“I don’t know what to say. Thanks very much.”

“No need to thank me; it was your idea to expand the product range. It’s a real gold mine.”

“Where would I moor it?”

“Leave it where it is. I’ve spoken with the marina management company, and they’ve allocated us these two berths.”

“What? Just like that?”

“I had to grease some palms, but it’ll be worth it. We can tour the other islands from here and even head back to Africa if we want.” Do you have any idea what you will call yours?

Gus had not considered a name, but one came to him quickly. “How about Matilda? After the woman who made our business expansion possible.”

“Nice touch. I will call mine Waltzing.”

Gus studied the yachts, standing side by side. “Isn’t yours a bit longer?”

“It was ever thus,” said Graham, punching his arm.

Gemma had arrived far too early. They were supposed to meet at eight, but it was not yet seven. She entered the bar, bought a large pinot and retreated to a table in the middle of the room. She chose the seat facing the door so she could see the arrivals. Her mobile buzzed, and she read a message ‘On my way, should be there by 7.30. See you then.’ She replied with a thumbs up.

Gemma had returned to Edinburgh early to take a job in a shoe shop on Princes Street. She would work in the weeks before she started her second year and then on weekends. It would be tough going, but the pay was reasonable, and it was an opportunity to meet people who were not students. There were plenty of good-looking blokes on campus, but they were much of a muchness. She was tired of talking about classes, dorm stories, and student loans. She made it her priority to find someone outside the university circles.

This was the first date she had been on with someone

from the real world in over a year. He had called in to buy football boots and bought the most expensive pair in the shop. He departed with the boots, trainers he never knew he needed, and a date for the following evening.

"Gemma, isn't it?"

She did not immediately recognise the girl.

"I'm Zoe. We are at the same university. We met at the quiz night in the union."

Recognition and realisation. "Of course, Zoe. How are you?"

Zoe looked about and then back at Gemma. "I'm good, thanks. What brings you here? This is a real locals' pub. Do you live in the area now?"

"No three of us are renting a flat close to campus. I'm here to meet someone."

"Boy or girl? Not that it is any of my business,"

Gemma chuckled. "It's no secret. It's a lad. I met him in the shop where I work."

"Where is he?"

"I'm a bit early. I misjudged the timings. He's due in half an hour."

"In that case, do you mind if I join you? I am meeting my boyfriend. He's been playing football this afternoon but will be here shortly.

The pair laughed and joked, chatting about anything and everything. Zoe bought a round of drinks, and Gemma was about to reciprocate when two men entered the pub.

"Here's Ian now. What is Mac doing with him?"

"Do you know Mac?"

"Yes, he and Ian work for my Dad, but he doesn't usually come here."

"He's here to meet me."

"You are kidding," said Zoe, stifling a giggle. "That's incredible."

"Why? Is there something wrong with him?"

"No, he's a great guy. It's just that it is a small world."

"Isn't it just?" Gemma replied as the men arrived at the table.

Will handed his wife a glass of wine and sat beside her on the sofa. "That went as well as could be expected."

Shirley nodded, wiped her eyes with the tissue in her spare hand and looked at him. "Yes, it was a lovely service. Thanks for all your help." She stretched over, and her lips met his cheek.

"Careful now. You'll disturb my make-up."

She playfully elbowed him in the ribs. "That's my line."

"Anyway, there's no need to thank me. I'm happy to help in any way I can. You know that."

"And I'm glad of your support. My father isn't much use. Bless him. His family could have helped more but left it all to us. I am not sure what I would have done without you."

"How is your mother? She seemed pretty upbeat today."

"Hmm, she did, but I wish she would come clean. I can't keep it from Dad much longer."

"But he's depressed enough as it is. How will he react if she tells him she wants a divorce?"

"I accept that, but how will he react when he discovers we knew about her affair but said nothing?"

Will sipped his wine. Shirley looked contemplative, nibbling her bottom lip. He felt she needed to say something else. "What is it?"

She looked him straight in the eye. "I know you have a busy life as a spy…."

"I was never a spy. I am a forensic specialist."

"Whatever, but how do you fancy doing your wife a favour."

He took another drink. "As I said, I'm happy to do what I can. What do you need?"

"How easy would it be to hide money so nobody could find it?"

"Depends on how much and how long you have."

"I want to hide some of my parents' money so that my mother's lawyers can't find it, and it needs to happen before Mum starts proceedings."

"But this is your mother, Shirl. She's entitled to half of everything."

"I know, and I don't begrudge her a penny, but I'll be damned if I let that snivelling little shit of a fitness instructor..."

"Personal trainer."

"He's still shit, and I won't let him waltz off with any of the money my parents worked so hard for."

"You can't be sure he intends to waltz off." He immediately realised his mistake.

Shirley glared at him. "Are you being serious? He's younger than me, for fuck's sake. How long do you think he'll stick around? It's obvious how much he enjoys the high life and spends a fortune when he goes out with his friends. Who pays for that? Mum. He's not with her for the long term. He knows when he is on to a good thing. It is just a shame she can't see it. She is smitten." Shirley looked at her hands cradling the glass, then downed half her wine in one gulp. "He'll wait until the divorce and then fleece my mother. She'll never see him again." She faced Will. "I am not talking about us stealing her share. I only want to put it somewhere so she has something to fall back on when he does the dirty on her. If miracles happen and he stays with her, we can hand it over in a few years."

"How do we explain that?"

"No idea yet, but we have time to think about it. In any case, I think he'll be gone as soon as the divorce comes through." She faced him again. "So, Gwilym Ira Hopkins, are you prepared to help your wife or not?"

DAY 8 - SATURDAY 31 JULY

Jon, Leah and family waited by the bus stop.

"I did not expect to see you," Leah said to the lady approaching. "Are you Going somewhere nice?"

"Ben wanted to see Santanyi, so I invited myself along. We stop at a few places, so it will be nice to see the island. What about you?"

"Soller. They take us to the market, and then we take the train to Palma."

"That'll be nice," replied Elizabeth.

"Do you think so?" Jon asked, struggling to get the boys to sit still. "In that case, you go with Leah, and I'll keep Ben company."

"Where's Lucia?" Daisy asked.

"She has to work. New guests are arriving today, and she'll be busy. I offered to help, but she told me it would be quicker if she did it alone. Honestly, that woman is so cheeky."

"She's nice, though," said Leah, looking at her daughter. "Lucia is great fun."

"She is," said Daisy. "Me gusta Lucía"

"Muy bien," said Elizabeth.

Gemma, Kylie, and Sara had a great time wandering around the shops. They handled and shared opinions on multiple items and tried on clothes and shoes but bought nothing.

"There might be better shops in Porto Cristo," said Sara.

"What time are you going?" Kylie asked.

"Probably lunchtime," said Gemma.

"Any idea what time you are coming back?"

"We won't be late. Nick might have to work tonight."

"In that case, me and Sara will come with you."

"I thought you were meeting the Chuckle brothers?"

"We are, but not until this evening."

"Great," said Gemma, confident that Nick would have no objection.

Nick looked around the bar's mishmash of equipment. It was antiquated compared to the stuff he used at work, but then his cousin had not received a substantial start-up grant from the Welsh Government and did not have Chris Shanklin's contacts.

None of the machines were in use.

The barman seemed oblivious to his arrival and concentrated on his mobile.

"Hi, I'm looking for Donny."

The eyes did not leave the little screen.

"Upstairs." A half-hearted hand wave showed him the direction. A wooden door with a digital lock looked like it would restrict Nick's entry to the first floor, but the barman told him it was open. Nick walked through and climbed the stairs.

The Kingston Communications (Majorca) empire spent little time or money on fixtures and fittings. The stairwell's walls were dirty, and the paint flaked off. The concrete on the uncovered stairs was heavily stained. The small window was filthy and had a cracked pane.

"Hello," Nick called out.

"In here." Donny's head appeared out of the second of three open doors along the wall. A fourth door at the end of the corridor was closed.

The main office area was open plan with two doors on the right side.

On the oversize counter in the centre of the room stood three desktop PCs and a laptop Donny had been using. All the monitors were off, but some base units were powered up. Nick thought they were connected to a larger server unit on the far wall.

Three large flat-screen monitors hung on the wall above the server. The first monitor displayed images of the downstairs bar. The barman hadn't moved since Nick arrived.

The second showed images from the security cameras around the building. Nick guessed there were three external cameras, two at the front and one at the back.

The third monitor was blank.

Donny sat and typed on the laptop. He pushed down the lid, but not quickly enough to stop Nick from seeing an unfinished email addressed to someone called Isabella.

A cork notice board hung on the wall by the door, containing several postcards, photographs, and two sheets of paper. One was an insurance document. The other had two columns comprising lists of numbers scribbled in pen, with several crossings out. A separate sheet showed several blocks of apparently random text.

"Nice setup."

"We like it."

Nick pointed at the sheets of paper on the board. "Are they scripts for code that you are writing?"

Donny snickered, "Fuck no; they are codes, but for the various security measures we have on the systems. I have a shit memory." He laughed aloud. "I wish I could write software code."

When Donny disappeared through the first door behind him, Nick followed him and saw his cousin in the kitchen. "So, how is business? There weren't many when I arrived."

"We are doing well, and things are still picking up. Our takings last month were 170 per cent up on the same time last year."

Nick would never have guessed that.

Donny collected two cans of beer, handed one to Nick, and ushered him back to the office.

The cousins discussed the machines' specifications and usage, and Nick tried his hardest to minimise his knowledge. His cousin was very proud that he had built the system from scratch and expanded it to meet all their business needs.

Donny led Nick into the adjoining room, which required a passcode to open. Donny explained that this was where they kept the important stuff. The room was full of computer parts, spare surveillance cameras, webcams, and monitors. Donny walked over to a shelf and put his hand on a metal frame.

"This is where we keep all the backups for our system."

Nick asked many questions, curious about how the business operated. Donny appeared to answer honestly, and Nick did not get the feeling his cousin was lying or hiding anything. He declined the offer of a second beer, saying he had barely touched the first. Donny fetched another for himself, tossing the empty in the direction of the bin. He shrugged when it missed, and liquid dripped over the floor.

By the time the tour was over and they had returned to the office, a light on one of the PCs had stopped flashing. Nick assumed this meant that whatever task it undertook had been completed. When Nick suggested this, Donny grunted and suddenly appeared anxious to get Nick off the premises.

He looked at his watch. "Shit, is that the time? I'd better get a move on. It's been great seeing you again, Nick. Perhaps we can grab a beer before you go home?"

"Yes, that would be great," said Nick, confident it would never happen. He checked the time. "I'd better be going too. I'm meeting Gemma in an hour."

Donny nodded knowingly and sat behind the desk, resisting the temptation to switch on the monitor until his cousin left the room.

Nick was curious about what else was in the building and ignored the signposted exit route. Instead, he went to the fourth door at the end of the corridor, which took him to another stairwell. Steps led up to a third floor and down to what he guessed was the back of the bar. Nick softly trotted up the stairs and discovered another door on the upper level. This one was secured with a padlock and a digital lock. Frustrated, he tip-toed back down the stairs to the ground floor.

The door he thought would lead to the back of the bar took him into a downstairs kitchen area. Nick glanced through the cloudy circular window and saw through to the bar. The barman was dealing with a customer and did not spot Nick opening an exterior door leading to the parking area. The door opened without so much as a squeak.

The space was empty, apart from bins full of bottles and other bar paraphernalia. The tarmac had become littered with rubbish and weeds. Nick thought this was the fire exit. He stepped back inside and quietly shut the door behind him.

Nick walked through the kitchen and strolled into the bar. He took the barman by surprise.

"You're not supposed to be here."

"Yeah, sorry, I took the wrong stairs. See you."

Jon and Leah had their work cut out to keep the children under control at the massive open-air market. The boys picked up and tried everything, while Daisy did not want to be restrained by holding her parents' hands. The crowds of people made it very difficult to make progress.

Reaching the field's outer limit, Jon spotted an ice cream parlour, and the family stopped for a well-earned break.

"Have you considered my proposal any further?" Leah sipped her latte and wiped strawberry ice cream from Charlie's nose.

"I haven't thought of anything else, to be honest." John removed the plastic lid from his coffee. "It sounds very tempting."

"Then let's do it. Let's tell the Cromwells where to go and do business on our own."

"It's appealing, but can we afford it?"

"We can if we sell our house."

"Yes, but we can't start converting your father's house until we get the money from ours. What are we supposed to live on?"

"We'll manage. You can do carpentry jobs. I can call a few

contacts and see if they have any design work. We'll be fine."

"I am not so sure. I might ask Rob if he's interested in investing."

"Don't you dare! That man makes your life enough misery as it is. I am not prepared to share this with him. The whole purpose of this new venture is to get you away from the Cromwells. I am certainly not working for them, and if I can do anything about it, you won't be working for them much longer. I said we'll manage, and we will."

She stopped speaking when she realised she had raised her voice and that four faces were staring at her. Three of the faces had ice cream on them, and the fourth had milky froth on its nose.

Snowy moved his newspaper and motioned for the waiter to put the coffee in its place on the table. He handed over a note, dismissed the offer of change and resumed his telephone conversation.

"That's right. Grigor and Graham live in the same house. It's bloody massive too. You can just about see it from the road. It's set right back on the headland." He listened to the caller's question. "No, not a sign of her. Nobody around here appears to know anything about her. She must have dumped them." Another comment. "Yeah, or they've dumped her."

He leaned forward as he tasted the coffee, still listening to the other man. He slapped his lips before replying. "It looks like Graham runs the businesses but goes to great lengths to ensure his business rivals don't invade his space. I'm told that he has videos made showing them in compromising situations." The man interrupted him. "Sorry? Yeah, insurance policies. You'll never guess who helps him make the videos." The other man had no clue. "Eddie Kingston's son and daughter...yes, that's right, Louise and Donald. With help from some Portuguese man."

He listened as the caller spoke again. "As well as helping Graham to set up his rivals, the terrible trio have a nice little sideline in sex tapes. It looks like they pick up girls and film them having sex...No, I am pretty sure the girls know nothing about it and do not consent." Snowy listened again. "Yes, that's right. I doubt that many know they have starred in a porno, but some get reminded. The wealthier ladies get a message when they leave telling them to pay up to avoid the video going public. My contact tells me many girls pay, but the video is still uploaded…Sorry? Yes, that's right, they run a website. It's called Mallorcan Memories…yeah, spelt the Spanish way… and a members' section called Mallorcan Mammories…Very tasteful."

The man closed by proposing to look at the site, and they would speak again later.

As soon as the two English girls entered the Sa Coma café bar and grill, with much flesh on display, Minoli, the head waitress, guessed it was payday. She wondered why the third girl was not with them but was not curious enough to vocalise her interest.

The three girls gathered here every month and drank coffee while they awaited the arrival of the slimy Englishman and his dishy Portuguese friend, who handed out the cash.

The order was usually the same, as was the lack of manners and the absence of tips.

"Bring them over," said Louise. "We'll be just there." She pointed without looking at the barista.

Minoli smiled politely, resisting the temptation to spit in the cup.

"How did it go last night, Cand?"

Candice shrugged, not overly keen to be reminded. "Okay, y'know, a typical middle-aged married man with a weekend pass…bit of a kid in a toy shop, keen to try everything but unable to get round to it all."

"Did he behave?"

"Yeah, he slapped me a bit, but only on the arse. Other than that, he was quite sweet. He kept calling me baby. I half expected him to tell me to call him daddy, but thank God he didn't."

Louise joined in with her sniggers. "That would have been weird."

"Where is Becky? She normally rings, so we meet before coming here, but I haven't heard from her. I rang her, but no answer."

"Graham wants her for a job next week, and I don't think she is happy about it."

"I see. Do you want me to have a word?"

"Do you think it would do any good? You know what a prima donna she is."

"I could reassure her that it is not that bad and it's not as if we must always do it. And you get tips. That bloke last night gave me €200 for my taxi home."

"That would be great," said Louise, disappointed that Candice had taken money without sharing it. She said nothing, but that little snippet might prove helpful later. Her face lit up as the boys arrived carrying a wad of cash.

The train to Soller took them through lemon groves and afforded spectacular views. Jon was in his element. His camera hardly stayed still as he tried to capture every image from every angle. Leah enjoyed the light breeze blowing through the carriage. Charlie fell asleep, resting his head on his mother's side while Daisy made up Spanish words to impress her other brother.

The coach pulled into a space outside a single-storey café that doubled as a service area.

Ben and Elizabeth ordered coffee and cake and went outside to eat it.

"You never mentioned what you do back home?" said Ben, ripping into his Danish pastry.

"Nor did you," said Elizabeth. "I suppose you could call me self-employed. I do a range of things. I bake, sew, knit and do anything else that raises a pound or two. Nick and I buy and sell things on auction sites."

"Very enterprising," said Ben. "Was this your idea?"

"I am afraid it is a case of necessity being the mother of invention." She did not wait for Ben to ask before giving him the background.

Ben was sympathetic and said that Elizabeth and Nick should be proud of themselves for not taking the easy way out. Many would have. If he had been in the same position, Ben feared he would have declared bankruptcy without a moment's hesitation.

Elizabeth was about to ask about Ben's background when a horn tooted, reminding them it was time to return to the coach.

Originally planned as a trip for two, the number of participants attending the outing to Porto Cristo expanded to four. Nick didn't mind, which was just as well, as he was not given a choice.

They alighted the bus at the bottom of the steep hill and wandered around the shops and small harbour before returning to the narrow beach. Local kids jumped off walls into the sea, and the girls tried to tempt Nick into trying it.

"Nah, it's not for me. I'm not much good at diving."

"Even better," said Kylie. "You can give us a good laugh."

"Hmm, thanks for that."

Two young men wearing yellow inflatable vests arrived and stood close by.

"Hola, Nick. Hi Gemma, how are you?"

Nick rose to shake hands. "Hola Sergio, hola Costas. Are you okay?"

Gemma smiled, said she was fine, and waved. Sara and Kylie sat upright, curious about the newcomers. Nick introduced the newcomers and explained to Gemma's friends that he had played football with the pair the previous evening.

"It was a good last night, no?" Sergio smiled at Sara, who

held his stare.

"Yes, great," said Nick.

"Where did you two go? You disappeared very quickly."

"We...er...went for a walk on the beach," said Nick as Gemma coughed into her hand.

"Very romantic," said Costas, who had now caught Kylie's eye. "It is a shame we are not playing again on Friday, as you could have joined us."

"That would have been nice," said Kylie.

"You could come too," said Sergio to Sara.

"It is a shame there is no game."

Calls from further down the beach forced the visitors to leave. "It is our turn on the banana," said Sergio. "We have to go."

"Hope to see you again," said Costas, running after his friend.

"I wouldn't mind a go on that, "said Kylie.

"What? The banana?" said Nick. "How much is it?"

"Not the banana, stupid. I meant Costas," said Kylie.

"You take him, and I'll have Sergio," said Sara.

"Ignore them," said Gemma to Nick. "This heat makes them horny."

"Hark, who's talking," said Kylie. "It wasn't us who went skinny dipping last night."

"Did Gemma get a long ride on your banana Nick?"

Kylie and Sara slapped hands and roared with laughter.

Nick looked at Gemma, who put the tip of her index finger to her lips. "I never said a word. Honest," she whispered through a bout of giggles.

"Here you are, Candice, your monthly share of the profits from MM productions." Christiano handed her an envelope.

Donny had popped a bottle of fizzy wine and poured it into four flutes.

"Thanks, hun." Candice quickly counted her cash.

"Wow, it has been a good month."

The other three agreed.

"And we couldn't have done it without you," said Donny, handing her a glass.

Candice winked at him. "Always nice to be of service."

"Well, you keep introducing them, and we'll keep filming them," said Donny. "When do your cousin and her friends arrive?"

"Sunday afternoon. I've Skyped them and told them we're all going out in the evening."

"How many friends?"

"Four."

Louise added a record to the calendar on her mobile. "In that case, we'd better keep Barty sober. We missed out on Gemma."

"Which reminds me that we need to offload the current two," said Donny.

Louise nodded in agreement. "I've checked, and they are not in well-paid jobs. Time to move on, I think."

"It will be a pleasure, "said Christiano. "I look forward to a new challenge. Kylie was too easy."

"Sara is too keen," said Donny. "I'll take a video tonight. I'm sure she will put on a good show."

Candice had more news to impart. "My sister's two friends arrive at the end of next week," she said. "She's picking them up next Thursday."

"What do they do?" Donny asked.

"One is a doctor, and the other works in the city. My sister said they liked to enjoy themselves, and they are all staying in the Mediterraneo, and that's not cheap."

Christiano raised his glass. "It looks like it could be another bumper month."

Ben and Elizabeth pointed at various sights and gasped at the beauty of the views. They still had an hour before the coach returned to Sa Coma, and Ben asked if Elizabeth fancied something to drink. He let her place her arm through his as they walked to a bar. He insisted she took a seat while he ordered.

"They always put too much ice in," said Elizabeth, taking three cubes from her gin and tonic and tossing them into the grass.

"And they freeze the beer glasses. I am afraid my lips will stick to the side."

"You didn't get to tell me what you do back home."

"I wondered when you'd bring that up." Ben smiled. "I am retired."

"Retired? How old are you? Sixty?"

"Fifty-eight, " said Ben.

"You must have had a good job to retire so young."

Ben said he owned a few food stores but had sold most of them. He admitted to missing the work and had always enjoyed running the business.

"So why did you sell?"

Ben took a slow sip, licked his lips and said, "My ex-wife persuaded me it was time for us to enjoy ourselves. We sold up, and then I discovered she was already enjoying herself too much with her personal trainer."

"Ouch," said Elizabeth.

"She took half of everything, not that I begrudged her a full share. She was instrumental in us starting the business." He rested his elbows on the bench and intertwined his fingers as if praying. "I wish she had told me her plans before she left. I could have bought her out and kept the business."

"Is she still with this personal trainer?"

"It looks like he has done a bunk. She called me crying, saying he had emptied his stuff and taken a sizeable amount of cash from their home."

"I take it he is a younger man?"

"He is younger than our daughter."

"Ouch again. Why did she ring you? Are you still close?"

"No, not at all. I hadn't heard from her in ages."

"Does she have other friends?"

"Yes, lots. She always had a busy social life."

"So why did she feel the need to tell you what had happened?"

Ben shrugged. "I've been thinking about that, and I wonder if she thinks we could start again."

"Will you?"

"Not a chance. She left me twice before, although those separations only lasted a few weeks. I'm not getting back with her this time. Cheryl has made her bed." He took a drink. "I have plans, and she doesn't feature in them."

Nick and the gang's return trip from Porto Cristo was only memorable for an incident involving a girl eating ice cream, a sudden jolt, and Nick's lap, resulting in his shorts having strawberry ice cream and sauce across his crutch area and down one side.

The little girl's mother was most apologetic. The other passengers were concerned, but Nick's female companions found it hilarious. He wore his bravest face and insisted he did not need anyone to wipe him down.

"I'll nip back to the apartment and change."

"Do you want me to come with you?" Gemma struggled to maintain a straight face.

"I'll be fine. I can ring Chris at the same time to see if I am needed tonight."

"Text me to let me know what's happening. It is my turn to buy provisions, so I'll visit the shop on my way back."

Jon, Leah and the kids were exhausted after their expedition.

"Shall I fetch us a pizza?" Jon asked, slipping on his sandals. "There's a place over the road."

"Good idea," said Leah, seeing Charlie's eyelids droop. "Better make it quick. I don't think the boys will be awake much longer."

Jon ordered the pizzas and sat at the bar, enjoying a complimentary glass of local wine. He was thinking about the possibilities that had recently opened up for him. He finally had the chance to start his own business.

The only stumbling block, and he had to accept it was a massive obstacle to overcome, was a lack of capital. They needed to raise enough money to tide them over until they sold their house and established the business. He knew he had a good credit rating but doubted that would be enough to help him raise the money without regular income.

He believed the Cromwells represented an excellent option. Rob was a sensible businessman and, Jon guessed, had lots of money. Jon would offer him a stake in his new business and offer to repay the investment as soon as possible.

He was unsure whether to ring Rob or wait to speak to him face to face on his return from holiday. Jon was confident his boss would see merit in his idea and support him. After all, Jon had been instrumental in helping them build the Cromwell business. He felt that the Cromwells were almost obliged to help him. It was only fair. He asked the waiter how long the pizza would be, and when he heard it would be another five minutes, Jon decided to ring Rob immediately.

He inserted the SIM card from Leah's spare purse and switched on the mobile. The screen lit up, telling him he had voicemails from Rob Cromwell. He became increasingly depressed as he listened to each message. By the end of the third one, he learned that the contract on renovating a block of housing association flats, another of Richard's projects, had gone awry because essential materials were missing. Switching the phone off, Jon wondered how to tell Leah that he no longer had a job with the Cromwells, let alone any prospect of borrowing money from them.

Gemma sent Nick a thumbs up and a smiley face in response to a text confirming he would be free that evening. He was going to shower and aimed to be at her hotel by seven. Meandering back from the hypermarket with a bagful of essential provisions, Gemma weighed up their options for the evening. She knew Kylie and Sara were heading straight out. They saw no need to change and could do their make-up in the bar while waiting for their beaus.

Gemma's initial idea was for Nick and her to go for something to eat before returning to the room, but then she thought about ordering pizza and enjoying the privacy.

It was a strange feeling, and Gemma Potter found it odd that she felt much happier at the prospect of seeing Nick that evening. She was very relieved when she got his text, and it dawned on her that she would have missed her new Welsh friend if he had had to work. They had spent five days together, and the time had flown. Gemma did not understand why she hadn't grown bored. A runner went by and reminded her of Nick, bringing a smile to her face.

Turning down the path toward the rear of the hotel, Gemma spotted Becky sitting on a low wall with hands to her face. She had been crying heavily. "Becky? What's the matter."

The youngster stood and started to run down the path away from Gemma.

"Wait. Come back." Gemma kicked off her flip-flops, rammed them into the carrier bag and chased after her.

Snowy's caller rang back and told him he had looked at the website and accessed other files linked to Mallorcan Memories. He had little trouble getting in. The setup was simplistic, with minimum security.

The operation worked as Snowy had suggested. Once they had the film, if the victim had money, she got contacted and invited to pay to ensure the video stayed off the website. If she had no money, the video got uploaded.

It looked like a lady in South Africa was next on their list of ladies to get blackmailed.

The pair agreed they needed to close the site, and Snowy would pay a visit to destroy any backup files. Snowy's colleague would contact the South African to tell her not to pay, as the files would disappear once Snowy was on the plane home.

"What's wrong, Becky? You can tell me. It won't go any further."

Gemma had caught up with the girl at the end of the road. Neither of them realised it was a dead end. Becky had turned and fallen into Gemma's arms, sobbing like a child. Gemma took her back to the hotel room, gave her a glass of cola, and texted Nick, suggesting he delay his arrival. She would tell him when the coast was clear. He replied with a sad face.

Becky was initially hesitant to say much. She dismissed her troubles as a storm in a teacup and suggested she was overreacting.

Gemma placed a hand on Becky's arm. "It must be something to make you cry like that. You'll feel better telling someone, and I promise it won't go any further."

After more persuasion, Becky told her about misreading her relationship with Christiano. She thought he cared for her, but he was only using her. Becky told Gemma about the video and how Christiano was using it to blackmail her into having sex with a stranger. The footage shocked her, but she was more upset by Christiano's deceit, demands, and threats.

"He didn't ask for consent to film?"

"No. It was all done by hidden cameras. I thought I was safe because I kept away from the Pleasure Palace."

"Pleasure palace? What's that?" Gemma needed a drink, so she removed the cork stopper from the wine bottle she had opened the night before.

"It's the apartment above the internet café. Chris and Donny take girls back there, film them and then blackmail them."

Gemma remembered Kylie speaking about the place. She was unsure if that was where Sara would be going that night.

"Blackmail?" Gemma did not like the pair but would never have imagined this. She held up the bottle for Becky to see.

"Yes, please, but just a small one. I don't like wine very much." Becky rubbed her eyes with a tissue. "They ask the victim for money to prevent the video from going onto their website.

"I thought the website was only photos of girls with their boobs out."

"That's Mallorcan Memories. They sell the images to tourists as a souvenir. The real action is on the members' pages. Mallorcan Mammories..."

"Classy name." Gemma had poured two glasses of wine and handed one to her visitor.

"They make a lot of money out of it. Not just from members but also rich girls who pay not to appear." She sipped her wine. "Not that it does any good. They post the videos anyway."

"The bastards." A question came from nowhere. "But if you knew about this, why haven't you told anyone?"

Becky downed the rest of her wine in one gulp and took a deep breath. "Candice and I get paid for introducing girls," she said.

"Paid? Do you get paid? You made money out of entrapping girls?"

The tears reappeared. "I do...I did, but I never thought... I never imagined..."

"What? That they would use you too?"

"I thought he cared for me."

"He only cares about how much he can make from you." Gemma topped up her glass and walked away as she sipped the liquid.

"I know that now." Becky started to howl as she sobbed. "But I never thought he would do this to me."

"Pity," said Gemma. "You didn't give a shit about the other girls, but now it is happening to you..."

"I know I have been stupid, but making money seemed

fun and easy. I work in my father's shop, and he doesn't pay me very much as he wants me to go to college."

"Sounds like your father has the right idea. Save me the sob story. I am more concerned about these poor girls having to hand over their hard-earned cash than some spoilt little brat who, some would argue, got what she deserved."

Becky stood, screamed and cried again. Gemma sighed, drank her wine, put her glass on the table and sat Becky on the sofa. She placed a sisterly arm around Becky's shoulders more out of instinct than concern. Kylie and Sara suddenly appeared in her thoughts. "This Pleasure Palace. Has Kylie been there?"

"Yes," said Becky, wiping her eyes. "I think Sara is going tonight. It will probably be the last time she sees Donny. The boys tend not to stick with the girls for more than a week."

"Use 'em and ditch 'em."

"At least they won't get blackmailed." Becky saw Gemma did not follow. "Louise doesn't think they can afford much. Their videos will go up as soon as they leave the island."

Gemma had forgotten about Louise. "What is her role in all this?"

"All this is her idea. She scrutinises the girls Candice and I recruit and then decides who goes with who."

"How does she know how much the girls can afford?"

"She talks to them, asking questions. Louise finds out what the girls do, how much they earn, whether they are in a relationship, etcetera. After that, she looks on social media and things like that."

Gemma recalled the first meeting and Louise's nosiness. "I did wonder why she was so interested."

"You were supposed to go with Barty, but he got pissed and missed his chance."

Gemma doubted the boy was ever in with a chance.

Becky continued, "Louise didn't like you. She thought you might be dangerous, so she told the boys to stay out of your way."

"Hmmm, she might have more sense than I thought. "

Despite her bravado, Sara was not the most experienced in sexual encounters. Most boys back home sought a quick fumble, wham-bam-thank you ma'am and then rode off into the sunset. One or two had been different. Sara thought initially they might be Stage 3 material, but it came to nothing. She was too young to consider settling down, so she found an excuse to drop them.

Donny was nothing like the boys back home, and Sara had initially been grateful that he never groped her and paid more attention to her needs than his own.

That gratitude was wearing thin.

She thought this would be a memorable evening when she saw the cupboard full of toys. However, Donny did not appear intent on using his sex aids to warm up. Once again, they would be the main event.

When Sara told him she had enough, he kissed her cheek, put on his shirt and left the room to get them a drink from downstairs.

Sara studied the toy cupboard and picked up two handcuffs, one pink and the other rainbow-coloured. She thought the boys would not miss a couple of pairs. She checked the keys were attached and dropped them into her beach bag.

She would not be sorry to never see this room again. It was a depressing place, and it was time to move on. When Donny returned, Sara would tell him that she'd enjoyed their time together, but all good things come to an end. She was on holiday and had not planned to spend all her time with one man.

Sara rested against the bookcase as she slipped on her clothes.

The bookcase shook, and a couple of novels toppled. Sara put them upright again and spotted a cable tucked behind the books. She traced the path and found the line ended at a speaker.

Working in the health service's IT department, Sara

knew the difference between an audio and optical cable. The latter was designed for recording and playing video.

She picked up the speaker and removed the back. Inside, she found a camera. Sara studied the line of sight and, as she expected, found the camera would have captured everything that happened on the bed.

A quick inspection of the vicinity discovered four more cameras focused on the sleeping area.

The cables from the other cameras were positioned to avoid detection and met in the corner. Have they never heard of wifi, she thought as she kneeled on the floor and put a hand under the box.

Sara found another line which went into a floorboard. She grabbed her bag, slipped on her shoes and walked down the stairs.

The door marked "Office - Private" had been left ajar, and she entered to see lights flashing and images on two screens. The first showed security camera images from inside and outside the building.

The second image, on a laptop, showed a still of her and Donny. Her hands were cuffed above her head as he operated a vibrator. Sara pressed a button on the mouse, and the video started.

Donny entered the room holding two glasses of rum and cola. "You are not supposed to be in here." He saw the movement on the monitor. "It's not what you think."

"Isn't it? You invited me here so you could record me getting off. What happens next? You put these images on a website without me knowing?"

"No, nothing like that. It is just for my use."

"Really? Then why didn't you ask?"

"I umm…find it more exciting to think you knew nothing about it."

"Pull the other one." Sara's fingers worked quickly, hitting the keyboard and manoeuvring the mouse.

Donny stepped closer. "You can't look at that. It's

nothing to do with you." He placed the drinks on the desk and rushed to Sara.

Her foot came fast and hard, catching him in the delicate area between his legs. He groaned and collapsed onto the floor.

"If you are filming me, it is my business." She applied one handcuff to Donny's foot, twisting his ankle when he wriggled, and the other to the base of the desk chair. "That'll slow you down."

Donny continued wincing, cradling his privates.

She examined the laptop. Donny had not connected it to the internet or another PC. The only thing it appeared linked to was the video cable.

Sara accessed settings and found it was not using wifi, so she was confident he had not had time to share her starring role. "Why didn't you just record this onto the server?"

Donny groaned. "I didn't have time. You arrived earlier than I expected."

"This early bird certainly caught a huge worm." She unplugged and closed the laptop and wrapped the power cable around it. "I'm taking this, and if I find any images of Kylie or me on your website, I will tell the world where they came from and make it my life's work to wipe you out. Do you understand?"

"Yes," Donny said, soothing his nerves. "Couldn't you just delete the video and leave the laptop? It was a present from my dad."

"I am sure you will replace it soon enough. I suppose I could delete the video, but I am guessing you have recovery software, and my performance would quickly reappear." She stepped over him. "I would like to say this has been fun, but finding out a pervert has used me has been a shock." She used her free hand to pour one drink into the other glass. "Thanks for the double rum and cola, though. I will enjoy that on the way back as I ponder what to do next."

Gemma's train of thought was interrupted by an angry

Sara storming into the room, holding a bottle of vodka and cursing. She stood to greet her friend. "I thought you had a date?"

"I did," said Sara, spotting they had company. "What is she doing here?"

"We'll get to that in a minute. What happened to you?"

Sara dropped the bag onto the floor. "I've just discovered Donny likes to make secret videos of the girls he has sex with… or doesn't have sex with, in my case."

Becky cried again.

Gemma said, "Neither Donny nor Christiano has behaved nicely. If it is any consolation, they have also shat on Becky." She updated Sara on developments and Becky's role in proceedings.

If Becky was expecting sisterly sympathy from Sara, she was mistaken. "So you knew what they were doing and did nothing to stop them? I've met many selfish bitches, but I doubt any of them were as bad as you."

Becky said nothing. She lowered her eyes to avert Sara's glare.

"Did it pay well? I fucking hope so. Not that it's done you any good. They used you just like they've used those other girls. It serves you fucking right. " Sara then looked at Gemma. "At least I know my video isn't going public."

"How? Did you delete it?"

"No, I took his laptop before he could upload it?"

"You did what? You stole his laptop? Won't he come looking for it?"

"Probably, but I'll tell him I have already sent all the files to my cloud account." Sara opened the bag and removed the laptop. She powered it up, surprised to learn it was not password protected. "He is more stupid than I realised. I thought I would have to download software to bypass the password, but he hasn't even secured the thing. What an arsehole."

"Is my video on there?" Becky asked.

"Wouldn't you like to know," said Sara. "If it is, it will cost you to keep it hidden."

"But I haven't got any money."

"Then tough shit."

Becky went to speak, but Gemma motioned for her to keep quiet. "Let's calm down. We must see what is on there and decide what to do next."

"I'm the only one who is going to look at this. "Sara patted the machine. "At least until I have wiped any trace of my sexploits."

Will and Shirley tried to relax as they sipped their drinks at the Happy Bar.

"I wonder how his trip went. I hope he's enjoyed it," said Will.

"Me too. It's worse than when the kids were little. I can't remember being this nervous when those two went off alone."

"It's been a long time since Ben showed interest in anything, let alone new places. You are bound to be worried about him."

Kylie Best stormed away from Cody's bar, ignoring the sniggering and laughter she had left behind. She was as fun-loving as the next girl, but there was no way she was letting Barty and Donny join her and Christiano for sex. The minute her date had mentioned the possibility, she realised the mask had slipped. Gemma had been right all along. Christiano and Donny were a pair of sneaky little shits. She was angry at herself for falling for their innocent little boy routines.

Louise's comments about not understanding why Kylie was upset after she had been such a willing participant nearly caused Kylie to explode. Christiano had obviously told Louise everything.

The bitch also suggested that Kylie had the makings of an excellent porn star as the camera loved her. That had proved to be her detonation point. Kylie lifted the table, tossed it toward the gang, showered them with spilt drinks, grabbed her bag and stormed off. That would show them.

Two hundred strides later, Kylie began to calm down and think things through. What did Louise mean by the porn star comment? How did she know the camera loved her? Had someone filmed her? Had Christiano filmed them together? Had he shown his friends footage of them having sex? If he had, then who else had seen it? She slackened her pace to a slow walking speed as the questions filled her mind. The situation might be worse than she initially feared.

Christiano worked on websites. Had he put a video on the website? Had he uploaded images of them having sex? Was she the star of a sex tape? Was she currently getting leered at by some sick porno-loving geek who had no chance of a real girlfriend? The thought infuriated her. Sex tapes were the domain of celebrities, not dental receptionists from Cheltenham. Would people back home get to see it? What would people say? What would her parents think if word got around? Why had she been so stupid? Why had she believed the lies?

Kylie hailed a passing taxi and took it to the hotel. She was seething as she entered the apartment to find Sara, Gemma and Becky holding glasses of vodka and coke.

"You too?" said Sara as Gemma invited Kylie to tell them what had happened.

Ben and Elizabeth called into the Happy Bar for supper and one last drink before retiring.

"Cheers," said Elizabeth, raising her glass. "I have had a lovely day. Thank you very much."

Their glasses clinked.

"I have too. Thank you for being a great companion." Ben sipped his wine. "Would you like to go out for a meal tomorrow evening? We can go to a place Will found. It's not very far away, and the food is delicious."

"I'm afraid I can't. Not tomorrow." Ben looked

disappointed. "Lucia has invited me around to her home. She said she would make paella."

"That's a shame."

"I tell you what. You can come too. I will speak to Lucia in the morning. I am sure she will be fine with it. If she's not, maybe we could meet on Monday evening?"

"That would be lovely," said Ben, beaming.

When Gemma hadn't made contact by 11 pm, Nick decided to walk to the hotel to check she was okay. He smiled as he saw his mother and Ben walking arm in arm. His first reaction was to shout and wave, but they seemed deep in conversation, oblivious to the world around them. He left them alone and continued his trek to Gemma's hotel.

Turning the corner to the entrance, he bumped into Candice, playing with her mobile on the hotel's steps.

"Hi, Nick."

"Hello. What are you doing here?"

"I have been looking for Becky. I thought she might be here."

"Is she?"

"I don't know. I couldn't get in. The receptionist keeps stopping me."

Nick made for the door. Candice caught his hand.

"If you are thinking about seeing Gemma, I would leave it if I were you."

"Why is that?"

"I just saw Kylie return, and she was furious. She told me to fuck off and threatened to rip my head off if I didn't get out of her way."

"Oh. Right."

"Christiano dumped her. If Becky is up there, she won't be thrilled either. Christiano wants her to do him a favour, but she doesn't want to. She thinks it is beneath her, the snotty cow."

"But what does this have to do with Gemma?"

"Nothing, but I am guessing the other two might be anti-men at the moment and not welcome a male presence."

"I see." Nick wanted more details but wasn't sure whether Candice was the one to ask. He would save his questions for Gemma. "So you think I would be better off seeing Gemma tomorrow."

"I do."

"You seem to know a lot."

"I was at the bar when Christiano dumped Kylie, and I knew about Becky earlier. Christiano asked me to track her down and remind her about the favour.

"Okay, well, I suppose I'd better get back." Nick wanted to be alone so he could contact Gemma to find out what happened.

"Are you walking back?"

"I am."

"Can I walk with you? I was going to get a taxi, but if you're going that way, I'll come with you if you don't mind?"

Nick did mind but would not admit it. "No, I suppose that would be okay."

Candice put her arm through his. "Wow. Gemma said you had muscles, but I didn't know they were that big." She squeezed his upper arm. "You've kept these big guns quiet, haven't you?"

"Not really. They are not exactly big guns, are they? Most people wouldn't notice them," he said. "But I don't let many people touch them."

"So I'm one of the lucky ones?"

"I suppose you are. Are you ready?"

Nick pulled his arm away and kept a couple of feet between him and Candice. As they reached the bend, Nick looked back toward Gemma's room but saw nothing other than a curtain blowing in the wind.

Having calmed Sara and Kylie and put a drunk Becky to sleep on the sofa, Gemma announced it was time for a drinking game involving whatever cheap alcohol they could get. While Gemma used the bathroom, her friends nipped to the local shop.

Their toilet lay directly above the main entrance to the hotel, but the street outside was surprisingly quiet. Gemma heard Nick's voice and was staggered by the fact that he was talking to Candice. She pushed open the little window, letting the curtain fall through the gap. It blew in the light breeze outside. Gemma saw Candice squeezing his arm. She gasped as the girl took his arm like Gemma had done five nights before. Gemma saw Nick's head turn and pulled herself away from the window.

What was Nick doing here? Had he just arrived on the off chance to see her, or had he come with Candice? Was Nick flirting with the girl? Did he say he didn't let many people touch his arms? Her mind overflowed with horrible thoughts. What if she had misjudged Nick? Was he more of a womaniser than she believed? Perhaps the Welsh virgin image was just a stunt he played time after time? She thought that made him a hell of an actor as he didn't have much of a clue that first night, but was that a part of his plan? Had it just been a ploy to get her into bed? If so, she had fallen for it hook, line and sinker. Perhaps Nick was no better than his cousins and their friends for all his nice words and actions. She thought of Nick's fracas with Barty the previous evening. He denied it was anything, but what if the other lad knew of the scam and had threatened to tell her? What if Donny and Nick had set it all up?

The thought of Donny brought her mind back to Sara and Kylie and then to Zoe. Gemma winced at the memory of the last time she saw Zoe nearly two months previously. She knew all too well what it felt like to be wrongly accused. When she saw Nick in the morning, she would ask him to explain himself. Her priority was to look after her friends. They would all get very drunk and, for a short while at least, forget about their troubles.

Candice's parents owned a villa two streets from the beach on the back road to Cala Millor. Candice was evidently in no rush to get home. She asked Nick many questions and tried several times to get him to stop for a drink. Nick refused. The sooner this journey was over, the happier he would be. It was bad enough that she kept touching. He had no desire to give her the wrong impression by conversing with her over a beer. He declined politely, saying that he rarely drank.

"It's this one here," she said, stopping him by tall metal gates.

"Oh, okay, well, it's been nice talking to you...err...sleep tight."

"You don't have to go anywhere just yet, do you?" said Candice, reaching for him. "You could come in if you wanted. My bedroom is right by the door, and my parents sleep at the back of the house."

He gently removed her hands from his head. "I'm seeing Gemma, in case you'd forgotten."

"But you're on holiday. You don't need to spend all your time with one girl, not when plenty of others are around." She tried to retake hold of him. "Come on, Nick. It'll be fun. I promise."

He eased her hands away from him. "Thank you, but I'm not interested," he said, turning to leave.

"Donny and Louise were so right about you. You are a mummy's boy. I bet you wouldn't have a clue what to do."

He kept on walking and ignored the comments. Her assumptions would have been correct a week ago, but he now had a better idea of what to do and who he wanted to do it with.

Elizabeth kissed Ben's cheek and walked to her apartment. The place was dark, and Elizabeth walked through to the balcony without putting on the lights. She opened the doors and then returned to the kitchen, where she mixed herself a gin and tonic to drink outside,

She enjoyed Ben's company but hoped he did not think there was the prospect of romance between them. She doubted he would. Elizabeth suspected she was not much of a catch at the moment.

He seemed like a nice guy, albeit a little sullen and prone to awkward silences, but she believed he might become a good friend. Her mother often told her she could never have enough friends.

Elizabeth sat in silence, listening to people enjoying themselves and wondering if it was time she found someone who could be more than just a friend.

Nick took a last look at the grounds. The complex was in complete darkness, with lights on in only a few apartments. His uncle's apartment was not one of them. He pulled the curtains across the patio door before making himself a coffee and sitting on the balcony. He sent a text to Gemma. She eventually replied, saying she would see him tomorrow unless he had something else he needed to do.

DAY 9 - SUNDAY 1 AUGUST

Kylie and Sara became increasingly incensed as Gemma provided further background about why Becky was in their room, her role in the blackmail, and why she was upset. Kylie thought it was no more than the bitch deserved, while Sara wanted to kill her while she was unconscious on the sofa.

The anger was palpable, and things needed calming down. Gemma gave an impromptu lecture in which she advised her friends to put recent developments behind them as there was no point getting angry. She told them that they deserved better than this, that there were plenty of other fish in the sea and that they still had a week of their holiday left. They would never have to set eyes on the two arseholes again if they didn't want to, but Gemma would ensure they enjoyed themselves. She deliberately kept Nick out of the conversation as she was not confident he would feature in their plans.

Sara borrowed a set of screwdrivers from the hotel handyman, pretending she needed to fix her glasses. She used them to remove the hard disk from the laptop. She smashed the disk several times with a rock before dumping it in the hotel's refuge,

The sun rose as Gemma, Kylie, and Sara walked the hung-over Becky back to her house. Their unexpected guest said she would spend the day in bed, her parents would be at the shop, and she could ignore any callers. On the way back, the girls stopped at the internet café to drop off the laptop.

Jon and Leah sat silently, sipping their coffee on the balcony as the kids played in the apartment.

"When are you going to tell me what's wrong?"

Jon forced a smile. "Nothing's wrong. I am just thinking about getting the money to start our business."

"Come off it, Jon. I know the difference between when you are thinking and when you are worrying. This is you worrying."

There was no point in arguing. Jon explained that he took the sim card and checked his messages while waiting for the pizza. He was startled when she asked, "Is that all?"

"Isn't it enough? I've lost my job, Leah."

"Thank God for that. Now you have no choice but to do what we said. I'll get a loan off Mum to tide us over, and we'll put the house on the market as soon as we get back."

"But..."

"No buts Jon. This is our chance to make a fresh start. It's our opportunity to do everything we have talked about for years. It will be the making of us."

"Hmm," said Jon, contemplating ringing Rob Cromwell and apologising.

"And no stupid ideas about calling Rob to ask for your job back because the terms will be worse, and they'll screw you every way they can. We'll never have another holiday."

"But we might not be able to afford one anyway."

"Maybe, but I have a good feeling about this. This is our big chance. We need to be bold and hold firm. Even if Rob Cromwell rings to apologise and offers you a partnership, you must turn him down."

"Okay," said Jon, unsure whether he would ever be that brave if the invitation came but confident that it would not.

Ben yawned as he said, "Good morning."

"Hi, Dad. You okay?"

"I'm fine, thanks." Ben filled the kettle and nodded at Will as he entered the room. "Morning."

"Don't you morning me. What time did you get in last night? We were worried sick. You know you are supposed to be in bed by ten." Will winked. "And if you weren't, you should have come home."

"Boom boom, " said Ben, tilting his head at Will while

speaking to Shirley. "He's in a good mood today."

"Always in a good mood, me," said Will. "Especially when my beloved father-in-law is about to make me a cup of tea. I like new experiences."

"Don't get too used to it," laughed Ben.

Gemma's lack of verbal communication suggested to Nick something was amiss, but no matter how often he asked her, she refused to elaborate.

"Nothing is the matter. Stop going on. You're like a stuck record."

"But you've hardly said a word since we got here. It's not like you."

"How would you know? You've only known me a week."

"A week is long enough if you carry on like this."

She didn't know if the threat was genuine, but she didn't want to take a risk until she heard his side of the story. Sitting up on her towel, she said, "It's just that I thought I would have seen or heard from you last night."

"I sent you messages, and I called at your hotel."

"What time was this? We were up late."

"It was about eleven. I didn't come up. I bumped into Candice. She was looking for Becky." Nick kept talking despite the lack of response. "Candice told me about Kylie getting dumped."

"So why didn't you come up?"

"She suggested I leave you in peace. She thought you had things to discuss with Kylie, and it might not be appropriate for me to show up. They might think we were rubbing their noses in it."

The honesty was reassuring. "Oh. Really? What did you do then?"

"I walked her back to her house, returned to the apartment, and surfed the net for a bit before going to bed."

"Didn't you take her for a drink or anything?"

Nick lay on his back, hands behind his head, and his face

turned towards her. “Nah, to be honest, I don’t like her. She’s too full of herself.”

The honesty was more than comforting. Gemma felt better with every word coming from his mouth. “So, you didn’t try anything?

“What me? With her? No chance. She invited me in, and I know I’m not the quickest on the uptake, but she made it clear what I could expect if I accepted.”

“What did you say?”

“Not a lot. I told her that I was seeing you and wasn’t interested in her.”

The honesty was positively uplifting. “Really?”

“Yeah.”

“How did she react to that?”

“She called me names as I walked off.”

The honesty deserved a reward. Gemma rolled on top of him and kissed him.

“Mummy and Daddy were doing that the other morning when I walked into their bedroom. Mummy had no knickers on,” said Daisy.

Jon and Leah stared at each other and gasped.

“They hang us every time,” said Jon.

Gemma rolled back onto her towel, trying not to laugh too loudly.

Daisy sat beside her. “Do you like my new wristband?” She asked, holding her arm up for Gemma to see.

“That’s lovely, very colourful. Did you make it?”

“Yes, Lucia gave me a kit when we met her for coffee. Would you like me to make you one?”

“What? A coffee? There’s nowhere to plug the kettle in?”

Daisy tittered, “Not a coffee, silly, a wristband.”

“Ah, right. Yes, please. Can I have one just like yours?”

“You can,” said Daisy. “I will make it this evening when the babies are in bed. I can’t use the pack when they are around. They get things everywhere.”

“I see,” said Gemma, stifling a giggle as Leah rolled her

eyes.

"Good morning," said Nick as the boys stood beside him. "Are you two going to behave yourselves today?"

"No," said Charlie.

Harry giggled as he shook his head.

"Oh, I'm going to have to watch out, am I?" Nick rose to a sitting position.

"Yes," said Harry, backing away.

Charlie turned, ready to run.

"Well, we'd better start by throwing you in the sea!"

Nick sprang up as the boys ran away. He chased them, grabbed them, and, with one under each arm, carried them into the sea. They roared as Nick threatened to drop them into the water.

Daisy collected her utensils and started building castles in the shade of the tree a few feet away. Jon fussed with the umbrella, and Leah unrolled their towels.

"I hope you don't mind us bothering you again," said Leah. "It's just that as soon as the kids spot you, they make a beeline to where you are."

"It's not a problem," said Gemma. "They are cool kids and great fun. You two are not bad company either, but the kids are more our age."

"Watch it!" said Leah, chuckling. "It wasn't long ago we were love's young dream like you too. Now, look at us."

Jon breathed in as he placed a hand on each hip. "Speak for yourself; I still am love's young dream."

"Of course you are, sweetheart. Well, in your world, you are anyway," said Leah, winking at Gemma. "But I am not sure your physique quite measures up to Nick's."

"You wait until I go back to the gym. I could be an Adonis as well."

"I am not sure I would call Nick an Adonis," said Gemma. "But he's fit, and he has great stamina."

"Oh right," Jon smirked as he did a double take.

"No, I don't mean it like that," said Gemma. "I mean, he

runs a lot…and can keep going…"

Leah put a hand on Gemma's shoulder. "It's okay, Gemma. When you are in a hole, it is best to stop digging. You don't have to explain yourself. He's a nice lad, and you're a lovely girl. You make a nice couple."

"Do you think so?"

"I do,"

Gemma's eyes followed Nick at the water's edge. "But we've only just met."

"Well, if you find a good one, what difference does it make when you find him? It's what you do with him that matters."

"Can we change the subject?" Jon asked. "It's a bit early in the morning for this talk."

"That's not what Daisy just told us," Gemma said.

Daisy heard her name mentioned but had no idea what the grown-ups had found so hilarious about it.

Ben and Shirley sat on the steps to their apartment block, waiting for Will to join them.

"Are you having a good time, Dad?"

"Yes, I am. Now, stop worrying about me and enjoy yourself."

"I can't help being concerned. You hardly left the house for the last few months, and I wonder if …well, you are trying too hard?"

Ben looked puzzled. "At what?"

"Showing me that you are having fun."

"I am having fun. Look around you, Shirl. We have glorious weather, a beautiful beach, a luxurious apartment, and lovely food, and I'm making new friends. How could I not enjoy myself?"

"I am …umm…pleased to hear that." She fidgeted on the step.

"Out with it. You are exactly like your mother when it comes to saying something you are unsure you should say. She stammers, fidgets and looks uncomfortable."

"It's just that I don't know what made you change your mind about coming here. You were dead against it for ages, but miraculously, you told us you'd like to come at almost the last minute."

"Your uncle had a word with me. He told me to stop being a miserable old fart. He reminded me how lucky I am to have a daughter like you and threatened to drag me to the airport and push me on the plane."

"And that's it? Depression over, just like that?"

"I was not depressed; I was just feeling sorry for myself. What have I got to be depressed about?"

"Losing your parents, wife and business in quick succession, possibly? Any of those things would be enough for most people."

"I must admit that losing your nan and grandad hurt me. It hurt me a lot. Your mother's departure was a surprise, but if I am honest, I knew something was up. " Ben raised a hand to tell Shirley not to interrupt. "I do miss the business more than I thought I would. It has taken me a while to adjust, but I think I'm getting over it now and know what I want to do next."

"Which is?"

"I won't tell you at the moment, but you'll know all about it by the time this holiday ends."

"Hmm, okay, but I think you need to talk to someone when we get home."

"Talk about what?"

"You know what, your depression, your feelings..."

"Give it a rest, Shirley. I've told you I am not depressed. I will not discuss personal feelings with a stranger."

"You wouldn't need to. We had a great counselling team in the business. I can get one of them to speak to you."

"Can you imagine me discussing my life with an ex-employee? They'd laugh me out of the room." Ben mocked. "What have you got to be miserable about? You're loaded."

"They don't think like that."

"There is no need to involve them or anybody else. I'm fine. Anyway, when did you become my mother?"

When my mum left...I worry about you, Dad. I don't want you to do anything silly."

"Like have a good time, you mean?"

"No. I am pleased if you really are enjoying this break. Of course I am, but you have been so low these last few months, and I am not sure you can cure...whatever has been wrong with you by self-diagnosis."

"There is nothing to cure. Honestly, love, I am fine." He stood and placed his hand on her shoulder. "All I needed was a kick up the bum. Your uncle gave me just that. There is nothing for you to worry about. There is nothing to diagnose. Before you say it, the fact that I have a few drinks on this trip doesn't mean I am self-medicating."

Will had joined the pair without either of them noticing. "I tried self-medication once, but it didn't work. When I sobered up, my problems were still with me."

Shirley stood and grabbed his arm. "I told you I wasn't going anywhere. You are stuck with me no matter what. You don't get rid of me that easily."

"You are never a problem." They kissed. "I don't know what I would do without you."

Ben shook his head theatrically. "Yuk! Please. Not in front of the child."

Donny was nervous about meeting their business partner alone in the office above the café. His sister was better at dealing with him but had gone to see Christiano. He hid the dismembered laptop and cursed himself for being so stupid. He should have connected the thing to his system. That was a harsh lesson to learn.

Graham and Donny watched the latest video, and Donny was mightily relieved when Graham told him he was ecstatic about the video's content, which showed Candice's liaison with his business contact.

Graham handed over a bundle of notes.“Here, have this. It includes a bonus. She is worth every penny.”

“Thank you,” said Donny, checking the bundle. He estimated he had three times more than the figure agreed.

“I think Marcus will have a lot to consider when I make him the offer. When will you finish the editing?”

“By the end of the week, is that okay?”

“That’s fine. He and his family are here until a week Saturday. I won’t approach him before then. I will send it when they go home..” He scratched his goatee. “Rewind to the bit where he slaps her.” Donny turned the dial. “That’s very good, very nice. She looks so young. How old is she?”

“Nineteen.”

“You could knock five years off that. Have we introduced this angel to our other friends at the Bull Ring?”

“No, we’ve kept her secret, using her only for special events. We’ve tried to ensure she doesn’t get too well known.”

“Good thinking. People pay good money for someone who looks as young as that, but she won’t stay that way forever. We need to take advantage of her looks and undoubted skills while we can. You should use her more.”

“Okay,” said Donny. “I’ll arrange it.”

“Have you booked someone special to be available on Wednesday?”

“Christiano has selected Becky for the job. It will be her first time with a client.”

“New blood. Good, very good. We may have to postpone it by a week, but I can confirm tomorrow. Are you and Chris all set for Ibiza next weekend?”

“Looking forward to it.”

“It should be fun. Louise mentioned I am having the café painted while we are away?”

“She did.”

“Good. It looks run down. Manuel can chirp it up a bit. I am not sure he was keen on the idea, but he saw sense. His boys will erect the scaffolding in the next couple of days" Graham's eyes ceased surveying the room and focused on Donny, who was ogling the bundle of cash. "Make sure you take a cut of that bonus. You've earned it. You've done very well."

"Thank you. I will. Don't worry about that." Donny had already decided that Candice would not get much of a share. He needed a new laptop.

Something was troubling Gemma, but Nick resisted pressing her for information. Halfway through their tapas, he got his first clue about her thoughts.

"What sort of security does your cousin's café have?"

Nick shrugged. "Not sure. Why?"

"You must have some idea. You visited the place. Do they have security cameras, remote sensors and stuff?"

"What, like they do in Mission Impossible, you mean? You do know that is mostly fiction."

"So what do they have?"

Nick stopped eating and thought about it. "They have CCTV on the outside and in the internet café. I didn't see anything in the office, but they probably keep the doors locked."

"Where do they keep the keys?"

"Why are you so interested?"

Gemma was drinking her milkshake through a straw and looked at him over the top of her sunglasses. She checked, and the other customers were not listening. "If I tell you something, will you promise not to tell anyone else?"

"Of course."

"Swear on your mother's life."

"I swear on my mother's life. I should say I don't believe in that crap."

"Nor do I, but I wasn't sure what else to say. The thing is..."

Gemma told him about the blackmail, his cousins' involvement and her friends' sex tapes. Between them, the girls thought they had identified what their subsequent actions needed to be. They planned to break into the internet café and crash the system. That way, they could be sure the videos of the other girls would no longer be public.

Nick warned against doing that. He thought that Donny and Co would guess who had crashed the system and come looking for Gemma and her friends. He thought wiping the files remotely after the girls had gone home would be better.

He recalled the notice board and the passwords and suggested he could get into the office and take a picture of the board. Nick was confident that would help them gain access to the system.

Before they did anything, he would speak to his boss, Chris, who could advise him on what needed to be done.

They agreed that Nick would make the call and catch up with the girls later.

Leah and Jon each held one of Harry's hands as he walked between them and gently swung him. The child cackled and told them to do it again.

Daisy and Charlie had walked to the complex's gates and waited patiently for their parents and brother to arrive.

"I spy with my little eye something beginning with g," Daisy said.

Charlie looked around. "Sand."

"No, silly. Sand begins with s. You want something starting with a gah."

"Gah gah green sand." Charlie chuckled and repeated his answer. "Green sand."

"You babies are too little to play grown-up games."

Arriving at his apartment block, Nick turned when someone called his name.

"Neek, Neek, what are you doing this evening?"

"I think we are going out with Kylie and Sara," Nick said, waiting for Javier to catch up. "Why do you ask?"

"My father is performing at a hotel in Porto Colom. Would you like to come with us? He likes us to attend. We help get people up dancing."

Nick immediately thought of Candice and Becky's help to his cousins but knew there was a big difference in the roles and outcome. "Performing? What does he do?"

"Flamenco. He and his friends play guitar and dance, and then the audience joins in. Sometimes it is very funny. You and Gemma seemed keen to dance last Friday."

"Hmm," said Nick.

"There is free food and cheap drink. It will be great fun."

Nick wasn't sure Gemma and her friends would be delighted at the news, but he did not want to upset his new friend. "That sounds different. I'll have a word. How would we get there?"

"I can pick you up at the Happy Bar in two hours. Sergio and Costas are coming too."

"Will we all fit in one car?"

"No, we will travel in two cars. They will be in Sergio's, but we can set off together."

He thought of something that might persuade Gemma it was worth going. "Do you think they could take Kylie and Sara?"

"I am sure that would be okay. I am meeting my girlfriend there, but the boys are going alone. They sometimes try very hard to meet the tourists. If you know what I mean."

They may not have to try that hard tonight, Nick thought, asking, "What time does it end?"

"Do you need a beauty sleep?"

"I think I'd need a coma! No, the girls are bound to ask."

"The show closes at midnight, but afterwards we can go to a club I know near the hotel. The prices are lower than around here. We can return whenever you are ready."

"Great," said Nick. "We'll see you in a couple of hours."

Nick provided as much detail as possible to Chris

Shanklin, who agreed this sounded a nasty business. He told Nick to think very carefully before taking action. They did not know who else might be involved. Christiano and Nick's cousins might work for a dangerous criminal.

Nick told his boss about Gemma's plan to visit the internet café and delete all the data. Chris doubted this was the wisest move. It would be better to wipe the films after Nick and Gemma left the island.

Nick said he knew where to get the passwords, but Chris asked him to wait until he explored the site. Chris wanted to check if he could get full access without the passwords.

Chris said he would be delighted to remove the incriminating films, provided Nick didn't try anything stupid. He repeated that he might not need the passwords, so Nick should not rush into action.

With the kids crashed out, Jon in the shower, and the wine uncorked and ready to drink, Leah took out her tablet and reviewed her list of barriers to setting up their business. Money remained the most significant problem. Leah knew that Mum would help, but she wanted her mother to enjoy her remaining years in comfort. She had to balance finishing the work quickly and leaving Mum with enough money to enjoy life. The loan would get repaid, but it might take time.

When Nick entered the hotel bar, he immediately heard the familiar sound of Sara laughing. He was relieved, as he feared a dark cloud might be hanging over proceedings.

"Hello, ladies,"

Kylie and Sara said hello. Gemma waited until he had kissed her. "Hello, you," she said.

"I hope you don't mind. I arranged with Javier that we will see his father perform a Flamenco show tonight."

Gemma did not look delighted. "But we said we would all go out."

"Don't worry about us," said Sara. "You go ahead and

enjoy yourselves."

"Sounds lovely." Kylie was also giggling.

"Have you two brought your dancing shoes?" Nick asked. "You're coming too."

"You what?" Kylie asked. "Why did you think we'd be interested in Spanish dancing?"

"Because it will be fun," said Nick. "They get people from the audience to have a go. Javier says some of them are hysterical."

"Sounds hilarious," said Kylie, stone-faced. "I repeat, why would you think we'd be interested?"

"There's free food and cheap drink."

"You're not selling it to us," said Sara.

"Okay, what if I told you I arranged for Sergio and Costas to collect you at seven, take you to the venue, and spend all evening with you? There would be no distractions." Nick sat next to Gemma.

Kylie and Sara stared at each other. Kylie checked her watch.

"Really?" Kylie asked.

"Really," said Nick.

Kylie's face lit up.

Sara trotted around the table and hugged Nick, kissing his cheek. "This bloke is the best," she said, kissing him again.

"I think so, too," said Kylie, kissing his spare cheek. "Come on, Sar, we'd better get our dancing gear on."

Elizabeth was waiting in the foyer as promised. "New hat?"

Ben nodded. "I bought it today. I could use a new one." He stretched the bottom of his shirt. "I got this too. It's not too big, is it?"

"Not at all. You look very smart."

"Thank you. You don't look too bad yourself." He spotted the flowers. "They are lovely. How much do I owe you."

"You can buy the wine. Lucia told me she likes Rioja and has written down the name of her favourite bottle."

Will threw his last dart and totted up his score. "That leaves me double eight."

"I need double sixteen." Shirley took aim, threw the dart and hit her target. "Three games to one to me."

"Best of seven?"

"Nah, let's have something to eat."

The pair left the darts on the board and took a table in the restaurant. The waiter was on them instantly, left them a couple of menus, and went to get their drinks.

"This holiday hasn't turned out as I had expected."

"In what way?"

"I thought your father would be with us all the time. He surprised me. It wasn't so long along that we had the work of the world to get him out of the house. Since he's been here, we can't keep him in."

Shirley wasn't sure if this development was wholly positive. "I just hope he doesn't make a fool of himself."

"Why should he? He is only having a bit of fun."

"I know that love, but…well, he's off with those two ladies. We don't know them from Adam, and they could be robbing him blind."

"Or they could be lovely and are doing him a world of good. Ben's not stupid. You said you'd rather he go out enjoying himself than stay home all day."

"I know, and I still think that, but he's acting like a teenager. He's been drinking to the early hours, going on trips, and buying new clothes today."

"A shirt and a hat hardly constitute a new wardrobe, do they?"

"No, but I hope he doesn't do something stupid."

"Good luck to him, I say. He deserves to be happy, and I am sure he will be fine."

"I suppose you are right. It is nice to see him smile. I

want Dad to be happy. My stupid, selfish mother has taken so much from him."

Will said nothing.

"By the way, we might need to access that money soon."

Will was surprised. "What's happened?"

"It looks like Captain Fitness has done a runner."

"When?"

"He hasn't been home for two days. Mum told me this morning. She said they hardly spoke in the last couple of weeks, and he has been out seeing friends a lot. When she returned from the hairdresser's this morning, his clothes, a stack of cash, and valuables were missing."

"Doesn't sound very promising. Poor old Cheryl. I can sort that out."

"Thanks. Mum has already told Dad, but he didn't seem interested."

"Do you think she wants to come back?"

"Probably. My mother doesn't do well on her own."

The waiter delivered two large beers and a saucer of nibbles. "Thank you. I never liked these things," said Will, taking an olive. "But now I think they're da iawn."

Nick and Gemma left the balcony area and found a quiet space in one of the hotel's bars. Gemma collected drinks and sat on the wicker chairs. "What did your boss say?"

Nick relayed the essence of his chat with Chris.

"How long do we give him? We are going home on Saturday."

"We'd better check with him on Thursday to make sure he has all the access he needs. If he does, we can leave it to him to do what is necessary while we return to the UK. If he doesn't, we would still have time to help him overcome any issues."

"It's a big gamble, and that does not help Becky, who is supposed to see that guy on Wednesday."

Nick sipped his lager. He was getting a taste for it. "I wouldn't have thought Becky was your main priority. She is one of the reasons Sara and Kylie are in the proverbial."

"I know that, but she is just a kid…"

"She's not much younger than us."

"Yes, but she's got a lot of growing up to do. She thought she was in love." Gemma stopped talking long enough to suck her drink through the straw. "I can't help comparing her to our Kate. She does some silly things. I would hate to think of anyone abusing her in this way."

"Your sister would probably be too sensible to get involved in anything like this."

"I'd like to think so, but who knows what she might do if some charmer came along and swept her off her feet."

"I tell you what, I'll call Chris in the morning to see if he has had any luck. If not, I'll get into the office and photograph the passwords. That should help him get access. I'll tell him to make Becky's video a priority. If the footage exists, I'll get him to wipe Kylie from the system. He will probably be able to make it look like the system failed."

"But won't they upload it again? Do they have backups?"

Nick remembered something he had not told Chris Shanklin. He leaned forward in his chair. "Shit, I forgot they keep backup drives in the store room. We need to do something with them." He put his elbow on the arm of the chair and his fingers to his mouth as he considered options.

"They are bound to notice they are gone?"

"Hmmm, probably. Perhaps Chris can tell me how to corrupt them and make them unusable. I'll have to think about the best way to get in."

"You are seriously thinking of breaking in?"

"I was hoping I could casually call in to see Donny and distract him while I snapped the passwords, but getting at the backups will be harder. Donny is hardly likely to let me walk out with his stuff."

"I'm coming with you."

"Hang on a second…"

"No. I will not let you put yourself at risk for my friends.

I've got you into this mess, and it's only fair I help you get us out of it."

"But if we get caught..."

Gemma picked up her glass and sipped again as she sat back. "We won't. I have complete trust in my Welsh guardian angel."

Nick smiled but was not convinced.

The sound of guitars was filtering through the outside terrace. Gemma stood and held out a hand for Nick to take. "We can worry about that tomorrow. Come on. We've got to show the Spanish how to dance," she said.

The meal at Lucia's was a great success. Afterwards, with her grandson fast asleep, the hostess joined the other two on her small balcony.

Elizabeth filled their glasses with wine. "That was delicious, Lucia. Thank you, and well done."

Lucia waved her arms in the air. "It was nothing. I am glad you enjoyed it."

Ben muttered agreement while studying a mosaic on the wall. "This is good," he said, running his hand over the tiles.

"My daughter, Gabriela, did that. She is very..." She spoke to Elizabeth. "Artistica?"

"Artistic".

Lucia nodded. "She is very artistic."

Ben took the last seat. "You have a lovely home."

"Thank you. It is small, and there are too many of us, but we make it comfortable. What is your house like Elizabeth?"

"It is called a cottage, but it is just a standard two up, two down." She expanded on her explanation for Lucia's benefit.

"What about you, Ben? How big is your house?"

He sipped his drink. "It has five bedrooms, six bathrooms, a kitchen and three reception rooms. Plus, I have a conservatory, double garage and a large garden, so it is quite big."

"Wow! You live in a grand villa," said Lucia. "You must

have a big family?"

"No, I live alone. My daughter and grandchildren live two hours down the road, and my wife lives elsewhere."

"Like my husband," said Lucia. "You must have plenty of guests and hold many parties."

"No, not many."

Lucia looked from Ben to Elizabeth and back again. "Then why do you need a big house?"

"It seemed like a good idea at the time."

"If you have such a big house, a lovely daughter and grandchildren, why do you always look so sad?"

Elizabeth almost choked on her wine. "Lucia. That is none of our business."

"He is in my home. He ate my food. He is drinking my wine…well, yes, he bought the wine, and we are talking. It is my business."

Elizabeth started to speak, but Ben held up a hand. "It's okay. I don't mind."

He explained how his parents died close together, his wife encouraging him to sell the business before running off, taking half of everything, and then his medical diagnosis. He said he had spent much time alone in his house, but his daughter had forced him to come on holiday. "I am enjoying myself, but I've still got a lot on my mind, " he said with a half-hearted smile.

"What? You think you have a bad life because of that?"

"Lucia, don't be so mean." Elizabeth patted Ben's arm. "I am sorry about that."

"Why do you apologise to him? He has nothing to be sad about. He is, how you say? A spoilt brat."

"Lucia!"

Ben was not embarrassed. He asked what made Lucia the expert on suffering.

Lucia denied she ever said she was an expert or was suffering. She thought Ben had no reason to be sad and should not worry so much. She told her companions that her father died when he was fifty, and her mother passed at forty-nine. Lucia was approaching forty-eight but did not have time to fret about what might happen. She had to take care of her family.

Gabriela had been a promising student but met a twenty-two-year-old boy who got her pregnant. The boy dumped her and wanted nothing more to do with her. Lucia's husband could not accept that his daughter was pregnant at fifteen and went to live with his sister. Her son, Javier, caught up with Gabriela's ex-boyfriend and beat him. Javier was arrested and sent to prison for three months. When he exited prison, her son used drugs and drank too much. Luckily, his uncle paid for Javier to visit a Palma clinic. Lucia's brother then hired his nephew and trained him as a baker. Gabriela had a lovely son but had to work to help pay for things when Lucia wanted her to continue her education and become an artist. Lucia did three jobs and disliked all of them. Her husband mellowed about the baby and tried to help, sometimes financially, but Gabriela wanted nothing to do with her father.

"And we live in a two-bedroom apartment overlooking a wasteland." Lucia cast an arm out toward the field. "Javier has to sleep on the couch." She picked up her wine but, before taking a drink, said, "I am the one who should be miserable."

Elizabeth and Lucia exchanged harsh words in Spanish, which Ben could not understand. The disagreement ended when Elizabeth stood and said she was leaving.

"Please stay." Lucia shook her head before sipping her wine. "I am sorry, Ben. Elizabeth is correct. It is not your fault. I have had bad news today, and I am upset and worried about what to do." She took another sip. "I should not put my burdens on you. I am sure we'll be okay."

"What's happened?" Elizabeth asked, reaching for Lucia's arm.

"Gabriela will soon be out of work, and nothing is around here unless she works all day. She cannot do that because of the baby, and I cannot afford not to work."

Lucia needed little persuasion to provide more details.

Gabriela's boss was selling the supermarket because it was not making enough money. Gabriela and Lucia had tried to tell him that he should open a bakery and vary his stock, but he wouldn't listen. He intended to close the supermarket at the end of August and would put the building on the market immediately.

Ben said he knew something about running a food store and offered to speak to the owner. He might be able to provide him with advice. Lucia said the owner was stubborn and had decided to sell, so that was it. She thanked Ben for the offer and apologised again for the outburst, although she added that she still believed he had no reason to be so miserable. "You have a wonderful life, Ben. You have a lovely house, a loving family and plenty of money. You must appreciate what you have. No está la felicidad en vivir, sino en saber vivir."

Elizabeth translated. "There is not happiness in living but knowing how to live."

The flamenco evening was indeed hilarious. The Brits were pathetic dancers compared to the Spanish but proved a source of much hilarity. During the intermission, Javier joined his father in an unrehearsed recital of traditional Spanish tunes on their acoustic guitars. In the show's second half, Javier demonstrated that he was also a natural at dancing. His girlfriend was no slouch either.

Gemma found it strange that Nick appeared to have no musicality and worked hard to loosen him up. Sergio and Costas seemed more interested in Sara and Kylie than dancing.

After the show, the eight went to a nearby club and danced less formally into the early hours.

"So, do you feel like you've been put in your place?"

Ben laughed and then nodded. "I most certainly have been. I don't think I have been spoken to like that since my father gave me a bollocking for missing an exam." He fell quiet, staring at the sea. "He had a point as well, though."

"You think Lucia has a point? I think she was out of order speaking to you like that."

"And you told her so. At least, I think you did. You were both going for it in Spanish. I had no chance. My Spanish is terrible. Thank you for sticking up for me."

"I don't think Lucia meant to be so harsh. She has a lot on her plate, and the Spanish take a different view of mental illness."

"Are you suggesting I have a mental illness?"

"I don't think there is any doubt. From where I stand, and I am no expert, I would say you have or have had depression."

"I was just a bit down…"

"I get down sometimes but don't spend long periods moping around the house." Elizabeth regretted her tone. "I didn't mean that to sound like it did."

"It's okay. Shirley keeps saying the same thing. She wants me to see a therapist when I get back."

"Will you?"

"I don't know. I find it hard to open up to strangers."

"You've spoken to Lucia and me."

"I suppose I have, but…"

"No buts. You need to speak to someone about how you feel."

"I'll be fine. I'm having a great time here. I feel much better even though my face might not show it."

"But what happens when you get home, and you are on your own again, having to face whatever treatment the doctors have planned."

"I am not sure I want to go home, and I don't think I can start the treatment." Elizabeth's jaw dropped. Ben continued. "My parents both died of cancer, and now I have it. Even if they get rid of it, it will probably reappear."

"You don't know that. You must give yourself the best chance of surviving."

"So everyone keeps telling me, but I'm a grown-up. I can

make my own decisions."

"You also have grown-up responsibilities. You should think of your daughter. Think of the pain and grief you will cause her."

"It will happen one day. I can't live forever."

"But she will have time to prepare. If you don't give the treatment a go, I dread how Shirley will react."

"You've hardly spoken to her. How do you know how she will react?"

"From what you say, she is a caring, loving daughter, so she'll be broken-hearted..." She sighed. Ben offered no response. Elizabeth tapped the side of his head. "Only you know what is going on in there. At the very least, think about it some more. Better still, talk to a professional when you get home. If you still decide not to have the treatment after that, then at least you have discussed it with someone else."

Ben stood and nodded. "Okay. I will give it some thought. I must admit, though, I was expecting a sterner rebuke."

Elizabeth smiled. "It's been a long day."

STRUGGLES
(SIX MONTHS BEFORE THE HOLIDAY)

"Nick, hello. How are you doing? How is your mother?"

"We're fine, thanks, Mark. It's been hard work, but we're getting there."

The pair shook hands, and Nick followed the man in a white overall into a glass-walled office. The room was empty except for two long tables across the centre, one of which was covered by two large cardboard boxes.

"You'll have to excuse us. We have the decorators in, and this room is next on the list." He pointed to the boxes. "Do you want to sift through that stuff here?"

"I'll probably just take it away if you don't mind."

"That's totally up to you. Can you let me know what you're looking for? I might be able to help."

"We are still trying to find Dad's laptop."

"There's nothing electrical in there, I'm afraid. Lots of papers but no laptop."

"That's a shame. The papers might give us clues about where the money went."

Mark Eastley, site director and Kenneth's ex-boss, said, "Good luck."

"It'll keep Mum and me busy for a few nights. Thanks for letting me know that you'd found them."

"Sorry, it took so long. Someone sent the boxes to the archive, and they came up for review. That's the only reason we found them."

He lifted the lid of the first box and looked inside.

"Are these all my dad's papers?"

"I think so. Sally looked through them, and she said they belonged to Kenneth. If anyone knew, it would be her. She was his PA for years. I don't know how useful they might be, but hopefully, they might shed some light on things."

"Thanks...I hope so. That would be brilliant." Nick looked at a photocopy of an expense form, which sparked a question. "I know it was long ago, but I don't suppose my father was owed any money from his expenses. I remember he was just back from Germany when the stroke hit him. Is he owed anything for that trip by any chance?"

Mark shook his head. "No, I don't think so."

"Can you check? I know it was a long time ago."

"I doubt there is anything to check."

Nick was not giving up. "But if I can identify any expenditure not covered by his work-related credit card statements, can you check if he got reimbursed? If not, can we still claim that money back? He may have made a couple of other trips, too. I remember that just before he went to Germany, he had been to Sweden and Denmark for a week. He might not have claimed for that?"

"I'm Sorry, Nick. Your father wasn't owed any expenses." Mark Eastley's expression was solemn.

"How can you be so sure?"

"Because he gave up the foreign visits after his last promotion. He hadn't been overseas with work for a couple of years before he was...taken ill."

Nick's mouth fell open as he struggled to take in this news.

"But that can't be right. He was away several times during his last year, sometimes for a week or longer. Are you sure it wasn't for work?"

"Yes, Nick, I am absolutely sure. Your father was desk-bound for the last two years of his time here. In that period, as far as I can remember, he never missed a day apart from holidays and the odd day off to spend time on his boat."

"But he told us he was overseas. Where would he have gone? What was he doing?" Nick knew Mark would have no answers to his questions, but he wished he had.

Ben opened his eyes and stared at the ceiling. Another night over, another nightmare day beginning. His sleep had been reasonably peaceful. He felt rested. If he had dreams, he could not recall them. His mind was blank, but that was not unusual these days.

His hand roamed the space that his wife once occupied. The timing of her departure had floored him. He had not anticipated that news coming his way so soon. She said the joy had gone out of their marriage. She criticised Ben for losing his mojo. What had happened to the old Ben? The one she loved? The one she had helped to build a business empire? Where had the real Ben gone? The one who never used to be afraid of trying new things.

His life had never recovered from a series of disasters. It was Cheryl's idea to sell the business. The offer was a generous one, but Ben wanted to decline. He loved his work and planned to extend their chain of shops into Lancashire and Yorkshire. The surveyors had identified scores of suitable buildings, but Cheryl had been insistent. It was time for them to relax and enjoy their lives. His parents' illnesses proved that nobody knew how long they had left. She said they should travel more. She wanted them to do what they always wanted, like going to the gym.

Ben presumed that Cheryl had met her "personal" trainer at the gym. He was so personable that he now shared her new home and drove around in a top-of-the-range Mercedes. Why hadn't she admitted that she wanted the money in the bank to make it easier to access her share when she walked away?

He still didn't know what she was talking about when she claimed that some of their money was missing. She must have spent it but forgotten what and where. He hadn't done anything with it. When did he get the chance? You only had to look at the state of the house, his shabby clothes and the state of his cars to realise he had not done much and certainly had not benefitted from any illicit transactions.

It was time to get up. Shirley and Will were right. Ben needed to move on. He just wished he could summon some enthusiasm. His daughter and son-in-law had provided tremendous support over the previous eighteen months. He was not sure he would have managed without them. As much as he loved them, he hoped they would stay away today. He was in no mood for visitors.

Jon Oliver tried again to get the boy to listen. Considering Richard had been brought in to make Jon's life easier, he proved very time-consuming.

"It's not rocket science. You need to list the invoices in date order so that we know when they are overdue."

"You said."

"Then why haven't you done it?"

"Why do I have to do this anyway? It's a secretary's job, not a director's."

Not this again. "Look, Rich, your dad wants you to learn the ropes so you can take over when he retires next year. You must understand every aspect of the business to learn how things work."

Richard's mobile rang.

"I thought I asked you to keep your mobile switched off in the office. You will never learn if you keep getting distracted."

"You did ask me, and I've decided to ignore you." Richard hit the button. "Hi gorgeous, what's up?"

Jon waited as Richard finished his call and was surprised when the lad rose from his seat and collected his coat.

"Where are you going now?"

"Lunch."

"But it's not eleven o'clock yet."

"Early lunch then." He left the office, slamming the door behind him.

"Did you speak to your Dad?" Will kissed his wife's cheek as she sat at the kitchen table.

"I rang, but he wasn't very talkative. He claimed to be engrossed in some cricket match or other."

"I never knew Ben liked cricket."

"Me neither, and I am sure I could hear the Archers' theme tune in the background."

"Shall we visit him on the weekend?"

"That would be nice, but we need an excuse for being in the area. Dad will get annoyed if he thinks we have travelled up to see him."

"I think there is racing at Chester on Saturday. We can tell him we came to see that."

Gemma Potter dropped her phone onto the bed, put her face into the pillow and howled. This was no ordinary cry. It was the wailing of a person in real pain. Gemma screamed at and thumped her pillow even though it was not to blame. Nobody was to blame, not really, but that knowledge did not make things any easier.

Her sister, Carrie, had been thrilled to learn she was having her first baby. Her parents were delighted at the prospect of becoming grandparents. Gemma and her sister, Kate, had teased each other about becoming maiden aunts. Carrie's husband bought his wife an enormous bouquet and fussed over her.

The families had drawn up plans covering essential equipment, clothing, childcare, schools and potential names but had made no plans in preparation for a miscarriage.

Gemma felt like shit but sensed her sister would be feeling far worse. She took some comfort from knowing that Carrie was surrounded by a strong support group who would ensure she was okay. Gemma would head south to lend her support first thing tomorrow. She could not do anything immediately. It was too late to travel, so Gemma cried alone.

DAY 10 - MONDAY 2 AUGUST

Ben had slept for less than three hours and yawned as he joined the others. He had said too much to the ladies and needed to find a way to ensure Shirley never heard what he had told Elizabeth about him not having the treatment.

"Morning, Ben, another fine day," said Will.

"Hmmm."

"Fancy a boiled egg, Dad, Will is just about to put some on."

"They'll never fit me," said Will.

Shirley groaned but then looked concerned at Ben's lack of any response. "Everything okay, Dad? I heard you walking about in the night. Anything wrong?"

"I'm fine. I had trouble sleeping, and I'm feeling it today."

"Too much partying, I expect," said Will. "Take a night off the ladies. You need a longer recovery time at your age."

Isabella Sanchez had just put a fly in the ear of one of her suppliers and was about to light her cigarette to celebrate.

Her office had a balcony providing exquisite views of her beloved Cape Town. Isabella liked nothing better than a coffee and a ciggie while taking in her favourite city's breathtaking beauty.

Her sightseeing was disturbed by the ringing of a telephone in the outer office. Her secretary put through the call. The voice was British, possibly English.

"Hello, am I speaking to Isabella?"

She did not recognise the voice, and the display showed "number withheld."

"You are, but who is this? How did you get this number?"

"I will explain in a moment. You don't know me, but please listen to what I say. I assure you I am trying to help, so please give me a minute."

"You want to help me? What do you mean? How can you help me?" She listened to the silence. "You have ten seconds."

The male caller took a deep breath. "You were in Majorca recently."

She was unaware this was public knowledge, but she had not kept it secret. "I was."

"And you stayed in Sa Coma."

"That might have been the name of the place. What is this about?"

"I think someone will be contacting you very soon. They will try to blackmail you."

"Blackmail me? Why? How?"

"They have a video of you."

"And?"

He was finding it challenging to be blunt. "The video shows you having sex with three men."

"What?" Isabella took support from the edge of her desk. "That's impossible. Who are you? What do you want?"

"I am trying to help you. Honestly, I am. I think...well, I know that someone is going to contact you asking you for money, probably demanding monthly payments, or they will bring the video to the attention of your friends and family and post it on porn sites."

Isabella took a deep breath. "How do you know this?"

"I am trying to help others in a similar position, and I discovered your video. The blackmailers have files containing your details. That's how I got your office number. I also have your mobile. "

She was finding this conversation surreal and challenging to comprehend. "Why do you think they will blackmail me?"

"Because it is what they have done with all the others. They wait until the victim leaves the island and, a short while later, send emails or texts requesting money. They have you marked down for a lot of money each month. They must think you are wealthy."

She knew they were correct in their assumption but said nothing. "If you can access the files, why not just destroy them?"

"I intend to, but I have to be careful not to leave any trace that allows them to find me. Some members of my team are still on the island, and I don't want anyone to hurt them or me. I believe there are evil people involved in this."

Isabella understood. "When do you propose to wipe these films?"

"At the weekend. On or around Saturday."

"Okay, and what do you want me to do?"

"Nothing."

"I don't understand. Why ring me if you don't want me to do anything?"

"It is imperative that when you get the email or text, or however they bring it to your attention, you don't do anything. Don't respond, don't pass it on to the authorities and certainly don't make any threats. We mustn't wind them up, or they may do something stupid. Just ignore them and leave it to me to get rid of the evidence."

"What if they call me?"

"They normally make contact by email or text; I don't think they would have the guts to speak to you."

The words 'spineless bastards' entered her mind. "How do I know you are telling the truth? Why should I trust you?"

"At the moment, I cannot think of any alternative. Please be assured that I am not doing this for personal gain. I am doing this to help you and the others. "

"You say others. How many others are there?"

"About forty in the last few years."

Her chair tilted as she moved her back. "That sounds like a lot. What do they do? How do these bastards get so many victims?"

"It looks to me like they pick up girls on holiday and persuade them to have sex, which they secretly film. I am not sure that all girls are willing participants. Some look like they are drugged.

"I have no memory of having sex with anyone on the island, so I guess I fall into the latter category. Am I correct?"

"Yes...sorry."

"It's not your fault. About forty you say?"

"Yeah, thirty-one have been uploaded. Another eight or nine, including yours, are waiting to go on the website."

She exhaled through a narrow gap in her lips. "They have been busy."

"They do well out of it."

"Not a business model I would wish to adopt."

"No...but I am hoping to bring that business to an end."

Isabella was reluctant to ask the question, but she had to know. "You say I am having sex with three men."

"Yes."

"What are we doing?"

"Honestly, you don't appear to be doing very much. It is as if you are dead to the world...sorry, That sounded terrible."

"It's okay. I'd rather you tell me." This was the news she had feared. She inhaled sharply. "What are they doing to me?"

"I'd rather not say."

"Why not?"

"Because...well, mainly because the video is too horrific."

"Am I that bad?" Isabella immediately apologised for her crass comment. "If I ask you questions, would you answer them? I will try to make it so you can answer in a few words."

"Okay."

"Do all three men have full penetrative sex with me?"

"No."

"How many?"

"Two."

"Am I engaged in anal sex?"

"Yes."

"With the same two men?"

"Yes."

She now knew why she had been uncomfortable. "Do they wear protection?"

"No."

That scared her. "Are the men English?"

"Two of the three men in the video are English, although one doesn't do much apart from showing off."

"Showing off? How, exactly?

"He waves his bits in front of your face while you are... err...but he never touches you. If he did, then it is not on the film."

"Can you tell the nationality of the other man?"

"He appears to be Spanish... having said that, he speaks in Spanish, but his accent is all over the place."

"You know a lot about him. How many times have you seen this video?"

"Just the once, but he talks a lot."

"Does either of the Englishmen have blonde hair?"

"No." She sighed with relief but gasped as the man added, "I think I know the one you mean, and he does appear in other films. Is his name Donny?"

"It is."

"In your case, I think he is doing the filming."

"How do you know that?"

"The recordings show everything from the names of the cameramen to filming location and the... er... details of the stars. Sorry, that was a very clumsy way of putting it."

"That's okay. Are these credits included on the video, like in the movies?"

"No. The details are contained in a file attached to each video."

Isabella had no idea why she asked that question. "From what you say, the bastards drugged me and then pimped me out so they could film me having sex with their friends. Is that your assessment?"

"Yes."

"What did I do to deserve this?"

"I don't know. You probably didn't do anything. They are chasing easy money."

"Do they use any toys or weapons on me?"

"No."

She wasn't sure that provided any reassurance. "Does the video show when filming took place?"

"It does. They recorded yours on Sunday, 25 July, between midnight and 3 am."

"The fucking bastards."

"I am sorry to bring you this news, but I promise to do my utmost to shut down the site. Before I do, I need to know if you want me to keep the film."

"Why the fuck would I?"

"I wasn't sure if you intended to notify the police. The video could be evidence."

There was no way anybody else was going to witness this atrocity, but she appreciated the offer. "Yes, yes, of course. I am sorry for snapping at you. Please delete it. I won't go to the police. I don't want the publicity."

"What will you do?"

Isabella had already decided on her next course of action. "The first thing I shall do is get myself checked out by a doctor. Then, once you have confirmed the video has been wiped, I will arrange punishment for these sick fucks."

"I understand."

"Do you know all the names of those in the video?

"I do. Do you have a pen?"

She scribbled down the details of Grigor, Raul and Barty. "Is pretty boy Donny the only person making the films?"

"No. There's also a friend called Christiano."

"In that case, give me whatever details you have for Donny and Christiano." Again, she made notes as Chris spoke. "Which of these men was showing off?"

"Barty, Bartholemew."

"I might go a little easier on him but not be so generous

with the other bastards."

"That is your prerogative. Absolutely your choice."

"Will you let me know when the video gets deleted?"

"If you want me to."

"I do. I intend to get my revenge on these bastards, but only when you have eradicated the evidence."

"Thank you. I will ring you on this number."

"Please call me on my mobile and, thank you, whoever you are. I wish you well in your venture and look forward to hearing from you soon."

With that, Isabella Sanchez, importer and exporter and owner of the largest chain of men-only clubs across South Africa, hung up and told her secretary to get her ex-boyfriend on the phone immediately and then leave the premises. She could have the day off.

Will and Shirley left for a walk, lunch, and to find the bus times to Palma. Ben sat on the balcony, staring at the sea. The conversations with the ladies echoed around his head, and he needed to decide what to do. Lucia's comments had gotten to him.

Everything had seemed so straightforward when he was on his own in that empty house, but here, with other people, things became complicated. He had to consider his fellow travellers. He still wanted to end his life but doubted that would happen in Majorca. He would find a convincing way to do it at home.

He only had a few more days of pretending. Ben was sure he could present a brave face. He needed something to occupy his mind and was relieved when an idea appeared.

Gemma saw the caller's details and wondered if she had been stupid to give Becky her mobile number.

Becky said Grigor had rearranged her liaison with the stranger, delaying it a week. She asked Gemma if she thought getting away from the island was possible and whether

Gemma had any ideas about where she might go. Becky asked what Cheltenham was like, and Gemma cut that discussion short. She said she doubted there would be any benefit to Becky running away. The video would still get posted, and her parents would find out. The best action was to tell her parents what had happened, but Becky suggested it would be suicide. Her father would kill her. Gemma said that Becky needed to pray for a miracle in that case.

Becky became upset when telling Gemma that Christiano was cold when he rang to tell her about the postponement. He took great delight in boasting about some new girls who had arrived on the island. Work would start that evening. He said he would have to work quickly as he was off to Magaluf with Grigor, Graham and Donny on Thursday before going to Ibiza for the weekend. Becky had not wished him a safe journey.

Edward Montgomery Kingston was a big fan of the writing of Jack London, the acclaimed journalist and author, but he was not such a fan of the man's politics or social observation. He disagreed with London's assertion, '*Show me a man with a tattoo, and I'll show you a man with an interesting past.*'

As far as Edward was concerned, tattoos better reflected who you were than what you had done. He thought they were an abomination that typified and stigmatised the working class. He could not recall any sensible, affluent people who had irrevocably scarred their bodies in such a way. Okay, various sportspeople and nouveau celebrities may have succumbed to the ink, but that reflected their lack of class and intelligence.

His father often repeated his assertion that people with position, authority and grace did not indulge in body art. Edward saw no reason to disagree. Much to his disdain, Louise brazenly admitted that she visited a tattooist. She claimed she had inked her breasts, but her father had no evidence of this. He could not avoid seeing the various small animals scattered around her legs and body and an elongated knot design sprawled across her lower back. Her girlfriends had similar ones and referred to them as their tramp stamps.

Edward made no secret of his thoughts on her choices and how common the tattoos made her look. She would regret her decision in later life. Louise was unrepentant and called him a snotty old dinosaur.

Thankfully, Donny had not succumbed, and Edward was pleased that his boy showed the class and sophistication associated with the Kingston name.

Looking down upon the people scattered around the communal areas, Edward spotted the Welshman had tattoos on his upper arms and chest. To him, this perfectly exemplified why these people should not be allowed to breed. If he had his way, the working classes would be barred from the complex. They lowered the tone. They set a bad example. He wished they didn't feel the need to talk to him. He also wondered why the man was so important that Edward's estate agent had begged him to let this peasant occupy his best apartment.

Gemma rang Nick as soon as she closed the call with Becky. The news that the boys would be out to play that evening and away for their final weekend in Majorca promised to make their task easier. Gemma suggested visiting the office and collecting the passcodes. Then, if Nick's boss had any problems deleting the files, they could make a return visit to do the necessary.

Nick was still not sure he liked the idea of Gemma helping him, but her plan made sense. He would contact Chris to tell him what they would do, and he would meet Gemma later to finalise arrangements.

"He seems like a nice bloke." Will put on his sunglasses and lay on the bed.

"Who's that love?"

Will pointed out Eddie. "Him, on the balcony over there,

he owns our apartment. I think he's related to Ben's friend Elizabeth." He couldn't adjust his towel whilst still resting on it. He stood and put it right. "He seems to have his fingers in many pies. He runs several businesses."

Shirley shielded her eyes with her hand, trying to get a better view. She didn't like the man's look. His quiff made him look like a fifties rocker, and his gold necklace, bracelets, and large rings on his fingers suggested someone who felt the need to display his opulence. She did not consider this to be a classy look. "Oh, right." She returned her attention to her book.

As expected, Chris was unhappy to learn that Nick planned to break into the office to retrieve the passwords. He suggested the pair give him time to look at the site and see what he could do remotely. Nick swore they would not do anything risky and only photograph the notice board. He assured Chris they would be fine.

Jon was curious about his daughter's actions. She took a step, poured water onto the sand, and then stepped into the damp patch, repeating this process. Daisy slowly progressed up the beach and was still about ten feet away.

"What are you doing, Dais?"

"The sand is too hot to walk on. I am trying to find a way back to you without hurting my feet."

"Why not wear your sandals?"

"Because I might want to go in the sea."

"That's the beauty of sandals. You can wear them in the water."

"But then they get covered in sand when I walk back here."

He could offer no argument.

"How will you manage if you want to go back?"

Daisy stopped, put her index finger to her bottom lip, and considered the problem. "I need two buckets of water," she said.

She emptied the remaining water, grabbed her brother's bucket, and ran to the sea, oblivious to the hot sand. Daisy quickly filled both buckets and started her journey again.

"Where do you two fancy eating tonight? My treat."

"In that case, I will google the most expensive place on the island," Will picked up his mobile.

"No problem," said Ben. "Wherever you like."

"Don't listen to him, Dad. How about we visit that Italian place again? You enjoyed it there."

"It's not about me. I want you to choose. This is my treat as a thank you."

"A couple of people by the pool were talking about a fish restaurant in Sillot. They said it was excellent."

"Where is that?" Shirley asked.

"No idea."

Ben grabbed the opportunity. "I tell you what. Will, we'll take a walk down to Sillot and see what's what."

"He's a poet now as well," said Will, looking at Shirley and thrusting a thumb in Ben's direction. "I've just got back. All that sunbathing has made me sleepy."

"There's a pint in it."

"He's on," said Shirley, delighted that her father wanted to go out. "Will, get your shoes back on."

"Having a good day?"

"Great, thanks. Quite a successful one, too."

"Do tell."

The caller updated him on his progress tracking the blackmail victims and his conversation with Isabella.

"These lads really are a pair of shits, aren't they?"

"Sooner we bring them down, the better."

"The father of one of them is a bit of a twat. I can see where Donny gets it from."

"How are you doing with the other job?"

"Good, I think. I am going in on the weekend while they

are away." Snowy waved away a bug that was flying too close to his nose. "Can you do me a favour?"

"If I can, what do you want?"

"Find out what you can about Grigor."

"I thought you said you know who he is?"

"I do, but why choose that name? There must be a connection somewhere."

"Probably a G thing."

"Huh?"

"Frankie Nuggets' kids are Graham, Gavin and Gloria, and his nephew is Gus."

"Gotcha, but Grigor sounds foreign. It's as if he is trying to make people think he is Russian. "

"Maybe he thinks it makes him more intimidating."

"Possibly, but it would be good to learn about Grigor's background and whether they based him on a real person or just made up the name. They might have other aliases. "

"I'll take a look. I'll focus on Majorca and Barcelona to start with."

"And Ibiza. They are heading there later this week."

"Any sign of Matilda yet?"

"None. Nobody I've spoken to has heard of her. It's as if she's disappeared."

"She might have stayed in Morocco?"

"Maybe, but it is a bit odd. Gus has named his boat after the woman, but there is no trace of her."

"I'll see what I can find out. How is the boy doing?

"He's loved up, I think. He and his girl seem to be very close."

"Good, I'm happy for him. Keep an eye on him for me. He's talking about breaking into that internet café to retrieve passwords."

"You haven't told him that I'm on the case?"

"No, because he would only want to speak with you and help you. The fewer who know why you are there, the better."

"Fair point. I'll keep an eye on him."

The restaurant was on the seafront, and the owner said he would find a space for three at eight-thirty.

Ben suggested they stop at the bar opposite the SPAR supermarket.

He handed the glass to his son-in-law and said, “Good health.”

“Iechyd Da,” replied Will, tasting the beer. “Now, Ben, what do you want to tell me?”

Ben feigned surprise. “Me? What makes you think I want to tell you anything? Can’t a man invite his son-in-law for a pint?”

“Of course, and this son-in-law is only too delighted to accept. However, when we left you at the apartment earlier, you were downbeat, tired, and had no idea what to do with yourself. Now you are smiling and upbeat and look like a man with a plan. We could have googled the restaurant's name, but you wanted to get me away from Shirley to speak about something. What is it?”

Ben put his glass back on the table and leaned in. “Promise me you won’t say anything to our Shirl, at least not yet.”

“I’ll decide after you tell me what it is.”

Nick and Gemma ran through their plan once again as they sat on the water’s edge.

“I think we know what to do,” said Gemma. “It’s quite exciting, don’t you think?”

“I’ll be happier when we do what we must and get out of there.”

Will called the barman and asked for two more pints, telling him to put them on Ben’s tab. “You are serious about this?”

“I am.”

“When did this idea come to you?”

“A few months ago, but I know it would be impossible at

home."

Will ran a hand through his hair. "I am not sure how Shirley is going to take this."

"That's why I don't want to tell her. At least, not until I've sorted a few things."

"Okay. I'll help, but if Shirl gets suspicious, I'll come clean immediately."

"Agreed," Ben raised his quarter-full pint toward Will.

The internet bar looked busy. Nick regarded this as good news, as the customers would keep the barman engaged. He checked to make sure Gemma had hidden her identity sufficiently, pulled the baseball cap over his head, and put on the loud plastic jacket he had purchased in the charity shop. The pair disappeared down the lane to the back of the shop.

Several floodlights lit the yard, but no cars were in sight. They kept their heads down as they crossed the yard. The door opened and shut quietly, and Nick led Gemma up the stairs. The office door was ajar, and computer and monitor lights flashed. The screen hosting the cameras switched from bar to entry to yard and back again.

Gemma kept guard as Nick took photos of the notice board. He tried the entrance of the store room but was disappointed but not surprised to find it locked. He was studying the passcodes on the board, hoping to find the right one, when Gemma told him someone was coming. They heard voices coming up the stairs, and Gemma motioned for them to hide behind the desk.

Nick glanced at the screen, which showed images from the video cameras, and spotted a jeep parked in the yard. He remembered Gemma mentioning Christiano's jeep, so perhaps he had forgotten something.

Two male and one female voices came closer. The female was giggling, and a male urged her to be careful. Nick recognised all three. The trio reached the point where Nick guessed they would be directly behind the door. Nick hoped they would proceed to the top floor, but they did not move.

Christiano laughed because their intended targets wanted nothing to do with him and Donny. Donny suggested they were stuck-up bitches, and if Grigor had not invited them to Ibiza, he would teach them a lesson. Louise told them to forget about the girls. They did not matter. On the positive side, the three could have a night together. Donny offered to get the champagne.

Gemma and Nick held their breath as Donny entered the office. Gemma put one hand over Nick's mouth and the other over hers. Neither could see Donny, but they heard him walk across the floor and open the kitchen door. Bottles got rattled before the kitchen door closed again. The pair winced and sighed in relief after Donny left the office to follow his friends up the stairs.

Nick checked the image on his mobile and showed it to Gemma. They had what they came for. She nodded and whispered they should leave it a moment before departing. The pair waited in silence until they heard laughter upstairs.

They were readying themselves to go when Nick spotted a light flashing on one of the computers, which he thought indicated that it had started recording. He switched on both monitors, and an image emerged on the right-hand screen, which Donny had kept off during his previous visit.

They gasped at seeing a naked Christiano and Louise looking directly at them. Christiano stood behind her. His actions made her tattooed breasts wobble. She offered no objection and appeared to be enjoying herself. A naked Donny walked into view and touched them both. It looked like he was awaiting his turn.

As Donny continued to stroke his friend and kiss his sister, Nick could not tell which of them Donny would choose first.

Leah pushed the mobile into her pocket and re-entered the lounge.

"What did she say?" Jon had been on tenterhooks.

"I couldn't ask her. It seems impersonal to call her to ask for money. I'll take the kids to see her next week."

"So we can't take things any further until next week."

"No, but that doesn't mean we can't enjoy the rest of our holiday. When the kids wake up, let's take them down to the beach for a kick about and then stop for a drink at that bar you like."

Elizabeth closed her eyes and let the breeze flow through her hair. She felt good. Nick told her that the money transfer would take place on Friday. She hoped it would be early in the morning so she could find somewhere to get her hair done and buy a new outfit for the journey home.

She looked at her feet. The salt water had benefitted the skin around the heels, but it was time for new shoes. She wondered whether Lucia would like to visit the shoe shop she had recommended.

Elizabeth took out her mobile and called her friend.

Carlos Mendez was not a killer. He was a businessman. Granted, he was not the most successful businessman, but he had always been honest and law-abiding and remained confident his luck would change.

Not all of his failures were his fault. His real estate venture showed great promise, but cash flow hampered his efforts.

Why hadn't Isabella allowed him an extension on his loan? He only needed to miss three months' repayments and would have been home and dry. He knew he was wrong to mistreat her after she had travelled such a long way, but he had been angry. He might have been hasty in breaking up with her, but what was the point of maintaining a relationship with someone who would not help in his hour of need?

When she called him earlier that afternoon, his first reaction was to ignore her, but he saw a chance to apologise. He needed to tell her he was sorry about how things ended. After all, he still owed her considerable money, and his businesses would die if she foreclosed on the loan.

Her tone was businesslike. She dismissed his attempts to say sorry and told Carlos to shut up and listen. She would wipe his slate clean, but he had to do something for her. It was something vital. He was the only one she could trust to get it done quickly and efficiently. It was his patch, and nobody knew the island and its inhabitants as well as he did.

Isabella wanted him to arrange for people to die.

Carlos said he did not want to be involved and threatened to hang up, but then she told him what the bastards had done to her and were about to do. He had never heard her cry like that before. She sounded scared and frequently repeated that she wished he was there with her to hold her and tell her everything would work out for the best.

Carlos became very emotional as she repeated how the Englishman and his cronies had made her feel. He could not believe human beings could behave that way to other humans. She said they were animals, and rogue animals deserved to die. He agreed to help, although he had no idea how to achieve her aims.

Isabella gave him five days to devise a plan. She wanted evidence he had resolved the problem, and once she received it, she would write off all his debt. She would also give him the money to complete his new development.

Isabella had insisted that he could not reveal to anyone but his brother why the men needed to die. He was relieved she had said this. Jorge was more street-wise and did not care about laws. He would know what to do.

On the walk back to his apartment, Gemma and Nick only discussed one subject. They knew Louise and the boys were good friends but had never thought they were that close. Nick could not believe what he had seen and wished he could unsee it. Gemma asked if Nick's boss could give her a copy of the video, and she would hand it to Becky to use as a bargaining tool.

Barty was delighted when Grigor offered to pay him to keep an eye on the Welshman. The cash supplemented his earnings from doing odd jobs.

He had followed the man most of the afternoon but did not have much to report. All the guy seemed to do was walk, shop, drink, make the odd phone call and buy junk off the beach walker. He had spent two hours standing on a corner while the Welshman and the older geezer drank in a bar. What was so important about him? Why was Grigor so interested?

"Enjoying the evening?" Nick rested his arms on the wall.

"Oh, hi Nick, hello again, Gemma. Yes. We are. Thanks." Jon slipped off his sandals. "Have you been up to much?"

Gemma coughed. Nick said, "Not really, we've just been for a walk. What about you?"

"We've been playing football on the beach. We've worn the kids out, and they are sleeping in there. We are just about to have a glass of wine."

"Good evening, you two. Have you been anywhere nice?" Leah placed a bowl of crisps on the patio table.

Gemma spoke before Nick could think of anything. "We had a meal in Cala Millor, walked around and then went for a drink in the Happy Bar."

"Do you remember those days, Jon? A meal and a drink without the kids...bliss." Leah started to pour wine into her glass. "Would you like some?"

Gemma spoke again, "Go on then. That would be lovely."

They climbed over the wall while Leah got more glasses, and Jon shifted the furniture to accommodate their guests.

The four chatted, sipped wine and enjoyed the tranquillity until Gemma had an idea she voiced before mentioning it to Nick. She turned to Leah.

"I tell you what: If you and Jon want to go to the bar for an hour or two, we'll keep an eye on the children."

"I couldn't ask you to do that."

"Nobody's asking. We're offering, aren't we, Nick?"

"Looks like it."

Jon and Leah exchanged looks.

"But what if they wake up?" Jon asked.

"We'll try to get them back to sleep. If that fails, we'll come and get you," said Gemma.

"Do they often wake up?" Nick asked.

"Every morning, unfortunately," said Jon.

"But not usually during the night." Leah was keen to accept the offer. "What do you think, Jon? The kids know Gemma and Nick, so if they did wake up, then they'd be fine. It's not as if we're going far, but it would be nice to have time together, just like we used to."

Jon looked at Nick. "Are you sure you don't mind?"

"We'll be fine," said Nick. "We'll probably sit here drinking the rest of your wine."

"It's yours," said Leah. "I'll just pop a dress on."

"We'll give you our mobile numbers so you can ring and check if you want," said Gemma.

"Thanks, we'll only be an hour," said Jon.

"Two at the most," said Leah.

With the target and his companions settled in the fish restaurant, Barty decided enough was enough for one day. He checked his watch. He still had time to get to Cody's bar in Cala Bona to enjoy the remainder of happy hour.

"Remind me why we are doing this?"

Gemma filled her glass. "I thought it would be a useful alibi. You know, where were you at such and such? We can say we looked after the kids for Leah and Jon."

"But who is going to suspect us? It's not as if Louise and her boyfriends knew we were there."

"I suppose you are right. It seemed like a nice thing to do, and it was a chance to do something normal after seeing that awful fucking video."

Ben ushered his companions into the happy bar, telling them he needed a moment. The meal had filled him, and a quick walk along the promenade would help. He sat on the wall facing the sea and thought again about his plan. It was a good one. Will promised to begin his part of the task early the next day so that by lunchtime, Ben would better understand what would happen next and when.

Leah sat on Jon's lap on the sofa in their apartment.

"It was great to have time alone, wasn't it?" She kissed him.

"Yeah, that was very nice of Nick and Gemma to babysit. I can't say I would have been too keen to look after someone else's children on my holiday."

"But we were only gone two hours."

"I know, but all the same."

"They are like an old married couple, aren't they? They already seem to know each other so well that it's hard to believe they only met last week."

"A bit like we were...."

Her shoulders moved away from his chest. "Are you joking? You couldn't stand me when we first met. You thought I was a stuck-up cow."

"I am not sure I used those words."

"I think you did. You told my friend you thought she was okay, but I was too full of myself!"

"Well, you were a bit...odd. A bit arty farty!"

"I was creative. I was paid to think outside the box, so it was only natural for me to act a bit differently."

"I know. How many more times must I apologise?"

"One more."

"I am sorry for calling you a stuck-up cow."

"Apology accepted…again." They kissed. "I couldn't have been that bad. You've stuck with me for twelve years."

"You're the best. It just took me a while to realise, and now we're about to embark on a new journey together. Providing we can get the money."

"We'll get the money. Don't you worry about that. We will not miss this opportunity to do what we want."

"It won't be easy. There will be some hard times."

"We'll survive."

"I am looking forward to getting my hands dirty again. I might even lose a bit of weight."

She slipped her hand into his shirt. "You'll get your muscles back."

"Hope so. I'll be as fit as Nick this time next year." He nibbled her neck.

"Calm down, big boy. Having dreams is very good, but it is important to make them achievable."

Nick and Gemma parted at the door to her hotel. "Can I see you tomorrow?" he asked.

"Now, let me think. Yes, you can." She pulled him closer and kissed him. "Shall we take the bus to Palma?"

"Yeah, great. Any idea what's there?"

"Nope, but you have just over nine hours to find out. Pick me up at nine?"

"Will do."

DISCLOSURE

(FIVE MONTHS BEFORE THE HOLIDAY)

Jon Oliver motioned for his new colleague to answer the ringing phone. Rich was determined not to look at him and did not take his eyes off the computer screen.

What was the point of installing an extra line if only one gets answered? Jon thought as he asked the person he spoke to if he would mind holding on a second. He put his call on hold. "Rich, you are supposed to answer your 'phone when it rings."

"I haven't been told what to say."

"Shit! How old are you? You pick up the receiver and say hello."

"There is no need for swearing. You know how my father hates bad language. He is not going to be very happy when I tell him."

"Nor will he be happy to hear that you don't answer the bloody 'phone when it rings."

"You should have trained me."

"Trained? How the f... flaming hell am I supposed to train you to do that? Look, this is a 'phone. Pick it up and say hello." Richard made no effort to comply. Jon grabbed the receiver. "Hello, Cromwell Construction. Jon speaking, how can I help?"

"Hi, is Ritchie there, please?"

"Who's calling?"

"It's his girlfriend. I would have called his mobile, but my 'phone is dead, so I didn't have his number."

Jon dropped the 'phone on the table and mumbled, "It's for you."

Elizabeth's brain tried to accept that the stitch she was doing was different from what she usually did. The lady in the market had asked her if she could knit a Christening jacket for her grandson, and Elizabeth had said she could before she saw the pattern. Now, she wished she had declined the offer. An unexpected telephone call caused her further confusion.

"Mrs Kingston, I am not sure if you remember me. My name is Sally. I was your husband's secretary."

"Hello Sally, yes, of course, I remember you. How are you?"

"I'm fine, thank you, Mrs Kingston. It's been a long time."

"It has, but please call me Elizabeth."

"Thanks. I know this is probably none of my business, but I bumped into Mark Eastley the other day, and he mentioned that Nick had called to collect his father's old papers. They were in boxes we found in the filing room. Mark was hopeful they would help you answer a few questions. "

"That's right. I am grateful you kept hold of the boxes, but I'm afraid they didn't tell us very much."

A short, awkward silence filled the earpiece.

"Er...Mark also mentioned that Nick didn't know that Kenneth had stopped travelling when he took up his promotion."

"Yes, I have to admit that came as a surprise. We never knew Kenneth had become desk-bound. He was frequently away from home and told us it was because of work. Now, we have another mystery. Not only has all the money disappeared, but we don't even know where he went."

The receiver fell silent again, and Elizabeth heard the lady breathing heavily.

"Sally, are you okay?"

"I am not sure I should be telling you this...it seems disloyal because your husband was always very good to me... but you and your son have a right to know...I should have told you years ago...I regret keeping it quiet now. I am sorry...please don't tell anyone I told you. I should not betray confidences like this ...please promise me you won't say who told you."

"Calm down, Sally. Of course, I won't say anything if you

don't want me to, but what do you want to tell me?"

Another heavy sigh filled the short void.

"I think...well, I know really...where your husband used to go."

Elizabeth discarded the knitting. "Go on."

"Kenneth was...I didn't think it would be so hard to tell you." She took a deep breath. "He was having an affair with a girl who used to work at the yacht club. Her name is Julia, and she lives in Sully."

Elizabeth's jaw dropped as she breathed, and the 'phone shook.

"Hello? Are you still there?" Sally asked.

"Yes...yes, I am. How do you know this?"

"Because he used to have things delivered to the house and had me book taxis to pick him up from there."

"So you believe he was having an affair?"

"I am sorry. I am sure of it. Kenneth used to joke about how he would be going off to live his other life for a few days, and if you or anyone else rang, I had to maintain the pretence that he was overseas."

"But he was here the whole time?"

"He was."

"How long did this go on?"

"A couple of years, although I think she lived somewhere else when it started. The deliveries and taxis only occurred about a year before Kenneth's stroke."

"I see. Thank you for telling me...."

Sally grew uncomfortable with the growing silence. "Are you okay, Elizabeth?"

"Yes, I am, but as you might imagine, this is devastating news."

"I cannot imagine what you are going through, and I should have told you sooner, but...."

"It's okay, Sally. It is not your fault. At least you have told us now. I don't suppose you have a name or an address, do you?"

"I do. That's why I rang..."

Elizabeth picked up the pattern book and a pen and found a white space. "Can you let me have it?"

"Julia Havens, 17 Schooner Close, Sully."

The sudden need to cough reminded Ben that Shirley had booked a doctor's appointment for that afternoon. She was driving to the area anyway to exchange clothes she had bought on her last visit.

Ben had seen through the deception. Nobody could have that many reasons to visit the area, and she had called in at least once a week over the past month.

On the last visit, she noticed him coughing and wanted to call the doctor. Ben had refused, but, typical Shirl, she rang the surgery from her home.

In a way, Ben was relieved she had. The cough refused to go away no matter what he tried. Ben hoped the doctor could prescribe something to help him get better. He had grown bored of the pain and the persistent breathlessness. He became tired very quickly.

"Jon! Jon! Where are we with the McGregor site?"

"No idea. That is one of Richard's."

"But he's not here, is he? So I'm asking you."

"What do you mean he is not here? Where is he? Where has he gone?"

"I gave him an hour off."

"That's great. You keep telling me I must manage Richard, and then you make decisions without letting me know."

"I am the boss."

Jon was not going down that road again. "Where's he gone anyway?"

"To get a haircut."

"A haircut? Couldn't that wait until lunch?"

"He's meeting Holly at lunchtime."

"Oh right ...couldn't that wait until after work?"

"He's meeting his mother to get a suit for the wedding."

"You are kidding?" Rob was not. "Excuse me a second. I need an hour off to go and cut my grass."

"I don't appreciate sarcasm, Jon."

"No, and I don't appreciate being treated like a fool. You told me you were taking on extra contractors because Richard would be available to manage them, but he does sod all, and I have to pick up the pieces!" He walked away from the desk.

"McGregor site?"

Jon opened the drawer, took out the folder and dropped it on the desk. His boss spoke before Jon got to his seat.

"There's nothing on here to show that you placed the order for tiles."

"Whether I placed the order? Why would I know? It's not my project."

"It is if I say it is," Rob closed the file and held it out for Jon to collect. "Make sure the tiles are on order and on-site by Friday. I can't afford any more delays."

As usual, Nick had gone to work, having no idea what his mother had planned for the day. He thought she might visit the cash and carry to collect more ingredients for the pies that had proved popular on the market, but after that, he had no clue where she would go.

Elizabeth was initially distraught at Sally's news, but the feeling of desperation did not last long. She had learned so much about her husband in the past six years that discovering he had a mistress was not a big deal.

Sitting on the bus, she felt she was on a voyage of discovery. At the very least, she would learn more about Kenneth's life; she might even understand where the money had gone. As the bus rambled through rural villages and passed pubs and restaurants she once frequented, she visualised how the scene might unfold. Elizabeth rehearsed conversations she might have with Julia. She tried to anticipate the woman's reaction and fully expected her to try to lie her way out of it.

Two bus journeys later, she arrived at the end of Schooner Close. It was a modern estate on the coast road, with a selection of detached, semi-detached and link houses.

Number 17 looked the same as the other large detached houses in the cul-de-sac; it even had the obligatory large 4x4 in the drive. The car was a new model and also had a tow bar. Elizabeth wondered what that would pull. She had her answer as she reached the front of the house. A sizeable touring caravan stood in the space beside the garage.

Her mouth was dry, and she felt her hands shake as she reached for the bell.

A shapely, blonde lady, who she estimated to be in her early thirties, opened the door.

"Hello, can I help you?" Her accent was not Welsh.

"Hello, are you Julia?"

"I am. Who are you?"

"I'm Elizabeth Kingston, Kenneth's wife."

The colour quickly drained from Julia's made-up cheeks. "You'd better come in."

Elizabeth followed her into a smartly decorated hallway. She admired the wallpaper and knew it was expensive. They used to have it at home in Cowbridge. The floor was spotless and made of wooden blocks. The long mirror, hanging by the foot of the stairs, had a silver surround and looked antique.

Julia led her into a sumptuous living room, where she invited Elizabeth to sit on a leather sofa while she sat in an upright leather chair.

"I had a feeling this day would come, but I thought less and less about it as time passed." She clenched her hands together. "The funny thing is that I thought about Kenny this morning. I should have seen it as an omen."

Kenny thought Elizabeth. He hated people calling him Ken, let alone Kenny. That would be entirely out of the question.

She had carefully considered what she would say, but now that she sat face to face with the other woman, Elizabeth scrapped her speech. "I understand you had an affair with Kenneth."

"Yes, you could call it that, but I always thought it was more than an affair. We were very close before his…illness."

"Call it what you like, but a married man lived here when his family thought he was working overseas. I cannot believe that you slept in separate rooms. By my reckoning, having sex with a married man who isn't your husband is having an affair, no matter how you try to dress it up to appease your conscience. "

Julia's eyebrows rose, and her eyes narrowed as she wondered how to respond. "Kenny never told me you were direct. Yes, we lived here together as a couple… on a part-time basis…and yes, it was an affair but not a sordid relationship. I genuinely loved Kenny; he loved me too, but not enough to leave you for me."

Elizabeth knew there was a good reason her husband had stayed with her. She studied the petite blonde, who was nothing like she had imagined her to be. Julia looked older indoors, and Elizabeth now believed she was only a few years younger than herself. Julia did have the benefit of expensive makeup, clothes, and hairdressers.

"How did you meet?"

Julia scooped a handful of hair from behind her head and brought it back over her shoulder, where she held it as she spoke.

"My husband… ex-husband, Lee, was on the committee at the yacht club. He helped Kenny choose his boat. Ken used to call around to see Lee to discuss the purchase, and we used to chat. He was very flirty, and…well…one thing led to another. One night, after a competition at the club, he kissed me. After that, he used to call around to see me when Lee was out."

"Very cosy. So when was this? When did it all start?"

"About eight years ago."

"And then what? You moved here?"

"Not straight away. That was only a year before Kenny had his stroke. Lee discovered that I was…seeing someone else and kicked me out. I had nowhere else to go, so Kenny helped secure this place. It was a new build, but the developer had trouble selling it, and Kenny offered to rent it. We had a six-month tenancy. At the end of that, Kenny bought it. He offered cash, and the builder bit his hand off."

"I bet he did. And this house is in your name?"

Julia's tongue appeared between her narrow lips as she pondered how to say what she had to say. "No, it is our son's name."

Elizabeth shook as she slumped back. "Your son? Kenneth's son?"

"Yes," she nodded. "Kenneth placed it in Archie's name…"

Elizabeth recognised the connection. Archibald Kenneth Edward Montgomery Kingston had been her father-in-law.

"…we were rowing a lot when Archie was born. I have no proof, but I believe Kenny had a few work worries. He insisted that we put the house in Archie's name. The trust agreement lets me stay here to look after him on the condition that I never try to sell it. The solicitor explained that when he reaches 21, the house is Archie's, and I could be out on the street." She giggled nervously.

"Who is your solicitor?"

"That's a strange question. It wasn't my solicitor. It was Kenny's. Douglas Watson, of Watson and Carnaby."

Elizabeth's stomach tightened, and she needed to inhale quickly.

Sally sensed her discomfort. "Are you okay? Do you want a drink or something?"

"No, I'm fine, thank you," said Elizabeth, regaining her composure. She wanted nothing from this woman but the truth. "Douglas Watson is my solicitor. His firm has represented my family for years, but I fear I am about to terminate that relationship."

The significance of the remark was not lost on Sally. "Oh, I see."

"Archie was born when?"

"He was eight months old when Kenny died."

Elizabeth realised that Julia had been pregnant when they first moved here. "Is that why your husband kicked you out?"

"Yeah, it was getting a bit obvious. Archie was a stupid mistake, really. Me and Lee hadn't had sex in ages, at least two years, and then I met Kenny. Well, I didn't think. Before I knew it, my periods had stopped, and I was in trouble. I offered to get rid of it, but it was too late. I was already four months gone..."

Elizabeth doubted Julia was as innocent as she tried to appear.

"...and then Lee told me he wouldn't look after another man's kid. I had nowhere else to turn. Kenny assured me we'd be okay, and that's when he found this place. We got the decorators in, and when Archie was born, he negotiated the purchase. If I am honest, I asked him to divorce you, but he said he couldn't. That was never an option. He never explained why. I realise now that he must have loved you more than me."

"I doubt it. Kenneth probably loved my money more than he loved me."

"Your money?"

"Yes, my husband had no money of his own."

"But I thought it was his money. He had a great job, a massive house, cars, a yacht, a place in France...not that I ever saw them, you understand."

"All those things were paid for on credit using his salary. The money was mine; it was what my father had left me. Kenny's family were never well off."

"He must have had money. He paid for this house in cash."

"Yes, using an insurance policy that I had purchased. He cashed it six months before he died, but at least I know where that money went. Can I ask, did he leave you anything else?"

Julia became suddenly edgy and anxious. "Why do you want to know?"

"Don't worry. I don't want it....it's too late for that now, and, in any case, if Kenneth is the father of your son..."

"He is."

"...then it is only correct that he makes provision for him." The words hurt her as Kenneth had made no such provision for Nicholas.

"He put a hundred and fifty thousand in a bank account. When I heard about Kenny, I put eighty grand of it in the trust fund for Archie."

Elizabeth guessed that was another job for Douglas Watson. "Good thinking," she said absently. She rubbed her eyes, thinking about what she had learned, and a chilling thought struck her. "Who did you get to do the decorating?"

"Eddie, Kenny's brother."

Her pain could not have been any worse had someone stabbed her.

"Eddie knew about you and Ken...Kenny?"

"Yeah, he used to call in quite a bit, especially after Archie was born. He and Kenny used to go into the study. That's when I started to worry about Kenny. I used to hear them arguing about money. Eddie needed a loan, but Kenny told him he could not get such a large amount. I thought he was lying, but if you held the pursestrings, he might have been telling the truth."

Elizabeth smiled and changed the subject. "Have you spoken to Eddie since?"

"Yeah, he called me a few times after Kenny died. He wanted to make sure I was okay and managing financially. He made me promise that if I needed anything, I had to get in touch, but I didn't want anything. I had my Archie and this house, and then I met someone else, so I was fine."

"Lucky you," said Elizabeth, struggling to keep calm.

"I did ring him once, not to ask for anything but to offer

him a job. My current partner, Gordy, needed some decoration at his office, but apparently, Eddie doesn't do the decorating anymore?"

"No, he sold his business and invested in other areas. He's done very well for himself. He spends much of his time in Munich and Majorca now."

"He's done well. Kenny always said he looked forward to Eddie's ship's arrival but never said why. Do you know why Eddie wanted the old laptop?"

"What laptop?"

"Kenny's laptop," she spoke slowly, remembering events. "Eddie came to see me when Kenny died and wanted the laptop. He was furious when I denied ever seeing it. Eddie searched the house but never found it. After he went home, I had a phone call saying it was in Kenny's locker at the yacht club. One of the girls brought it around. I never mentioned it to Eddie. It was quite old then. I thought it might be helpful for Archie, but I couldn't get into it. I didn't know Kenny's password, so I bought a new one."

"And you still have his old laptop?"

"Yes, but I haven't used it. Gordy looked at it once but didn't get anywhere. He told me to throw it out, but I left it in the wardrobe. Do you want it? We have no use for it. Archie has his laptop and tablet. Gordy uses the PC in the study, and I use my phone to play games.

Quite the modern family thought Elizabeth. "Yes, I would like to take it if I could. My son Nick is desperate for a laptop."

"Couldn't you just get him a new one..." said Sally, rising from her chair. "...what with your family having all that money?"

Elizabeth shrugged, saying nothing.

"I will fetch it for you now...by the way, if Nicholas wants to meet his brother..."

"Half-brother."

"Of course, half-brother, but if he wants to see him, tell

him to call around. I've told Archie about his extended family, and he quite likes the thought of having a big brother."

Will looked up from his paper as Shirley entered the room. She had been out far longer than he had expected. "Everything okay? I expected you back ages ago. How is your dad?"

"Not great. The doctor sent him for an X-ray and wants him to have more tests. She will arrange a meeting with a consultant."

"Did she mention what it might be?"

"No, she suggested a few possibilities, but Dad is sure he's got cancer."

"Oh God, what did you say to that?"

"I told him it was too early to say, but even if it is, he can get treatment." She sat across from him and rested her elbows on the table with her chin on her hands. "He is fearing the worst after what happened to my grandparents."

Will rose from his seat to put on the kettle. "I can imagine."

"My mother isn't helping either. She is still bugging him for the money she thinks is missing. I told him to tell her the solicitors would sort out the settlement. Are you sure they won't find that money?"

He dropped teabags into two cups. "As sure as I can be. I had Chris review the accounts, and he didn't find anything, so we should be okay."

"That's good. Can I have one of those doughnuts with that, or did you eat them all?"

"Cheeky! As if I would do that," said Will, relieved he had left one in the bag.

The journey back on the bus was slow, frustrating and incredibly emotional for Elizabeth. She wanted to cry, but this was neither the time nor the place. It had been a voyage of discovery, and the findings had come at a cost. They had proved painful.

Not only had her bastard of a husband taken a mistress, but they also had a child. If that wasn't enough, Kenny the shit had cashed in a life insurance policy she had paid for to buy his new family a spanking new house by the sea and, presumably, had left them with the balance to live on. Then, to make matters even worse, the sneaky twat had used the family solicitor to set it all up. Douglas Watson could look out if she ever saw him again. The snivelling bastard with his '*our families have been friends for years*' bullshit would not know what had hit him.

The bus was approaching her stop. Elizabeth checked her purse and added up the contents.

I've just enough for a large bottle of vodka and a couple of cans of tonic. I've earned that, she thought, pressing the stop button.

DAY 11 - TUESDAY 3 AUGUST

The bus moved slowly through the narrow streets, and rather than follow it all the way, Barty decided to overtake it and wait for his targets to arrive in Palma. He knew a good place to park the car, which just happened to be near a decent burger bar. He could have an early lunch before the bus arrived, and he needed something greasy to help him get over his hangover.

Ben leaned on the balcony as his mind replayed what Will had told him. His plan was taking shape. Before heading home, he would speak to Elizabeth and Lucia in person and outline his proposals.

"The Cathedral of Santa Lucia of Palma, more commonly referred to as La Seu, is a Gothic Roman Catholic cathedral. It is built on the site of a pre-existing Arab mosque. The cathedral is 121 metres long and 55 metres wide, and its nave is 44 metres tall. To illustrate how this compares to other world-famous cathedrals, the central nave at Notre Dame, that's in Paris, you know, is 33m, 38m in Reims, 42m in Notre-Dame d'Amiens and 48m in Saint-Pierre de Beauvais, which is the highest of all Gothic cathedrals. The Cathedral was designed in the Catalan Gothic style but with Northern European influences. Building begun by King James 1 of Aragon around 1229 but wasn't finished until 1601...."

"1229 to 1601. So, a king built this in under four hours. He must have been one hell of a bricklayer."

Nick ignored the sarcasm and continued. "This cathedral sits within the old city of Palma. We are standing on top of a former citadel of the Roman city, between the Royal Palace of La Almudainai and the episcopal palace." He stretched his arms to highlight the vista. "Here, we overlook the Parc de la Mar and the Mediterranean Sea. Apparently, in 1901..."

"Just after seven?"

Nick shook his head. "Fifty years after the cathedral restoration had started, Anton Gaudi was invited to take over the project. While some of his ideas were adopted, such as moving the choir stalls from the middle nave to be closer to the altar and introducing a large canopy, Gaudí abandoned his work in 1914 after an argument with the contractor. The planned changes were essentially cosmetic rather than structural, and the project was cancelled soon afterwards. Anton Gaudi returned to his day job as a right winger at Barcelona."

"I wished I'd never asked," said Gemma. "Fair play to you, though. You are better than a tour guide. You have all this stored on your mobile?"

"Nah, not really. The online encyclopaedias are useful sometimes so long as you remember that not everything they say is correct." Nick cast his eye over the horizon and pointed to the harbour. "There's a cruise ship."

"Which one is it?"

"The big white one with the balconies on it."

"I know that, stupid. I am asking what the ship is called. My mother and I used to watch documentaries on cruise ships, and I'd like to know which one that is."

"No idea. It's too far away to see."

"Well, Mr Oracle, I am disappointed. You mean to tell me that your 'phone can't tell you everything?"

"Ha ha, very funny. You can get an app, but that would be too sad even for me." He looked up at the cathedral. "Do you want to go inside?"

"No thanks. I've been to Notre Dame, Lincoln Cathedral and York Minister. Once you've seen inside one church, you've seen them all."

"Too true. My father would drag me around all these places of culture, bombarding me with his version of history and one-sided views on why things are so important. It was all bollocks. He didn't know half of what he thought he did. I'd ask my mother or grandfather if I wanted to know something."

"So your mother's family has the brains, then?"

"Very much so. Mum's father, my Grampa Ned, was a knowledgeable bloke, not that he had formal schooling and never went to university. He would get a book if he needed to find the answer. He was always reading, and he had this way of passing on information that made it interesting y'know?"

Gemma nodded.

"But he was the same when he would read to me. He put so much expression into the words that I felt I was there. I hung on to every word. The number of novels I know without actually having opened the book."

"You've never read them for yourself?"

"Nah, it wouldn't be the same."

"Which was your favourite story?"

"Robin Hood. He read me that book many times and would make up his own stories. He never wrote them down but always remembered what he had told me and never repeated the same tale. I didn't know how he did it."

"Nor me," said Gemma with a mischievous smile. "I wish you'd inherited that, as I've only known you a week, and you've told me the same thing three times already."

Nick laughed. "Well, I know you swede bashers have turnips for brains, so have little or no memory retention. I said that I know you swede bashers...."

Gemma slapped his hand. "Watch it you." She took his arm, placed it around her shoulders, and put hers around his waist. "Shall we get some lunch?"

"Yeah, go on then. Burger?"

"No way. I think you are the one with memory retention problems. How many times have I told you that I have not come to the middle of the Med to have food that I can get back home?"

His free hand pointed out to the sea. "Technically, the

middle of the Med is 870 miles over there."

"How do you know that?"

"I don't. I made it up, but that's the kind of rubbish my father used to spout."

Gemma smiled. "So, what do you fancy eating?"

"Chips. No, not really," Nick said as Gemma's fingers squeezed his side. "Let's see what we find."

The bus arrived, and the passengers disembarked before Barty remembered why he was in Palma. The burger had been tasty, but it hadn't cured his hangover. His head was banging, and his stomach was unsure what to do.

He rushed, well walked as quickly as possible, around the more popular tourist haunts, stopping often fearing he was about to be sick, and caught sight of the couple before they separated with a kiss. Barty felt better believing he was prime private investigator material.

His target headed toward the marina. Barty had no time for boats. Knowing there was only one way in and out, he stopped at a bar to use their facilities and await the man's return. The hair of the dog might be in order.

Palma Marina was a hive of activity. While others fussed around, a few people bustled about loading, unloading, cleaning, and polishing. Waltzing and Matilda were right at the end of a jetty. Unfortunately, a man on a neighbouring boat spotted the stranger immediately and spoke to him in Spanish.

"I am sorry I don't understand," Snowy replied.

The man put his words together slowly. "What are you doing down here? This area is for owners only."

"I am here to look over Waltzing and Matilda. The owners, Grigor and Graham, are supposed to meet me here. I am thinking about buying one, possibly both boats."

The man smiled. "They are selling?"

"Maybe. It all depends on whether we can agree on a price. Have you seen them around?"

"Not for a few days."

Snowy looked at his watch. "I told them I was in a hurry. I am leaving for Monaco this evening and wanted to look over the boats before I go."

"Can you come back?"

"Not really. If I like the boats, we plan to meet in Ibiza at the weekend to conclude the deal. The deal is off if I cannot look over the boat."

"What do you do?"

"Sorry?"

"How do you work?"

"I am a broker." The man looked perplexed. "I buy items that I hope my clients would like and then sell them for a higher price."

"So you would not own the boat?"

"No chance I stick to the land. I have clients interested in buying the boats, providing the price is right."

"Would your clients moor the boats here?"

"Unlikely. One lives in Greece, the other in Mexico." Snowy had no idea whether yachts were popular in Mexico.

The man stepped down the short ladder from the bridge to the deck. "So these two spaces might be free soon?"

"Possibly. Does that bother you?"

"Not at all. This marina has a waiting list for spaces, but that did not apply to these two. They have plenty of money and can bend the rules. My friends have been waiting a long time to get a berth here. I will tell them of this opportunity."

"Don't get your hopes up. If I cannot look over the boats, there is no sale. If Grigor and Graham don't arrive soon, I am afraid your friends will have to wait longer."

Snowy held up his mobile. "Sorry, I have to take this." He played out an elaborate one-sided conversation in which he expressed disappointment that Grigor and Graham could not make the meeting and the deal was off.

"Ah well, that's the way it goes, I suppose. The owners aren't coming, so I am afraid your friends have to wait. I am not buying without viewing." He waved as he turned to leave.

"Don't go." The man joined him on the jetty. "There are spare keys in the office. I can get them for you. Wait here."

"But Grigor and Graham might be angry that you let me on the boat without them."

"I won't tell them if you don't."

The bus arrived seven minutes before its departure, and the orderly queue disintegrated into a free-for-all, even though there was room for everyone onboard. Gemma and Nick stood back, enjoying the spectacle. They stepped up, presented their tickets, and selected a double seat near the back.

"I'm a bit sleepy," said Gemma. "I didn't get much sleep last night."

"I was there, remember."

"How could I forget?" She stood, swivelled and plopped herself on his lap. Wake me up at Sa Coma."

Nick put his arms around her, keeping her steady, as she rested her head on his shoulder. "Okay."

"Barty, how are you? Where are you? What's happening?"

"Oh, hi, Grigor. I'm just leaving Palma. I've been following that man as you asked."

"Did you learn anything?"

"Not really, this visit was a touristy thing. He wandered around looking at the sights."

"Anything, in particular, catch his eye?"

"Not as far as I could see." It was better not to mention the time spent on the marina. Grigor was bound to ask for information Barty did not have, and it was not as if anything happened.

Sara counted out the euros in her purse. "Jesus, Kylie, this fortnight has cost me more than the holiday in Ibiza."

"I told you we should have gone all-inclusive. This

hotel is nice, but it's only a bed and breakfast, and eating is expensive."

"The burger place is cheap enough."

"Yeah, but who wants to eat meat every night?"

"I wouldn't say no!" Sara smirked.

"Donny said as much."

"Ho ho," Sara and Kylie slapped hands. "But I wouldn't survive on his. It was hardly more than a starter.... it wasn't even hard-ly sometimes if you know what I mean."

"Too much information....again!" Kylie shook her head. "Being on holiday with you is like getting stuck in one of those Carry-On films we used to watch at my gran's."

Sara adopted a camp but posh voice, "Oh, I say, do you come here often, madam? Would you like a cockatoo? My wife asked me for a double-entendre, so I gave her one, fnarr fnarr!"

"Enough," Kylie tried hard to stop giggling. "Haven't you got any coins to count?"

Nick and Gemma held hands as they walked from the restaurant.

"Lucia was right. The food was stunning," she said. "

"I loved it," said Nick. "I am not sure you'll want to kiss me after that. My mouth reeks of garlic."

"Let me see."

She turned, and they kissed.

"Tastes fine to me. I am very impressed that you knew the name of that vegetable they served with it."

"It was probably one of the only benefits of having a father like mine. He used to take us to the poshest places, although, more often than not, it was my mother who knew what the dishes were. Dad used to bluff his way through."

"Don't you miss him at all?"

"I did initially, but only because when the money dried up, I had to change schools." Gemma wanted more information. "I started at a private school..."

"Ooeerr hark at Mr Posh Bollocks."

"That's pretty much what they called me in my first year at the comp."

She pulled him closer. "Did they give my little gimp a hard time?"

"Just a tad. I was easy meat. This one boy, in particular, took great delight in beating me up. He even pissed on me at one stage."

"Seriously? Oh my God, that's gross. What did you do?"

"I started training with the Samurai. He didn't pick on me very much after that."

"So he gave you piss rather than take it out of you."

"He did both."

"At least you had the last word. I hear urine is good for the skin, which is probably why you have such a glowing complexion."

"I think that's too much sun."

They walked on. Nick broke the short silence.

"Do you want to go to another club or a bar?"

Gemma shook her head. "Not really. The girls are meeting their new Spanish friends and are probably already out. Do you fancy coming back to mine?"

"Brilliant."

She grabbed his shirt. "Don't get any ideas. There is no way I'm going to piss on you."

The only benefit of searching the boats was that it established that Graham and Grigor kept nothing on them. Snowy managed to distract his guide long enough to search cupboards and drawers but found nothing useful. He was growing more confident that everything he needed would be in the house.

REVELATION
(THREE MONTHS BEFORE THE HOLIDAY)

It didn't feel as though he was signing his life away. It was only fair that Cheryl got compensation for her efforts. He would have more than enough money to live his life. If push came to shove, he could start a new business. That thought did not excite him as much as it would have years ago. For now, he wanted to rest.

The solicitor pointed to where he had to put his mark, and Ben did so without hesitation. The solicitor's secretary signed as a witness. Shirley appeared by his side.

"Okay, Dad? Too late for regrets now."

He smiled as he put his arm around her. "No regrets. It is only fair. Talking of fairness, I've arranged with Mr Carlisle to give money to you and Will."

"You've done what? Why?" Shirley pulled away from him. "What are you going to live on? Why didn't you say something?"

"I wanted it to be a surprise. It's only right that I gave you something. After all, you maintained the businesses while I was…out of commission. This sale means I am slashing your income."

"But we've got plenty…"

Ben held up a hand. "I know, but you shouldn't suffer for my mistakes."

"You haven't done anything wrong. We both know who is to blame."

"She's still your mother, Shirl."

"Don't I know it? I'll never forgive her for what she did, but I don't want your money. You've already given us a house, and we've still got the garages, so we'll be fine. I just want you to be happy."

"I am happy. You'd have had the money anyway once I've gone, and I'd rather you have it now while I can watch you spend it."

"But what are you going to live on? You are still young."

Ben waved away her fears. "I've got more than enough. I've hardly spent anything in the last couple of years and invested heavily in a pension scheme. I still have my shares and some insurance policies to cash in. Your mother agreed that she wouldn't touch that. I'll be fine."

"Are you sure she can't return for more once you've finalised the divorce?"

"I am. The solicitors have sorted it all out. It'll be fine."

"And will you?" She hugged him.

"Will I be what?"

"Fine?"

"I will," he said, kissing her head.

"I'd still like you to come away with us. A holiday might do you good."

"We'll see."

Even after two months on the job, Nick Kingston still found it strange to know he was getting paid for sitting behind a desk. The hours were a bonus: 9 am to 5 pm, Monday through Friday, with Wednesdays off to attend college, much better than his previous employment.

The weather outside was glorious, quite unusual for a day in May, and the lack of ventilation in his office in the old bank building made him sleepy. His concentration was waning, but he was startled back to life by a buzzing intercom. He rubbed his face and picked up the receiver.

"Yes, can I help you?"

"Mr Laing to see Chris Shanklin."

Nick glanced at the appointments listed on the whiteboard. Mr Laing's name was there. He checked the clock; the visitor was punctual.

"Be right with you."

His boss was drinking tea while looking out the office window. The refurbishment of this room was complete, and the air conditioning made it a lot cooler than Nick's office. "Mr Laing is here to see you."

"Yes, I know. I saw them arrive."

"Them? I assumed he was on his own. Shall I let them in?"

"Yes, take them to the board room..." another room with air-con, "...and offer them a drink. Get your tablet and join us. Make a note of anything you find interesting."

The four exchanged handshakes before they sat in pairs on opposite sides of a large meeting table, with plastic beakers of water in front of them.

The younger visitor made the introductions. He was dressed smartly in a crisp white shirt and navy suit.

"Thanks for seeing us, Mr Shanklin. As I just mentioned, this is my father, Francis Laing, and I'm his younger son, Gavin."

Chris Shanklin studied the pair for a moment as his brain made connections.

"Thank you for coming. How do you think we can help?"

The older man, who looked lost, lifted his hand and pointed at Nick. "Who is he? Why is he here?"

"This is Nick. He's recently joined us, and I am keen to make sure he gets to see every aspect of our business."

The older man folded his arms and sat back, lips fast.

"My father does not like discussing business in front of strangers. I've explained about you, but he was not expecting to see Nick. Can he leave?"

"He can, but you would have to leave too. It is not company policy that customers get seen alone."

Nick knew this was a lie but said nothing and did not move.

"If you are worried that we are here to hurt you, please be assured we are not. We want to employ your services, but it is a rather delicate matter that we would prefer to keep secret."

“I am not sure why you think I might be worried. I would have to know something about you before I could be worried about you. However, if you are here to cause trouble or make threats, I should advise you that it is company policy to record all conversations. We are recording this discussion on video and audio recorders. If you were to hurt either of us, then others would get to know about it.”

This news was a surprise to Nick. He had not seen any cameras installed during the refurbishment.

The younger visitor looked suitably impressed as he examined the room.

Shanklin continued, “…but we pride ourselves on our confidentiality. Whatever gets said between us stays between us. The surveillance protects us, but we may use it as evidence in case of problems.”

“Fair enough. Let’s get down to business.” He sipped water as he prepared his comments. “A few years ago, you helped my ex-stepmother, Matilda, obtain details of…how shall I say this? Offshore investments that helped her secure a much-increased divorce settlement.”

“I can neither confirm nor deny involvement in such matters, but please remember that we have only recently established this business.”

“We were told by her solicitors…who we have retained to work for us. They advised you used to work freelance with a small team of investigators.”

“Again, I cannot comment on what I might or might not have done before starting here.”

“Understood. If you were involved, you did a thorough job. Every aspect of that job was impressive. You managed to convince my cousin, Gus, to help you. At that time, he was the last person we expected to betray us, but we know better now. Your preparation was extraordinarily comprehensive. From the row in a public place to how your fellow staged the fight, it was all pure genius. If the police arrested your man for hitting my brother, he would have claimed he was upset. Who was he, by the way? Graham told us that the mystery attacker was a swift mover for a bulky man. He shuddered when he thought about his chin hitting that knee."

Shanklin said nothing. His poker face was intact.

"That divorce cost my father a fortune, but he now accepts that he should never have tried to hide the money. They were legitimate investments that he built up before my mother died. By right, there was no way that bit... my ex-stepmother should have had any of it, but the Courts took a dim view of my father's deceit. I often wonder how you found out about them?"

Shanklin shrugged. "As I said, I can neither...."

"Okay, okay, I get it. I just wanted to congratulate you on a job well done. Hopefully, you will be as successful with our case as we are."

Nick was intrigued but remained calm, ensuring he did not fidget.

Mr Shanklin sipped his water, ran his tongue over his lips and said, "How do you think we can help."

"My ex-stepmother, Matilda, walked away with a fortune, but that is history now. My father has accepted it and bears no malice. In his business, he quickly restored his fortune."

"What is his business?" asked Mr Shanklin.

The younger Laing nodded knowingly. "Sorry, I should have said. My father used to run fast-food ventures across the southwest. Regrettably, a few years ago, Dad was diagnosed with dementia and can no longer manage independently. Some days, he is more lucid than others, but his decisions are erratic, and he cannot always remember what was agreed. My elder brother, Graham, who met with your operative, left to run a business he started in Majorca. I look after the shops and our most recent ventures, including hotels, pubs and nightclubs. My sister manages our taxi firms, laundries, and betting offices."

"Cash-rich businesses."

"Yes, I suppose they are, but people are keen on card payments these days." He waited for a reaction but did not get one.

"You mentioned a cousin?"

"Gus. Yes. He's no longer part of the family, I'm afraid.

"Oh really?" Shanklin feared the worst. "Is he okay?"

Laing Jr picked up on his tone. "Nothing like that. When dear Matilda told my father that she was leaving the country to be with another man, it was her step-nephew, Gus, to whom she was running. He is the same age as her but as thick as a dog's muck. Gus is very easy to manipulate, as well, you know."

Shanklin did not bite. "Very sorry to hear your family's bad news, but can I just ask how this affects me?"

"When he left to join Matilda, Gus took a few things that were very important to my father...."

"Such as?"

"A hard drive containing videos my father obtained and kept as security to ensure his enemies would not hurt him."

"His insurance policy?"

"Exactly, that is a much better way of describing it. In addition to his insurance policy, Gus took a box of discs. I am unsure if they were CDs or DVDs, but they are important to my father for several reasons."

"Why? What's on them?"

"You don't need to know that."

"Then I don't want your business." Shanklin rose from his chair. "Thank you for visiting."

Gavin looked at his father, who muttered. "Tell him."

Shanklin took his seat.

"They contain family videos taken when my mother was alive, family holidays, birthdays, parties at the house, etcetera."

"And?"

"That's it."

"Again, thank you for visiting. I hope you have a pleasant journey back." He stood again.

Frankie Laing spoke. "Sit down, Mr Shanklin. My son refuses to tell you that the discs contain details of hidden bank accounts. I put half the details on the discs and kept the remaining information in my notebook. I used to know the numbers off by heart, but…now…I cannot recall them. I try hard, but I can't get them." He bent over and covered his face in his hands. "295…"

"It's okay, Dad." Gavin put his hand on his father's shoulder. "Don't be upset. It's not important. Mr Shanklin will find them. You said he was good. Now relax, take a deep breath and sit back."

Frankie looked at his son and nodded, slowly sitting back.

Shanklin took another drink of water and asked the visitors if they wanted any more. Both shook their heads.

"When did you discover these were missing?"

"Just after Gus walked out about three and a half years ago."

"And only now are you looking for them?"

"My father insisted he could remember them, so he wasn't bothered apart from the sentimental value. He refused to write down the complete account details for fear of you, or someone like you, getting hold of them again. Now that we want to access the accounts, he cannot remember the details. He is becoming more sullen and angry, and showing him old family videos calms him down. He has seen the ones we have so many times he gets frustrated that he cannot see the rest. He knows they exist and is like a dog with a bone."

"What about the insurance policies? Why do you need them now?"

"One of our competitors is beginning to push his luck. We think he knows that Gus took the evidence."

"Where are Gus and Matilda?"

"We have no idea. We have tried everything. We've contacted old friends and friends of friends, searched social media, and visited her old favourite haunts, but there is no sign. Someone told us they spotted her in Morocco, so we searched but found nothing. We have no idea where they are."

"What would you like us to do exactly?"

"Get it all back. We don't want to know how you get the disks or where Matilda and my dickhead cousin are. We want our property back while Dad is still around to enjoy it."

Shanklin asked them many questions and made notes of old email addresses, pseudonyms, and social media details. Gavin agreed to send photographs of the pair and any other supporting information they might have. He showed the Laings off the property and was surprised when Frankie turned to him, shook his hand and said, "Please find them."

Shanklin walked in carrying a laptop.

"Here you are, Nick. I've cracked the log-on password but haven't tried to open anything else. I didn't want to poke my nose in."

Nick had been thinking about the Laing visit and how he would find the missing nephew and ex-wife. His boss's arrival quickly brought Nick's attention back to the room.

"Thanks, Mr Shanklin," he said, taking the computer. "That didn't take you very long."

"Well, it is what I trained to do, so it shouldn't come as that much of a surprise. By the way, Nick, please stop calling me Mr Shanklin. We are not in school now. Call me Chris. Mr Shanklin sounds so formal, especially when we have customers around."

"Yeah, of course, I will do…er…Chris."

"That's better. Now, I expect you'll want to go home with your mother and explore your father's machine."

"But it's only three o'clock."

"Well, I won't tell if you don't." His boss winked as he smiled. "Anyway, it's far too hot here today, and whatever we haven't done can wait until next week. Do you need a lift?"

"No thanks, I have my bike. The laptop will fit in my backpack."

"Right, I'll go and shut up shop and see you Monday. Enjoy the weekend."

"Just one thing." Shanklin stopped, and Nick added, "Why did you say the conversation with the Laings was getting recorded?"

"That was just a bit of a bluff to ensure they behaved."

"Good thinking."

"I can't take any credit for it. My brother-in-law is very good at it. We call it SBS talk."

"SBS? Was he in the special services?"

"Not as far as I know, but he would never say anything even if he was. His nickname is Snowy, and it stands for Snowy's Bull Shit talk. I'll see you Monday."

Rob Cromwell would not listen. "Look, Jon, you know the score. Ritchie needs to learn the ropes, and who better to teach him than you? You know the business as well as anyone. You've been with me since we expanded, and you know the projects inside out. I know it will take time, but you must be patient with him."

"But Rob, he's not interested. All he wants to do is sit at his desk texting that girlfriend of his. I try to get him to work, but he won't listen."

"Well, you must make him listen to you. You can't keep running to me with problems. You are the general manager here."

"I thought I was project manager?"

"That as well, but the key task is to be a manager. You don't manage by running to the boss all the time. You must make Rich do the work; otherwise, you can never gain his respect."

"What respect is he going to have for me when he knows that one day he will be running the show?"

"Total respect if you tell him what's what. You must start engaging him in things instead of keeping him out."

"I do try to engage him, but he's not interested. I have

given him projects, easy ones to start with...."

"That's it, then. It would help if you challenged him. Richard has been through university, and he needs challenges. Give him the more difficult projects."

"But how would he manage the bigger projects if he can't even do the easy ones? I've got no fucking chance."

"That's enough of that language. Thank you, Jon. Please remember that I am still the one paying the wages here. May I also remind you that only three months ago, you agreed to mentor my son and guide him when he takes over the business? In exchange for showing him the ropes, I agreed to award you a significant pay raise that you need to start earning."

"But I haven't seen a penny of it yet. "

"That is because you have not yet taught him anything. When I see signs that my son is improving and it is evident that you are bringing him on, I will give you the extra cash."

"But how can I bring him on if he doesn't do what I ask?"

"You'd better find a way if you want to see that extra cash. Now I've got to go. I'm taking my wife to choose her new car and, by the way, I need an update on the flats for tomorrow. I am meeting the directors of the housing association."

"That's one of Rich's. Ask him for the update."

"You are still the project manager, and I am telling you what I need."

"But it's gone six now. I am supposed to be going home."

"Do it in the morning, then. I won't need it until 8. We tee off at 8.30."

That was not what Jon wanted to hear. He didn't usually work on Saturday.

Gemma Potter downed a second glass of wine and sighed. Mac would be there any moment, and she was not looking forward to his arrival. They were not getting on as well as they did, and Gemma recognised it was her fault. Mac wanted more from their relationship than she would give.

When her parents visited over Easter, she resisted his attempts to meet them and join in the sightseeing. It had not pleased him to be left out. He questioned what Gemma wanted from the relationship and whether she thought he was good enough for her and her family. Gemma repeated that they were not in a serious relationship. She thought they had agreed to keep things on a casual basis. Mac said he had never agreed to that and wanted her to move in with him. Her laughter hadn't helped the situation.

A girly weekend, Carrie and Kate's visit placed additional strain on Mac and her. He had turned up at one of the bars the girls were visiting, and she had to tell him that he was not welcome. This was a sisters-only event. He stormed off and did not contact her for a fortnight. She hoped he was sending her a message that they were no longer together, but that hope ended when he texted her to apologise and ask her to attend a concert with him. She had been a fool to accept because since then, he talked about them taking things to the next stage and tried to get her to agree to go on holiday with him. That thought did not excite her. It reminded Gemma that she had not told him she was going to Majorca with Zoe and two other friends in July. She would break that news tonight.

Gemma walked a few steps to the bar and ordered another drink. As she waited for the barman to serve her, she stared at herself in the mirror behind the optics. Gemma nodded at her reflection as she made her decision. She would end things with Mac. He was a great guy, but she had never anticipated him getting so serious about her. He wanted commitments Gemma was not ready to make. Why couldn't he accept it was a bit of fun? She was only twenty and not looking for domestic bliss. He was barely three years older and should be out enjoying himself.

She would tell him tonight.

Nick munched on his sandwich as his mother examined the email exchanges for the umpteenth time.

"You recovered these emails from the hard drive?"

"Yes. Someone had deleted them all."

"And the account information confirms the amounts, dates, and the account into which the money went?"

Nick swallowed his food. "Hmm... yes... the money left your bank accounts and was transferred to Dad's account in Gibraltar."

"What was he doing with an account there?"

Nick shrugged.

"No idea, but it looks like it had been dormant for years. Only a few hundred pounds were in it until Dad emptied the accounts."

"He must have opened it when he worked in the Gulf. I recall him saying something about an offshore account to avoid tax. I didn't know it was in Gibraltar, though."

"Whenever he opened it, the money went there, and he transferred the whole amount in the weeks before the stroke. "

"And that was after the threatening emails arrived?"

"Yes, that's what it looks like."

"The bastard, how could he do that to us?"

"Well, now we know, we can do something about it. I will get the solicitor on to it on Monday morning."

"Hang on a minute, Nick. Let's think about this." Her son's expression told her he wanted her to continue. "Solicitors cost money, and it could take ages to get anywhere. Let's see if we can finish this by ourselves. We've come this far without any help from anyone. How good would it feel to get to the bottom of this and sort it out on our own?"

Nick nodded and smiled. "Yes, I would love to see the look on certain faces. Let's do this as they say in those television programmes you like. Let's work out a plan."

Chris Shanklin said goodbye and closed the call. Snowy would let him know whether he fancied getting reacquainted with the Laings. It had gone like clockwork the last time, but things were different now. For one thing, could they trust that the Laings had spoken the truth on their recent visit? They might be setting a trap. For another thing, they had lost the element of surprise. Gus would certainly recognise Snowy, putting them at an advantage. Finally, they had no idea where the pair had gone; even if they found them, they would probably need to retrieve the items from overseas. Shanklin was nervous about that. He knew Snowy loved taking risks, but Shanklin was uncomfortable because guns would be readily available in certain countries.

DAY 12 - WEDNESDAY 4 AUGUST

"Mummy, mummy, I need an aeroplane," Harry shouted. He had watched another child throw the balsa wood toy across the beach, and it looked fun.

"Not now, Harry. That little boy is older than you. I can't let you run around the beach chasing it like that."

"But mummy, I need an aeroplane."

"No, you don't. You might want one, but you don't need one."

"Yes, yes, I do. I need an aeroplane."

"You don't need one, Harry. You simply want one."

"Well, I want one, then."

"Let's see how well you behave. At the moment, you don't deserve one."

He looked frustrated.

Daisy joined him and his mother. "Mum, I need a wee."

"You might want one, but you don't need one." Harry stormed off to join his brother.

Nick and Gemma returned from the shops, holding hands and carrying plastic bags.

"It's a shame we are going home in three days."

"It is. I've had a fab time."

"Me too, thanks. You'll have to give me your address," said Nick. "I'll pop over to visit you." Before Gemma had time to answer, Nick's attention had moved elsewhere. "What's going on?"

"What?"

Nick pointed to the internet café surrounded by scaffolding. "There, Donny's place. I wonder what they are doing."

"Do you care? Really?"

"I'm just being nosey. Come on."

They entered the café to find the miserable bar steward reading a comic book.

"Where's Donny?" Nick asked.

"He's probably packing his suitcase."

"Packing? Where's he going?"

"Ibiza. He and Christiano are going with Grigor and Graham for the weekend."

"Nice," said Nick.

"It is okay for some. The painters start work tomorrow, so I won't be able to work. I have to take a few days off."

"Lucky you," Gemma said.

"Not really. I won't get paid."

"Couldn't you work while they paint outside?" Nick asked.

"No, they will be painting here starting Friday. Before then, I have to pack everything up and store it upstairs. Barty is supposed to be helping me, but he will probably turn up late, if he turns up at all. He spends all his time pretending to be a private eye."

"Why can't Donny and whatsisname do it?"

The man laughed. "That is a good one. They do as little as possible around here. They travel to Palma tomorrow, attend a Magaluf party, and leave for Ibiza on Friday."

Nick looked at Gemma and smiled. "If we'd known, we could have gone with them."

"I'd rather have needles in my eyes," said Gemma, meaning every word.

Barty followed Snowy and the older man, leaving the estate agency holding sheets of paper at a safe distance. Barty thought they had booked tickets for a trip and wondered if his father would lend him the car at short notice should he need to follow them. He deliberated whether to enquire at the agency to find out where the pair were going, but he worried word might get to Snowy, blowing Barty's cover.

Ben and Will waited in the hypermarket café as Shirley ordered the coffee.

"It's nice and cool in here. It must cost them a fortune in aircon."

Ben pointed at the main shopping area. "I can't imagine they are that bothered. Look how busy it is."

"You could have opened one of these back home."

"Nah, new places like this are soulless tin boxes. I always liked the atmosphere of an old building. I also felt that I was helping save the planet in my little way by recycling rather than building new."

"It's a shame your products had such a noticeable carbon footprint. Half of your household goods came from China, and you imported a lot of fruit and vegetables."

"It's what the customer wanted. Thanks, love." Ben took the cup from Shirley's tray and sipped it before placing it on the table. "That's nice. Anyway, it's too late to concern ourselves with all that now. I'll leave someone else to worry about it."

"No news on when our Welsh friend intends to visit us?" Grigor flopped onto the sofa.

"Not yet. Barty said he booked a trip today and thinks he will be away tomorrow. I guess he will visit us on Friday when we are in Palma."

"Assuming he knows our plans."

"Shit, I can't imagine anyone in Sa Coma hasn't heard about our trip. Donny and Chris have been telling everyone."

Grigor cackled. "They are very excited. By the way, he dislikes being called Chris. It's Christiano."

Graham stood and picked up the mug from the table. "Pretentious Portugese Prick. I'll call him what I fucking well like." He showed the cup to Grigor. "When is Lucia due to visit?"

"Not until Monday. I didn't see the point of her coming in when we were away."

"Bollocks. I suppose I'd better wash this myself then."

"Or leave it for Barty to do. He'll call in later expecting payment."

"Brilliant. I'll do that." He put the cup down. "Come on, let's go and visit Alfie's. You can give me a hiding at pool."

"We need to be more careful."

"I need to be more careful, you mean. You are not the one who lost a laptop."

"At least we still have Kylie's movie." Christiano smoothed his companion's hair.

"Some consolation, I suppose. I am not happy that Sara will get away scot-free. That bitch needs to get taught a lesson."

"You win some. You lose some."

They kissed.

"Come on. Let's go shopping. I need to look my best if we have a weekend of partying." Christiano got out of bed, grabbed his shorts, and then sat back down to put them on. "We can sort out this other stuff when we get back."

"You always know how to cheer me up," said Donny, kissing his friend's shoulder.

The last person Lucia expected to serve in the shop was Ben.

"Elizabeth said you'd be here."

"That woman, she has trouble keeping this shut." She zipped her mouth.

"I am not sure she thought it was a secret."

"I am only joking. How are you? I did not see you yesterday. I thought I had upset you with my words."

"You're okay. I have thick skin." Ben looked around. The shelves were messy, and some vegetables looked like they had been there a while. "I see what you mean about the shop needing attention. Are those avocados?"

"Si, but they have been left too long. I would put them in

the bin, but he will make me pay for it."

"What about the shelves? There is stuff all over the place." Ben stepped away from the counter and picked up three tins. "Tomatoes and beans on the same shelf, I can understand, but rice pudding? Does anyone actually eat rice pudding these days?"

"He thinks people like to see a whole meal in one place." She shook her head. "He bought a lot of tins of that Ambrosia for the tourists, but they don't come here as he won't sell other English products. He purchases cheap varieties and charges a lot. He then complains that we don't sell enough. It is little wonder he loses money. Gabriela tries to tell him, but he won't listen. He is a stubborn man."

"What are you doing this evening?"

"Me? I am looking after my grandson so Gabriela can work."

"Elizabeth said that would be the case. How would you feel if Elizabeth looked after the baby and you came for a meal with me?"

"How does Elizabeth feel about this?"

"It is her idea."

"Just me and you? Out for a meal?"

"Yes."

"Where?"

"Wherever you like. My treat."

"Why?"

"I want to tell you something and to say thank you."

"Thank me? What for?"

"For being there and telling me straight."

Lucia wasn't sure what that meant but smiled and nodded. "It is a long time since I go out. I am not sure I have anything to wear."

"You look fine as you are."

"Now that is a lie." She put her hands on the counter and stretched her arms. "I will find something. What time?"

"I am at your disposal."

Charlie was determined to hold the pool cue even though he could not reach the table. Jon pulled a chair across for his son to stand on and tried again to help him, but the lad was adamant. "No, I will do it."

His brother pushed another chair closer to the table and clambered up, leaning over the opposite side.

"You be careful now, Harry. You will hurt yourself if you fall."

"I'm okay."

Charlie hit the white ball, rolling it down the table. It missed most of the balls but tapped a yellow ball."

"Unlucky," Jon said, putting his hands on Charlie's hips and getting ready to put him on the floor.

Harry pushed the yellow ball into a pocket. "Good shot."

Charlie dropped the cue and stood with his hands in the air. "Yes."

Jon shrugged at Leah, who covered her mouth as she giggled.

"I have no chance with these two," said Jon. "Right. What ball are you going for next?"

Ben Moran held open the door for his companion and followed her into the restaurant. "Have you been here before?"

"No. A friend told me about it."

A waitress appeared, took their names and led them up the stairs. Ben had expected to sit on the ground floor and was worried they would end up at some out-of-the-way table. He relaxed as he entered a candlelit dining room with views over the sea. The restaurant was busy, but the waitress took them to a quiet spot by the open patio doors.

"Is this okay?" The waitress asked.

Ben looked at his companion, who nodded and said, "Perfect, thanks."

Shirley sipped her beer. "I wonder what he's ordered." She checked her watch. "They booked the table for eight, and it's half past now, so they must be into their starters, don't you think?"

"Aye, I reckon he's gone for garlic mushrooms if they have them, something safe."

"Or maybe soup," said Shirley. "He likes a nice drop of soup."

"He does, but we can be sure he won't go for anything Spanish or fishy. I reckon his main course will be chicken."

"Steak if he wants to impress," said Shirley. "I hope they do it well done."

"Remember that steak we had in Harrogate? It only had the slightest trace of blood, but he complained like hell."

"He enjoyed the tacos we had the following night, though." Shirley smiled as she recalled when her father had a fire in his belly and an interest in everything new.

The waiter took their order and promised to return with their wine. Ben looked over his companions' shoulders to the promenade's lights and the sea beyond them.

"This is a delightful place."

"I think so."

"The view is stunning from where I am sitting, and the scenery behind you isn't bad either."

Lucia chuckled. "You are very cheeky, but I will take it. It has been a long time since anyone gave me a compliment. Thank you, Ben."

Elizabeth sat quietly watching English television programmes dubbed into Spanish, the grandson sleeping peacefully nearby. She was happy to think of her new friends enjoying themselves at the restaurant.

It was time she got out more. She did not think she needed a man in that sense, but a companion would be good. Someone to go for a meal with, visit theatres, and go on trips. Nick was forging a new life and, before too much longer, would be off doing all the things he hadn't been able to do since his father died. It was time to regain her life.

When she got home, she would look up old friends and see what they were doing and if they'd fancy catching up. She wondered if Chris Shanklin would like to go to the theatre. Nick said his boss got lonely sometimes.

She checked the internet to see what shows were coming to Cardiff.

Ben asked for a second bottle of Rioja.

"Are you trying to get me drunk?"

"No, not necessarily. I am just having a good time."

"Me too, but I don't need wine to enjoy myself."

"Nor me, but it is an excellent wine."

"The best in all of Spain."

Scaffolding poles and planks obstructed the security camera, and Nick opened the rear door and stepped inside. He was relieved the door was open. He was unsure what he would have done if he found it locked. The staircase was dark. Stepping quickly and silently, Nick reached the top of the stairs and opened the office door. The blinds had been partially drawn, letting in light from outside. Nick chose not to put on any internal lights. The room looked as though nothing had moved since the previous Saturday. Nick felt uneasy but did not know whether that was because he worried about being caught or knowing what had happened in the building. Either way, he would spend no longer there than was necessary.

Nick entered the storage area and reached to collect the backups, but he did not get to touch them. A gloved hand covered his mouth and pulled him backwards, and another handheld something against his neck.

"Don't say a word. Understand? Not a word."

The man's voice sounded Welsh, but he had spoken in barely more than a whisper. Nick nodded, and the man released his grip, allowing Nick to turn and face him.

"What are you doing here?"

"Saving you from making stupid mistakes."

"How did you know I was here?"

Will pointed a finger at his temple. "Experience." He nodded knowingly. "You don't have to whisper, by the way. He's never going to hear us up here."

"Then why were you whispering?"

Will shrugged. "For effect mostly. It sounds more sinister, don't you think?"

"Possibly. What are you doing here?"

"I told you. I'm saving you from making stupid mistakes. Chris asked me to keep an eye on you."

"What? Why?"

"He was worried about you."

"There was no need. I have everything under control."

"That's nice to know. So tell me, why did you not disable the CCTV camera?"

"It couldn't see anything. The planks of wood blocked the view."

"I see. What about the temporary ones installed on the scaffolding?"

"What temporary ones?"

"The one that you missed." He sensed Nick did not believe him. "Come with me."

Nick followed him to the office, where the man switched on a monitor and fiddled with a mouse. Nick saw himself entering the car park. Pressing a button switched the view to the camera pointing at the rear door. There was Nick as he entered the building, looking around sheepishly. Will moved the mouse, pressed the enter button, and accepted the offer to delete.

"You need to be a lot more careful. Situations change minute by minute, day by day. What's broken on your first visit can be fixed and catch you out the next. It would help if you were more thorough with your research and preparation. You mustn't rush things. I am glad to see you remembered to wear gloves, though."

"Won't that camera film us as we leave?"

"Not when I set it to delete and adjust the timer. Your friends will blame an installation error."

"They are no friends of mine."

"It was only a figure of speech. Keep your hair on."

Nick nodded and mumbled, "Sorry."

"No worries. Shall we go?"

"Hang on. I need to retrieve something."

"If you are talking about the backups, don't worry. I have already erased them and, for good measure, ensured they can never work again."

"Wouldn't it be better to take them?"

"And put what in their place?"

"Nothing. Nobody will be here over the weekend."

"What happens when they get back?"

"I'll be long gone."

"And you don't think it might look a tad suspicious that their website went down and someone stole their backups the very weekend they were away? They will know it was an inside job. If we leave things where they are, they might assume that the discs got corrupted because they haven't been used for so long. Chris intends to make it look like a rival has hacked the site."

"How would he..."

"No idea. He'll think of something."

"How do you know him?"

"I've known Chris for years. Buy me a pint, and I'll tell you about it. Let's get out of here before someone finds us."

Ben and Elizabeth strolled across the sand back to the apartment block. She held her shoes in one hand and her cardigan in another as she paddled in the sea by the water's edge.

"You enjoyed the meal then?" She asked.

"It was great, thank you. The octopus salad starter was superb, as was the grilled bream. I cannot remember the last time I tasted fish as good as that."

"And you said you don't like to try new things."

"I know. I don't think Shirley and Will will believe me when I tell them. How was your meal?"

"Lovely, you can't beat homemade lasagne even if it was reheated."

"It's been a lovely evening. I thoroughly enjoyed myself. Thank you so much, Elizabeth."

"There's no need to thank me. I'm just pleased you had a good time. Did you manage to discuss your plans?"

"I did, but I am sure Lucia thinks I am crazy. She cannot believe I would take such a risk."

"I'm sure you know what you are doing."

"Thank you. I do, too, although I still have to tell Shirley."

Nick was fascinated to learn that Will was his ex-teacher's brother-in-law. He would never have imagined meeting Snowy, whom Chris often spoke about. The description was spot on. Snowy was a character.

Will had always been a rebel, and it was no surprise to his parents and two sisters that he fell in with the wrong crowd. His father suggested that Will might benefit from spending time in boxing classes. Will found that he loved the discipline of sport and won several competitions. When he left school, Will followed the path trodden by his father and joined the Navy. He served at home and abroad.

Chris met Will's sister, Eluned, when she was on vacation in Washington, where he worked for Microsoft. They maintained a long-distance relationship because she was a special needs teacher who loved her job so much that there was no chance of her giving it up to live in the States. Chris took the opportunity to move to the company's European offices just outside Dublin, and the pair married. They bought the house in Cowbridge, and Chris came home every weekend.

By a stroke of luck, Microsoft, working in partnership with another company, developed communication software for military operatives. Will got involved in the testing and was eventually introduced to one of the software engineers. He was staggered to see his sister's boyfriend in the same room, but they got on well, and Chris taught him a lot.

Sadly, Eluned developed MND, which ravaged her body. She quickly became dependent on others to look after her. Chris gave up his job to become a full-time carer, but Eluned passed shortly after his return home.

Chris was lost for a few years until he began teaching and slowly regained his interest in software. He developed the forensic software that made his fortune.

A UK police force needed help tracking the funds from a drugs and weapons operation and called in Chris for advice on the best use of his software. Chris invited Will to work with him, and the rest was history. Will had always been happier working 'in the field,' believing his role to be a quasi-private investigator. The work resulted in him meeting his wife and becoming a stepdad to her two children. He suggested this might be his last job as he wanted to spend more time at home.

Nick told his story and said that Chris had greatly supported him. He mentioned that he had recently become involved in one of Chris's forensic cases involving a man who disappeared with items belonging to his uncle. Will laughed and revealed that he had been tasked with finding Gus and Matilda Laing, which was why he was on the island. He briefly outlined his progress to date and his next steps.

"Do you need any help?" Nick asked.

"No thanks. It should be straightforward from now on. Graham and Grigor, aka Gus, are heading to Magaluf tomorrow for a party. On Friday, they go to Ibiza until Monday. I'll double-check they've gone and then enter the property on Friday morning to retrieve the goods."

"What if the goods, as you call them, aren't in the house? You could waste a lot of time searching. Four hands and all that?"

Having searched the boats, Will was confident the items

were at the house. If they weren't, they had to be stored somewhere else, possibly in a safe deposit box. He had no idea where to find one or how to get into it, and time was running out. He needed the stuff to be at the house, but his job might be easier if he had an assistant. It would be an easy task. What could go wrong? "Okay, here's what we will do..."

BOOKINGS AND CANCELLATIONS

(THREE WEEKS BEFORE THE HOLIDAY)

Gemma Potter stood beside the bed to pull her top over her head. Her partner stirred.

"What time is it?"

"It's early. Go back to sleep."

He sat up with his back against the pillow. "What time are you meeting your folks?"

"Their flight gets in at ten."

"What time is your graduation?"

"They expect our group to be on about three-ish."

"I can still come along if you want. I can take a duvet day."

Not this again, she thought. "No, you're okay. You go to work."

"For fuck's sake, Gem, I'm your boyfriend. I'm supposed to meet your family."

Gemma had put on her jeans and was bending to tie up the laces on her boots. She left that task and stood to face him, hands on hips. "Mac, we have been over and over this, you and me…it's fun, but nothing serious."

"It's pretty serious to me. We've been together for nearly two years."

"We've hardly been together, together, have we? At most, we only see each other once a week."

"And whose fault is that? I want to see you more often, but you keep telling me you are too busy. I asked you to move in here, but you refused. I've started to think you only want to see me for sex."

Gemma thought that suggestion might be valid but said, "Don't be silly. It's just that I told you I didn't want anything serious. I am not ready to be tied down. It's too soon for me to think about commitment. You said you understood, but now you're more clingy than ever."

"I didn't know it was bad to want to be with someone and get to know their family."

"It's not, but it gives the wrong signals."

"Why, though? I am not asking you to marry me. I want to be with you."

"I told you I'm not looking for anything serious."

"It wouldn't have to interrupt your plans."

"What about your plans?" Changing the focus of the discussion had worked in the past. "You love Edinburgh. You've barely been outside Scotland."

"And your point is?"

"I return home to Cheltenham tomorrow."

"But you'll be back; you're doing your Masters up here."

She tilted her head to gaze at the ceiling and exhaled loudly. "I've already explained that I'll do most of the work at home. I only have to come up here for the odd discussion and occasional tutorial."

"I could see you when you come back, and I can visit you. Mickey is a good boss. He would let me get away Friday lunchtime and come back Monday. I'll make up the hours through the week."

This offer was not new. "I've told you I will work for my dad. He's getting busier and needs my help. I don't want to have to miss work to entertain you."

"Entertain? Is that how you see me, someone to be entertained? What am I? A fucking five-year-old?"

"Well, you're acting like one. Grow up!" She immediately regretted her words.

"For fuck's sake, Gemma. Give it to me straight, why don't you." He slid back down the bed and grabbed a pillow to hug.

She exhaled again. "Look, Mac, I like you, but that's all. I don't love you, and I don't see us having a long-term relationship. It's been fun. It has, but now it is time to go our separate ways."

"You said that last week and the week before. Yet, you are in my room again, having spent the night in my bed."

He had a point, but she kept falling for his false promises. The drink might have affected her common sense. As soon as she entered his flat and heard his expressions of love, Gemma knew he wasn't committed to the notion of one last fling. "This has been a mistake."

"You said that before."

I mean it this time." She opened the bedroom door. "Bye, Mac, be happy, and maybe I'll see you around."

"Fuck off, you English bitch."

Going private was a lot different from dealing with the NHS. He was seen on time, in comfortable surroundings and greeted by staff who appeared to have all the time in the world. The doctor sat the three down, outlined her prognosis, and explained the treatment options. The result would have been the same on the NHS but would have cost less.

The advice was that Ben needed chemotherapy. This would be an intense treatment to be followed by further sessions depending on the success of the first. There may be side effects, and it was not always a comfortable treatment, but there was every reason to believe it would be successful. They had spotted the tumour early, and there was no sign of any secondary cancers.

Ben smiled and nodded, hiding his disbelief at what he was hearing. In his experience, cancer was neither treatable nor beatable. His parents had started their treatments with tremendous optimism, but the disease had beaten them. Why did anyone think his outcome would be different?

He had already decided not to have the treatment and would look for a way to end his life that was quick, painless and did not look like suicide. He doubted his death would be a significant loss. His family would be better off with him dead. They could move on with their lives and not have to watch him deteriorate as he had with his parents. It was important to him that his life insurance company paid out on the multiple policies that had cost a fortune.

Ben mentioned the forthcoming trip to Majorca and asked if he could delay treatment until after that. He did not want to miss the holiday. The doctor said she could offer no guarantees and would prefer the treatment to start immediately. That said, nothing suggested the tumour was aggressive; if Ben wanted to wait a few weeks, that was his choice. However, he would need to have the first course immediately upon his return.

As they returned to the car, Will and Shirl said they were thrilled Ben would accompany them to Majorca. A couple of weeks in the sun would probably do him good. It would certainly do him no harm.

Gemma's parents only visited for a day and had gone to the airport for their return flight to Bristol. Gemma returned her hired garments, a cap and gown, changed her clothes, and was sat in the Café Royal, enjoying a cocktail.

"Cheers," she said, clinking her glass against Zoe's.

"Slainte Mhath," said Zoe.

Gemma had delayed her return home by 24 hours to attend Zoe's 21st birthday party. The pair awaited the arrival of other guests.

"I feel like getting rat-arsed tonight," said Gemma.

"You weren't exactly sober last night. How did Cally's parents take it? They are not keen on their daughter imbibing the devil's brew. "

"No idea."

"Weren't they at home?"

"No idea." Zoe expected an explanation."I never made it back to Cally's."

"So, where did you...not with Mac? Please tell me you didn't end up at his place?"

"Well, he was in the Conan Doyle, and we started

talking."

Zoe's expression suggested she thought Gemma was crazy. "Gemma, this is me you are talking to, Zoe Crosby, daughter of Mickey Crosby, general builder, Mac's boss. My father said that Mac was practically in tears all last week because you had broken up with him again. Mac thinks the world of you. How could you be so cruel as to string him along?"

"I didn't mean to, but he turned up and asked if we could talk. One thing led to another. He assured me he would not read too much into it, so I went to his for old times' sake."

"And did he read anything into it?"

Gemma placed her fingers on her chin in mock contemplation. "Now, let me think about that. Can you guess his parting words after I refused his offer to meet my parents this morning?"

"Be happy."

"Close. Fuck off, you English bitch."

"He took it well then."

"I was a hard-nosed C U Next Tuesday last time."

"Mac has always had a way with words. He could have been a poet, you know." Gemma giggled at the absurdity of the statement. Zoe added, "Do me a favour, though; don't say a word about this to my father when you see him tonight. Mac was a right pain in his arse last time. Dad will not be happy to learn he will go through the same again."

"My lips are sealed. It's not something I would brag about." She raised her glass to her mouth. "I wish Mac was not so clingy. I tried to tell him I was not looking for anything serious. I like my freedom too much."

"I'll drink to that," said Zoe, and they did.

Jon arrived home exhausted. His boss had gone on a golfing trip to Portugal, and his assistant had disappeared to spend time with his girlfriend.

Leah had made a shepherd's pie but had expected him

home an hour earlier. The cheese was brown and crispy, although Jon assured her it was tasty.

The children played in the lounge, and when he joined them, they insisted on bringing their father up to speed with their activities that day. The boys sat on one leg while Daisy took the other. Jon asked questions and made jokes, but all he wanted to do was sleep.

Leah announced it was time for bed, and Jon rose to take them upstairs. He felt light-headed as he stood and wasn't sure if he felt a pain in his chest. Jon did not mention it to his wife; she would only worry. He was probably just overtired. They were going away in a few weeks, and the break would do him good.

Zac caught Nick with a spinning backkick that knocked him to the floor.

"Nice shot," Nick said as he pulled himself up. "I did not see that coming."

"I've been practising," said Zac. "Are you coming to the party this weekend?"

"No. I'm working."

"But I thought you had a full-time job working for Mr Shanklin."

"I do, but I still need the cash. Pizza delivery on the weekend gives you great tips."

"I suppose you'll be borrowing my car again?"

"Is that okay?"

"Of course, just don't leave any crusts on the seats. The kids find them and nag me for pizza."

"I can get you a good discount."

The party was a great success. The club rocked, with Zoe's friends and family dancing and drinking into the wee hours. Gemma was a popular dancing partner, and several of Zoe's family members asked to dance with her. Sean, Zoe's brother-in-law, insisted on several dances.

Elizabeth still wasn't convinced they needed travel insurance for a trip to Majorca. They would both be there and if anything nasty happened, they would go together. The cost seemed a luxury they could not afford.

Nick had a point when he said they needed protection against lost luggage and delayed or cancelled flights. They could ill afford to replace clothes or pay for new flights.

If everything went as they hoped, they would be considerably richer by the time they got home, but she supposed it was better to be safe than sorry.

She entered her debit card details and hit pay.

At almost four in the morning, Gemma arrived at Zoe's parents' house, an elegant four-bedroomed, three-story Georgian townhouse. Mickey wanted to keep the party going, but Gemma had drunk enough. She was ready for bed. Zoe showed her to one of the attic bedrooms, hugged her, and wished her good night.

Gemma woke with a start, realising someone had climbed in beside her. A hand caressed her breast."

"What the..."

"Shh, they'll hear us."

Gemma sat up and switched on the bedside light.

"Sean! What are you doing here?"

"I thought you'd like some company. Mac told me you enjoy a good time."

He tried easing her backwards, but Gemma pushed him away and leapt out of bed.

"I think you'd better go."

"Come on, Gemma. You've been giving me the come-on all evening. There is no need to be coy now."

She placed her left hand across her body until her palm rested on her right shoulder. Using her right hand to point at the door, she said, "Out! Piss off."

Sean did not leave. He moved closer. He pressed himself

against her. Gemma could tell he was raring for action. "Come on, Gemma. Nobody ever needs to know."

He held her tightly and tried to kiss her.

The lights went up at that moment, and Zoe's father stood in the doorway. There was much shuffling on the landing behind.

"What the fuck is going on?"

DAY 13 - THURSDAY 5 AUGUST

It had been an enjoyable evening. Nick's mum was very entertaining and welcoming, and the lad himself was attentive, generous, tactile and complimentary. Gemma felt very much at home and at ease in their company. It felt good to be with them. She liked Nick a lot. So why was she convinced that ending things now was the right decision?

Part of her concern stemmed from knowing that Nick had never been with anyone else. Everybody knew that men needed different partners before settling down; they were more likely to stray if they didn't.

Many of her friends suggested that men could not be monogamous. She doubted that was the case. Her parents had been with each other for aeons and did everything together. Men just needed time to find the right one. Nick needed to experience other women.

"You can't be serious."

"I am."

"But why? It makes no sense."

"It does to me."

"You are going to finish with him. Why exactly?"

"Because it would never work. We live too far apart."

"Rubbish. I know Wales is in the dark ages, but he can get a flight to Edinburgh within an hour."

"I might not be in Edinburgh. I might be at home."

"That's even nearer."

Kylie entered the room and told her friends to be quiet. "I can hear you shouting down the corridor. What are you barking about?"

"Gemma plans to dump Nick," said Sara.

Kylie's volume went close to maximum. "What? You're joking. Why?"

"I am not going to dump him, as you so eloquently put it. I will tell him I don't want a long-term relationship. It ends at Stage Two."

"Why?" Kylie repeated.

"Because, as I told her," she pointed at Sara, " we live too far apart."

"Rubbish," said Kylie. "What's the real reason?"

"I've just told you."

"That's crap, and you know it." She lowered her voice. "Look, Gem, we three have been mates since junior school, and we know you as well as anyone. I cannot remember you looking as happy as you have this last fortnight..."

"Nine days," said Gemma.

"I might have guessed you would have counted them," said Kylie. "What's wrong? You make each other laugh, have similar interests, and get along better than many couples who have known each other for years. You like him, and he likes you. What is your problem?"

Gemma could not explain that he had never been with a girl before. She would never betray that confidence, not even to her best friends. She sat at the dining table, hands before her, fiddling with Daisy's wristband.

"I am just not ready to move to stage three. We are too young. I must focus on my education and helping Dad build his business. You are right. I like him, but it's not the right time."

Sara and Kylie also sat.

"So, when do you think will be the right time?" Kylie asked.

"You could see him occasionally, see how it goes," Sara suggested.

"It will never work. We have spent practically every moment together for nine days, but the day after tomorrow, we go home to live hundreds of miles apart. I know there are planes, trains, and automobiles, but I will live at one end of the country, and he will be at the other. It will be difficult for us to spend every minute of every day together, and I am sure that, over time, we will grow apart."

"But why should that happen? There are plenty of ways to keep in touch. There's an airport in Cardiff with flights to Edinburgh. You can make it work," said Sara.

Gemma was not persuaded. "Once this holiday is over and he doesn't see me every minute of every day, he will move on. Holiday romances are meant to be just that. For the holidays. I am not looking for anything else."

Sara and Kylie looked at each other, frowned and shook their heads.

"Utter crap," said Kylie.

"Complete bullshit," said Sara.

"It's the truth," Gemma insisted.

Kylie nibbled her bottom lip before speaking. "What? You are seriously going to finish with the man of your dreams..."

"I am not sure I would ever call him that. That's pushing it," said Gemma.

"Okay, the best man you have met for a long time... possibly ever," said Sara.

"One of them," said Gemma.

"And all because you don't think you are ready for a serious relationship. Perhaps he's not looking for anything serious either."

I doubt he knows what he is looking for, thought Gemma. "My mind is made up," she said.

"I'm not sure you'll ever have a serious relationship," Kylie sighed.

"We'll see," said Gemma

"What if he gets upset?" Sara asked.

This was the one thing she hoped would not happen. "He won't. I don't think anybody has ever got upset about me."

"There's no way I'm feeling sorry for you," said Kylie.

"You are talking bollocks," said Sara. "Gary Cobbley was heartbroken when you finished with him."

"So heartbroken he went off with Kylie straight away."

"How did you..." Kylie said.

"He rang to tell me that he had shagged you."

"Really? The bastard. I wonder if he told anyone else."

"Probably," said Sara. "He told me too."

"But I told you?" said Kylie

"He told me first."

"Well, that's only two people," said Kylie optimistically.

Sara stretched her mouth and tightened her neck. "Err... I was in Tesco when he told me, and I knew many people in the queue. Most of the girls that work there live down our way."

"Shit! So, do you think everyone knows? That's not good." Kylie feared for her reputation. "That's so bad."

"But not as bad as what our friend here is about to do," said Sara.

"I don't know why you are so bothered," said Gemma. "You called him a gimp."

"I admit it," Sara said. "I did call him that, but that was before I got to know him. I regret speaking of Nick in such terms. Now I know him better. I like him. The fact that he is as fit as fuck has nothing to do with why I think you would be bonkers to finish with him."

Kylie agreed. "I feel the same, including the bit about him being fit as fuck. I'd have him. The clothes I can cope with as I wouldn't let him wear them for long."

Gemma shook her head in disbelief.

Sara spoke again. "Gem, go home, try the long-distance relationship thing and see how it goes. If it doesn't work out, end it, but if it does, who knows where it might lead. Think about what you are doing. Take your time."

Gemma shrugged but said nothing. She did not need time to think.

Charlie was feeling poorly, and Jon offered to stay in the apartment while Leah took the other two to the pool.

He placed a damp flannel over his son's head and told him not to cry. The medicine the emergency doctor had given him would soon work, and he would be right as rain.

Eventually, Charlie fell asleep on the sofa, and Jon moved a chair to look into the pool from the living area while remaining close to his son.

He saw Leah clapping as Harry swam from the middle to the edge of the big pool. Daisy was not impressed. She jumped in and splashed water over her brother and mother.

Jon gently touched Charlie's shoulder and leaned over to kiss the sleeping head. "We'll be in there tomorrow. Just wait and see," he said.

"I thought you liked me."

"I do like you, Nick. I like you a lot."

"Then why are you doing this? I don't understand."

"You're a great bloke, but I don't want a long-term relationship. I have too much going on at the moment. I start my Masters in a few weeks and want to help my father build his business."

"I can help you with those things."

"You can't, Nick. You'll be in Barry with your mother and friends, and I'll split my time between Edinburgh and Cheltenham. We'd never see each other."

"I can move."

"What? You'd move away to be with someone you've only known for a fortnight? Don't be ridiculous."

"I would."

"No, you wouldn't. I won't let you. This is what I was worried about. You are fanny-struck. You think you're in love with me because I'm the first girl you've had sex with."

"I never said I was in love with you, and it's not about the sex. I like being with you. You're funny, easy to talk to, and we get on well."

"But I'm the first girl you've been with. I bet there are loads of other girls who would make you feel the same."

"I doubt it."

"But you don't know that for sure, do you?"

"Nor do you."

"Fair point, but if I commit to someone, I need to know that they are with me for the right reasons, not because they don't know any different. You could be the one for me, but how do you know I'm the one for you? You've got no one to compare me to. In a few years, you'd probably start looking for someone else to see what you've missed."

"I won't."

"You probably will. Go out, sow your oats, bang a few other girls, and then see what you want. If you still feel the same after a few months, you have my number. Give me a ring, and we'll take it from there."

Nick threw up his arms and sighed. There was no point in continuing this conversation. Gemma had decided, and he had no idea how to change her mind.

"If that's what you want," he said. "Thanks for a lovely time. It's been great knowing you." He tried to smile and then walked out of the room.

"You too," she said.

Nick was the sweetest guy. He made her laugh and kept her interest, and it felt right being with him. They had a connection. She even got along well with his mother. So why was she so sure this was the right thing to do?

"Hola Donny, hola Chrissy." Graham walked up his extensive drive to meet his guests.

Christiano did not look happy but said nothing. He waved at Graham.

"Are you all set?" Donny asked. "What time are we going?"

"I need to sort something first, but come on inside, and I can explain.

Ben and Elizabeth were drinking coffee when she saw her son jog by.

"That's weird."

"What is?"

"Nick said he was spending the day with Gemma. They wouldn't see each other tomorrow; today would be their last day together. "

"Perhaps they changed their plans. The best-made plans can change in the blink of an eye."

"Very philosophical. Is that your way of telling me you've changed your mind and will start the treatment?"

"I still haven't decided about treatment, but Will has arranged for me to meet his therapist friend. He's coming to see me next week."

"That's something. " She squeezed his hand and then patted his knuckles. "I'm no expert, and don't answer this if you don't want to, but do you know when you became so unhappy?"

"Actually, I think I do. It kicked off when we sold the shops. I know Cheryl left at the same time, but I could have coped with that. Losing the shops meant I did not have enough to keep my mind active, so I ... started to overthink. I looked back at my life and realised I had done some horrible things."

"You probably aren't the only one. I imagine most successful businessmen have done something they are not proud of."

"Yes, but I felt good about those things at the time."

"What changed?"

"I realised things happen for a reason. My father died suddenly, and my mother became ill shortly afterwards. I think it had something to do with me. I had to pay the price for my sins."

"Well, I have no idea what I did to deserve so much shit," Elizabeth said. "Sorry, bad joke. You were upset about your parents' death but cannot blame yourself. These things happen. Nobody is to blame, and I doubt things would have been different had you changed your actions."

"You may be right." He stared into the distance. "By the time we knew Mum was ill, we had moved to Cheshire. We had expanded the business. We loved the area and the people, but Mum wouldn't move from Birmingham, no matter how much I tried. She used to have this saying…." He lapsed into a broad West Midlands accent. 'Once a Brummie, always a Brummie, and you'll never get me to leave'. We never did. I still miss my mum." He sipped his coffee. "I think now that I should have moved back. I thought about it then but told myself I needed to oversee the expansion programme. By that time, my role in the business had diminished. I used to sit in my office at home making calls, working away on the computer, pretending I was still a vital cog in the wheels of Matty's Corner Shops, but I was merely a figurehead. We had teams of people sorting everything out: accountants, warehouse workers, logistics experts, and HR departments. I could have lived anywhere. I should have moved back to look after Mum."

"Would your wife have moved with you? Do you think you would have stayed together?"

"Unlikely. Unbeknownst to me, Cheryl was already seeing her new man, so if I had decided to relocate, I would have probably lost the house, too. Once we got approached by a larger competitor offering to buy most of our bigger stores, Cheryl was very keen to make a deal."

"And you sold them?"

"Yeah… I know why now, but at the time, I believed her stories about us enjoying our retirement. We agreed to give the remaining stores and garages, the ones the buyer did not want, to Shirley and Will to manage. I thought Cheryl was acting for our benefit, not just hers."

"The sale happened just after your mother died of cancer?"

"Yes, she actually died of a heart attack. She had breast cancer, but her heart packed up. Bless her. There was nothing left of her in the end. She was such a tiny thing…" He wandered off mentally.

"Were you with your Mum when she passed?"

"That's the thing, I wasn't, but I should have been. We

knew it was coming, and I was preparing myself, but my soon-to-be ex-wife booked a trip to Bruges."

"I like Bruges. It's a lovely place."

"I've never seen it. We never got there. We'd reached Brussels when we had a call saying Mum had a heart attack and we had to rush back. We got to the local train station and waited for a taxi. My brother and sister offered to pick us up, but I wanted them to stay with my mum. When the taxi arrived, a bloke came out of nowhere and took it. He was very abusive. I felt so useless, I should have argued with him, but I just wanted to cry. My mum had just died when we got to the hospital."

"And you've never forgiven yourself?"

"Something like that. Some of the bad things I did in business, like bribing people, gazumping, and using dirty tricks to get my way, returned to haunt me. What do they call it? Karma?" he saw Elizabeth nod. "If I had been a better person, I would have got that taxi and been with my mum as she died."

"You can't know that for sure. There might have been a hold-up on the journey. Some things happen, and you can't control them."

"It's not just that. I feel that God is punishing me for all my evil deeds. My parents fell ill and died, my marriage ended, and I have cancer."

Elizabeth sat back in her seat. "Yup, that sounds like the work of a vengeful God. I had no idea you are religious."

"I'm not, but I couldn't think of anyone else who would have the power to hit me with all these things at once."

"We all do things we regret, but there is no escaping the fact that life is shit sometimes. It is nobody's fault. There is no rhyme or reason to it. Things happen. Apart from your wife leaving you, nothing that happened to you was within your control. It wasn't a sign or a punishment. It was just bad luck. Tough shit, as my father used to say."

"You should do a course in therapy." Ben laughed.

"I am simply saying it as I see it. Your problems are nobody's fault, especially not yours, whereas I have done something unforgivable and will soon pay a heavy price." She pushed her cup to the middle of the table.

"It's all you, you, isn't it?" He waited until Elizabeth's expression softened, and she smiled. "Can I ask what you've done?"

"I can hardly say no after forcing you to open up." She took a deep breath. "For the last six and a half years, I have lived a lie and forced my son to live it with me unknowingly. However, I must come clean very soon, and I don't know how Nick will react."

Ben put his elbows on the table as he moved closer to her. "What have you done?"

"I told you my husband died, and then we discovered all our money had disappeared?"

"Yes, you mentioned it. You've both done well to pay it back."

"Nick did not need to work so hard or give up school. He will inherit a fortune from my late father when he turns 21 in a few months."

"But the inheritance wouldn't have done him any good until he's 21."

"That's just the thing. Nick could have taken the money at any point with my consent, but I chose not to tell him about it."

"Why would you do that? Why struggle when you didn't need to?"

"I wanted to teach him the value of money. My father came from nothing and made something of his life. He valued every penny, moment, and person he met. He was never flash, and to look at him, you'd never think he had anything. On the other hand, if you met Nick's father, my late husband, you would swear he had been born with a silver spoon in his mouth. His family was never as wealthy as he and his brother would have you believe. Their father set up businesses, took in cash and then went bust. He did it time after time. Kenneth was lucky enough to get a job in the petrochemical industry and did very well, but he never cared about anyone but himself. Don't get me wrong, he could be very generous, but only because he thought that by splashing the cash, he could make himself popular and prove something to others. Kenneth was deluded. All people did was take from him, and he never saw that they were using him. I saw through him eventually. My father saw it immediately but, bless him, never said anything until years later. When I asked why he never commented, he said it had been painful, but he had to let me make my own mistakes." She reached for her coffee cup but saw it was empty. Ben ordered another round. "I knew that I would inherit the lot after my father. My mother passed away when I was a teenager, so there was only me. I also knew that if Kenneth knew about it, he would want to control it. He would also turn Nicholas, he never called him Nick, into a spoilt, pampered, ill-tempered brat like him. I wanted to ensure Kenneth never gained access to the bulk of my father's money."

"You put it in a trust fund."

"I had my father do it secretly, using a different solicitor. Kenneth had gotten very close to the one we normally used, and I didn't want him to find out. So when Nick is 21, he inherits the lot. As well as the houses, there is a stack of unspent rent, cash and shares."

"Houses? How many did your father have?"

"About a dozen. My father liked the idea of owning land. He was old-fashioned and said land was a solid investment because 'God ain't making any more'. When he started work, he saved every penny he had to buy a house. After that, he kept going. They weren't big or flashy properties, but he kept them smart and let them. Third-generation tenants occupy some of the houses. As long as they kept the place neat and tidy, didn't cause any problems to the neighbours and paid their rent, they could stay as long as they wanted."

"He sounds like a good man."

"He was a lovely man, an absolute gem. I miss him terribly." She brought her lips together and took a moment before continuing. "His father worked on the docks and spent all his money in the pub. His mum did whatever she could to provide for Dad and his sister, my Auntie Phyllis. Dad said they collected old bottles and returned them to pubs to make a few bob. Later on, when he left school, he got a job on the docks and started to make connections between the goods coming in and what businesses in the town could use."

"He used to steal from the docks?" Ben chuckled. "He must have been quite a character."

"He was. As I said, he did whatever was needed to get by, and then when he had enough money, he bought a house and rented it out. He didn't tell his family what he was doing because his father would want a share."

"He didn't tell his mother or sister?"

"No, because he didn't want his mother to lie, and he knew his sister was very close to their father. She went the same way as her dad and died of liver failure. My grandmother lived long enough to see Nicholas born. My father died ten years ago."

"What would you have done if your husband had lived?"

"I am not sure. There's not much I could have done apart from hope and praying that Nicholas became a better man than his father. I know he has done, but I am not confident I would have had much influence had Kenneth been around."

"Was your husband aggressive?"

"No, not aggressive. He was abusive, not physically, but in a manner that was more akin to mental abuse. He would say mean things and constantly put me down. I should have stood up to him, but…I don't know. I suppose that I lost my confidence. I became a subservient wife. To put it bluntly, it was a bit of a relief when he died."

"How did you meet?"

"I was his translator at an event in London." Ben looked impressed. "I studied languages at university and then travelled across Europe honing my skills. When I returned, a girlfriend asked me to do some translation, which led to a company supplying translation facilities offering me a job. That's how I met Kenneth. We went out a few times, and I believed his stories, and we eventually married. He had a good job but spent money faster than he could earn it. We had a massive house and flash cars. You name it, and we probably had it at one time. Unbeknown to me, Kenneth had started borrowing from the bank to pay for his extravagances. Dad insisted on leaving me a large sum of money to use as my pension fund and thought he had arranged things so that Kenneth could not access it. He found a way, and when I needed that cash, it was no longer there."

"That must have been terrible."

"You'd have thought so, wouldn't you? Perversely, I have enjoyed the challenge. It was hard at first. We went right back to basics. I did whatever was needed: baking, sewing, ironing, gardening. I'd do most things if there was a pound or two in it, providing it was legal."

"Wouldn't translating have paid better than baking?"

"I'm not sure these days. I wanted to forget what I had become and build something new. I was happy pottering about and wanted to be there for Nick. The whole charade was all about helping him. I refused to touch my father's money, but I did occupy one of his houses, pretending it was rented. Nick got several part-time jobs, and as I said, over time, we sold what we could, scrimped and saved until we eventually paid most of what Kenneth owed. We had some great times, brilliant memories, and happy days. Nick has changed greatly in the last six years, and watching him blossom has been a privilege. He's a kind, caring boy and a great judge of character. He is nobody's fool. He has made good friends who are normal people, you know? Not those pretentious hooray Henry types he met at private school. He's also gained a lot of confidence, and, as difficult as things have been, he has some great experiences to look back on."

The waiter arrived with the refills.

"The big test for me now is how Nick reacts to having money, and I am not sure he will be too happy when he hears about his inheritance."

"Well," said Ben, raising his cup. "If he is anything like you think he is, I am sure things will turn out fine. I think you've done a fabulous job. You've taught your son some valuable life lessons. He sounds like a lovely boy and a credit to his mother."

"Thank you. I hope he thinks his mother is a credit to him when he learns the truth."

Nick had no idea how far he had run. He guessed he had covered several miles, but the time had passed quickly.

He stood staring out at the sea, trying to think of what he might have done wrong, which of his actions had caused Gemma to react as she did. Nothing obvious sprang to mind.

He would have to tread carefully over the next forty-eight hours to avoid meeting her. He could not face that. He hoped she was not laughing about him with her friends, and he imagined he was the subject of much ridicule.

He thought they were good. He thought they were tight. He cared about her and thought she felt the same about him. He had thought wrong.

Nick turned to retrace his steps, hoping he would never see or hear from Gemma Potter again.

"How did he take it, Gem?" Kylie sat up on the towel, awaiting a reply.

She did not look up from her book. "Fine, yeah. He…er… understood and agreed with my decision. We'll keep in touch. He's a great bloke, and I like him, so there's no reason we can't be friends." It was time to move the conversation along. "Where do you fancy going tonight? Which of the dodgy places you've been without me are we visiting first?"

Will promised Shirley that he would return from his

walk with something for lunch. As he waited for the food to be prepared, he made a call.

Chris Shanklin heard Will had just witnessed a Range Rover and the green Ferrari containing five people between them leaving the house. He had only expected four but guessed one of the girls had joined the party. He thought he spotted a female wearing a baseball cap. The darkened windows on the cars made it difficult to identify the passengers.

He would revisit the house that evening to check it was empty before returning the next day to collect the goods. Will was confident he would find the items there. The things were not on the boat. He had visited the club, and so many visitors frequented the office he could not imagine it would make a secure hiding place. Grigor and Graham appeared to keep a tight rein on callers to the house. Nobody got in or out without their say-so. Apart from Will, that is.

Shanklin wished him well and told him to keep in touch. Will promised he would, but he decided against mentioning he would have an accomplice. That would remain a surprise until after the event.

Grigor stopped to let Louise and Candice out of the Range Rover. Candice removed the borrowed baseball cap and threw it into the rear seat footwell. Louise left her straw Panama on her head. She quite liked it.

"Thank you, ladies," said Grigor, handing notes to Louise. "Share this. Get yourselves a nice meal or a drink on me."

"Enjoy your trip," said Louise.

"Have a great time," said Candice, studying how Louise divided the cash.

The Range Rover drove away, and the green Ferrari behind it tooted as it passed.

Louise blew kisses to Christiano and Donny before shouting, "See you Monday."

Charlie wanted pizza. The family sat around the laminate table, ripping slices from the overlarge box at the centre. Jon once again marvelled at the child's recovery powers.

"Slow down, Charlie. There's plenty left."

"Harry has had two slices."

"I know, but you don't want to make yourself ill again. Take your time. There is no rush." He pulled the box closer to him. "Look, Daddy will make sure that you get two slices too."

"Mum, Daddy wants to eat it all," said Harry, his mouth covered in tomato and cheese sauce.

It might have been Gemma's imagination, but the atmosphere in the Cavern seemed much better without Christiano, Donny and company. She knew the boys had gone to Magaluf but had expected to see the girls.

Becky had called earlier and asked whether anything had been done about her video. It dawned on Gemma that the only way she would find out would be by ringing Nick. She was confident it would be a civilised conversation and would ring him on Saturday when she got home.

She asked the barman if Louise would come in later and was pleased when he replied, "I hope not. That girl is trouble." Gemma quickly emphasised that Louise was not a friend of hers.

The Cheltenham three drank and danced until Sergio and Costas joined them. The lads were surprised to learn Nick was no longer on the scene and introduced Gemma to their friend Gavi. He was shorter than Gemma, but she danced with him anyway.

"Chris is ready to make the transfer, Mum. Shall I give him the go-ahead?"

"What do you think? Shall we go for it?"

"Why not? We are only taking back what is ours."

"Go on then. Lucia said she could get me an appointment

with Gabriela's hairdresser tomorrow, so I'll need a few euros."

"Go for it."

"We are going shopping afterwards. I want to get some new shoes."

"About time too. Those clogs have seen better days."

Elizabeth removed a shoe and looked at it. "We've been through some hard times."

"We have, but hopefully, that's behind us now."

"I was talking to my shoe."

Ben, Shirley and Will had developed a taste for the brandy, and Ben ordered three more.

"This will be my last," said Will. "I need a clear head in the morning."

"What for?" Shirley asked. "You're on holiday, although most days seem to be a holiday for you."

"Haha. I have some business to attend to, so I'll be gone most of the morning."

"You did say," said Shirley, rising from her seat. "I'll just nip to the loo. Dad, make sure he doesn't pinch my drink."

"No problem," said Ben. Once Shirley was out of earshot, he added, "I thought we were meeting tomorrow afternoon?"

"We are. I have something else to attend to first. A mate of mine wants me to take some stuff back to England. I'll collect it in the morning."

"I've got something to do tomorrow, Mum."

"Meeting Gemma?"

"Something like that, but I'll be back in the afternoon if you want to spread the good news."

"I would like nothing better."

Gavi eased a hand up Gemma's top as they kissed in his car. His touch was gentle, but Gemma did not share his intentions. "I am sorry, Gavi. I have a bit of a headache. I'm going to lie down."

"Shall I lie down with you to keep you company?"

Nice try, she thought, kissing him. “Thank you for a lovely evening.”

DAY 14 - FRIDAY 6 AUGUST

Gemma woke to find herself alone. It was just after seven. She rested on her elbows while observing the room from her bed. The other beds were undisturbed. She guessed that Kylie and Sara had struck it lucky with their Spanish friends. She knew she had a chance with Gavi but did not regret not taking it. He was not her type. He was too short, lacked any discernible physique and was not much of a talker. It dawned on her that she was criticising Gavi for not being Nick.

She smiled at pleasant memories before letting her head fall back onto the pillow.

The pair climbed over a fence at the bottom end of the garden and hid under the cover of the trees.

Will used his binoculars to study the house and grounds. Confident there was nobody at home, the pair walked across the lawn to the carport outside the back door.

Lucia had called to tell Elizabeth that if she wanted a haircut, she needed to be at the salon by 8.30. She had awoken early, but not before Nick. He had already gone on his errand, whatever that might be.

Elizabeth made good speed and stopped at the cash point to check the balance. The sight of her bank balance made her heart flutter. She was going to enjoy today. Taking the cash from the dispenser, she noticed her fingernails and wondered if the salon also did manicures.

Grigor steered Matilda out of the marina while Donny and Christiano sat beside him.

"How long will this take?" Christiano looked like he would be sick. "Did we have to leave so early?"

"I told you to go easy on the alcohol," laughed Donny.

"You are not used to it."

"I want to get there for lunch," said Grigor. "It will take around three hours to get to Marina Botafoch."

"Great, I'm starving," said Donny.

"How can you even think of food," said a queasy Christiano.

"It's the sea air."

"There is plenty of drink and a few snacks downstairs. Help yourselves. Later, if you want, we can stop to swim."

Donny rushed to the stairs.

Christiano took a deep breath. "What time is Graham's meeting?"

Grigor checked his watch. "Probably very soon."

"It is a shame he's not coming with us."

"He's had a last-minute business opportunity, and, you know Graham, he can't let a good thing go."

"He'll probably make a killing."

You're probably right, thought Grigor, determined not to laugh. "Once he does his business, he will follow us over."

Jon was surprised when Leah held out her mobile. "It's for you."

"Hello."

"Hi, it's Mike Clemence. I am sorry to bother you on holiday, but..."

Mike owned the largest construction company in the Worcester area. He told Jon that word had spread about his departure from Cromwells and asked if he fancied a job.

"Doing what?"

"Pretty much what you were doing at Cromwells. You'd be my right-hand man and don't worry, I'll give you what you get now, but treat you much better than Rob did. For one thing, I won't disappear to play golf all the time. I hate golf."

Jon ran his free hand over his mouth. "I don't know what to say. Thank you. I'm stunned. Can I discuss it with Leah and get back to you when I get home?"

"Of course. I heard about your situation yesterday and tried to ring you before anyone else got hold of you."

"Yeah, I'm sorry. My mobile has been out of action, and I need to get it fixed."

"It took several calls to get Leah's number."

"Who else will be trying to reach me?"

"Probably every other building firm in our area. Rob is stupid to let you go. Just remember that I asked first."

"Will do, of course. Thank you, Mike."

Nick zipped up the front of his disposable coverall and pulled the hood over his head. "With this on, I feel like someone out of CSI. It's a bit hot, though."

His companion only had his legs in his suit and struggled with his arms. "It serves a purpose. We want to avoid leaving clues if we can help it." With a heave, he pulled his suit over his shoulders, pulled up the zip, and eased the hood around his face.

"Ready then?"

Will held Nick by the shoulder and told him to be patient. "You know what we're looking for?"

"I do."

"Take your time. The house is empty and will be for the whole day at least. Make sure you check every wall, cupboard, nook, and cranny. Remembering..."

"I know, to put things back as I found them."

"Gloves on?"

Nick held up his hands. "Check."

"Shoes covered?"

"Yup."

"Right, let's do this." He unlocked the door and checked the alarm system. It had not been activated. "I will search down here."

Nick looked confused. "Why?"

"Because you are younger than me, you get to search upstairs."

Nick did as instructed.

Will searched the hall but found nothing of use. He entered the living room and stopped dead.

Nick crept up the stairs even though Will had said the house would be empty. The first room upstairs was a lavatory. Nick doubted there would be much in there. The second door was ajar, and he pushed it open wide. It was a non-descript bedroom with no wall hangings, minimal furniture and no built-in cupboards. He moved to the third door.

The lever was a little stiff, but the door itself opened quickly. Nick's eyes left the handle and looked into the room. A bat slammed into his midriff, pushing him backwards. Subsequent blows to his body, legs and arms followed quickly.

Before he could comprehend what was happening, Nick was in acute pain and curled up in a ball on the floor. The beating stopped.

Gemma, Kylie and Sara sat in their room drinking coffee.

"What are we going to do today?" Kylie asked.

"Sleep, please, " said Sara. "I'm knackered."

"Well, if you will stay out shagging all night, that's your problem," Gemma replied. "I want to make the most of our last day."

"Ah, but we haven't been shagging all night." Kylie had her friend's attention. "We went to a club and were dancing. Weren't we Sar?"

"You were dancing," Sara said. "My feet were knackered after three."

Gemma nodded in admiration. "Well, I never expected you to say that. Dancing until eight in the morning. Well done to the pair of you."

"We only danced until five," said Sara. "The rest of the time, we were shagging."

Will was speechless to see Graham sitting in a comfy chair, pointing a gun, with a silencer already fixed, at him.

He motioned for Will to take a seat. Two chairs had been positioned so they faced him.

"Come in, Mr Bound. I've been expecting you."

Will took the seat nearer the door. "Where's your white cat, Mr Blofeld?"

"I must admit that line sounded better when I rehearsed it."

"I hate to be the bearer of bad news, but my name isn't Bound. That was just an alias we used to book the B&B. Mr and Mrs Eggerton Bound, Egg Bound. Get it?"

"Very droll."

"The hotel receptionist didn't get it either. I thought it was funny, but perhaps not everyone shares my sense of humour."

"I know who you really are, Will Hopkins, a.k.a. Snowy. I also know who you work for and have a good idea of why you are here." Graham gave Will a once-over and said, "You've lost weight."

Unlike you, Will thought. Up close, he could see that Graham had swapped muscle for fat. "I've shaved since you saw me last. That always takes pounds off me."

"No, you look slimmer. That makes me more wary of you. You were quick enough before."

"Only because Gus probably told you to make it easy for me."

"Don't be so modest, Will. You're among friends. Gus gave me no warning."

A repetitive beat came through the ceiling. It sounded like someone was getting bounced across the floor. Will hoped Nick was okay.

"Did Gavin tip you off that I was coming?"

"My little brother? No chance. I have minimal contact with the family nowadays. They think I live in Barcelona. I prefer it like that. They have no idea what I am doing. Gav once rang to ask if I knew where Gus lived, but I told him nothing. He said they were considering employing a detective to chase down the drive and DVDs, but I had no idea it would be you."

"So, how did you know I was coming?"

"You were spotted at the apartment. We weren't sure it was you until Gus heard your voice."

"Always gives me away."

"I can imagine."

"We had Barty follow you, and that's when we discovered that you had spoken to Banda. After that, it was easy to plant false information."

"Banda?"

"Don't be so coy, Will. Banda is safe for now, but he will receive his just rewards when we've gotten rid of you."

Will tried to remain nonchalant. "How did you know I would call today?"

"I didn't know for sure, but it seemed logical to assume you would leave it until the last moment. I know you go home tomorrow, and I guessed you would look here first to give yourself time to look elsewhere if you didn't find what you wanted."

"And will I find what I want here?"

He waved the gun in the direction of the television. "It's over there, so near and yet so far."

"And you gave Ibiza a miss just to tell me that. I don't know what to say."

"It is my pleasure. I have looked forward to this moment for years. I'll travel over later after we are done here."

"I have always enjoyed a nice boat trip." Will smiled.

"We have room for two more, but I didn't expect you to have company."

The banging noise from upstairs had stopped, replaced by heavy movement down the stairs,

Will scanned the room. "Aren't you worried about blood stains on the carpet? It looks expensive."

"Not really. You've done me a favour by wearing those ridiculous suits. You'll leave no evidence. Anyway, I'm not planning on killing you here. We'll do that outside. "

"I could have sworn I saw five people in two cars." He slapped his palm against his forehead. "You used dummies."

"I am not sure the girls would like to be called that, but yes, we did."

"As the Ferrari and the Range Rover are on their way to Palma, how will you move us?"

"Sadly, we will travel in Barty's father's car, but I am sure you won't mind." Graham turned his attention to the shuffling in the hall. "Barty, is everything okay?"

"Yes, fine. Just bringing this wanker down a peg or two."

Nick came tumbling into the room and fell on Will. His coverall was intact, and his face was unmarked.

"Well done, Barty. Great job. No blood and not a mark visible."

"Are you okay, Nick?" Will asked. Nick was in apparent pain, so Will stood and helped Nick into the seat.

"I've been better."

Will started to sit but then stopped to stare at Barty. "You look more like Blowjob than Oddjob."

Barty took two steps forward, baseball bat raised.

"Relax, man. He is just trying to wind you up. He probably wants you to step nearer to him. Be careful; he's a swift mover. You are no use to me as a hostage."

Will cursed a missed opportunity. He needed another idea.

Barty stepped back, blocking the doorway behind Will. Slowly, he swang his baseball bat, trying to intimidate him.

Graham smiled at Nick. "I don't think we've been introduced. What's your name?"

"Nick."

"What are you doing here, Nick?"

"I blackmailed him," Will said. "I caught him breaking into the internet café and told him I would tell the owners about it."

Nick gave Will a look, suggesting he could murder him.

"What?" asked Will. "It makes no difference now. We've

both been caught."

Graham smirked. "That's right, Mr Bound."

"Bound?" asked Nick."I thought your surname was Hopkins."

"It is. Bound was the name I used the last time I met this jerk, or should I say, Graham Laing?"

"Graham?" asked Nick. "That's not a very macho name."

Barty forced a cough to disguise his sniggering.

Will continued, "Sadly, you cannot choose the name you were born with. Talking of names, can I ask why Gus calls himself Grigor?"

"Has anyone ever told you that you are a nosey bastard?"

Nick thought of Gemma but said nothing, lowering his gaze. He let Will continue the conversation.

"I am guessing he thinks Grigor sounds scarier. Gus is such a limp name; it's less manly than Graham, and that's saying something."

"Ha fucking ha. Grigor was the name of the Russian Matty fell in love with in Casablanca."

"In all the gin joints..." said Will.

"Indeed. We actually did meet him at a club he owns... sorry, owned in the city," said Graham.

"So Matilda fell in love with someone else."

"Hmm, I doubt it. She probably thought Grigor could help to protect her. What we knew, and she didn't, was that our gentle Russian friend had no connections in the underworld. He was what they call a bona fida businessman. His staff were a bit dodgy, but, from what we saw, Grigor was as clean as a whistle."

"He held no threat."

"We were never frightened of Grigor. Now, it is my turn to ask the questions. How did you find us?"

"It wasn't difficult when I put my mind to it. I have a friend who can access flight logs. He traced your arrival in Morocco and your departure with your companion, Grigor Yashin. He told me that you sat next to each other on the flight.

Grigor Yashin! What sort of name is that?"

"That was the best our Moroccan man could supply quickly. It worked, though. It got us into Spain. And here we are. I am curious about your little friend." Graham wagged the gun at Nick, "Why were you breaking into the café?"

Nick had not expected to be spoken to and mumbled, "Who? Me?" He saw Graham looking at him. "Christiano filmed a girlfriend, and I thought I could get access to destroy the video," he said.

"But you failed?"

"Yeah, because of dickhead here. He caught me attempting to get in."

"Better it was me than the police or those two perverts," said Will.

Nick shook his head in disbelief, "That's right because I am much better off now, right?"

Graham cackled. "You don't have much luck, do you? I hope you got a quick shag as a reward for your efforts?"

Nick shook his head.

"That's bad. You know you could have saved yourself a lot of effort if you had just come to see me?"

Nick looked at Will and then at Graham. "I didn't even know you existed until a few minutes ago." He pointed a thumb at Will, and pain shot through his arm. "After stopping me from helping my friend, this joker told me we were robbing this place because his ex-wife had been a scam victim, and her video would be in this house. He told me you kept all the videos here. "

"Honestly, Snowy, you are such a liar." Graham's focus was on Nick again. "Did he mention his ex-wife's name?"

Nick said, "Mary," the first name that came to mind.

Graham looked at Will. His white teeth glowed as he smiled. "Mary Hopkins. You and your joke names," he said.

"Those were the days," said Will as his eyes explored the room. The space was compartmentalised. One corner was filled with photos of boats and yachting memorabilia, another with images and mementoes of cars and the third crammed with top-end entertainment systems. He did not see anything that might facilitate an escape. He hid his anxiety in his usual way. "Are you a bit OCD?"

"Why do you ask?"

"It's just the room is very organised. I imagine all the car documents get stored there," He pointed at the images of top-of-the-range cars. "Your IT stuff is in the entertainment quarter, and everything relating to the ships gets stored in that unit under the photos on that wall. Where are the fake passports you promised your salespeople?"

"In the office in a box marked passports."

"You are extremely anal-retentive."

"I like order. By the way, Waltzing and Matilda are boats, not ships."

"I served in the mob long enough to know a ship when I see one. They are huge, too big to be boats."

"I'm glad you think so. They are rather large. Waltzing is mine, and it is longer by three feet."

Size clearly matters, Will thought. "Where is Matilda, by the way?"

"Do you mean the yacht or the person?"

"Your ex-stepmother," said Will. He had already guessed what had happened but wanted to continue the conversation until he found a way out.

A sneer emerged on Graham's face. "She is somewhere off the coast of Tangiers."

"Might she re-emerge someday?"

"I doubt it. She and the real Grigor were so heavy when we left them that I can't see them moving very far."

"How did you arrange it?"

"We followed them to his boat and ...well, you can guess the rest."

"Didn't his friends and family come looking for him?"

"No idea. I found a buyer for the boat, and we gathered as much as possible before we left Morocco in a hurry. We've never been back."

"And nobody came here to look for Grigor?"

"Why would they? Gus borrowed his first name but used a different surname. We bought the clubs and boats, and life here has benefitted us. We now have businesses all over Spain and the Balearics."

"I love a happy ending," said Will. "And you did all this just to get your father's money?"

"I didn't need it as I am still part of the family, so I can get a handout whenever I want one. We had to help Tilda get away, and when Gus took the blame. I had to help him. We have always been very close."

"As in lovers?" Will asked.

"Good God, no, close as brothers. Which is what we are."

Will had seen a resemblance but had not expected that news.

Graham told how Frankie Laing had a brother named Felix. The brothers married sisters, but Felix couldn't have children. Frankie had sex with his sister-in-law to give his brother a child. When Felix and his wife died in a car crash, Frankie brought Gus up as his own.

"Bless him. He has a heart of gold, that man." Will said. "Frankie and Felix, Graham and Gus, Gavin and Gaynor. Are your family working through the dictionary?"

"Ha ha, if I ever have kids, I'll have to call them Hilary, Heather, or Harry. It is a shame I won't be around to see Zack, Zelda and Zebedee.

"Poor old Zeus will be less memorable." Will rested his chin on his hand. "Can I ask you another question?"

"Feel free."

"Was Gus in love with Matilda?"

"Is that what my dear old dad told you?"

Will nodded.

"We both were, to tell you the truth. Tilda was fascinating, to begin with. Dad was way too old, and she needed younger company. We were happy to oblige. Tilda had a healthy appetite if you know what I mean."

Will did.

"Here's a question for you. Can you guess why we called her Tilda?"

Will shook his head. "No idea."

"She didn't like being called mum or stepmum, so Dad suggested 'Step Matilda', which we pronounced Stepma Tilda. We shortened that to Tilda, and it stuck."

"Ingenious," said Will. "It must have been a laugh a minute in your house."

Graham ignored the sarcasm. "We were happy enough until dear old Dad learned that Tilda wanted to file for divorce. He became determined she would not get her hands on his money. One day, Dad gave out little gifts etched with details of the accounts he used to stash money to ensure Tilda never got her hands on it. We told Tilda, who then employed your firm, and the rest is history. You played your part perfectly. Thank you."

"But then Tilda became surplus to requirements."

"She did, but it was her own fault. She spent money like it was going out of fashion. We tried to rein her in, and her response was to go with Grigor and hide behind him. We could not let her leave. You never know. You might end up next to her."

Nick had imagined Graham would call the police, but the man's last comment scared him. He realised Graham planned to kill them and dump their bodies in the ocean. He thought of his mum and his friends.

Nick did not want to die - not yet. He knew he had to do something but could achieve little while sitting in the chair. He extended his legs and winced. "Sorry, my legs are seizing up." He pointed at the table between their seats. Three orb-shaped orange glass paperweights rested on an ornate glass tray. "Nice paperweights," Nick groaned again as he stretched his back. "My mum used to collect them. Are they Murano?"

"You have a good eye. Yes, they are. An orange grower

friend from Valencia had them blown, especially for me."

"They must have cost him."

"It was a thank you for getting him workers at short notice."

Nick shifted forward in his seat. "Do you mind if I stand? My back and legs are killing me, thanks to Barty and his baton."

Barty smirked.

Graham said, "Yes, please do. I am growing bored now."

"Just like Blofeld," said Will. "He always keeps Bond waiting for the execution. Mind that you don't cock it up like he always did." Will could not see a way out that did not result in either him or Nick getting shot.

He had to neutralise the gun. When the time was right, he would rush at Graham. If he could knock the gun onto the floor, Nick could get it and disable Barty. The police would sort the rest. Thinking and delivering were different things. Graham had carefully positioned the seats to avoid getting rushed. He would have plenty of warning if either of them made a move.

"I won't. James Bond is fictional. This is reality." He threw a set of handcuffs at Nick. "Put them on him."

Will stood and looked around. Barty had not moved. There was no way to get to Graham without the gun going off. Nick was in agony and would not be much use. The situation was becoming desperate. Will decided their escape was better left until they were in the car. He could see no way they could both get away from the house. "Don't worry. *I'll think of something. Just do what he tells you,"* he whispered to Nick.

"What did you say?" Graham asked.

"I told him to be gentle with me," replied Will.

Will's thoughts had moved to the car. He would ensure a guard sat in the back with a prisoner if he were in charge. If his captors thought the same way, Nick or Will would likely sit by Graham in the back. After all, he was the one with the gun. This would expose Barty in the front. Will was confident he could do enough to nullify whomever he sat next to. He would seek to crash the car if he were in the front seat. Will held out his arms.

Nick wrapped the metal bands around Will's wrist and was about to close the lock when Graham shouted. "No, secure them behind his back. I'm not having his hands free to cause mischief."

Shit, thought Will. He wondered whether he would have enough room to use his feet.

Graham spoke to Nick again. "Once you've done that, Barty will sort your cuffs, and then he'll give you something to keep you quiet during the journey." He nodded at two syringes and two small bottles on a unit.

Bollocks thought Will. He had not considered he might be unconscious. Still, he was not beaten yet. He turned arms behind him and said, "Just one thing, though. I believe in full disclosure, so I need to tell you that I have already sent photos of you, Gus and your crew to friends of mine in the UK. These friends will not take kindly to anything happening to us, so they will come looking. Once they find you, they will kill you."

"Is that supposed to scare me?"

"No, but it might cause Barty to shit himself."

"Fuck off," Barty grunted, holding up his bat.

"Come a bit closer," said Will. "I'll ram that stick where the sun doesn't shine."

"*Brace yourself*," mumbled Nick.

Will felt Nick's hands on his back, pushing him hard. He plunged forward onto the floor. Graham let off two shots, yelped and then fired a third.

"What the...." Will clambered upright and spotted Graham's upper body slumped over the chair's arm. It looked like a bullet had gone through Graham's head. The blood had splattered over the wall behind him. An orange glass ball rested in his lap.

Nick stood motionless, staring across the room. Will had forgotten about Barty, and his eyes followed Nick's gaze, fearing Barty also had a gun.

Bartholomew Smith was no longer a threat to anyone. His body lay on its side, blood pouring from his chest and head. His baseball bat had rolled away. Barty groaned for Nick to help him before he gasped for one last breath. His empty eyes peered into nothingness.

Nick could not take his eyes off Barty's dead body. He puffed heavily and quickly.

"Are you okay? Well done. That was brilliant." Will put his arm around Nick's shoulder, told him to take a slow, deep breath and led him out of the door into the hallway, where he sat him on the stairs. "Try not to be sick. We can't leave any trace evidence. Breathe in through your nose and let it out of your mouth slowly. That's it and again."

Barty's body was still visible from Nick's seat. He swallowed hard, trying to focus on his breathing. "I didn't like him, but he didn't deserve that."

"Nobody does."

"Fuck. That was..." he forced air from his mouth, "...not good."

"It could have gone better." Will sat on the lower step.

Nick was struggling to cope with what he had witnessed."Did I just kill Graham?"

"Not unless that glass orange had a bomb in it. He shot himself." Nick gasped. Will patted his knee. "It was not your fault he pulled a gun on us."

"But I threw the paperweight."

"Yes, you did, and it was a bloody good job you did. If you hadn't done that, we would both be dead."

"Do you think?"

"I'm certain. Graham has killed before and seemed relaxed about doing it again. What happened here...is not your...it's not our fault. We're blameless."

"The police won't see it like that."

"I'm not going to tell them, are you?"

Nick shook his head. "No, but someone must have heard the shots."

"We are a long way from the road and the nearest property. Everyone thinks the gang has gone to Ibiza, so they won't be looking for them. The cleaner doesn't work weekends. We'll be long gone before anyone finds the bodies."

"And after that? The police could still come looking for us."

"I see no reason why they would think we were here. We have not left any forensic evidence, and with a little work, I think I can make it look like Graham shot his mate and then killed himself."

"Grigor will know Graham was expecting you. He might say something."

"I can't imagine Grigor...Gus will want to say too much about me. He'll probably want to kill me, but we'll cross that bridge...He wouldn't know you were here, so you'll be okay."

Nick nodded slowly and put his head back in his hands. The pair sat silently until Nick spoke. "Have you ever killed anyone?"

"I did when I was in the forces."

"How did you cope?"

"I felt better by thinking it was either them or me. It's the same today."

"Barty was not a threat. We could have taken him."

"But we didn't kill him. Graham did when he was trying to shoot us." He checked his watch and then stood. "We need to get moving. You sit for a moment while I find what we came for, adjust the scene a little and double-check there is no trace of us being here."

Nick sat quietly, trying to control the shake that was surging through his body. He could not shift his thoughts from Graham and Barty. He put his gloved hands to his head and rubbed his eyes, hoping to erase images.

The first dead body he had seen was his Grampa Ned. His father had made young Nicholas view the open coffin and instructed him not to cry. Kenneth Kingston regarded tears as weakness, but Nick failed to fulfil his father's instructions. The second dead body Nick saw was his father, but he felt no urge to cry on that occasion. He thought he should feel guilty that the death of two relative strangers had upset him more than the passing of the man who helped bring him into the world.

Nick partly unzipped the coverall and cried into his t-shirt.

Will placed Barty's hand around the orange and put the glass ornament back where it had landed after Nick had thrown it. He stuffed the hard drive, discs, a batch of papers, passports, keys and a large amount of cash into his backpack. He collected documents relating to the boat and the car before returning to his accomplice. "That should appease the authorities."

Nick was traumatised by the event and clearly in pain, but he needed to speak. "For a moment, I was scared I'd never see home again."

"Only a moment? I was shitting myself the whole time."

"It didn't look like it."

"It was an act. What made you think of the orange?"

"I'm not sure. I just knew I had to try something. I played baseball in school and was lucky I hadn't lost the muscle memory."

"You did brilliantly. I would never have thought of that. By the way, it was a great throw."

"Thanks." Nick took the air in through his nose, slowly letting it out of his mouth. "I've never seen death before. I've seen dead people, but never anyone actually dying."

Will zipped up the bag. "It doesn't get easier. We cannot avoid it, but you never become immune to it." He helped Nick through the door and locked it behind them. They walked to the carport, removed the coveralls and shoe covers, and put both sets in a black bin liner.

"The best thing you can do is to remind yourself that none of this was your fault. If you don't, it will eat away at you. What happened in there was out of our control. Just be grateful we got out," Will said, tying a knot in the bin bag.

Nick nodded slowly, knowing he would not easily forget the events. "What happens next?"

"We get on with our holiday and fly home tomorrow to get on with our lives." Will shrugged, unsure what other comfort he could offer. "I have to help my father-in-law this afternoon, and we are taking Shirley for a curry tonight. What about you?"

Nick's mind had gone blank. "I'm…um..celebrating with Mum tonight."

"What are you celebrating?"

"The return of something we thought we had lost."

"Nice," said Will. "If you see us, stop and have a drink." He saw Nick blink hard. "Do you fancy a pint now?"

"I could do with something. I feel a bit sick. I can't go back to the apartment like this."

"You'll need to process what happened, and that might take a while. Come on, let's get that beer."

"Do you have time?"

"Always have time for a pint; I know just the place. It's close to the hotel where Banda stays."

"Shit! Banda. What will happen to him? Do you think Grigor will hurt him when he gets back?"

Will nodded. "Banda will have to get off the island. I think I know how we can help him. Come on, we'll discuss it on the way to the pub, and then you can buy me that pint."

"You'll have to fetch them. I am not sure I can carry very much."

"Any excuse."

Daisy appeared at Jon's shoulder and tapped his upper arm.

"Mum said that she is making lunch. Come to the apartment if you fancy a sandwich and a beer."

Jon had made no progress with the book and was no nearer finishing it. He could not stop thinking about the offer and how to tell Leah he would work for Mike. He had fobbed her off with a lie about Mike trying to get an update on a job Cromwell had been sub-contracted into.

Jon knew that Leah was excited about starting their own business, and he was in no rush to break her heart. Accepting the offer made sense, as they could not afford to go their own way just yet.

He closed the book and left it under the towel. There was always the afternoon, but then the twins would be around. It was possibly time to accept defeat. He had set himself the objective of reading two books on this holiday but had not yet completed one. He had, however, found a new job.

"That sounds lovely." He slipped his feet into his sandals. "Have you enjoyed your morning?" Jon waved at Leah, who had watched her daughter's every step.

"Yes, thank you. We went to Cala Millor, where Mum and I did some shopping and let the babies play on some swings. You know how much they like that."

Jon smiled. "I know children can be funny like that, can't they?"

Daisy nodded as she caught her father's hand.

Lucia clapped. *"Wow! Elizabeth, you look your age at last."*

"Charming. I thought you would say I look ten years younger."

"You look twenty years younger than you did."

Elizabeth held out her hand. *"What do you think of my nails?"*

"Very nice, but around here, that colour is only used by prostitutes."

Elizabeth laughed at the lady at the counter's expression. *"It's okay. My friend is obsessed with sex."* She handed over payment plus a large tip. *"Let's go and find some shoes and a new dress."*

"Do you want to go where the prostitutes go?"

"If that's where you usually shop. I'm in your hands."

Ben and Shirley had chosen Mallorcan pearl earrings as an extra gift for Rosie. Thomas would be made up with his Barcelona football shirt. Ben had moved to the next counter.

"You thinking of buying some for Mum?"

"I think she's had enough, don't you?" He caught his daughter's eye. "Did she tell you about lover boy?"

"She did. She was distraught."

"It's a terrible feeling, betrayal."

"Has she suggested reconciliation?"

Ben shrugged. "That is never going to work. The damage is done."

Shirley nodded and thanked the shop assistant who handed her the package. She put her arm through her dad's. "Let's get some lunch before you go on your top-secret mission with Will," she said.

"I'm surprised he hasn't told you what it is."

"Not a word, which is surprising when you think how much he likes to yak."

"So that's settled then. You'll do the talking. I'm aching like hell. It hurts when I breathe."

"Don't breathe then."

"I'll try my best."

"We made a good team," said Will, placing the rucksack on the seat next to Nick. He had disposed of the black bag in a back street bin. "How did you come up with Mary? Have you heard her sing?"

"No. I was thinking about my Kendo classes. The trainer's name is Mary. She is the wife of my martial arts instructor." The waiter arrived and left with an order for two large beers. "Who is Mary Hopkins anyway?"

"Hopkin. Her name is Hopkin. She was a popular singer back in the day."

"Was she any good?"

"Of course. She's Welsh."

Will briefly left Nick nursing his injuries and crossed the road to the dilapidated hotel. He asked for Banda, and when the lady told him she would send him over, Will returned to Nick.

"What did Clemence want?"

"I told you. He wanted an update on a job he gave us but couldn't reach Rob."

Leah momentarily turned away from the children and looked at Jon sceptically. "Really? Clemence hates Rob and would never throw any work his way. Everyone knows that. What did he want?"

Jon told her about the job offer and his future role as Clemence's right-hand man. He thought it was a great offer and was inclined to accept. He was thrilled that Clemence had taken the time to speak to him.

The children sat on the grass and played one of Daisy's improvised games involving a tennis ball.

Leah controlled her anger and spoke in a harsh whisper. "You were going to accept without discussing it with me?"

"I was going to tell you when we get home."

"What about our plans?"

"This will give us a chance to do up the house, and then we can start a business in a few years."

"If you are still around."

"What is that supposed to mean?"

Leah's feet swang off the sunbed as she sat upright, facing her husband. "You know what I mean. Clemence is going to work you even harder than Cromwell. His business is much larger, and he has contracts up and down the country. We'll never see you. When we do, you'll want to work on the house. You'll be dead before we ever start a business."

"That's pessimistic."

"I think it's realistic." Tears had formed on her eyelids. "I know you are flattered that Clemence rang you, and it is great that he wants you to work for him, but please take your time before giving him an answer. Let me speak to Mum, and if she says no, then take the job. If she agrees to lend us the cash, you can tell Clemence to throw a few contracts our way."

Jon doubted life would be that simple but wrapped his arms around her. "If that's what you want. When can you ask your mum?"

"Sunday."

"Okay, I told him I'd give him an answer early next week."

Banda looked like he had just got out of bed. "Why did you want to see me?" As he got closer, he saw Nick was not his usual self. "What is the matter, my friend?"

"It's nothing," said Nick. "I'm just a bit under the weather."

Banda looked bewildered, unable to understand the phrase. When Nick flinched, Banda asked, "Are you hurt?"

"I had an accident, but I'll be fine."

"Would you like a beer?" Will asked.

Banda shook his head. "No, thank you. I do not drink alcohol. Why am I here?" He eyed Will, who was taking out documents and cash. "What is that?"

"These are the passports prepared for you and your friends. This is some of the money Graham and Grigor owe you."

Banda leaned away. "How did you acquire these things?"

"We were looking for something else, and...let's just say that they fell into our laps," said Nick.

Banda's hand covered his mouth, and his palm rubbed his cheeks and chin. "Why are you pushing them at me? Why would I want them? Why should I trust you?"

"They are no use to us," said Will. "This is your property. You paid for it. We cannot force you to take this, and you have no reason to trust us, but I assure you we are trying to help you and your friends." He drank from his pint. "We wanted you to know you'll be out of work on Monday. Grigor is out of town and is not likely to be happy with what he finds when he returns. You and all your friends could be in real danger."

"What sort of danger?"

"The worst kind," said Will.

"How do you know this?"

"I told you that I came here to recover goods stolen from Graham's father?" Banda nodded. "Well, we discovered much more than expected, and the authorities will learn about everything on Monday. That means you have until Sunday evening to get away."

Nick picked up his beer, emptied it and indicated to the barman that they wanted another round. "Will means it when he says you are all in danger and must get away before Monday. After that, Grigor returns, the police will arrive, and, as we say in Wales, the shit will hit the fan. All hell is going to break loose. So you have to make up your mind quickly."

Banda sat quietly, trying to read his companions' expressions. "You are serious about this?"

"Deadly, " said Will.

"We are," Nick added.

"You will give me my passport..."

Will pushed the items further across the table."Take it and take your friends' passports, too. Have the money as well. It will be more useful to you."

Banda examined the pile of notes. "There are many thousands of Euros here."

"It's yours." Will wiped his forehead. He wished they had sat in the shade. He tapped the small pile of papers. "These are the ownership documents for Graham's yacht and car. The boat will be in the Palma marina."

"I know where that is. I have been there with Grigor to collect goods. You are telling me to take it?"

"It is there if you want it," Will said.

"It might help you all get home," suggested Nick.

"Does Graham know about this?"

"No. He's got a lot on his mind," said Will, who

whispered an apology to Nick when he saw him wince. "Grigor is in Ibiza. They will think Graham has gone to meet him as planned."

"Where is Graham?"

"He's safe. He's not going anywhere. He's certainly not going to cause anyone any bother...for a while," Nick replied. "I don't know what the security is like at the marina, but you can tell them you bought the boat."

"They know me there. I visit regularly to collect things, so that will not be a problem."

Will pointed to the car key. "This will get you into the Ferrari. I imagine it is parked close to where Gus keeps his boat. There is also a Range Rover, although I couldn't find the ownership papers, and we don't have the key."

"I know where they park their cars. I won't need a Range Rover."

"Good. You're sorted, then. I think these keys are for the warehouse in Palma, where they store their goods. I assume you know where that is, too?"

Banda nodded. "How did you get all this?"

"As we said, when we went to recover the stolen items, these just happened to be there." Nick thanked the lady for delivering the drinks.

"What will you do with the car?" Will asked.

Banda answered immediately. "I know a man who is desperate to own a Ferrari. He won't care that it is a horrible colour." He flicked through the passports until he found the one he wanted. He smiled as he opened it. "Mikel knows boats. He used to be a fisherman."

"There you are then," said Will. "Graham was supposed to take it out this morning, so it should be full of fuel. If you act quickly, you can empty the warehouse of anything valuable and sell everything when you get back home."

"And you are doing all this for me? Why?"

"Because you are in danger because of me, " said Will. "I want to keep you safe."

"And your daughter needs you," added Nick. "I know what it is like not to have a father around."

"What if I stay?"

Will pondered for a second. "As far as I can see, the least that will happen to you is that you will get hauled in when the police swarm around, and they will be swarming, believe me. If you are released, you will be out of a job. Grigor and Graham's businesses are going down the pan, and there will be no more work. You will be stuck on this island with no income. The worst that might happen is that Grigor discovers Graham has been...caught, and the police want to interview him. Everyone Grigor has used in his business dealings will potentially threaten his freedom, so Grigor will want them all to disappear, including you."

Nick nodded. "We advise you to get out now while you can. Take your friends with you, but be gone by Monday."

Banda studied their faces. They seemed to think he had nothing to lose, but what if they lied? He was inclined to believe them. Why would they give him a passport and money if they were setting him up? He leaned across the table and shook their hands. "It is a deal, my friends."

Both Will and Nick relaxed.

"Thank God for that, " said Will.

Banda took out his mobile. "But I want a photograph to show my daughter the very kind Welshmen who brought me home.."

He was surprised when Will snatched his mobile. "Sorry, Banda, we cannot let you do that."

Nick and Banda glared at him.

"If you get caught leaving the island, the police will want to know who helped you and will search all your belongings. They might find the photo. We cannot take that risk."

Nick cringed as he extracted his mobile. "I tell you what. Take a picture with my phone and then give me your number. I'll send it to you when this is all over."

Will thought that a reasonable compromise and

moved closer to Nick. Banda nodded and stood. He called the barmaid and asked if she would snap the three of them. When she agreed, he said, "Diolch yn fawr," and put his head between the other two.

Will sat in the corner of the office while Ben discussed his business with Will's contact. The words he heard were going in one ear and out the other. Will could not stop thinking about the events of that morning. He had been sloppy. He had not done his homework correctly and nearly killed them both. They had been fortunate. They would be dead if Nick's pitch had been an inch or two out.

The shitstorm was not yet over. He hoped nobody discovered the bodies until Monday, but he did not know if that would be the case. What if Barty's father wanted his car back and went looking? Will hadn't seen the car on entering but guessed Graham would have hidden it. It could be in the garage. It could be anywhere.

Gus would be back in a couple of days. He knew Will was in the area and why, so it was a safe bet that he would come looking. Will was not bothered about his safety but worried for Shirley and the kids. What would he tell Shirl? How could Will protect his family? Gus had no problem arranging new identities to travel wherever he wanted.

The obvious thing to do was tell Frankie Nuggets about Gus and Graham working together, but how did he explain the deaths? Would he throw himself from the frying pan into the proverbial fire?

Will liked a tidy ending, but he had left too many unresolved issues because he made too many mistakes. He had already decided that this would be his last job. Now he worried he might not get to enjoy his retirement.

Edward Kingston poured his sister-in-law a glass of orange juice and handed it to her. His nephew had already helped himself to a bottle of water from the balcony chiller.

"You are looking much better now than when you arrived. The holiday has done you good. Have you enjoyed yourselves?"

Nick nodded as his mother spoke. "We have indeed, Edward. It's been lovely. Thank you. However, there is something we need to discuss with you. I feel awkward mentioning it after you have been so kind."

"We are family. You can say what you like."

"We want to know when you will pay us back the money you borrowed from Kenneth."

Unless you closely observed him, you would not have noticed the tiniest tremor in Edward's hand. "What do you mean, Elizabeth? What money?"

"The money you blackmailed your brother into lending you."

"I am sorry, Elizabeth. I don't know what you are talking about."

Elizabeth nodded to Nick, who took papers from his pocket and handed them to Edward. The movement stirred the impact of the beating to return, and he silently grimaced, determined not to show he was hurting.

Edward studied the sheet. "What is this?"

"The email exchange between you and your brother in which you threatened to tell me about his other relationship unless he lends you all the money you wanted - three hundred thousand pounds," said Elizabeth matter-of-factly.

"This must be fake? Where did you get it?"

Nick spoke. "It was on my father's laptop."

"I thought that was missing. Where did you find it?"

Elizabeth said, "We discovered Julia, and luckily, she had kept it."

Edward's eyes roamed the room as he sought a response.

Elizabeth beat him to it. "We had a lovely little chat. She told us you visited her and asked if the laptop had turned up. By the way, she wondered whether you fancy doing another decorating job. I suggested you've diversified since then."

Eddie sat on the arm of a chair. "This is all nonsense. I

don't know this, Julia, and, in any case, why would you take the word of a woman who stole your husband rather than your brother-in-law, someone who has tried to help you?"

Elizabeth looked at Nick and smiled. "Funny how he knows what Julia has done but doesn't know her, isn't it, Nick?"

"It is extraordinary."

"Kenneth told me he was having an affair. I told him not to be so stupid. He had a great life with you and shouldn't spoil that."

"Ah, bless you. You are quite correct. Kenneth did have a good life with us. Sadly, Nick and I did not have such a good life with him. He made things even worse for us after he died."

"I can't comment, but why would you think Kenneth loaned me money? I admit that I asked him, but he refused. He said he needed all his money for his new life with Julia."

"Not just his money. He also spent all my money."

"What money did you have? You hadn't worked for years."

"Money that my father left me and my husband loaned to you. I want it back. Incidentally, forcing your brother to lend you my money probably led to his death. Does that make you feel good?"

"I had nothing to do with this. There is no evidence that any money was paid or received. How do you know Kenneth didn't spend it on something else?"

"Because we have the email exchanges and bank transfer details."

"What details?"

"The transfer of three hundred thousand to your account in Gibraltar."

"Nice try." Edward smiled smugly. "There were years between this alleged transfer and you finding the laptop. The bank would have expunged the records?"

"Probably," said Nick. "But Dad saved copies of all his important documents, and the transfer details are here." He handed his uncle another sheet of paper." He waited while

Edward digested the information. "It's all there. We want to know when you intend to repay the debt?"

"How can you be sure there is a debt?" He stood to face his visitors. "I am sorry to tell you this, but Kenneth was in such deep financial trouble that he begged me to repay the loan, and I did. I'm sure the transfer is on my computer somewhere."

"It isn't," said Nick confidently.

"How do you know?" It only took Edward a moment to realise there was no point in bluffing. "You accessed my records." He pointed at his nephew. "That day my computer went down, you set me up."

"Sorry, unc, but we guessed you would be difficult. There is no record of any money being repaid on my dad's computer or yours."

"I gave it to him in cash, just like he asked."

"You must have moved quickly because Edward had a stroke within days of giving you that money."

"I gave it to Julia."

Nick held up a hand. "Enough of this bullshit. You have not paid back a single penny to Julia or us. You thought you had gotten away with it when your brother died. Your one and only brother, and you killed him."

"Hang on a second..."

"It's all documented, Eddie. Your threats, blackmail, intimidation, call it what you want. We even have a copy of the thank you email that you sent. It arrived the same day as Dad had his stroke."

Edward squeezed his cheeks, desperately considering his options. "Just say that I was in a generous mood and wanted to help out the family of my only brother. I am not sure I could get three hundred thousand, so what settlement would you expect?

"We want the lot plus interest," said Nick.

"You cannot be serious?"

"Oh yes, we can. You borrowed three hundred thousand

six years ago. That money was in an account that paid 5% interest. By our estimates, you now owe us four hundred and twenty-five thousand pounds." Elizabeth folded her arms, awaiting his response. "That is compound interest, and you are welcome to check our calculations."

Edward Kingston spread his arms. "Hold on a minute, be reasonable. I don't have that sort of money."

"You can get it," said Nick.

Edward's expression changed as an idea formed. "You are seriously expecting me to simply hand over the money?" He laughed when they nodded. "You're deranged, the pair of you. You waltz in here demanding money when you don't have anything with which to threaten me. You are having a laugh."

"We could contact your customers and suppliers to tell them what sort of person you are," said Nick.

"I'm scared, I'm scared," said Edward mockingly, resting his bottom on the arm of a chair.

"We could notify the police and the wider authorities."

"Go ahead. This alleged incident happened many years ago, and, in any case, the authorities would probably class it as a family dispute. I would argue that Kenneth gave me the money as a gift. I had no idea how he got it. You cannot claim it is a crime simply because after your husband made a gift to his brother, you changed your mind. I would maintain that the emails are fake and, as you are now a whizz with IT, that would be believable. You would have to take it through the Courts, provided you can afford a lawyer. There would then be discussions about jurisdiction. It would take years to get to Court."

"Okay then. What if we took what we think you owe us without asking?" Nick asked.

Kenneth's mouth stretched into a wide smirk. "I don't keep that amount of money in an internet access account."

"Not in one account, no. But we've discovered you have over five hundred thousand spread over various accounts and Donny's business accounts. We have only taken what you owe us."

Kenneth lost his smugness. "You've done what?"

"You heard," said Elizabeth.

"You've taken that money from my accounts and Donny's?"

"Yes."

"How did you get access to Donny's records?"

"It wasn't difficult."

Edward thought about the monthly payments he had to make to Graham and Grigor after he had laundered their drug monies. "But much of that money belongs to someone else."

"The money you forced Kenneth to give you was mine," said Elizabeth. "I think that makes us even."

"Do you know what you've done?"

"Yep," said his nephew.

"I'll be in deep shit for this."

Elizabeth looked at her son. "That's a shame, isn't it?"

"Not really, said Nick."

"They'll come after you."

"We'll deny any knowledge. We'll say you repaid us what you owed but have no idea where the money came from. We knew you were loaded."

"But you've stolen from them." Edward sat in the chair.

"Where's your proof?" Elizabeth asked. "You accessed the accounts. You are the only one with the account details and passwords. What did we have to do with anything? You cannot claim it is a crime simply because you changed your mind after returning our money."

Edward's tongue ran along his lips. "You realise I have friends on this island who are not nice. I could make you disappear."

"You could, but you'd never get any of your money back, and we would not be around to stop the remainder of your cash going to charities and those incriminating emails from being sent," said Nick.

"What emails?"

Nick shrugged. "You know those emails exchanged between you and various business contacts listed in your inbox boasting about how you bribed senior people to secure contracts and overcome problems? Plus, the other emails where you refer to ripping off your dodgy friends by under-declaring revenue streams and posting that money to your other personal accounts. "

"There are no such emails. They don't exist."

"They were there when I'd finished searching. Your life won't be worth living when they land in people's inboxes."

Edward held his head in his hand. "You've been very thorough."

"We've had plenty of time."

Edward rubbed his eyes as he swore.

"Well, we've got one more night before our flight. Thanks again, Edward, but please don't bother coming to see us or wave us off tomorrow. I'd be quite happy never to set eyes on you again." Elizabeth left the room.

"If you try anything, those emails will appear before you can say Adios Amigo." Nick patted his uncle on the head and followed his mother through the door.

Edward massaged his temples. "Hang on a second. What if anything happens to you by accident?"

Nick stepped back into the room and shrugged.

Mother and son walked the short distance to their apartment.

"When did you get to write those incriminating emails?"

"I didn't," said Nick. "It's called SBS talk. A friend of mine came up with the idea."

"Are you hoping to see Nick?" Kylie asked as Gemma surveyed the beach and promenade.

"No, not at all. I was appreciating the view. This time next week, I'll be staring at a big steel drum."

"I'll be checking Mrs Lowther in for her clean and polish," said Kylie. "That woman has a huge mouth."

"At least you won't have to listen to Craig Martin go on and on about the meals he's cooked that week."

"Is he still single?" Kylie asked. "Perhaps he's trying to impress you."

"He has no chance," Sara said. "I won't eat one of his sausage rolls, no matter how delicious they are."

"He must be bad," said Gemma, dodging a flying flip-flop.

Evelyn Kingston was not impressed to find her husband drinking a large glass of whisky. It was not yet five o'clock. "That's becoming a habit. What's your excuse this time?"

"Shut up, woman." Her husband shouted.

"Don't speak to me like that!"

Edward put his nose to hers and barked, "I will speak to you how I fucking well like."

She slapped his face. "We'll see about that." Evelyn took his glass off him and threw it against the wall. Seeing it break into tiny particles, leaving whisky splattered around the place, she retraced her path to the car and drove away.

Jon pulled a face at Leah. "Sounds like someone isn't happy."

Leah coyly looked over to the Kingston apartment, where she heard a man shouting and furniture getting roughly moved around, but said nothing about it. "It's nearly five. Shall we have another half hour and then go for a siesta?"

The children played quietly in the shade. The boys giggled at something Daisy said.

"Fine. I might get to finish another chapter."

Elizabeth Kingston listened as Nick told her how and why he had divided the money. It all seemed logical, and she congratulated him on a well-done job before asking, "Where are you going tonight? Anywhere special?"

"No. I might go for a swim in a minute." He remembered his bruises. "I didn't say anything earlier, but I had a bit of a tumble this morning, and I've badly bruised myself. It"s nothing serious, but a swim might help."

"You need to be more careful. Lucia has invited us to her niece's birthday party. Would you like to come along?"

Nick had gone into the bathroom to change his shorts. "Where and how old is she? I am not sure I want to play musical chairs as I had to with Zac's kids that day."

"It will be nothing like that. She's twenty-one, and there is food and drink at Lucia's brother's house, but then you youngsters will go to the Cavern until late. Javier will be there."

"I'll think about it while I'm doing my laps." He emerged without a shirt.

Elizabeth stared open-mouthed at the brown marks across his torso and legs. "A bit of a tumble? You look like you've fallen from an aeroplane."

"I…err…tried a shortcut and slipped down a bank. As I said, it's fine. It looks worse than it is. It doesn't hurt." Much, he thought.

"Well, be more careful and take your key. I told Lucia I would get there to help with the preparations, and I'll be leaving shortly."

"Will do," Nick grabbed the key and his towel. "Where is the house?"

"It's the big one on the other side of Sillot. Apparently, you can't miss it."

"Okay, I might see you later."

Nick waved at the Olivers, dived into the pool to avoid conversations about his bruises, and started swimming. His body ached, and his arms seemed reluctant to stretch, but he eventually found a rhythm and forgot his troubles as he moved up and down the pool.

"You fucking bitch, what right do you have to do this to me?" Edward Kingston ran across the grass toward his sister-in-law, who had stopped to speak with Leah.

Jon stood, intercepted Edward and dragged him into the

water.

The splash made a wave that caused Nick to stop swimming. He waded across the pool. His uncle was about to punch Jon, but Nick grabbed his hand and twisted Edward's arm behind his back. Seeing that his uncle had calmed a little, Nick swept his legs away, and Edward went back under the water. Nick put his spare hand on Edward's head. "Are you going to behave now?"

His uncle spluttered. Nick pulled him by the hair, noticing for the first time that Edward had a bald patch he usually kept hidden by combing over.

"You realise that little outburst is going to cost you." Nick had turned Edward's head to face him.

"I don't know what came over me. I just lost it."

"Well, you certainly know how to make an entrance. I think everyone in the complex knows what a dick you are."

Nick pushed his way to get to the ladder first. "Thanks, Jon."

Oliver was drying himself. "I didn't do much. I wasn't going to let him hit your mother."

With head bowed, Edward climbed out of the pool and walked toward his apartment.

Nick ran at him and jumped up, kicking his uncle in the face. Edward hit the water again.

"I've wanted to do that for ages, " Nick admitted.

"That's enough, Nick. You are scaring the children," said Elizabeth.

Three stunned faces stared at Nick from their mother's lounger.

"It's okay. I was practising my karate." Nick squatted beside them and pointed at his uncle, climbing the ladder on the other side of the pool. "See, he's fine. I didn't hurt him at all. It looked worse than it was."

"What are those marks on your body?" Daisy asked as the boys inched forward to inspect more closely.

"They are nothing. I had a bump earlier, but I'm fine." He

turned to Leah. "Can I get you all a drink or an ice cream?"

"I could murder a beer," said Jon.

"Me too, please," said Leah as the children placed their orders.

Herr Sneider had been unsure whether to accept when his new neighbours, the Bennetts, invited him and his wife for an afternoon sherry. He was not a fan of sherry, but his wife suggested they attend to get to know some other owners.

The Sneiders had saved for years to buy a place in the sun. Majorca had always been the preferred destination, even though one of the Costas would have been a far cheaper alternative.

Sitting on the Bennetts' balcony, watching other British residents fighting and pushing one another into the pool, Herr Sneider wondered whether he should have bought a place on the mainland.

Gemma, Kylie and Sara clubbed together all their remaining cash and mapped out a plan for the evening. They would have a pub crawl before hitting the English bar, with a disco and karaoke.

Plans changed when Sergio called to invite them to the Cavern to celebrate Javier's cousin's birthday. There would be free alcohol, and entry was by invitation only, so they would not bump into Barty, Donny or Christiano. Sergio also confirmed that Gavi would not be there. He was working.

The free alcohol appealed to Kylie and Sara, who assured Gemma they would not leave her on her own.

Nobody could have failed to notice a party was occurring at Lucia's brother's house. There were balloons, banners and bunting everywhere. Nick arrived to be greeted by Javier.

"I wondered why there was no cage tonight," Nick said in Spanish.

"My cousin is an only child. Her father is rich, so if she wants a party." Javier spread his arms. *"He is my boss and uncle. I have*

to be here. It is good to see you, Nick. You are very welcome." Javier scanned the garden. *"No Gemma?"*

"No, that's err..."

"It is okay. You don't need to tell me. These things happen. Now let's have fun. Are you coming to the Cavern later?"

"We'll see how it goes."

Chris Shanklin shut down his machine, rubbed his eyes and stretched. It had been a long session, but the outcome had been more than satisfactory.

He had moved the Kingston cash from Mallorcan Mammories to Kingston Communications and then onto an account in the Cayman Islands before it came back into the UK shared between Nick and Elizabeth's accounts. Having been involved in this kind of activity for a long time, it was almost second nature to him. He was confident nobody would trace it.

He then focused his attention on the video business. Just over half of the women targeted for blackmail had paid a ransom. Developing a workaround that allowed him to repay the money, plus interest, from funds that remained in the Mallorcan Memories account was easy. Finding suitable words to explain to victims what he had done proved more problematic.

After sending the money, he destroyed all videos and files and closed the website. He then rang his contact in South Africa to confirm the site was no longer open and that all the information had been wiped. She was ecstatic, grateful, and relieved. She offered to pay him for his services. He refused, saying he was only correcting a wrong. In truth, he did not want Isabella to know anything about him.

It was time to relax. He kicked off his shoes and lay on the oversized sofa, remote control in hand.

Nick was introduced to Javier's cousin, Carmen, and wished her happy birthday. Her boyfriend stayed close, wary of the stranger. Carmen's other cousin, Isobel, on her mother's side, had flown in from the mainland with her brother. She showed no caution around Nick. Isobel was pretty, petite, and witty and would not leave Nick out of her sight. She told him she wanted to get to know him to help improve her English but spoke to him only in Spanish.

"Neek, are you ready? We are going to the club."

"I'm not sure..."

"Of course you are. You cannot let me go on my own. Carmen will have many guests. Javier and his friends are meeting their girlfriends. My brother will be dancing with who knows who. I do not know anyone, so you must keep me company."

Javier appeared beside him and whispered, "I have just spoken to Sergio. Gemma's friends will be there."

The thought of bumping into Kylie and Sara filled Nick with dread. It would be worse if Gemma were also there. Nick was trying to think of a suitable excuse when Javier said, "We will sit in the private area. You will not have to talk with them if you do not want to."

Elizabeth was having fun.

Lucia and her brother were a hilarious double act, keeping the guests happy with stories of the past. When they took a break, Lucia's husband entertained them with dancing.

Elizabeth felt sad about returning home the next day, but she supposed all good things...

She determined not to wait so long for the next good thing.

This was nothing like the school disco. The loud music bounced off the walls. The lights were bright, doubly so when they hit the mirror balls on the ceiling. People filled the dance floor.

Nick saw Isobel, Carmen and Gabriela dancing with other guests. He followed Javier to the VIP area, a raised platform with a wooden railing. A man wearing an identity badge stood ready to stop unwanted visitors.

To the right of the VIP area, Nick spotted Kylie and Sara sitting in a booth on one side and Gemma on the other. She had her back to him. Kylie raised her hand to acknowledge she had seen him. Sara repeated the action, causing Gemma to turn and nod at him. Nick waved shyly and stepped up into the reserved space.

Open bottles of sparkling wine rested in ice buckets surrounded by champagne flutes. Half barrels filled with ice and bottled beers stood on the fringes. Javier passed a bottle to Nick and handed him a bottle opener with 'The Cavern Club, Sa Coma' on the side.

"You can take this home as a souvenir," said Javier with a smile

"I might just do that." Nick flicked off the lid. *"These beers will not last long. Shall I get more?"*

Javier laughed. *"No, when these are gone, the barman will refill the barrel. My uncle is paying tonight, so put your money away."*

Gemma smiled to herself, happy that Nick had landed on his feet. His Spanish friends treated him much better than his family had. He deserved a break. She turned to see what he was doing,

"Not pining for him already?" Kylie asked.

"You could have been there, Gem, if you hadn't been so hasty."

"I'm fine here," said Gemma, who felt like a voyeur when the pretty Spaniard girl sat on Nick's lap. Fucking hell, he doesn't hang about, she thought, quickly facing the other way.

Ben and Will settled on the comfier seats at the rear of the bar. They had eaten at the Indian restaurant, but Ben wanted somewhere more private to share some news. Will put their drinks on the table.

"What's all this about, Dad?"

"I have some news for you. You may not be happy with

what I am about to say."

"Well, come on, spit it out," said his daughter."

"I'm buying a supermarket."

"What? You are not serious?"

"I told you that you might not be happy." Ben sipped his San Miguel.

Shirley asked, "What brought this on."

"I need something to occupy my mind, and I think it will be a good investment."

"Fair enough, but I thought you agreed not to open a new shop within five years of the sale?"

"That's in the UK. I'm buying a shop here, in Sillot."

"You are doing what? Are you off your head? What made you think that is a good idea? Who will manage it? Don't say us because we have enough to do, and you can't do it, not while you're having treatment."

Ben didn't mention that the jury was still out on that score, "Lucia's daughter, Gabriela, with help from Lucia and her brother, Javier."

Shirley looked at Will. "I told you they were after his money. There is no fool..."

"They don't know yet. I haven't told them."

"So, who does know?"

"Well, you, the estate agent and..."

"Me," said Will.

Shirley glared at Will. "You? How...do you know when I didn't? How long have you known?"

"A couple of days." Will raised his eyebrows as he took a drink.

Shirley grabbed her wine glass. She remained silent long enough to drink half the contents. "What brought this on?"

Ben told his daughter about his discussions with Lucia and how he liked Gabriela's ideas. He had spoken to the estate agent, who had not yet advertised the property. At his request, the agent talked to the owner, who was receptive to the suggestion of a quick sale. "The property next door is also available, so I might buy the two and expand the supermarket to give more room for a bakery. The agent does not think that would be difficult to arrange. What do you think?"

"It's a bit bloody late to ask my opinion. It sounds like you've already made up your mind." The rest of her wine disappeared.

"I'll get you another." Will stood to go to the bar. "That went better than I imagined." He winked at Ben and kissed Shirley's cheek. "Be back in a tick."

Isobel dragged Nick up to dance and would not let him go. After three songs, he needed something to drink, and she caught his hand as they left the dancefloor.

Kylie passed them on her way to the loo. "Good on you, Nick. You didn't hang around. Don't do anything I wouldn't do." She blew him a kiss.

"Who is that?" Isobel asked, giving Kylie a once over.

"Just a friend." Nick sat.

Isobel placed her bottom on his lap and her arms around his neck. *"Can I be your friend, too?"* she asked, staring into his eyes.

Jon and Leah zipped up their cases and checked that everything was ready for the next day.

"The bus is at two, so we'll be at the bus stop ten minutes before."

"Check," said Jon. They had already agreed on the timetable. "Do you think taking the children out for breakfast is a good idea? The boys are bound to get in a mess."

"We have to occupy them somehow. I have clean T-shirts in my hand luggage. Their shorts will be fine."

"I am not looking forward to the journey home."

"Why? Because you don't want the holiday to end?

"Partly that, but mainly because the boys are guaranteed to be a pain in my arse."

Isobel nibbled Nick's neck and said, *"I have had enough of this place. Will you take me home?"*

"Of course. Where are you staying?"

"In my aunt's house, where we met. They put me in the room above the garage. It is very private."

"I'm ready when you are." Nick smiled as he stood.

Isobel pulled him closer to whisper in his ear. *"Do you have any condoms?"*

"I don't think so," said Nick, not expecting to hear those words.

"No problem, I know where to get some. Wait here. I'll only be a minute." She kissed him again, grabbed her bag and went to the ladies.

"Do you think I ought to go over and say hello?"

Sara's expression made it clear she did not think that was a good idea. "No."

"Won't he think it's odd that I didn't speak to him?"

"You waved at him. He knows you've seen him. Leave it at that."

"I am not sure. I think I ought to..."

"Don't do this Gem."

"Do what?"

"Go over and suggest you have one last waltz for old-time's sake."

"I do NOT do that."

"You do. You've done it a few times."

"When? With whom?"

Sara reeled off four names, leaving Gemma dumbstruck. "I didn't waltz with the first two," she said.

"I didn't say you did, but having finished with them, you met up with them and made it look like you were back together, only to dump them again."

Gemma thought about the last time she saw Mac. "Shit, I never realised that was my thing. Anyway, I'm not thinking of one for the road with Nick. He seems quite happy with his new friend. I just wanted to make sure there were no hard feelings."

"I believe you."

"What do you believe?" Kylie returned from the bar.

"That Gemma is just going over to ensure there are no hard feelings between her and Nick."

"Not the one last time, for old times' sake routine again," said Kylie, making Gemma's jaw drop. "It's a bit late for that. I just said goodnight to him. He's gone off with the pretty Spaniard."

Elizabeth checked that the path was clear before leaving the taxi and walking to her apartment. She did not want to repeat the earlier events.

Once inside, she made herself a coffee and started to pack up her things. Tomorrow was the first day of the rest of her life. She hoped it would begin a massive improvement in their fortunes. She needed to convince Nick that the last six years had not been wasted.

Tracey Stone finished an extended shift at the hospital and was waiting for her bus. She opened her purse. There was just enough money to last her until payday, but she would have to rely on sandwiches for supper again. She wished her boyfriend would buy something other than cheese and ham. Tracey craved something different. She shook herself. Her desire for change had gotten her into this mess.

The thought prompted her to check her bank balance. She had to ensure that the payment to the Spanish Shits had gone; she had no wish for them to contact her again. Her thumbs hit her phone until her account details appeared, and Tracey's eyes lit up as he stared at her balance. She looked up and down the street before rechecking the figures. The amount had not changed.

A message appeared. Tracey half-expected a grovelling apology from Donny, but the news was much better. The anonymous contact told her that the site was no more, she was getting a refund on her payments plus interest, and there would be no further contact. Tracey punched the air, kissed the screen, and thanked her God.

There will be no cheese and ham supper for her tonight. Tracey was buying takeaway. Should she have an Indian curry? A pizza? Then she thought a Chinese meal would be nice. No, she decided she fancied an Indian curry.

Tracey checked her watch. Jordan would be home from work in an hour. She would get his favourite, chicken biriani with madras sauce. Tracey would have chicken tikka masala with pilau rice. If the bus was on time, she could nip into the convenience store for a bottle of wine and some cans.

She hoped Jordan would be pleased, but he could never know what they were celebrating.

Will put his palms on his face and pulled them down until his fingertips rested on his chin. A deep sigh left his mouth. He interlocked his fingers, placed them behind his head and stretched out his legs. The wooden chair creaked as he leaned back.

He could not get over what a close call it had been. Too close for his liking. Far too close. Will could not believe that he had been so careless. His complacency had almost made him pay the ultimate price. If that wasn't bad enough, he had put Nick at risk. Nick should never have been allowed to join in, let alone have to save his life. He saved both their lives. Maybe it was fate. Whatever it was, it did not forgive his sloppiness.

Will revisited seeing the Ferrari and Gus' car leaving the property and had assumed the cars contained the men going in the boat. What was that saying about why it was never safe to assume? He remembered something else. When he opened the front door of Graham's house, the alarm was off. Why did he not notice that? That should have warned him something was wrong. Will should have stopped rather than wading straight in. He had rebuked Nick for his mistake at the internet café but then made significantly greater errors himself. The younger Snowy would not have been so slapdash. What was the matter with him?

He was getting too old for this. He reached over the table and grabbed the bottle of brandy, bringing it nearer to his glass. Will poured himself a considerable measure and downed most of it, toasting the end of his career in the field. From that moment forward, he would remain indoors, out of sight and miles from the action. He sat drinking, wondering if young Nick might replace him. He seemed to have an aptitude for the work, and Will could teach him all he needed to know. He could also show him how to avoid mistakes.

It was time for bed. Will emptied his glass and put the bottle back in the cupboard. He rinsed his glass and left it on the drainer. Checking all the lights were off. He walked to the bedroom. He heard Shirley lightly snoring. Further down the hall, he saw Ben had shut his door, but there was no noise behind it.

Ben had also taken a potentially life-changing decision. Shirley had not been impressed. Will knew she would come around. She was only smarting because she hated being the last to know.

Good for you Ben. Go for it. You are a long time dead, Will thought. He shivered as if someone had walked over his grave.

"Neek, Neek, are you okay?"

Nick opened his eyes and saw Isobel over him. *"Yes, I'm fine. What happened?"*

"You were calling out in your sleep, and your body shook. I was worried."

He took her in his arms. *"It's okay. It was just a bad dream. I am fine now."* Isobel cuddled up close. Nick kissed her head. *"I'd better get some sleep. I have to be up early. I go home tomorrow."*

"Don't remind me." Isobel patted his bum. *"Night night, sleep tight."*

Nick wasn't sure he wanted to sleep now that he knew

what to expect from his dreams.

DEPARTURES AND ARRIVALS

Eddie Kingston's head pounded, his neck ached, and his stomach gurgled. He had slept on the sofa and looked like he had missed the opportunity to go to the loo. His shorts were soaking wet. He felt something pressing into his side and retrieved an empty whisky bottle. Slowly leaning forward, he put it on the coffee table with the other.

"Where are we going?" Jon asked.

"To the Red Lion."

"What? Why? We've had breakfast; the only money left is to cover us if we need anything at the airport. "

"Elizabeth asked us to meet her and Nick at the Red Lion. She wants to tell us something."

"Couldn't this have waited until we got home?"

"She must have her reasons."

They found Elizabeth and Nick sitting at a large table. In front of them was an ice bucket containing a bottle of champagne and a selection of soft drinks. Nick had partially filled four flutes. He gave one to Leah and Jon and handed plastic bottles to the children.

"Thanks for coming, "said Elizabeth. "I'll try to keep this brief."

"Please do," said Jon. "What is this about?"

"It's about a business proposition," said Elizabeth.

"Cheers." Jon sipped the liquid and then wiped his mouth. "What business proposition?

"I'm coming to that, " said Elizabeth. "I have been trying to think of a way to thank you for your bravery yesterday. Not many men would have done what you did."

"I didn't think about it, to be honest. I'm just glad you are okay. Did you patch things up with whatshisname?"

"No, I have no plans to speak to him ever again. Anyway, thank you." Elizabeth raised her glass.

"You could have just spoken to us. You didn't need to go to all this fuss."

"We haven't finished yet," said Nick. "Go on, Mum."

"We would like to help you start your own business."

"I'm not being funny, but how can you help us? You told Leah all your money had gone when your husband died."

"Jon…" said Leah, looking embarrassed.

"It's okay, Leah, he's quite correct to be suspicious," said Elizabeth. "We found out that my husband loaned his brother, whatshisname, a sizeable chunk of our money, and he has now, um, how shall I put this, paid us back with interest."

"And you are going to help us? Just because I pushed a man into the pool?"

"You didn't have to do anything," Elizabeth said, sipping her drink. "And yes, we want to help you."

How much are you thinking?" asked a sceptical Jon.

Elizabeth sipped more champagne and let the taste develop in her mouth before answering. "How much would you need to renovate the house?"

"I don't know, but I'm guessing it is likely to be tens of thousands rather than thousands," said Jon. "We'll get the money back when we sell the other house, so it would only be a bridging loan."

"How about fifty thousand to begin with?"

Leah and Jon's mouths dropped open. Leah spoke first. "What? Are you being serious?"

Jon joined in. "It would take us ages to pay that back. How do you know I am any good at what I do?"

"Yes, we are serious and know you are good," said Elizabeth. "Nick and I were up early this morning looking at the Cromwell Construction website. The before and after images showed great work, and the client reviews praised you. We are not helping you because we want to be charitable. We believe we can all make money out of this. That's why we don't want the money paid back. Nick and I want to be your partners in a new venture. We thought that we could set up a company. Each family would have a 50% share. You can buy your share when you sell your existing property."

Jon eyed the lady distrustfully."What would this company do?"

"Pretty much what you do now: construction and property renovation. We could also buy houses and renovate them. Leah can design the interiors, etcetera."

Leah's mouth had not closed.

Jon spoke again. "Could we get properties for the money we could afford to contribute?"

"We have enough to start us off when you are ready. There are plenty of empty houses around needing a little TLC. Property prices are lower in Wales," said Elizabeth

"So we buy one, do it up and then what?"

"We can rent or sell it and move on to the next one."

The business model was not unique, and Jon knew it had worked for others. "In return for what?"

"If the business takes off, we expect 50% of profits..."

"And if it fails?"

"Then we dissolve the business, share the property and start again. If you are half the man your wife thinks you are, then this won't fail."

Leah grabbed his hand. "What do you think Jon?"

He puffed out his cheeks and lips and sighed as he looked at Elizabeth.

Jon nodded. "I'm interested, but how do we know this is real? How do we know you are not bullshitting us?"

"Jon!" Leah looked horrified. "Do you think Elizabeth and Nick would be that devious? Why would they do that?"

"I don't know," said Jon. "This still seems a bit too good to be true. One minute they have no money, the next...."

Nick held up his mobile. "This is our current account balance this morning."

"Lucky you," said Jon. "Should I be impressed? That

could be fake. You probably want us to hand over the deeds to our house before you disappear."

"Jon!" Leah's expression quickly softened to appease the children, who looked anxious.

"We can sort this very quickly," said Nick. "You have internet banking?"

"Yes," said Jon.

"Well, give me your account details.

"Hold on a second, " Jon turned to Leah. "See, I told you, this is a scam."

"Here," said Leah, handing her debit card to Nick.

"Leah!" Jon was not impressed.

"Can you access your account on your 'phone?"

"Yes," Jon said, pressing buttons on his mobile and handing it to Leah. "She knows more about it than me."

"Okay," said Nick, trying hard to ignore the pain in his arms and chest. "I'll transfer £500 to your account. I know this account transfers money immediately because I did it this morning."

They sipped champagne while they waited for the technology to do its work. Jon's mobile pinged.

"It's there," said Leah. "Look."

Nick showed Jon his screen. "See, our balance has gone down..."

"And ours has gone up." Said Leah.

"Do you want that back?" asked Leah.

"No. Consider it as a first instalment," said Elizabeth.

Jon puffed out his cheeks. Things were moving faster than anticipated, and excitement was building in his belly. "Thank you for the offer, but we don't have any work if it has escaped your attention."

"Not yet, but we'll get some," said Elizabeth. "You have to do up your house first."

"You are happy for us to focus on that?" Jon saw two heads nod. He turned to his wife. "What do you think, love?"

"I'm in," said Leah, raising her glass. "Here's to our new

business venture.

"Come off it, Leah. Stop sitting on the fence and tell me what you think."

"I think that my brave husband needs to channel his newfound courage and take the chance. We'll never get another opportunity like this."

Jon looked at his wife and then at the Kingstons. "I think we have a deal."

They shook hands

"I'll drink to that," said a smiling Elizabeth.

"Will you want any role in the business?" Jon asked.

"No," said Elizabeth. "We might organise a few jobs and ask you to do the work. The day-to-day management will be your responsibility."

"What happens next?"

"We'll draw up an agreement, then register a company and transfer the money."

"This is amazing," said Leah as Jon studied the newly arrived credit.

Nick grabbed the champagne bottle and topped up their glasses. "Cheers."

Jon kissed the phone's screen. "It certainly looks like we're in business," he said before asking Elizabeth if he could use some of the advance to pay for a taxi to the airport.

Will and Shirley left Ben in the airport bar while they went to select some reading materials. Ben promised to get the drinks in by the time they returned. It was not like Will asking for coffee; he must have drunk too much the previous evening.

The barman took his order, and Ben returned to the corner table, watching the passengers wander by, looking for their departure gates. Ben checked his watch. They had another hour and a half until flight time.

He wanted to call Lucia to give her the news but would wait until everything progressed. The agent had made the offers on his behalf, and both were accepted, but Ben wanted a survey done and also needed to ensure the authorities had no problem with his plans. He had his fingers burned for not doing things by the book.

Will's therapist friend would call on Monday to set up a session. Ben was unsure he needed it, but Shirley insisted that he at least talk to the man. Ben's resolve had more or less capitulated, and he would have the treatment. Shirley would contact the consultant to discuss the next steps.

His companions were coming. Will held up a music magazine for Ben to see. "There's an article in here about Led Zeppelin. I loved that band."

"You'd be better off with a nice bit of jazz," said Ben.

"If you are going to wind me up, I'd better have a pint," Will replied.

Nick Kingston was unusually sullen on the 'plane home. His mother guessed the reason.

"Are you missing her already?"

He felt uncomfortable having this discussion, not least because his body ached. His torso and legs were blue with bruises, and he would have liked some space to stretch. "Ah, you know."

"You'll see her again soon enough."

"I don't think so. Gemma finished with me."

"What? When?"

"Thursday."

Then where were you last night? On second thoughts, I don't want to know. Why did she do that?"

"She told me the other evening that this was only a holiday fling. She doesn't want to see me when we get back home. She thinks I need to see other girls. I should never have told her that she was my first girlfriend."

"Well, you had to be honest with her, and I think she might have noticed. It's not good to start a relationship with a lie." Elizabeth resisted the temptation to tell him that he would get over it. "I think that shows a lot of maturity on her part."

"Why would you think that?"

"Because she wants you to be sure of your feelings. It's a big risk for a girl to commit to a man who hasn't…as Grampa Ned used to say, played a few tunes on different pianos. There is always a fear that he will want to tickle a few new ivories at some point." His mother smiled. "I shouldn't tell you this, but I told my best friend at university what my Dad said, and she always quoted it. She adapted it and used to rate the men in her life by the tunes they could play."

"Tunes?"

"Yes, she equated sexual activities with tunes. She finished with one lad because he only knew two tunes. She married her husband because he could recite the whole songbook." Elizabeth laughed but then fell solemn. "He left her to join a new band!"

"So I need to play a few pianos and learn new tunes. How do you know when you've found a piano you want to play forever?"

Elizabeth chuckled. "You'll know. There is a big difference between lust and love. Lust can be temporary, but love can last a lifetime, whether you want it to or not. You will know when you feel it."

"I wasn't asking Gemma to commit to anything. I just liked the idea of seeing her now and again. She is funny and great company."

"I could see you thought a lot of her. All I can say is that faint heart never won fair lady. You might have to work at it if you want her back."

"I wouldn't know where to start; I don't even have her address."

"You have her 'phone number?"

"But I wouldn't know what to say."

She had a few ideas but did not mention them. Nick had to work out this on his own. "You'll think of something. You're a bright lad. You've come a long way in the last fortnight; let's see what the next few weeks bring." She took a deep breath, having decided this was the time to pass on some news of her own. "I've got some news that might cheer you up."

"I didn't know I was miserable."

"It might make you even happier."

"What's that?"

"Well, you'll be 21 soon."

"I know that, mum."

"Before he died, Grampa Ned prepared a surprise for you." She paused, unsure how to continue.

"The trust fund, you mean. I know all about that."

"How?"

"He told me."

"When?"

"I'm not sure now. It was one of my weekend stays. He introduced me to a few of his tenants and said I would be their landlord in the future."

"You never mentioned it."

"He told me not to."

"What else did he tell you?"

"I was always to treat the tenants fairly and with respect. I was to look after you, making sure you were provided for. With your consent, I could access the trust fund whenever I wanted. I had to promise him that Dad would never get his hands on it."

Elizabeth's hands covered her mouth. "You never said a word."

"Nor did you."

"But you could have asked me for the money instead of going without."

"I know, but I didn't need it. I guessed that you were trying to teach me something. I wasn't sure what at the time, but I thought it had to do with valuing money. I always knew the fund was there, but I also recognised that you were determined to pay Dad's debts on your terms. I was happy to go along with it. You and I did well, and it's been a mad ride. I've learned a lot, and I've got you to thank for that."

Tears welled in Elizabeth's eyes. "I put you through so much..."

"Nah, you didn't. My arsehole of a father did that. You've been brilliant, Mum. You've worked hard. You've always looked after me. You are my best friend."

"But I made you sacrifice so much. I can never give you back everything you've missed out on."

"I don't think I missed anything. It's been a blast. I owe you everything."

She pulled him to her and kissed the top of his head. "Oh, Nick, you owe me nothing. I would do it all again if I had to." Her tears fell onto his hair.

The sudden movement caused pain to shoot across his body. "Careful," he said. "You're spoiling my style. This haircut cost a fortune, although Gemma and her friends paid for it." Nick eased himself upright, trying not to squirm.

"You'll make a fine piano player. Just wait and see."

Nick did not mention that he had learned a few valuable tunes from Isobel. There were some things his mother did not need to know.

It had been a hard, long day for Lucia García-Ramírez. It was too hot, even for her, and she had lived on the island all her life. This weather was not conducive to good cleaning. If the owners want good cleaning in hot weather, they should install air-conditioning. Electric fans were okay, but air-conditioning was essential on sweltering days like today.

She had said goodbye to Elizabeth and Nick at their hotel and cried when they left on the bus. They had promised to keep in touch and invited Lucia to Wales, but she could see no way that would happen anytime soon.

She opened her front door and announced her arrival in Spanish. Her daughter shouted from the kitchen. Lucia walked over to her grandson, kissed him on the forehead and asked how he was feeling. He could not reply, but it made no difference. She always spoke to him.

Her daughter shouted again. She said something about

a delivery on her bed. Lucia checked her room, and her heart skipped a beat as she spotted an open box containing chocolates, wine, the sandals she had fancied in the shoe shop, and an enormous bouquet. The stems rested in a large plastic bowl bearing an envelope with her name.

She opened the envelope carefully and extracted a card. Lucia put on her glasses and read the words written in her native tongue.

"Lucia, thank you for making our holiday so special. We appreciate everything you and your wonderful family did for us. Accept these as small tokens of our love and appreciation. We will see you again soon. Elizabeth and Nick xx.

Lucia held the card to her chest as she thought about her friends. Her mood had improved so much that she felt so happy she could cry, and she did.

"Bloody hell, Kylie, cheer up, Will you? You've got a face like a slapped arse." Sara was at her sympathetic best.

"I don't want to go home. I wish I could live in Majorca."

"Last year, it was Ibiza. You say these things, but you'll be glad you live in Cheltenham next week," said Gemma. "It was very eventful, though."

"It's not every day I get to star in a porn film without knowing," said Kylie.

"Life is all about new experiences," Gemma said with a cheeky look.

"Do you think Nick managed to wipe the hard drives and shut the site?"

"I think so. I looked this morning and couldn't find the website."

"But you haven't asked him?" Kylie shifted along the row to let two other travellers sit together. As the airport became busier, seats were filling up.

"I'll message him now." Her thumbs hit the screen. "I was going to ask him last night, but then you pair went on about how I'm Last Waltz Gemma."

"Liar," said Sara, lifting her face from the magazine. "That wasn't the reason you wanted to talk to him."

"I still think you were stupid, though," said Kylie. "You obviously liked him. You don't normally throw yourself at a guy that quickly."

"I hardly threw myself at him."

Sara chuckled. "Didn't you?"

"No."

"From where we were standing, you did," said Kylie. "You saw him practically every minute of every day; you couldn't stop gushing about him, and when you were together, you couldn't keep your hands off him."

"I was not that bad."

"You so were," said Sara. "That was the most in love... or lust we have ever seen you."

"He was easy to like," said Gemma.

"So why have you dumped him?" asked Kylie.

"I didn't dump him - not really. I told him I wasn't ready for commitment and that he should get on with his life."

Kylie's expressions spoke for her, but Sara wanted to articulate her thoughts. "That reminds me of something," she said, looking at Kylie and then back at Gemma. "Now, what is it?" She put her index finger on her lips as she thought for a second. "I've got it - someone getting dumped!"

"It's for the best. It was the right thing to do," said Gemma.

"I can see that," said Kylie. "In my experience doing the right things in life usually leaves you in the shit."

"Probably too late now anyway. Nick's found himself a nice little senorita." Sara put the magazine on her seat. "Make sure nobody takes my space. I'm going to the loo."

Leah heard her husband returning before she could see him. He was singing his favourite Oasis song. Badly. She opened the door in readiness for his arrival.

"Hello, my love. What a wonderful day! You are my

Wonderwall." He kissed her cheek, and she smelled the alcohol on his breath. "I have Chinese food."

She had no heart to tell him that she and the kids had already eaten. "Great. I thought you were only going to call in for a drink."

"I was, but then I caught up with some regulars and had a few more. I knew you wouldn't mind."

How could she? The funding offer had been monumental news. She would have liked to have celebrated it too, but someone had to look after the children. "No, I don't mind. I've opened a bottle of wine, but what I don't drink will keep until tomorrow."

"Thanks, love, you are the best."

She took the food off him and resisted a giggle as he wobbled down the hallway, colliding with the walls. Daisy was in the dining room, busily colouring in. "Hi-ya Dais, what's happening?

Daisy stared at him with a concerned expression. Leah assured her that Daddy was okay. He was just happy.

Jon staggered into the lounge, fell on the sofa and spoke to the boys playing on the floor. "How are you doing, boys? Have you missed me?"

"No," said Charlie with a glint in his eye.

"Daddy dunk," said Harry, climbing up to sit on his father.

Gemma Potter sat with her sister, watching a rom-com on the TV. When Kate left the room to get crisps, Gemma's mobile rattled, and she grabbed it. She did not recognise the number—it was a landline. She thought it might be Nick.

"Hello."

"Hi, Gemma, how are you? Did you have a lovely holiday?"

It was her ex-friend Zoe. Her tone was friendly and not the least bit aggressive. Gemma replied in the same manner. "I'm fine, thank you, and yes, I had a great time." Had they been on friendlier terms, she would have readily gushed about the holiday, but they weren't. "You should have been there."

"I know, I wish now that I had come....look, Gemma, I am in Cardiff visiting a cousin, and I wondered if I could call over to see you tomorrow."

"Why? The last time we spoke, you made it abundantly clear that you never wanted to see me again. Your family hates me."

Kate tried to get her attention. "Who is it?"

She waved her away, listening for Zoe's response.

"I'm really sorry about that. That's why I want to see you so I can apologise face to face. We should have believed you, but we know we were wrong."

"You've changed your tune."

"My sister found out Sean's been seeing other women. One told my father Sean was in bed with her when he should have been working. Sean had dumped her for a lady in another house they were renovating. Dad confronted him about it, and Sean admitted it. He even confessed to climbing into bed with you. He said he was trying to help Mac."

"What a bastard."

"Something like that. Mia agreed to talk to him and expected him to plead for forgiveness, but he told her it was all her fault. If she had been more adventurous, then he would never have strayed.

"The complete bastard."

"I am so sorry we didn't believe you."

"Why? I would have done the same. He's family, and you had known him longer."

"It's okay, Gem. You don't have to make apologies to us. We all know we messed up. Can we meet tomorrow? I could buy you lunch, and we could have a catch-up. She paused, hoping for a quick reply, but all she heard was an intake of breath. She quickly continued. "My parents are also desperate for the chance to apologise and to make it up to you."

"Yes, okay then, why not? What time?"

"Shall I get to yours by eleven? You can choose the venue. My treat."

They closed with Zoe, saying she was looking forward to seeing Gemma again.

Kate saw her sister end the call. "So who was it?"

"That was Zoe. It looks like we're mates again. She's invited me to lunch."

"When?"

"Tomorrow."

"Don't go rushing into anything. She needs to earn your forgiveness."

Gemma hugged her sister. "When did you get so wise?" she asked, rubbing her head with her knuckles as she used to when Kate was younger.

"Ouch! You're a bully."

The comment made her think of Nick. Why hadn't he been in touch?

It was after midnight in Ibiza, and Gus was bored. One club was like another; the guests were identical, and all places charged exorbitant prices for entry and drinks. He told his friends he was heading back to the boat.

Where the hell was Graham? Gus knew they had agreed not to call each other because Graham believed a local police inspector was having doubts about the Laings' activities and might be eavesdropping. Still, he thought Graham would have sent a thumbs-up or something similar.

When they bought the boats, Graham and Gus paid for elaborate tracker systems to trace the vessels if they got stolen or if one became lost at sea. Gus yawned as the tablet searched for Waltzing's coordinates. The yacht was heading south, towards Malaga. What the fuck was Graham up to?

Nick fist-bumped Zac as he and his mother left the car. "Thanks for the lift. I owe you."

"No problem. You coming training on Tuesday?"

Nick patted his belly. “I think I better had. I’ve done nothing but eat and drink for the last fortnight.”

“Sounds like bliss,” said Zac.

Nick patted the top of the car as it moved away.

Elizabeth had opened the door and picked up the mail on the welcome mat. “Mostly advertising bumpf,” she said. “If you take the bags upstairs, I’ll get the kettle on.”

“Okay. I'll charge my mobile, and then I’ll take the bags up."

The sea was calm, the sky was black, and the yacht was silent. Banda stared over the rail, watching the Spanish coastline pass in the distance. He knew nothing about boats even though he technically now owned one. As it happened, Mikel, the man he had appointed Captain, did not know much more than him. Mikel could start, manoeuvre, and steer the boat but had no idea how to navigate it. Banda suggested they follow the coastline to southern Spain and then turn left. That would get them nearer their destination.

Ben was pleased when Shirley and Will accepted the invitation to stay at his house. He welcomed the company.

Will searched the cupboards and freezer for something to eat. “Bloody hell, Ben, you’d never believe you made a living out of food. You’ve got nothing in.” He closed the fridge door. “Looks like a takeaway again, then.”

Ben shrugged. Why would he stock up when he had no intention of coming home?

Gemma felt good being back in her bed with a comfy pillow. Her brain was starting to switch off when her mobile pinged. She had a message from Nick. It consisted of two words, ‘All done’.

MONDAY 9TH AUGUST

Isabella Sanchez's ex-boyfriend, Carlos, was not surprised to hear from her again. Their relationship may have ended, but the not-insignificant matter of the money he owed her remained. He could lose the debt by doing her a favour. She had called the day after Graham and one of his henchmen, a young man named Bartholemew, had been found dead in Graham's mansion.

Her call told him it was time to deliver.

Elizabeth Kingston wasted no time setting about finding a new home for her and Nick. It made sense to act quickly and helped enhance the feeling of a fresh start. Her ability to pay in cash would help them secure a bargain, and she would visit the City for a shopping expedition to celebrate. Elizabeth decided to revert to her maiden name, Burgess.

Nick said he would focus on his new property portfolio and discuss priorities with the managing agents. If houses required significant refurbishment, he would employ Jon and Leah.

He rang Chris Shanklin to resign from his post but was persuaded to work part-time on other projects. Chris mentioned it had been Will's idea.

Nick suggested Zac could take his place.

From speaking to the cleaner, who had discovered the bodies when she arrived on Monday morning, a friend in the police and several local contacts, Carlos had a reasonable idea of what had transpired.

The police provisionally categorised it as a murder-suicide. They surmised that the pair had argued. Graham pulled a gun, and the other man threw a paperweight, trying to defend himself. Graham might have taken his own life, but the weapon could have gone off accidentally when Barty threw the paperweight. The police had no idea why they had turned on each other, but the presence of a baseball bat suggested Barty came ready to defend himself. There was no sign that anything was missing, and it did not appear that anyone else was present.

The police wanted to speak to Grigor, Donny, and Christiano, who had conveniently left the island at the time. They would also question Louise, Becky, and Candice, three known associates.

Inspector Mortez had a permanent smug grin on his face. He had always known that Laing and the Russian were up to something. All he had to do now was find out what. His superiors could not block his enquiries this time.

Grigor, Donny and Christiano transferred the cargo from Matilda to the back of the Range Rover. The Ferrari had gone, and Waltzing had not returned. Grigor had no answers to the infantile questions from the other two. He was more concerned with what Graham had done and where he had gone.

The three went to the house and were astonished to be met by a police cordon and officers awaiting their arrival. Donny and Christiano became twitchy at the prospect of police enquiries. They got taken to the local police station, a modern, flat-roofed building in Sa Coma, where they were left to stew in a meeting room.

The police asked them what they knew about the deaths of the two males and appeared not to believe their stories. Grigor refused the police's requests to access the Range Rover and called his lawyer. There was no evidence to suggest he had done anything wrong.

The lawyer arrived quickly and said a warrant was required before the police could search the vehicle. He and Grigor listened to the officers summarise their thoughts and then insisted the three could not have been involved in the tragic events. The police had no grounds to detain them. Grigor said Waltzing was gone when they returned to the marina, but he did not consider this suspicious as Graham often took out his boat. Grigor said nothing about his suspicions that Waltzing's absence was due to Graham using it to dispose of Snowy's body.

Inspector Mortez ignored their pleas and said he could hold them until he had verified their movements over the previous 48 hours. Mortez was gutted when the three alibis held firm. The Ibiza contacts confirmed the three visited several clubs and many bars.

After six hours of detention, the three were released from police custody, pending further investigations. They agreed to surrender their passports. Matilda was to remain where it was until further notice. Grigor knew his boat was clean. He told the police they were welcome to search it once they had their warrant and told them where to find his passport. The house was off-limits to him, so they would need to get it themselves. He said he was happy to help them with any further enquiries.

Grigor insisted he wanted to solve the mystery and offered a reward for any information that might help the investigation. The police gratefully declined his offer.

He did not believe the police's suggested sequence of events but did not desire to incriminate himself by explaining the background. How could he admit that someone had sent a henchman to recover goods Grigor had stolen from his father? Grigor sensed Snowy was involved in the deaths but could not know for sure until he checked what was missing.

There was plenty of time to decide what retribution was required. Grigor knew enough people and had a good idea of where to find Snowy. His immediate priority was to get the drugs they brought from Ibiza out of the boot of his car. These would need to be transferred to his office at the club at the earliest opportunity.

Carlos watched as four men left the police station. His police officer friend told him when that would happen. His brother, Jorge, told his driver to follow the lawyer's car. Carlos was nervous, and his mouth dried as their targets arrived at the Range Rover and the lawyer drove away.

Jorge's driver pulled the van alongside, blocking their way. The door in the side panel slid across, and a pistol persuaded Christiano and Donny not to flee.

Grigor projected calmness and looked into the back of the van. "What is this about?"

"Get in, and I'll tell you." Carlos initially tried to disguise his voice but realised there was no need. The men did not know him, and he was unlikely to hear from them again. As soon as Donny took his place, the door slammed shut.

Carlos leaned toward Grigor. "I understand that you and your associates are involved in pornography and blackmail."

Christiano fidgeted while Donny freaked.

"I think you have mistaken us for somebody else," said Grigor. "I run several businesses on the island, but they are all legitimate."

Jorge held up his mobile and pressed play. The video of Isabella appeared with Grigor's face prominent.

"I thought you pixelated that," Grigor said to Christiano.

" I did. How did you..." Christiano shut up when Carlos shouted for silence.

"Let's just say we acquired the rights to the director's cut."

Nick appeared in Donny's thoughts. "Did Nick Kingston give you this?" he asked, wondering what other damage his cousin had done.

"If he did, then you need to know he's involved. He's setting us up," said Christiano.

"Is he in this video?"

"No, but..."

"No buts. I am only interested in the men who made and

starred in this video. I understand that Bartholemew is one of the unfortunate victims of the shooting."

Grigor nodded. "That's right, along with my cousin."

"I am sorry for your loss. Is the other man in this video Raul, a business associate of you and your cousin?"

Grigor wondered if these men were involved in shooting Graham and Barty. If so, how much had they told him before they died? Grigor would speak the truth, hoping they would go easier on him. "Yes, it is Raul," he said.

"You two are responsible for making this video and the blackmail?"

"We didn't mean..."

"Don't lie," said Grigor. "There is no point in denying it. Just tell him the truth. Yes, they made the video and set up the blackmail, and we all enjoyed the proceeds,"

"Thank you, that is all I needed to know. Please sit back, relax and enjoy the ride."

Edward Kingston had no idea what to do when a blubbering Candice arrived at his door demanding to speak to Louise. His response that Louise was out resulted in a volley of information from Candice that terrified Edward.

He had no advice for the girl about whether she should go to the police station alone. The officer who called her said they would send someone around, but she hadn't waited. She suggested she would wait for Louise's return.

Edward wanted her off his property. It would not take long for someone to learn of his activities. He needed to get away. He slammed the door on a wailing Candice and gathered together as much as he could fit into a van.

Oh shit, it's Becky thought Gemma accepting the call. "Hi."

Becky told her the police had telephoned to speak to her about Graham and Barty's deaths. Their bodies had been discovered by the cleaner that morning.

Gemma was upset to hear that news and shocked to hear that it might be a murder-suicide case.

Becky had agreed to speak with Inspector Mortez, who came from Sillot but worked mainly in Palma. Before having that discussion, Becky wanted to know if Nick's contact had deleted the incriminating files. The answer to that question would influence how she played things. It would be easier to deny any association if the video was not available to catch her out.

The girl's audacity amazed Gemma, who wondered if the little girl's lost routine was all a ruse. She told Becky she needed to be careful, as the police would undoubtedly speak to Louise and Candice, and their evidence might count against Becky. Gemma reminded her that Grigor, Donny, and Christiano might also reveal something that implicated Becky. Her advice was that Becky should tell the truth, but there was no need to mention the video. That had been taken care of.

The building site lay on a dust track off the Manacor road. It was an isolated spot with only partially completed buildings as far as the eye could see.

The Mercedes van progressed slowly, pulling up beside a Jeep.

"Come, boys. Your friend is waiting."

The driver of the Jeep rested against the bonnet. He held a gun. Another man emerged from the shell of the house, also armed.

Carlos motioned for his guests to follow him.

The expanded group walked into a shell with scaffolding along all four walls. There were no doors or windows, and the open space had a deep, wide hole in the floor and a digger nearby.

"Stop there," said Carlos

The three did as instructed and jumped as Raul landed on the floor beside them. He had taken a beating.

"Why are you doing this?" Grigor asked.

"I owe someone a lot of money."

"If you need money, I can give you what you need and more. I come from a wealthy family in England. How much do you want? Take my money, and you will never hear from us again. You don't need to hurt us."

"Oh, but I do," said Carlos. "The lady you blackmailed has great power, and I owe her much money. However, when she gets this video, I will no longer owe her a euro." He pointed at one of the men recording the scene on the phone. "All set?"

The man held up a thumb.

"We didn't want to make that film," said Christiano, tears rolling down his cheeks.

"We were forced into it," Donny said with water running down his leg.

"In that case," said Jorge waving his gun at Gus and Raul, "You two fucked with the wrong woman and you two..." He smiled at Donny and Christiano, "...you simply fucked up."

Louise left the police station and considered her options. She could only think of two. Stay and get implicated in all the shit about to come her way, or go and try her luck elsewhere. The police had no evidence to incriminate her at the moment. It was a no-brainer.

The state of the apartment suggested her darling Daddy had reached the same conclusion. She thought about waiting for Donny and Christiano but had heard they climbed into the back of a black van with Grigor. She guessed they had already planned their escape.

What was it about the men in her life? They were all selfish bastards.

Jon emptied his desk and walked across Cromwell's car park carrying a cardboard box.

"Jon, Jon, hang on a second." Rob Cromwell had just pulled up in his Mercedes SUV. "I wanted a word."

Ordinarily, Jon would have walked to his ex-boss, but

this time, he concentrated on putting the box in his car. He heard footsteps on the tarmac. "Jon, I was calling you. I need to speak to you. Did you enjoy the holiday?"

Jon placed his bottom on the boot of his car and folded his arms. "Yes, thanks. We had a great time," he said.

"Good, good. I'm glad I got back in time to see you."

"How did you know…oh, I get it. That's why Richard left to make a call. He was phoning you." He checked out Cromwells' trousers and sweater. "Another busy day on the golf course. I'm surprised you could spare me the time to say goodbye."

"There is no need for that attitude."

"With respect, Rob, how I act is fuck all to do with you. I can have all the attitude I like."

"I thought you might be angry," Cromwell said, stepping back. "Can we start again? I wanted to apologise for my outbursts last week. I realise you need this job, and I should have thought about your predicament before acting so hastily. You, me, and Richard are a good team, and we should let bygones be bygones. Take your stuff back inside, and we'll continue as if nothing happened."

"Really? You sacked me, calling me all the names under the sun, but now you are inviting me back? Just like that? I don't know what to say."

"You don't need to say anything. You are correct, though. It won't be entirely just like that. I will put an official warning on your record, and I might have to cut your pay for a while. Nothing too severe, but people can't think I've gone soft."

"Very generous of you, Rob. I am not sure how to say what I'm thinking."

Rob placed a hand on Jon's shoulder. "As I said, there is no need to say anything. Just come back inside, and we'll carry on as normal."

Jon shook to free himself from Cromwell's hand. "I've got it. I know what to say. Go fuck yourself, Rob." Cromwell was speechless. "I have already received a very generous offer from Mike Clemence, and I promised him an answer today."

"You don't want to work for that charlatan."

"Maybe I do, maybe I don't, but Leah just told me I've had other calls from people wanting to talk to me about a job."

"I always knew you'd do well, but remember, this is where you made your name."

"This is where I made your name, you mean."

"Now, Jon, don't do anything hasty. Let's go inside and talk. I'm sure we can agree on a new package. We've been friends a long time...."

"Friends? Friends? We were never friends. You were my boss. Friends don't ring and sack you while you're on holiday, the first holiday I had in years."

"I can tell you are upset. Go home, speak to Leah, and we'll discuss it tomorrow."

"No need Rob. You've sacked me, and I won't return today, tomorrow or any other day. I look forward to getting what you owe me, and I expect a formal termination letter. I should warn you that I reserve the right to sue for wrongful dismissal once I have discussed this with an employment lawyer." Jon had no idea whether he had a case but felt much better leaving that threat in the air. He patted Rob's upper arm. "Take care, Rob, good luck and tell Richard I won't miss him."

Inspector Mortez did not understand how three key suspects could disappear so quickly. His men had found Grigor's car and had spoken to witnesses who saw the men step into the back of a black Mercedes van. The ports and airports had been alerted, but there was no evidence to suggest they had left the island. Mortez felt sure they were still on Majorca, probably hiding with an accomplice. His superior officer had previously stopped his efforts to investigate the British and Russian activities. Had he been allowed to act, Mortez was confident the pair would have gotten detained without anyone dying.

He had a solid suspicion that corrupt officers were complicit in helping to hide the illegal activities in Sa Coma. This was his chance to expose that corruption. His men would search every inch of the island to find the three fugitives, irrespective of cost or competing priorities.

LATER

Banda's daughter showed him the bag her mother had bought in the market. He smiled and turned his face so the little girl could kiss his cheek. He was delighted to be home but accepted that she required time to adapt. She had not seen her father for three years, and they needed to build a bond. His wife caught up with them, and the little girl walked between her parents, holding their hands as they walked down the road.

A ping caused Banda to stop. He took out his mobile and smiled broadly as the image of him and the Welshmen appeared. His wife and daughter asked what he looked at, and Banda showed them the picture.

"*Two friends I met in Spain. They brought me home.*"

Edward Kingston was not a happy man. His son and his friend were still missing. His daughter had fled to Italy, where she worked at a hotel, and his wife refused to speak with him. She returned to the UK. He wished he could have gone with her, but that would have resulted in his arrest. Europol had circulated his details concerning his alleged human smuggling and trafficking activities. He was safer in Morocco, waiting for his plans to come to fruition without fearing extradition.

It was an incredibly cheap place to live. Eddie had grabbed whatever money he had left, transferring some to new bank accounts and taking the rest in cash, but he needed to be frugal. He would not be earning for a while.

Ben and Lucia spoke regularly. He updated her on his treatment; the latest scan suggested the tumour had shrunk, and she informed him of progress with the shop refitting. She still could not believe what he had done. She and her children were very excited about the future, and Lucia looked forward to Ben seeing the changes.

Ben did not tell her his other news. Will's estate agent friend had advised him that all three of Eddie Kingston's apartments were available at a knockdown price. Eddie had disappeared, and his wife needed the cash. The properties were in her name, and she wanted to get rid of them. Ben had offers accepted on all three. He would give Lucia an option to move into one of them. They would have to discuss rent levels.

Will and Shirley would head to the island to close the deal on Ben's behalf. Will was not keen on visiting as he was concerned about possible repercussions. Gus, Donny, and Christiano had disappeared, and the police had no clue where they had gone. Will's efforts to track them also came to nothing.

The last time anyone saw the three on Majorca, they stepped into a black van. Will would need to keep his eyes open but felt a little happier at Chris' assertion that the three would not remain in an area where they were well known.

The new glasses and uniform did nothing for Louise. She had never liked combining black and white. Her hair was tied up in a bun with her waitress hat wrapped around it. The French maid's uniform made her look plain and dowdy. It did not stop her from getting unwanted attention from customers.

The only consolation was that she was confident not even her father would recognise her.

Jon Oliver was unimpressed with the finish on the wall.

"Rob. This wall needs repainting. It's a bit patchy."

"Okay, Jon, I'll get the painters back. Is there anything else?"

"Yes. I thought the kids' bathroom was supposed to be finished by the middle of this week."

"I think it should be. I'll speak to the plumbers. The flooring goes down on Thursday, so they'll need to complete the first fit by then."

"I'm a bit worried that things are falling behind. You agreed on the project plan, and we want to move in on the agreed-upon date."

"I don't see a problem. I can work later if required."

"Good."

It had been a hectic two months for the Olivers. The investment came through as promised, and they wasted no time spending it to make their dreams a reality.

A few weeks later, word spread that Rob Cromwell had revised his plans for semi-retirement and was working harder than ever. He spent much of his time trying to rectify the mistakes made by his son. The firm's reputation became tarnished. They lost multiple contracts, and Rob was left to manage the fallout alone. Richard and his girlfriend went travelling.

Jon offered Cromwell the contract for the work on their house, having already prepared specifications and fixed a price.

"I still can't believe how different you look, Nick. I hardly recognised you."

"I thought it was about time I changed my image."

"I can see that. You look terrific."

"Thanks, you don't look so bad yourself."

"It's strange that you called when you did. I was thinking about you the other day, wondering what had become of you."

"Why did you think about me?"

"I dug out some old photos from school, and you were in them."

"You kept them?"

"Of course. Didn't you?"

"Not sure I had them in the first place." Nick did not say that he doubted he would have had the money to waste on school photographs. "Do you see many of our old schoolmates?"

"Nah, not really. I spend most of my time in Cardiff now.

I haven't been out in Barry for ages. What about you?"

"I still see Simon, Julian and Zac. We train together twice a week."

"What did you call yourselves? The four Samurai?"

"We did...still do, to be honest."

She smiled. "Saddos."

"Yup, I know."

She scratched her chin with long fingernails. "I always had a bit of a crush on you, y'know?"

"Get off. You're pulling my leg. Why would you have a crush on me? You were...are gorgeous. You had all the cool dudes after you."

"Cool dudes! How old are you?" She laughed. "Anyway, what cool dudes? I seem to recall that most of the boys were total losers?"

"Hmm."

"Apart from you, you were always a mystery man."

"Me? I wasn't, not at all. There was more mystery in the school dinners than in me."

"Come off it. Nobody knew what you'd do next. One minute you were being pissed on by that idiot Wilco. The next, you knocked him over on the rugby pitch and made him look small. Everybody talked about it. Nobody could believe that sweet, innocent little Nicholas Kingston would fight back like that."

Nick smiled at the memory. "Many things changed that year, and I had to stand up for myself."

"And you stood up for many other people, too, from what I remember. If anyone got bullied, they ran to Nick. You were a hero."

"Hardly a hero."

"Well, you were always my hero. I used to think about asking you out."

He gave her a look that suggested he did not believe her.

She nodded. "It's true."

"Perhaps you should have."

"Would you have accepted?"

"Like a shot, not that I would have known what to do."

"You look like you would now."

The flirting reminded him of Gemma. "Well, let's just say I have had my moments, not enough to write a book about, though."

"Not yet, eh? There's still time. So, mystery man. Who were your heroes when we were in school?"

He did not hesitate in his response. "Robin Hood, he's always been a hero of mine, ever since my grandfather used to read me the stories when I was little.

"You do know he's not real?"

"Does it matter? It's a great philosophy to steal from the rich and help the poor."

"I suppose it is. Shall we have another drink and then head to the centre."

"Yeah, fine. Same again?"

Nick had dated four girls since the holiday. He had known three of them since school and met the other while working. This was the fifth, Sue Wilson. They had reconnected when Nick had to resolve a problem with a tenant, and Sue came to help.

He remembered her as a bright, intelligent girl who had always been part of the in-crowd. All the boys at school fancied her, and several asked her out. Nick would never have had the nerve, although Sue would always speak and sit beside him in their shared classes. She was always kind to him.

He recalled that they shared a common interest in a famous band of the time. The lead singer of this band had recently embarked on a solo tour, with a gig in Cardiff. Nick bought tickets, and Sue agreed to accompany him.

Sue was single, working for a housing charity in the city and shared a house with two other girls. This surprised Nick. He was convinced she would have a high-flying job in a large corporation.

Inspector Mortez knew that somebody was hiding something. How was it possible for so many people to leave the island without a trace?

He had found the yacht, Waltzing. It had been spotted in a harbour in Malta. The Maltese police confirmed that the owner possessed all the necessary paperwork, which looked like a genuine sale. There was nothing Mortez could do.

Nobody had seen the green Ferrari, although a similar model, in black, was filmed leaving the ferry in Barcelona in the week following the shooting.

Matilda was still moored at Palma Marina. The Laing family wanted to collect the boat, but Mortez insisted on retaining it as evidence. The substances discovered in the back of the Range Rover were enough to suggest the vessel was instrumental in bringing the drugs to the island. Mortez believed that proceeds of crime had helped pay for the boats. The yacht was relocated to a less prominent location, but this did not stop Mortez's superiors from being horrified about the fees payable.

The police's repeated visits to the marina were not fruitful. Other boat owners had seen a group of men carrying packages to the boat before it departed. This was nothing unusual; it happened often. Mortez believed these men had been involved in a burglary at a nearby warehouse with no registered owner. It must have been an inside job, as there were no signs of forced entry.

After speaking to several business associates, Mortez better understood Graham and Grigor's business activities. They dealt drugs and fake goods and were involved in prostitution, pornography, blackmail and, probably, people trafficking. Mortez's initial suspicions about Graham and Grigor related to his belief the pair were having sex with young girls. He could never have imagined opening such a massive can of worms.

Mortez needed a result, and soon. His priority was to

find the missing people. Someone must know something. He just had to ask the right person.

Gemma Potter downed one of the shots Kylie had placed before her. It promised to be an eventful evening.

Sara had given her apologies. A colleague at work had invited her out. It would be their third date. Gemma teased that her friend would soon be at level three.

"What time is your flight tomorrow?" Kylie rearranged the glasses, ensuring they had full ones in front of them.

"Not until eight in the evening. Plenty of time to recover."

"Shit. Don't look now, but that bloke you went with from the tyre fitters is over there."

"I haven't been with any bloke from the tyre fitters." Gemma looked over and caught the boy's eye.

"Must have been me then. Oh shit, he's coming over." Kylie grabbed her next drink. "Cheers!"

Nick climbed out of bed carefully. He did not want to wake his companion, but he felt an urge to walk about. It was that nightmare again. It frequently reappeared since the incident in Majorca. He didn't think he had screamed this time.

Standing in the window looking out onto the city, Nick reflected on the previous eight hours. He hadn't intended to stay at the hotel, but matters developed faster than anticipated, and they had limited options. Sue was happy for them to spend the night together but they couldn't return to her shared flat. His place was out of the question as his mother and aunt were there. The hotel made an ideal compromise.

The following day, the pair would visit each other's places to get fresh clothes before heading to the coast to celebrate his birthday. That had also been an impulsive suggestion, which she quickly accepted. The forecast was good, and he looked forward to the trip. He might even swim in the sea.

Thoughts of the beach stirred memories of the night on the Majorcan beach and Gemma. He smiled, thinking about their recent exchanges. Gemma had befriended him on social media and regularly liked and commented on his posts. He saw the shirt Gemma had sent him for his birthday resting on the back of the hotel chair. It had become a favourite.

"What's the matter?"

"Nothing. I couldn't sleep. Sorry, I didn't mean to wake you."

"Well, I am awake now. Come back to bed."

Little Bri had been Frankie Nuggets' chief enforcer for many years, and his father had held the position before him.

Brian had retired and moved to Lanzarote, claiming it was because his wife would benefit from a warmer climate. The truth was the younger Laings were taking the business in a new direction, and Brian did not want to be part of it. Graham, Frankie's oldest son, felt the same way and offered Brian a role that was too lucrative to refuse.

Brian became the co-ordinator of Graham's people smuggling operation. His job was to arrange collection, departure times, and destinations for the illegal immigrants and drugs shipped into the Canary Islands for distribution in Spain.

The role suited Bri. The job was part-time for full-time pay and allowed Brian ample time to indulge his love of fishing. He was happy being the invisible man in a highly profitable operation. Most people involved did not know his name, what he looked like or where he lived.

When word reached him that the police had intercepted the latest consignment in Majorca and Graham was dead, Brian assumed his retirement had become a reality. His last task would be to ensure the police had no trail to follow.

He hit a problem straight away. There was money missing. A lot of money. Then came the call from a stressed and angry Eddie Kingston, fellow transport consultant and money launderer. Brian knew he had more work to do.

Eddie said his nephew had accessed the accounts and had stolen the cash. There was nothing to worry about. Eddie had a plan to recover every penny. He was getting a new passport in Morrocco but would arrive in Lanzarote in a few weeks, where his daughter would join him. They needed Brian's help to get into the UK, where they would correct a few wrongs and recover the cash before returning to Spain to restart the business. He hoped Brian could help arrange discrete travel to and from England and supply two pistols to be collected on their arrival in Blighty.

Neither of these tasks presented any difficulty for Brian. It would cost him, but he was paid well enough and would take his expenses out of Kingston's share. What bothered him was that Kingston had called him directly. Contact had always been via Graham or Gus.

Brian had not thought about the idiot for months. How did Eddie get Bri's number? Why was he coming to the island? Was he working with the police?

Either way, Brian and his family might be at risk. If Kingston had become a police informant, he would try to trap Brian, so he had to be careful what he said. If Kingston was on the run, then successfully eluding capture did not equate to the authorities not knowing where he was. Bri had to ensure Kingston was not followed.
This amateurish activity was something he could not tolerate.

Brian also resented Kingston taking him for a fool. Little Bri was seething when he visited the bank and discovered monies had left the business account and paid into Kingston's. Did Eddie genuinely believe Brian would not find out? He hadn't even bothered trying to cover his tracks. The transferred cash went to the same account from whence it came.

There was another facet of this deceit that concerned Brian. Could it be a coincidence that Graham dies, Gus disappears, and Kingston arrives needing transport to the UK?

From what Graham had told him, Kingston was a greedy bastard, and Brian had never liked the sound of him. The feeling in Brian's gut was that Eddie wanted control of the whole enterprise. There was no intention to visit the UK. Kingston and his daughter were coming to remove Brian, but he would not go down without a fight.

LATER STILL

Gemma was happy living her life. She spent her time finishing her Master's thesis, helping her father grow his business, and, when possible, socialising. She met and went out with men but didn't stick around long. She felt no connection, no spark. Most did not reach Stage 2.

Things changed when Kylie told her about finding a profile for *Nick of the 4 Samurai* on social media. Kylie had been looking at her Spanish friends' posts and saw a link.

Gemma had not seen Nick for seven months but befriended him and became a keen follower of his activities. She liked his posts and often commented on them. Nick was witty but never cruel, always encouraging rather than disparaging. Seeing that Nick had posted something brought a smile to her face.

She messaged him, and these exchanges became more frequent. Gemma sent Nick stupid jokes and emailed silly things to him. She was delighted when he reciprocated.

For his 21st birthday, she sent him a shirt, a card and a box of random items. He texted to thank her for the gifts, promising to send her something special for her 21st in May.

Their contact became more frequent, and Gemma became impatient if Nick's message or reply took too long to reach her.

Gemma was surprised at how deflated she felt when an old school friend of his, Sue Arnold, posted an update about a visit to Tenby. The girl was pretty - perhaps too pretty. They looked happy - perhaps too happy. Gemma thought they looked good together. He looked fabulous in the photo, and the shirt Gemma had sent was a perfect fit.

She felt a little jealous seeing the most recent photos. She remembered the holiday and enjoyed thinking of what they did. She hated to admit it, but Kylie and Sara might have correctly suggested she had made a mistake. She should have given him a bit more time.

There was nothing she could do. Nick was now otherwise involved. Gemma would have to accept that she had blown her chance. She knew there would be plenty more fish once she found where to look for them.

Gavin Laing took the hard drive and the DVDs with a grin and offered his thanks. Chris Shanklin said he appreciated the speed with which Gavin settled his bill. Shanklin forced a smile. He wanted his visitor off his premises, preferably out of town, as quickly as possible. He sensed more questions were coming and tried to exude an air of patience.

"So, when exactly did Snowy..."

"I never mentioned any names. The person you refer to as Snowy has long since retired."

"Okay, when did your operative get the disks."

"Two weeks ago," Chris lied.

Gavin was not convinced. "Really? Why did it take so long?"

"The original plan was to make the extraction on the Saturday your brother was meant to be in Ibiza." Releasing how events had actually unfolded was of no benefit.

"The police suggested he intended to travel on the Friday."

"That's correct, but we considered gaining access the following day the better option. It shortened the time between extraction and departure, reducing the likelihood of capture."

"Why didn't you go ahead? My brother was already dead by then."

"My colleagues entered the property on Saturday afternoon as planned, but when they saw what had occurred, they left. They flew home later that evening, handing the job to another team. The second team could not access the house, which had become a crime scene. There was no way of getting in and out. We aborted our quest and sought to obtain the goods by alternative means."

"Which were?"

"Let's just say that we used our contacts to secure the early release of certain personal possessions."

"You bribed the police?"

"I can neither confirm nor deny that suggestion."

"Well, thank you anyway."

"Do the police have any idea what might have happened?"

Gavin shook his head. "No. They think Graham and one of his henchmen, Bartholemew somebody, had a falling out. The assailant went around there with a baseball bat. Graham pulled a gun. Somewhere in all the confusion, a paperweight got thrown..."

"A paperweight?"

"Yes, a round thing, I think. The investigating officer believes Graham fired his gun. His attacker dropped the bat and threw the glass thing, which hit Graham on the head. When Graham saw he had killed the man, he turned the gun on himself."

"That's quite a convenient sequence of events."

"I agree. The police have kept the case file open. They want to speak to Gus and their two associates, Christiano and Donny. They have gone to ground somewhere, and the police believe it'll only be a matter of time before they reappear."

"Where were they at the time of the incident?"

"In Ibiza. They told the police they had expected Graham to join them, but he must have changed his mind. When they got back on the Monday, they learned the truth."

"So the police have spoken to them? I thought you said they had disappeared."

"They have. The police held them in custody for a few hours, but the three of them disappeared as soon as they got released."

None of this was news to Shanklin, but he maintained

the pretence. “Do the police think Gus is involved in Graham’s death?”

“They didn’t initially, but his disappearance has cast a few doubts. The police are also interested in speaking to Edward Kingston. Isn’t that the uncle of your former employee?”

This guy had done his homework. “Now you mention it. I think he is. Why do the police want to speak to him?” Shanklin was testing how much more Laing knew.

“It appears he was working with Graham and Gus to smuggle people, counterfeit goods and drugs into Europe. He used his exhibition business to cover his activities. The police believe he brought migrants in from Africa. Once they were in Spanish territory, he ferried them around the country to get the best deal.”

It was as if he had listened to Shanklin’s earlier conversation with Will. “Why ever would anyone get involved in that business? I understand it from the migrants' point of view, but your brother and cousin were successful businessmen."

"As we already know, they were greedy and did not always act honourably. Kingston was probably just a conduit. Gus can be very manipulative.”

“Do you have any idea where Gus or Kingston might be?”

“None whatsoever.”

The offer to attend a business meeting at a posh country hotel outside Tewkesbury was too good for Gemma to refuse. Her father had been searching for a backer to help him expand, and a business consultant had identified someone prepared to help. The potential investors were a new business called Oliver Burgess. The support would come in two forms. The investor would provide money and premises. The Potters were over the moon at this news.

The Tewkesbury Park hotel is set in 176 acres of parkland, just a ten-minute walk from the Abbey. It boasts a spa, pool, and a renowned golf course. It is perched on a hill with views across the town and surrounding countryside.

"Didn't Carrie want to have her wedding here?"

Geoff Potter nodded. "It was on her list, but it was more than we could afford then." His eyes surveyed the grounds. "It is a fabulous place. Perhaps you can have yours here?"

"Fat chance. I haven't even got a boyfriend at the moment. In any case, I don't want a big do." She chuckled mischievously. "On the other hand, could you imagine Carrie's face if I had what she couldn't?" She nodded appreciatively. "It is a stunning hotel. I can see why you chose it to meet your secret investor."

"I didn't," said Geoff. "The lady I spoke to has travelled from Worcester and chose this as it is equidistant."

"Oh, it's equidistant, is it? You've suddenly become very posh. This place has gone to your head." Geoff shook his head as Gemma asked, "Is she paying, or are you?"

"I hadn't thought about it. Why?"

"Because if she's paying, I'll have a glass of wine, but if you are, I'll have tap water."

"You could swear I was a skinflint."

"No comment."

"Charming. You can have what you like but get a receipt. It's probably tax deductible."

Geoff parked the car and stretched as he got out. "Okay, here goes. Have you got your papers?"

Gemma showed him the document case. "You'll be fine Dad. Calm down. You are making me nervous."

"Sorry, love. I need to create a good impression. This deal is a good one. It could be the making of us."

"You'll be fine." Gemma spotted a shabby yellow Fiat parked three cars away. "Talking about making a good impression. You'd have thought the hotel wanted that car kept out of sight. It doesn't paint a good picture of the clientele."

"Your mother has always told you never to judge a book..."

"I know, but I wouldn't pick up a book if the cover was falling off and the pages were stained."

"You might if it was rare and valuable. Come on, let's get this done. She said to meet her in the lounge overlooking the golf course."

"What time are we meeting?"

"Eleven."

"It's only a quarter to now. I've got time to nip to the loo."

Gemma hated to admit it, but she felt butterflies in her belly as she entered the corridor to the nearest toilets. She desperately wanted this meeting to go well, as the family had spoken about nothing else for days.

The old hospital on the edge of town would make an ideal base for their brewery. They had the first call on the premises and were offered additional funding to refurbish and kit it out. This was almost too good to be true, certainly too good to miss.

Gemma knew her primary role was to offer moral support, but she hoped she might impress with her plans to build the business's distilling side.

"Feeling nervous? I'll be gentle with you," said a voice from behind.

"Nick. What are you doing here?"

"I'm discussing a potential investment with a craft beer maker from Cheltenham," he said, smiling.

Gemma's expression grew sterner as her mind processed this information.

"You...you bastard."

Nick recoiled. "What have I..."

Gemma's finger was pointing at him. "You complete and utter bastard. If you wanted to get back at me, then you should have. You didn't need to involve my father. He will be heartbroken to learn this is all a fucking scam so that you can get your revenge."

"What? What are you on about?"

"YOU KNOW WHAT I'M ON ABOUT, YOU FUCKER. I

knew this was too good to be true. Full funding, equity stakes, premises, no hassle...HOW COULD I NOT SEE IT? YOU EVIL, EVIL BASTARD."

"Gemma, what are you on about?"

"Don't play the innocent with me. You've pretended to be someone else to get us here so you can enact some childish revenge. I would never have expected this from you. YOU COMPLETE AND UTTER...FUCKING SHIT!"

Her father appeared from a side room. "Gemma, what's the matter? We can hear you shouting from the other side of the room. It's a good job that we have the place to ourselves. What is going on?"

"We've been scammed, Dad. There is no money. There is no deal. This is a set-up." She looked at Nick with the face of someone who felt severely let down.

Her father spoke, "But the accountant checked this out. The money is there. We have guarantees."

"THAT GUARANTEE IS WORTHLESS, DAD. THIS... CREEP HAS STITCHED US UP."

A lady appeared and stood beside Geoff. "What's all this noise about? You are worse than my kids."

Gemma gaped at Leah. "What are you doing here?"

"I work with Nick."

"So, you are in on this too."

"I am. I do the designs, and then Jon, you remember Jon, my husband, gets the building work done."

Geoff Potter had no idea what was going on. He looked at Nick and held out a hand. "By the way, I'm Geoff. We haven't been introduced."

"I'm Nick. I was Nick Kingston, but now I'm Nick Burgess." He sensed confusion. "I will explain later."

"Nick? Nick..." He gazed at the lad and then turned his attention to his daughter. "This is Nick from your holiday. I thought you said he was skint."

"I did, and he is. This is his way of getting revenge."

Nick had heard enough. "Just shut up a minute. I've had

enough of your ranting. I was skint, but I am not any longer. Do you remember me telling you that we hoped to recover some of the money my father lost?

Gemma nodded.

"Well, we did. We got back everything we were owed. Then when I turned 21, I was given access to a trust fund that my granddad set up for me, my mother's father, not the shitty side of my family."

"How much was that worth?"

"Enough, plus he left me his rental properties."

"How many?"

"Fourteen in and around Barry. We've added two more since."

Gemma's eyes could not stretch any wider. "So you are a property magnet?"

"Not exactly. The houses need modernising, but the rent pot hasn't been touched. Leah and Jon are helping me with a refurbishment plan. Don't worry. There will be more than enough left to invest in your father's business."

Gemma had no words.

"It's nice to see you again, by the way," Leah said, holding out her arms as she walked to Gemma to hug her. "I've drawn up some plans that I would like you and your dad to look at, but if there's anything you don't like, we can change it."

Gemma covered her mouth with her hand and lowered her head to Leah's shoulder. "I am so sorry."

"It's okay."

Gemma looked at Nick. "I don't know what to say."

"You don't need to say anything. Let's go on through and have a drink. You look lovely, by the way," said Nick

Gemma smiled as he wiped her eye. "This old thing? I only wear it when I can't be arsed worrying about how I look. Please remember this is a business meeting, and you are not supposed to make sexist remarks like that. I am a professional businesswoman who deserves to be treated with respect."

Nick put up his hands. "Sorry. I did not wish to offend

you."

"That's okay then, and thank you for saying it. You don't look too bad yourself, you Welsh gimp. By the way, I liked it when you were being firm." She winked at him. "I have to use the facilities. You go on, and I'll have a large glass of Pinot."

Gemma entered the room to find a waiter delivering wine and coffee to their table. Her father and Leah were deep in conversation and studying plans while Nick watched Gemma's every move. He had a broad smile on his face. Gemma frequently caught him staring and poked out her tongue at him.

The greeting was hardly cordial. "Hi, Dad. Why have you dragged me here?"

"Hello, love. You look well." He took her elbow and walked to a bench. "I want to tell you about my plans for a new business and ask you to help me get revenge on your cousin and auntie."

"Why would I want revenge on them?"

"Because they've stolen your inheritance."

"No, Dad, you stole Nick's inheritance, and he took it back."

Eddie realised his wife and daughter had spoken but would not relent. "But they stole everything from us. Getting that back will take a while, but I have a plan. First, I want to get rid of them."

"And that's why I needed to come to this island at short notice? So that you can ask for my help to kill two family members? You are more fucking deranged than I realised."

"Look, it's simple. We get on a flight to the UK, find them, deal with them, and head back here before going to Spain."

"You think killing someone will be that easy? The only simple thing around here is you."

"Lou, I have sorted out new identities, and when we return to Spain, we can reopen the business. Crossings have paused since Graham's death, and we have a long waiting list.

My contact here has everything ready. Come and meet him, then decide."

"No, Dad, I am not interested. I thought you were inviting me so that we could hand ourselves in. I am tired of running. I am fed up with doing shitty jobs. I am bored of having my arse pinched by randy Italians. I would rather go back to Majorca and face the music. I wasn't involved in Graham's death. All I did was procure girls for their videos. That is hardly a hanging offence. I have no idea why I ran." She rubbed her temples. "I suppose I panicked."

"I can't go back, Lou. I helped Graham in his business, and the police are looking for a scapegoat. Donny, Grigor and Christiano have disappeared, so I'm probably the only one left…apart from my contact here."

"Well, good luck Dad. I wish you well, but I'm not interested. I'll spend a few days here before returning to Majorca."

He dipped into his jacket pocket and removed two items. "Well, let me know if you change your mind. We are in the same hotel." He handed her a passport and a bank card. "The PIN for this card is your birthday. That money should last you a while."

Louise studied the card. "Thanks, Dad. Be careful."

The business concluded. The foursome settled on designs. After consulting with Jon, a final budget and work timetable would follow.

Geoff shook hands with his new investor and designer and told his daughter it was time to leave. He was keen to share the good news with his wider family. His daughter appeared to be in no rush to go anywhere.

"Do you have to leave right away, Nick? We could have a catch-up?"

"That sounds lovely, but Leah and I have to meet with Jon this afternoon to discuss a few projects."

Gemma's smile disappeared.

"One of which is the brewery," said Leah. "Why don't you join us? You are a major partner in the project, after all."

The disappointment lifted off Gemma's face. "Are you sure?" She looked for reassurance from Nick. He was smiling and nodding.

"Plus, the kids would love to see you," said Leah.

A practical thought hit her. "How would I get back?"

"I can drop you off," said Nick. "If that's okay?"

"Great," said Gemma.

Leah and Geoff walked back to their cars together before shaking hands again. As they departed, they each waved to Gemma and Nick.

"Hark at you with your smart sweater, posh jeans and expensive boots. What happened to the gimp?"

Nick pointed at his chest. "He's still here. He hasn't gone anywhere."

Gemma smiled and said, "Good. I am pleased to hear it."

Nick stopped by the yellow Fiat.

"You are fucking kidding me?"

"What? Why?" said Nick.

"This is your car? All that money, and you buy this… heap of shit!"

Nick chuckled. "It's not mine. It's Zac's. He lets me borrow it."

"Surely you could afford your own car?"

"I could, but do I need one? My properties are in and around Barry, so I can walk or catch a bus. I take a train or a bus to Cardiff. From there, I can get to most places in the UK. The airport is on my doorstep if I need to go abroad. Why do I need a car?"

"Well, you will probably need one if you come to Cheltenham to see… my dad, of course."

"You might be right." He unlocked the doors.

They got in the car and secured their seatbelts. The car engine fought a little before springing into life.

"Where is your daughter?" Brian asked as Eddie came aboard his fishing boat.

"She didn't want to help me. She's not interested. Lou is returning to Majorca. She'll probably go to the police."

Brian handed him a beer before freeing the boat from its mooring. "That's the way it goes, I suppose. Where is she now?"

"At the hotel, I imagine. She is spending a few days here, and knowing Lou, she'll spend her time partying."

"Typical youngsters," said Brian, steering the boat out to sea. "Right, let's go fishing."

"Great," said Eddie, sipping the cold lager. "I'm looking forward to this."

"I just wanted to check something. You didn't mention my name, did you? If your daughter hands herself in and mentions me, it could cause me problems."

"No, I'm not stupid. As soon as I saw Louise was not interested, I gave up. I only referred to you as my contact here."

"Phew," said Brian, only half joking.

The pair chatted and frequently chortled as Nick drove out of the hotel grounds and eventually joined the Worcester road. The gears did not always play nicely, and the car occasionally jumped. Gemma found this hilarious.

"Did you borrow this when you visited Tenby to celebrate your 21st? That must have made a great impression."

"No. There is a regular train service from Cardiff."

"I see. Were there any ladies present on this trip?"

"You know there was. You read my timeline."

"Who was she, anyone special?"

"A gentleman does not kiss and tell."

"So you had sex?"

"As I've said, a gentleman…."

"Gentleman! You aren't a gentleman. You're a taffy gimp."

"Yes, but in Welsh, taffy gimp means gentleman."

She dug her fingers into his thigh. "Fibber!"

Nick caught her hand and gently squeezed her fingers.

"Why won't you tell me who she was?"

"You know who she was; her name was below the photograph. Sue Arnold."

"I know who she is but not who she is. Is she important to you?"

"Sue is a good friend from school. She was one of the few girls who were nice to me. We went to a concert, had a meal together and then went away for my birthday."

"And you shagged her?"

"No comment."

"Are you still together?"

"No. Sue wasn't looking for commitment. What is it about me that the girls I like don't want to commit."

"Well, a girl can always change her mind." Their eyes met, and Gemma smiled. "So, how many women have you been with since the holiday?"

"Oh, you know, I know enough to know more about what to do but nowhere near enough to write a book. I haven't broken any records."

She playfully punched him. "That's my line."

"It was, but it's mine now." He rubbed his side. "I see you are still a bully."

Gemma became serious. "I wanted to say thank you for helping us. My father is over the moon. He told me that he thinks you are a lovely lad."

"Thank him. Tell him I think he's a good bloke. Not sure what he's done to have a daughter like you, though." Nick squirmed in the seat, trying to avoid a finger poke to his ribs.

Eddie Kingston had slumped onto the boat deck, unconscious from the drugs in his beer. Brian secured the weights to his guest's feet, scanned the horizon, and slowly eased the body over the side.

He would have to dispose of Louise by a different means. She was unlikely to be smitten with the appeal of catching fish. Brian knew her new false name and the name of her hotel. He would sort her out in the morning.

Four small hands converged on Nick's shoulders.

"Nick," shouted Charlie.

"Monster," said Harry.

"Look out. It's the terrible twosome. How are you."

"Hi, Nick," Jon also said hello to Gemma. "I am sorry for them running in like that, but they fled as soon as they spotted you. Leah is getting some lunch ready. I offered to do it, but she thought you might be in a hurry, so we'd better discuss those plans.

The boys came to the front of the seat. Nick pointed to his companion. "You remember Gemma?"

"Yes," said Harry.

"I do," said Charlie.

"Hello," they said together.

Daisy held onto her dad's hand and shyly sheltered by his legs.

Gemma held out her hand. "Hello, you. Have you still got your bracelet? I won't take mine off."

"I have." She gently twisted it around her wrist before hugging Gemma.

Leah brought coffee, told them lunch would follow shortly and took the children to the playroom, leaving the other three to discuss their business. It didn't take Jon long to realise that Nick was only half listening to him. His mind was elsewhere.

Lucia walked out of the arrivals gate straight into Ben's waiting arms.

"Hello, " he said, kissing her cheek.

"Good afternoon." She lifted off his hat. "Your hair is not so bad. It is thinner than it was, but who needs fat hair?"

"Thank you for coming over. I appreciate it very much. It is lovely to see you, and you look very pretty," said Ben in stuttering Spanish.

"I think you need to practice your lying. But your Spanish is not so bad."

Will arrived to collect Lucia's bag and greeted her in English only: "Come on, let's get to the car before the parking ticket runs out."

Louise Kingston spent a long time at the airport studying her new passport. There was no way she looked like a Justine. She had no clue how she should pronounce her new surname.

The taxi ride to Puerto del Carmen was over quickly, ending at the steps of her hotel. Louise did not check-in. Staying on the island would have resulted in more pestering from her father, and she was not in the mood for that.

Louise found an ATM to check the balance on her new account. Her father had been very generous. She had no idea how he managed to escape with so much money.

She would go to Fuerteventura, where she had friends who knew Christiano. She had kept in touch with some since they visited Majorca. A ferry service ran between the islands. Louise made a sizeable cash withdrawal and hailed a taxi to Playa Blanca marina.

"I meant to ask, how did you find out about the old cottage hospital?"

"Will told me about it."

"Who? Will from Majorca? How did he know?"

Nick told her about Will's links with Shanklin, Ben's previous acquisitions and how Will was tasked with reducing Ben's land and property holdings. Ben hoped to open a chain of supermarkets in the Balearics and needed to raise funds.

"Did it cost a lot to buy it?"

"Mind your own business." Nick smiled. "Will and I are

in partnership, so the costs get halved. We want to utilise as much available space as possible."

"I'll tell Dad. Or you could tell him yourself, we'll be at my house in twenty minutes, and I feel like we haven't had a proper chat."

"You haven't shut up. I couldn't get a word in edgeways."

"Watch it, Taffy." She gave him her most fierce stare, but it didn't last long. "How is your mum?"

"She's fine, thank you. Doing great. She's excited about Lucia coming next week."

"Lucia? From Sa Coma?" Gemma's eyes stretched. "I didn't expect you to say that."

Nick smiled. "They've become best friends. They talk on the phone all the time."

"So she's coming for a holiday?"

"This is a bit of one. Lucia and her daughter will manage the first of Ben's supermarkets in Sillot. She's come over to sort out paperwork, and then she's visiting Mum. God help Barry and Cardiff with those two on the loose."

Gemma chuckled, then fell silent for a moment. "I was serious when I said we haven't had a proper chat. I was thinking you could stay over," she said.

"Yeah?"

She nodded, awaiting his reply.

"I suppose I could. Do you know of a decent hotel?"

"Hotel? Do you think Mum would let you stay in a hotel? You'll be the guest of honour. However, I must warn you that you'll face a barrage of questions and be under the spotlight."

"In that case, I'll disappear."

"You'd better bloody not!" She stretched across and held his hand on the steering wheel. "I'll protect you."

Nick beamed. "Thank you."

"Besides, you've still got to meet Carrie and Kate. Kate will love you because she is going through this phase of fancying older, strange-looking men."

"Cheers for that."

"Carrie is pregnant and can get a bit moody. She'll hate you, though. She hasn't forgiven you for making fun of her name."

"Can I drop you here?"

Lucia loved her room but could not believe the size of the house and the number of bathrooms. "I thought you were lying."

Ben shrugged. "It was what I wanted at the time."

A table was booked at a nearby gastropub. Will dropped them off, and the pair would have a taxi back.

After completing his transport duties, Will joined Shirley to relax in Ben's lounge. Shirley's daughter had just phoned. She was staying home alone, and her brother had patched things up with his girlfriend, so he was at her place.

"I'd never imagined you telling me we had to act as chaperones," he said, rising to go to the kitchen.

"Dad wanted to reassure Lucia that he had no ulterior motive."

"Pull the other one. He's probably scared to death. I saw how passionate these Spanish girls can be."

"Might be some truth in that too."

Will and Shirley were binge-watching a crime series on one of the many streaming channels Ben subscribed to. He topped up their wine glasses between episodes and placed a tray of nibbles on the coffee table.

"Is that how you would have done it?"

"Done what?"

"Accessed that room. He put a machine on the box, identifying the entry code."

"That would be an option, but I cannot believe the machine would get the code that quickly. There could be millions of combinations." He leaned forward to take a crisp. "I think it would have taken me longer. I would probably have set up a monitoring device to record people entering the room, or if that failed, I would look through diaries and the like to see if the passcodes had been written down."

"Do people still do that?"

"You would be surprised at how stupid people can be regarding their security."

Shirl took a sip of wine and replaced her glass. "Do you think you'll miss being a spy?"

"I told you I was never a spy. I was a forensic investigator."

"You give it a new title every time I mention it."

"I can't help it if my job description kept changing," he said, lifting his glass. "I don't think I will regret my decision. That last job scared me a lot."

"You weren't to know he would be armed."

"I should have at least considered the possibility, though. I think I had become too cocksure of myself. I could have gotten myself and Nick killed. So no, I don't think I will miss that side of things, but I might miss the IT stuff. I loved the thrill of the search."

"I wouldn't be happy with you getting so closely involved in a case again, but I wouldn't mind if you could work from home. Does Chris have any jobs that would allow you to do that?"

He remembered the call from Chris earlier that afternoon. "It's funny you should mention that..."

Jon and Leah made the most of the sunny weather and extra space by having a barbecue in the garden. The children played, stopping to eat when the mood took them, as their parents sat on their garden chairs, watching.

"Do you think Gemma and her father liked the designs?"

Leah giggled. "I think Gemma had her designs on Nick. You should have seen them. They couldn't take their eyes off each other. Her Dad was very impressed, though. I told you he'd go for the brewery shop."

"You did. What about converting the other buildings?"

"He's happy to do that over time. I mentioned your

suggestion about opening it up to other food producers; he loved that idea. He was smitten with the thought of turning half the space into a food hub with various stalls and producers and supplying the liquid refreshments. His wife is a good cook. They might start a second business."

"There's plenty of space." Jon stood. "I know we said we would cut back on alcohol, but do you fancy a glass of wine?"

"We haven't any left. I didn't buy it after we agreed to go dry for a spell."

Jon pointed. "That's one of the advantages of having a supermarket on your doorstep. I'll be back in a tick."

Elizabeth thoroughly enjoyed the play. She had always loved Agatha Christie's stories, had read the book and thought the performance did it justice. It had been first class.

They took his car back to a pub near where she lived.

"Thank you, Chris. I've had a lovely evening. Perhaps we could do it again?"

"I hope so. I thoroughly enjoyed myself."

Glasses clinked.

Chris spoke again. "I wouldn't mind going to see that new Spielberg movie. It opens next weekend."

"Now you're talking," said Elizabeth. "I haven't been to the cinema for over twenty years."

"Then you are in for a treat," said Chris Shanklin.

"I will look forward to it. My father used to take me to the Saturday matinees. He'd always say we were going to the pictures."

Later that same evening, Gemma and Nick huddled while walking back to her parents' house. They had visited a pub that sold Potter's Ales.

Even though it had been a warm spring day, an icy wind blew down the road, causing Gemma to put her face into Nick's shoulder.

"You are not cold, are you?" He asked.

"I'm fine, thanks. You are nice and warm."

"Good." Nick stopped walking for a second. "I just want to be clear. I agreed to help your father because I liked his business plans. It was not meant as a sweetener to get back with you."

"I hope it wasn't because if I didn't want to be here now, I wouldn't be. I'm not like Banda and his imaginary camels. You can't buy me."

"Good to hear. He's doing well, by the way."

"Who? Banda?"

"Yes. He's back home with his wife and daughter, and their business is doing well."

Gemma stopped and stared at him. "What is it with you? You and your mother gather people as you go along. You go on holiday for two weeks and return with an extended Kingston… sorry, Burgess Collective. Us, Leah and Jon, Banda, Lucia, Ben, and his son and daughter-in-law."

Nick laughed, choosing not to discuss his other work with Will. "We also lost some along the way. We've still not heard from my uncle or my cousins."

"It is weird how people can disappear like that."

"My aunt thinks my loving uncle has gone to North Africa. Louise fled to Italy, but there was no news on Donny. He and Christiano have disappeared. They have probably legged it to Ibiza with Grigor or Gus, whatever his name is."

"They are no great loss. You still speak to your aunt, then?"

"Yes, she didn't know what my uncle had done and had no idea how warped her kids had become. She's staying with us for a while."

"Another one!"

Nick laughed. "She will take over the tenancy when we move."

"Are you moving far?"

"No, just a couple of miles. Over a cup of tea, I'll show you some pictures of the new place."

"Bugger that. My father always has a few bottles at home, and my mother usually has wine. You can show me the photos while we enjoy more alcohol." She dragged him along the pavement until they leaned against a bus shelter. She kissed him and said, "Don't drink too much. I want to see if you've learned any new moves during your extracurricular activities."

"I've mostly used the ones that you taught me."

"Mostly?" She stopped again. "Did they mostly work?"

"No complaints..."

She smacked his arm. "I probably taught you too well. Although, we have only covered stages one and two. Stage three might be tricky. Do you want to go for it?"

"I think I'd like that. Much depends on what I have to do."

"To be honest, I haven't a clue. It will be my first time, too ." Gemma held his face in her hands. "There are no rules. We can do whatever we like and take as long as we want."

ACKNOWLEDGEMENT

As always, MASSIVE thanks to the ever-patient and extremely supportive Annemarie Thorn and Stephen Phipps who take the time to read and comment on my first drafts. Your cheques are in the post but they will bounce...

Lashings of love and hugs to family, friends and readers - especially those who bought the previous books. I hope you enjoy this one.

Keep safe, keep well, keep smiling,

WSA x

Printed in Great Britain
by Amazon

40111418R00278